The City of

Your Final Destination

The City of
Your Final Destination

PETER CAMERON

FARRAR, STRAUS AND GIROUX

NEW YORK

Cameron

Farrar, Straus and Giroux
19 Union Square West, New York 10003

Copyright © 2002 by Peter Cameron
All rights reserved
Distributed in Canada by Douglas & McIntyre Ltd.
Printed in the United States of America
First edition, 2002

A portion of this novel originally appeared in *The Yale Review.*

Library of Congress Cataloging-in-Publication Data
Cameron, Peter, 1959–
    The city of your final destination / Peter Cameron.— 1st ed.
        p.   cm.
    ISBN 0-374-28197-1 (hardcover : alk. paper)
    1. Biography as a literary form—Fiction.   2. Americans—Uruguay—
Fiction.   3. Graduate students—Fiction.   4. Biographers—Fiction.
5. Uruguay—Fiction.   6. Kansas—Fiction.   I. Title.

PS3553.A4344 C58 2002
813'.54—dc21

                                                          2001051127

Designed by Jonathan D. Lippincott

www.fsgbooks.com

1   3   5   7   9   10   8   6   4   2

The author wishes to express his gratitude to Andrew Cameron, James Harms, Edward Swift, Irene Skolnick, John Glusman, the MacDowell Colony, and the Corporation of Yaddo.

FOR
NORBERTO

PART ONE

We are unhappy because we do not see how our unhappiness can end; whereas what we really fail to see
is that unhappiness cannot last, since even a continu-
ance of the same condition will bring about a change
of mood. For the same reason happiness does not last.
    —William Gerhardie, *Of Mortal Love*

CHAPTER ONE

September 13, 1995

Ms. Caroline Gund
Ms. Arden Langdon
Mr. Adam Gund
Ochos Rios
Tranqueras, Uruguay

Dear Ms. Gund, Ms. Langdon, and Mr. Gund:
I am writing to you because I have been told you are the executors of Jules Gund's literary estate. I am seeking permission to write an authorized biography of Mr. Gund.
I am a doctoral student at the University of Kansas. On the basis of my thesis, "Remember That? Well Forget It: The Articulation of Cultural Displacement and Linguistic Dismemberment in the Work of Jules Gund," I have been awarded the Dolores Faye and Bertram Siebert Petrie Award for Biographical Studies. This award, which includes publication by the University of Kansas Press of the Gund biography as well

3

as a generous research stipend, is contingent upon my receiving authorization from my subject's estate. I hope you will agree that a well-researched biography of Jules Gund written by me would be in the best interest of his estate. I feel sure that the biography I plan to write, coupled with the burgeoning interest in Holocaust studies and Latin American literature, would markedly increase the amount of attention paid to the presently overlooked work of Jules Gund. This attention would enhance and secure the reputation of Mr. Gund, which would invariably result in increased sales of his book.

In order that you may fully consider my request, I am enclosing a sample chapter and table of contents of my thesis. (Of course, I would be happy to send you the entire thesis if you would like to see it.) I am also enclosing a copy of my curriculum vitae, and the letter endorsing this project from the University of Kansas Press. I hope that after perusing this material, you will agree that I am uniquely qualified to research and write the comprehensive and sympathetic biography that Mr. Gund undoubtedly deserves.

Because I must furnish proof of authorization to the Fellowship Committee by November 1 in order for them to process the initial payment by year's end, I would appreciate your earliest possible response. I have taken the liberty of enclosing an authorization form herewith, should you feel ready to grant authorization at this time. Please feel free to contact me with any questions or concerns you may have about this project. You may call me, collect, at the number above.

Thank you for your consideration of this request. I look forward to your response.

Sincerely,
Omar Razaghi

CHAPTER TWO

Adam stood before the mirror and tried to tie his bow tie. He was having an unhappy time of it. Some of his difficulty could be attributed to the fact that his hands shook, but it also appeared as though he had forgotten how to create a bow. Yet he persisted, unloosening the unsatisfactory and ugly knots he formed, straightening the fabric wings, and beginning again. And again and again. He did not seem to grow aggravated at his lack of success; he seemed to have the belief that at some time, almost despite himself, a bow might form.

Pete, who was leaning over the banister on the third-floor landing, watched with no expression for about five minutes and then began down the stairs. At the sound of his descent Adam stopped his struggle with the tie but did not look up.

Pete appeared behind Adam and, standing so that they almost touched, reached around and grasped the tie. As their two faces watched in the mirror, he created a perfect bow out of the formerly recalcitrant fabric. Although the bow was perfect Pete adjusted it a little and then readjusted it (to restore its perfection) and then patted it lightly and said, "There you are."

"Thank you," said Adam. He touched Pete's hand, and held it against the bow. "Where would I be without you?"

"Right here, probably," said Pete.

"Yes. But sans tie. Or at least sans bow."

"So you would be better off. I don't know why you're wearing a tie."

"I was taught that one should always wear a tie when one ventures forth into society."

"Is dinner with Arden and Caroline society?" asked Pete.

"It is practically all the society we have," said Adam. "Or I should say I. Perhaps you have society of which I know not. Do you?"

"No," said Pete. They were still both looking into the mirror, talking to their reflections. Pete leaned his head closer and rested his chin on Adam's shoulder. Adam reached up and stroked Pete's dark hair. He had lovely long hair, Pete. They observed their reflection: an old man of European lineage, a young man of Asian descent.

And then Pete raised his head and stepped a bit away, so that his face disappeared from the tiny world of the mirror.

"Ready to go?" asked Adam.

"Yes," said Pete. "Do you want to walk, or should we drive?"

"It is a lovely evening," said Adam. "I want to walk."

"But what about coming back? Will you want to walk then?"

"I don't know," said Adam.

"Because if you'll want to drive home, we should take the car now."

"Why?"

"So that we will have it there, to drive back in."

"But you could always walk back for it, and drive up to get me."

"Yes, but it would be easier to take it now."

"I'm not sure I follow you," said Adam. "If we walk home, we walk home. And if we decide to drive you'll walk back for the car. So either way you will walk back, won't you?"

"Not if we drive up."

"Oh, but I want to walk up. Of that I am sure."

"Are you sure? How's your leg?"

"It is the same as always."

"Why don't you see the doctor?"

"Because he is a terrible doctor and there is nothing really wrong with me."

"Your hands shake. And your legs ache."

"And I am old. It all corresponds."

"So we should drive."

"No. I am old, but I can walk to the big house, and perhaps, depending how late it is and how much I eat and drink and what sort of mood I am in, walk back. We shall see." He looked back into the mirror. "Thank you for tying my tie. I look very handsome in it, I think. I have always liked this tie. I bought it in Venice, in fifty-five. It is important to buy beautiful things when you are happy. I look at this tie"—Adam touched the bow at his throat—"and I remember how happy I once was."

"Why were you happy?"

"I forget. Who knows? It is enough to remember the fact of the happiness. I'm sure I was happy. Otherwise I would never have bought such a beautiful tie."

"It's not so beautiful now," said Pete. "It's stained."

"Is it?" Adam leaned toward his reflection. "It looks fine to me. I am really happy to be losing my sight. Everything looks fine to me. It is the best evidence I know that there is a God."

"What?"

"That he dims our vision as we age. Otherwise it would be too horrible to bear. Especially for those who were beautiful when they were young."

"Were you beautiful when you were young?"

"I wasn't so terribly ancient when we met. I thought I still retained some of my beauty then. I must have. Otherwise, how could I ever have attracted you?"

Pete did not answer. Adam turned away from the mirror and faced his companion. Pete had opened the door. The evening light fell upon his handsome face. He was looking out at the little cobbled yard in front of the millhouse. A cat sat at the foot of the steps.

"Chuco wants his dinner," said Adam.

"Chuco can wait. If we're going to walk, we should leave now, or we will be late," said Pete.

Adam realized Pete was angry. Lately he seemed angry all the time, but it was an odd, private, submerged anger. He must be very angry not to feed Chuco, whom he loved. He will not feed Chuco to punish me, thought Adam. "We can take the car now," said Adam. "Perhaps I am too tired to walk."

Pete turned away from the door and looked at him. "No," he said. He bent down and picked up the cat. The cat looked away. "Just let me feed this little pig."

Portia was sitting at the round table in the courtyard drawing and labeling a map of South America. It was an assignment for school. She was a day student at the convent school in Tranqueras. The courtyard was surrounded on three sides by wings of the large house and on the fourth side by a stone wall. There was an archway in the center of the wall, and a small, round fountain in the middle of the courtyard. Arden, her mother, came out of the kitchen door, her hands full of tablecloth and napkins and cutlery, and stood behind Portia for a moment, watching her color Uruguay gold. The rest of South America was green, all different shades of green, like fields seen from an airplane.

"Why are you making it gold?" Arden asked.

For a moment Portia did not answer. She was eight years old and had recently discovered that the withholding of information is a kind of power. "Because," she finally said.

"But it doesn't match the rest of South America," said Arden.

"It's not supposed to," said Portia.

It made Arden happy to watch Portia carefully color Uruguay gold. "It's very pretty," she said.

"It's not supposed to be pretty," said Portia.

"Yes, but it can be," said Arden. "And is, I think. Like you." She bent down and kissed the top of her daughter's head. "Your hair smells of gasoline," she said. "What have you been doing?"

"Nothing," said Portia.

"Have you been playing in the garage?"

"No," Portia decided, after a moment's thought.

"Well, you shall have a shampoo tonight," said Arden. "Even if we have no hot water. Could you move that, darling? Just for a moment, while I set the table?"

"Why do we need a tablecloth?" asked Portia.

"Because Adam and Pete are coming to dinner and I want the table to look nice. And really, you should always have a tablecloth. There is no reason not to have a tablecloth. But when it's just us I get lazy."

"Do I have to eat with you?"

"Don't you want to?"

"No. I'd rather eat in the kitchen."

"Why?"

"Because you all talk too much."

"But that's what people do when they eat together—talk."

"But it's boring. Especially with Uncle Adam."

"All right. But help me with the tablecloth."

"I don't see why you should always have a tablecloth. It just gets dirty and has to be washed and that causes pollution," said Portia. "When it's just the table you can wipe the crumbs off, and let the birds eat them. It's much more elogical."

"Ecological, you mean," said Arden. "But life isn't always— well, some of the nice things about life aren't always the most practical or ecological, are they? And having a tablecloth does no great harm, so it's okay."

"Sister Domina says it is the little harms, the little sins, that matter most, because they add up. God adds them all up."

"I suppose you're right, but we shall still use the tablecloth. When you get a bit older you can join the nuns and live as simply as they do."

"You don't have to join the nuns to live simply," observed Portia.

"But it is easier, I think, when one is apart from the world."

"Sister Domina says that their world is the real world. And we live apart from it."

"Well, everything is a matter of perspective, I suppose," said Arden. "Now will you move your map and the pencils?"

Portia complied, and helped her mother set the table. After a moment they heard some voices from inside the house. "Listen," said Arden. "That must be Uncle Adam and Pete. Go tell them we're out here."

Portia disappeared through the French doors, and returned a moment later with Pete, who said good evening and kissed Arden. "Where's Adam?" she asked.

"He's inside," said Pete. "He wanted to look at the newspapers."

"Can I get you a drink?" Arden asked Pete.

"Yes," said Pete. "Thank you."

"Gin?"

"Yes, thanks," said Pete.

Arden entered the house through the French doors opening into a large front hall, the high ceiling of which was crowned with a cupola. Opposite the French doors was the large wooden front door; two galleries ran along the back wall from which doors led to the hallways on the second and third floors, and a curved staircase led up to the first gallery from each side of the room. Directly off the entrance hall were doors that led to the pantry and kitchen hallway, a small toilet, and two large, square rooms in the front of the house: one was a library, one was a sitting room. Arden paused at the library door. "Good evening, Adam," she said. "I won't disturb you now except to see if you'd like a drink. Pete and I are having gins."

"Oh, how I would adore a nice little glass of gin," said Adam.

"Lime?" asked Arden.

"Yes, of course," said Adam. "Lots of lime, if you can spare it."

Arden returned a moment later with a tray of drinks. She put Adam's on the little table beside his seat. "Thank you, my dear," he said, without looking up from the newspaper.

Arden returned to the courtyard, but Pete and Portia had disappeared. She put the tray down on the table, took her drink, and walked over and sat on the rim of the fountain. It was full of dark water and lily pads and fat, listless carp. They appeared and loitered at the surface near her, but she had nothing to feed them. After a moment they nonchalantly sank, as if they had never really expected to be fed at all.

Arden put her fingers in the water and some fish returned to nibble at the pellets of air that clung to them. Jules had used to nibble her fingertips, pretending he was—what? Not a fish. A child, perhaps. And suck them too.

After a while, Portia and Pete appeared through the archway. They came and sat beside Arden at the fountain. For a moment no one said anything, but it was a comfortable silence. Then Arden said, "Your drink's on the table, Pete. Portia, why don't you get it for him?"

"I'll get it," said Pete.

Portia was kneeling beside the basin, trailing the ends of her long hair through the water, trying to entice the fish.

"Don't," said Arden.

"Why? You already said I'll have a shampoo tonight," said Portia.

"Yes," said Arden.

Pete returned with his drink.

"Where did you go?" asked Arden.

Portia looked at Pete. "Nowhere," she said.

"A secret," said Pete.

Adam emerged from the house and sat at the table, the newspaper neatly folded into quarters. "Come here and help me with the Jumble," he called to Portia.

Portia stood up and joined her uncle at the table. This left Arden and Pete at the fountain. They sipped their drinks, and watched the fish move slowly through the dark green water.

Caroline looked down at them from her studio in the tower. It was not really a tower, just a room built above the attic, with dormers and windows on both sides. Jules had built it for her, because the rest of the house was so dark: in an effort to re-create Bavaria, Jules's parents had planted thousands of trees—Norwegian spruce, Austrian pine, juniper, larch—and the resulting forest now perpetually shadowed the big house. Caroline watched Pete and Arden sit on the fountain and say nothing to each other. Then she turned away from the window and looked at her canvas. Since she had realized—or admitted—years ago that she would never paint anything original or good, she had only made copies of great paintings. It was more sensible that way. Otherwise she would have stopped painting, and she liked to paint. She was now copying Bellini's *Madonna of the Meadow*. She crossed the room and looked out the other side, out across the tops of trees. She looked up: the sky was still a very pale blue, a tired, ancient blue. There were no clouds. She heard gravel crunching and saw Diego walking down the drive. He had come up from the village to fix the hot water heater. Perhaps they would have hot water tonight. She could take a bath. She watched him walk all the way down the long drive. He stood at the end smoking a cigarette, waiting for his son. She went back and

looked at her painting as if it might have changed, reconfigured itself, in her brief absence. It had not. She heard a car and returned to
the front windows and watched Diego get into his son's car. The car
drove away. She crossed the room and looked out the window at
the courtyard. They were eating now, all seated at the table. Candles and a tablecloth. Even though she had been asked, and refused,
to join them, she felt excluded. That the exclusion was her of them
rather than them of her made it no less keenly felt.

"Are we not being joined by Caroline?" asked Adam, as they began
eating.

"No," said Arden. "She's working and didn't want the interruption."

"I should go up later," said Adam. "After dinner."

"I'm sure she would like to see you," said Arden.

"She works very hard," said Adam. "Still, after all these years."

Arden agreed that she did.

"She wasn't a bad painter once, you know. Terribly derivative,
but not bad. Of course, all women artists tend to be derivative."

Arden refused to be baited. "I like her paintings," she said. "At
least the ones I've seen."

"Yes, you would," said Adam. "You know nothing about art, do
you?"

"No." Arden laughed. "Absolutely nothing." And then, to
change the subject, she said, "I received an interesting letter today."

"Did you? How nice for you," said Adam. "It has been ages—
years, perhaps—since I have received any correspondence that
could be called interesting. Who wrote you this interesting letter?"

"A student. A graduate student, from a university in the States.
He's written some sort of thesis on Jules, and he wants to turn it
into a biography. He's received a grant to fund his research and the
university press would publish it."

"And the reason he wrote you?"

"Well, he wants me—he wants us to authorize it. He needs our authorization to continue."

"Someone wants to write a biography of Jules Gund?"

"Yes," said Arden. "Apparently."

"Is this person reputable?" asked Adam.

"I don't know," said Arden. "I assume so. He's affiliated with a university."

"Which one?"

"I don't remember. A state university. Kansas, I think. Or Nebraska."

"May I see the letter?" asked Adam.

"Of course," said Arden. She went into the house and returned with the letter. She handed it across the table to Adam, who held it close to the candle and read it. Arden and Pete watched him.

After a moment Adam set the letter down on the table. "Well, a biography could be very good for us," he said.

"Could it? How?"

"By increasing interest in Jules. And thereby increasing sales."

"Yes, he mentions that in his letter. But surely that's no reason to authorize a biography . . . simply to increase sales. And there's no guarantee that it will, is there?"

"No," said Adam, "but it can't hurt."

"Can't it?" said Arden.

"I don't see how," said Adam.

"It could hurt Jules," said Arden.

"Jules is dead."

"I mean his reputation."

"I think you mean that it could hurt you," said Adam.

"No, I didn't mean that," said Arden. "How could it hurt me?"

"It would expose you—your life, after all, was entwined with his."

"Yes, it was, and in no way that shames me. So how could I be hurt? Besides, I'm not thinking of myself. I'm thinking about Jules.

14

Would Jules want this? Would he want a biography? I don't think so."

"Jules is dead. I don't think he is wanting or not wanting much of anything these days."

Arden frowned, but said nothing.

"Have you spoken with Caroline?"

"Yes," said Arden. "She said no. She would not authorize a biography. She wants no such thing."

"Why?"

"She did not say."

"How like Caroline."

"I think I agree with her."

"How can you agree with her without knowing her reasons?"

"I agree with her decision. And we outnumber you, so you will be outvoted."

"Are we to allow the continuing reputation of Jules Gund to be decided by something so stupid as democracy?"

"How else can we decide? It is certainly the easiest way."

"The easiest way! Don't you want to do what is best for the estate?"

"Yes," said Arden. "Of course, but also what is best for Jules."

"I hasten to remind you that Jules is dead."

"I know that. But that is not a reason to stop considering him."

"Isn't it? I would think it is a very good reason. I am hardhearted, I suppose."

Arden did not reply. She stood and began to stack the plates.

Adam leaned back in his chair and then said, "May I ask you again why you do not wish to encourage this biography? Perhaps you can explain your reasons to me."

"I don't believe in biography," Arden said.

"You don't believe in biography?"

"No," said Arden. "Well, not the biography of artists. Or writers. I think their work should speak for itself. I think their work is their life, at least publicly. And biography can only interfere with the work—it taints the work somehow."

"How?"

"By offering an alternative narrative. To have that out there, set alongside his work, for us to countenance that, and perhaps benefit from that—I feel that is wrong."

"Wrong? How wrong?"

"Just wrong. I don't know; I can't explain. I'm not an intellectual. I'm sorry I can't be clearer. It's just something I feel, strongly."

"I understand and appreciate your feeling," said Adam. "But think for a moment. You may not be an intellectual but you are a thoughtful and intelligent person. Think: we have before us the request to write an authorized biography." He touched the letter on the table. "Do you understand what that means?"

"It means he can't write it without our permission," said Arden.

"No," said Adam, "it does not. It means that in exchange for our permission and cooperation, in exchange for our making available to him Jules's papers and our reminiscences of him, we have control of the content of the book. We can withhold, or cause to be withheld, any information we do not wish, for any reason, to be included. This young man writes the book, yes, but its content is entirely controlled and vetted by us. That is an authorized biography. That is what this young man is proposing to write. If we decide, as you propose, not to cooperate with him, to withhold authorization, there is nothing to prevent him from writing his biography anyway. It would be more difficult, of course, without our help, but he would in that case be free to write whatever he wanted. We would, in effect, be handing the story of Jules over to him carte blanche. We would be sacrificing Jules out of pride, stubbornness, stupidity."

"I don't think he could write a biography without our cooperation," said Arden. "How could he?"

"That is the job of biographers. They are clever, vindictive, ruthless people. You must see that our withholding authorization is like throwing him the gauntlet. It is much better if he is on our side."

"Perhaps I'm naive," said Arden. "In fact, I'm sure I am. But I don't see the world like that. I don't presuppose that people will act ruthlessly or vindictively. I think people are reasonable and respect privacy. It's a nice letter, the letter he wrote. Polite, and respectful." She reached out and touched it. "You are too cynical, I think, Adam."

"Well, about one thing, at least, you are correct."

"What?"

"You are naive."

Arden picked up the stacked plates and carried them into the house. Pete stood up and walked across the courtyard, out through the archway, into the night. Adam sat alone for a moment. He looked up at the light in Caroline's room. He could hear Arden and Portia talking in the kitchen. He went looking for Pete. He found him smoking near the garden. They stood beside each other for a moment, not talking, and then Pete said, "You were nasty, I think."

Adam took the cigarette from him and dragged on it. He gave it back. Exhaled. "Was I?" he said.

"Yes," said Pete. "I think you'd have a better chance of changing her mind if you were a little kinder."

"Oh, please," said Adam. "Arden knows I am not kind."

Pete flicked his cigarette to the ground and stepped on it. Then he picked up the butt and put it in his shirt pocket. "I don't suppose you want to walk home?" he asked.

"No," said Adam. "I'm tired. And I've got to talk to Caroline."

"So you want me to get the car?"

"Yes," said Adam. "Please."

Pete began walking around the house, toward the drive.

"Wait!" Adam called. "Do you want me to get you a torch?"

"No," said Pete.

"It's dark," said Adam.

"It's okay," said Pete. "I know the way."

Adam made his slow way up the steps to Caroline's studio. She was working at the easel and did not turn around as he entered the room. He had the feeling she had not been working, that she had assumed this position only at the sound of his footsteps on the stairs; certainly his slow ascent had given her plenty of time. He stood behind her and watched her paint. Her intentness seemed artificial. He found a chair and sat down.

"It looks quite good," he said. "Although the colors are all wrong."

"Good evening, Adam," said Caroline. She did not turn around.

"Good evening," said Adam.

"Please don't say anything more about my painting," said Caroline.

"All right," said Adam. "Except really, the colors—"

"Please," said Caroline. She turned around and smiled brightly at him. "Did you come up for a drink?"

"No," said Adam. "I was left alone, and saw your light."

"And so you came up for a drink," said Caroline.

"I wouldn't refuse a drink," said Adam.

Caroline poured two glasses of scotch and gave one to Adam.

"I wish you and Arden would coordinate your liquor," Adam said. He sipped his scotch and looked again at the painting. "It's Bellini, isn't it?" he asked.

"Yes," said Caroline. "But please don't look at it."

"You can draw very well," said Adam.

"Yes," said Caroline. "I can draw. But I cannot paint."

"Yes you can," said Adam. "Or you could, at least. I was just telling Arden what a good painter you were."

"Yes," said Caroline. "Were. Can we not talk about the painting?"

18

They were silent a moment, and then Caroline said, "Did Arden show you the letter?"

"Yes," said Adam.

"And what do you think?"

"I think I am old and tired. I think this scotch is excellent. Where did you get it?"

"Sebastian brought it. What do you think of the letter?"

"I think what any sensible person would think," said Adam.

"And what is that?"

"It is an excellent opportunity for us. We would be fools not to encourage him."

"Ah," said Caroline.

"I understand you think differently."

"Yes," said Caroline. "I am not as sensible as you."

"Apparently no one is," said Adam. "Or at least no one to whom this matters."

"Not Arden?"

"Arden sees this as a romantic opportunity—to be the noble grieving widow, protecting her husband's good name. It is absurd."

"Why?"

"For several reasons. First of all, if anyone should play that role—which no one should—it is you. Second, it is stupid and impractical. And selfish. I could go on and on."

"I've no doubt you could."

"And I think, for some strange reason I can't fathom, she wants to align herself with you in this matter. And so I depend upon you to be sensible."

"You keep mentioning sensibility, as if you are the arbiter of it. You are not, Adam. We make our own sensibilities. You cannot impose yours on others. At least not upon me."

"Why don't you want this biography?"

"It is of no great concern to me. It is not something I want or don't want."

"Then why did you tell Arden you did not want it."

19

"I told her I would not grant authorization."

"Why did you tell her that?"

"Because Jules did not want a biography. He told me that once."

"When?"

"Years ago. When *The Gondola* was first published."

"That was over twenty years ago."

"Yes. Ages ago. Aeons. But when he said it is not important."

"And because of something Jules may have said to you twenty years ago, you are now going to refuse to authorize a biography that is undoubtedly in all of our best interests?"

"Yes," said Caroline. "It seems logical to me. Sensible, even."

"I'm sure Jules said many things to you twenty years ago," said Adam. "For instance, he said he would love you always, didn't he, when you were married?"

"Yes," said Caroline.

"And you did not hold him to that," said Adam.

"I did not need to. Jules didn't stop loving me. He stayed married to me."

"What you had, at the end, was not a marriage," said Adam.

"Was it not? Who are you to say? Again, I think it is a matter of sensibilities. And what does any of this have to do with the biography? Nothing, I think. Or, I might add, with you."

"I think it does," said Adam. "I was his brother. I was not his wife, or his mistress. Ours was a fairly dispassionate relationship, and I think I can see this present situation a little more clearly than either you or Arden. And I think it is a situation that needs to be looked at clearly. Dispassionately."

"And you are the one to do it," said Caroline.

"I'm sorry if I have offended you," said Adam. "That was not my intention."

"You haven't," said Caroline. "We just think differently about this, that is all."

They heard a car and saw its lights coming up the drive.

20

"Here is Pete," said Adam. "And it is late. Perhaps we should talk about this some more, the three of us, and come to a decision. We must respond to the letter, after all."

"Well, my mind is made up."

Adam stood up. "Please don't say that, Caroline. At least have the grace to listen to what I have to say, and consider it. I expect that rigidity of Arden, but not of you."

"Of course I will listen to you," said Caroline. "I did not mean that."

"Tomorrow, then. Will you come to lunch? And bring Arden with you? And we can discuss this all calmly and rationally."

"I'll come to lunch," said Caroline. "And bring Arden with me, but whether we can discuss this calmly and rationally is another matter."

"We can try," said Adam.

"Yes," said Caroline.

"You'll tell Arden?"

"Yes. Go now. Pete is waiting. How is Pete?"

"Pete is unhappy. Surly. He is getting tired of living in the middle of nowhere with a nasty old man."

"I don't believe it," said Caroline. "Pete loves you."

"And I love Pete. But nevertheless, he is unhappy. Good night."

Adam kissed her. She closed the door and listened to him go slowly down the stairs. She heard the car door open and close and then she heard the car drive away. It was quiet. Then she could hear, from somewhere lower in the house, a bath filling. Good, she thought, there must be hot water.

Arden was saying good night to Portia. She sat on the bed and combed Portia's hair, which was still damp from her shampoo, "Where did you go before, with Pete?" she asked.

"What?" asked Portia.

"Before dinner. You and Pete disappeared. Where did you go?"

"Nowhere," said Portia. "For a little walk."

"Yes, but where?"

"To the beehive," said Portia.

"You are supposed to stay away from the hive," said Arden. "You could get stung."

"I know. But I thought with Pete it would be all right. We wanted to see the bees fly home. They come back at sunset."

"Yes," said Arden, "I know."

"And then we listened to the hive. We didn't stand too close. We were behind the well. We could hear it from there. The humming." She made a purring noise low in her throat. "Pete says the bees talk to each other, and dance."

"Yes," said Arden. "I've heard that they do. There. Your hair is nice and dry. And it smells lovely. Get into bed."

"First I must say my prayers," said Portia.

"I forgot. Yes. Say your prayers, if you want."

Portia knelt beside the bed, but looked over her shoulder at her mother. "Go away," she said. "Don't listen. Prayers are private. They are between God and me."

"All right," said Arden. "But God can't tuck you in. Call me when you're ready."

She went out into the hall, from where she could hear her daughter mumbling a very long and complicated prayer, the particulars of which she could not, in spite of her efforts, discern.

Although Arden and Caroline lived in the same house they saw each other infrequently. Without ever having discussed or acknowledged it, they had come to an arrangement of passing through the house, of inhabiting certain rooms at certain times, of rising, eating, sleeping, and bathing, that allowed for little or, on some days, no contact.

Caroline's habit was to stay awake much of the night and sleep far into the day. After Adam left her she drank another scotch and sat looking at her rendition of *Madonna of the Meadow*. She was copying it from a large color plate in a book on Bellini that had been published in Dresden in 1920. It was one in a series of books that had been brought over by Jules's parents. Of course the colors were all wrong; probably printed poorly to begin with and now faded even further. She had tried in her version to replicate the colors she supposed were in the original painting—the brightness of the past—but she knew she had failed.

She waited until all the lights were out in the house until she descended from the attic and crossed the dark courtyard. The fountain had been turned off but the fish moved sleeplessly through the water. She stood for a moment, watching them, and then entered the house.

It was all still and dark. Her rooms were on the second floor and she had almost passed through the front hall toward the stairs when something made her turn around and study the shadows across the room. A woman was sitting in the dark, watching her.

"It's me," said Arden. "I'm sorry if I scared you."

"You startled me," said Caroline. "I thought you were in bed."

"I was," said Arden, "but I couldn't sleep."

I could say good night and continue up the stairs, thought Caroline. Or I could go and sit beside her. But her pause to think this was somehow decisive; it precluded the first alternative. "Perhaps you should have a drink," she said. "It may help you sleep."

"Actually, I already have one," said Arden. She raised her hands from her lap, revealing a small glass cupped in them.

Caroline sat down across the room, on the bottom stair. For a moment, neither of them said anything.

Then Caroline said, "Did Diego fix the heater? Do we have hot water?"

"No," said Arden. "He says he needs another part. He said he would come back tomorrow, if he can get it in town."

"How I long for a hot bath," said Caroline.

"Yes," said Arden. "I know."

They were silent a moment, and then Arden asked, "How is your painting coming?"

Caroline made a noise that indicated both impatience and dismissal.

Arden sipped from her little glass.

What is she drinking? wondered Caroline. Is she a drunk? Has Arden become a drunk? She bent down and unstrapped her sandals. "Adam has invited us to lunch tomorrow. He wishes to discuss the biography."

"I thought you didn't want it," said Arden.

"I don't," said Caroline. "But the least we can do is listen to Adam. We owe him that."

"Why?" said Arden. "He doesn't listen to others."

Caroline stood up. "Well, I said we would have lunch with him. You can not come if you wish."

"Of course I'll come," said Arden. "I just wish he weren't such a bully."

"It's rather pointless to wish that," said Caroline. "Should we walk down together?"

"Yes," said Arden.

"I'll look for you about noon, then. Good night."

"Good night," said Arden.

Caroline turned and went up the stairs. Arden sat alone a while longer, finishing her drink. Then she, too, went to bed.

CHAPTER THREE

Arden and Caroline walked along the shaded verge of the road. They both wore sleeveless dresses and sandals; Caroline wore a straw hat with a large, sloping brim. It tied with ribbons beneath her chin, but the ribbons were loose and fluttered at the periphery of her gaze.

It was about a mile downhill from the big house at Ochos Rios to the millhouse. The road was quiet, seldom traveled by automobiles. They walked past a field of wildflowers above which a cloud of butterflies delicately hovered. Then they turned off onto the dirt road that dipped down, shadowed by trees, toward the dell in which the millhouse stood, and the air was suddenly fresh.

From the window of the study Adam could see two women walking along the road. A little cloud of dust got kicked up around them. Fools, he thought. Mad dogs and Englishmen. He looked again at the women, who had drawn closer. One of them wore a coolie hat, trailing ribbons. And then he thought: Damn it, it's Caroline and Arden, coming to lunch. I forgot.

The millhouse was a round stone building that had been rather crudely transformed into a domicile. A large living room and small kitchen and bathroom occupied the first floor, the second floor was a large, unfinished room where Pete stored the secondhand and cast-off furniture he collected and sold to a dealer from New York City. A bedroom and study were on the third floor. Adam went out to the landing and called for Pete.

"What?" Pete called back up.

"I forgot to tell you. Caroline and Arden are coming to lunch."

"When?" asked Pete.

"Now," said Adam.

"What?" Pete appeared in the open space below, gazing up.

"I forgot to tell you that I invited Caroline and Arden to lunch. And they are coming up the road. Or actually, they are coming down the road. Do we have anything to feed them?"

"No," said Pete.

"There must be something," said Adam. "What were you planning for our lunch?"

"I didn't know I was planning our lunch."

"Of course you were. You always do. Don't taunt me."

"I thought we might have soup. A tin of soup. But it won't go four ways," said Pete.

"There must be another tin," said Adam.

"There isn't," said Pete.

"Could we stretch it?"

"What do you mean?"

"Add water till there's enough for four. What kind of soup is it?"

"Chicken," said Pete. "With rice."

"Oh, that will be fine," said Adam. "Just add some water and some milk. You can make it a sort of cream of chicken rice. Those tinned soups are made to be stretched. And we have bread, don't we?"

"A little," said Pete.

"Well, slice it thinly."

"Why did you invite them to lunch? We were just there last night."

"In order to discuss this business of the biography. I thought it might help to get them here, on my turf, so to speak. Otherwise they will stay home and plot things. And we don't want Arden and Caroline plotting behind our backs, do we?"

"That might be interesting," said Pete. "I would not mind it so much."

"Well, I would," said Adam. "And remember that you are on my side. You must charm them. I am incapable of that, so I depend upon you."

"Should I be charming before or after I make the lunch?" asked Pete.

"What?"

"I just want to make sure I understand your orders: feed them lunch and be charming. Anything else?"

There was a knock on the door.

"Don't be difficult," said Adam. "Open the door."

"Feed them lunch, be charming, don't be difficult, open the door. Anything else?"

Adam laughed. "Not at the moment," he said.

Pete opened the door. The two ladies entered and were greeted. Adam descended the stairs, and they entered the living room and found seats, all a little bit away from one another. The act of sitting down and arranging themselves took some time and attention, and was followed by a silence. Then Adam said, "I am sorry to say that Pete has burned the lunch. So I am afraid we have only the soup left to feed you."

"Soup sounds perfect," said Caroline. "I am not hungry for a big lunch."

"Neither am I," said Arden. And then she said, "It's much cooler down here near the stream. How lucky you are."

Caroline said, "I have always loved this room and now, for the first time, I understand why. There is something about a room with rounded walls, with no corners, that makes me feel safe and happy. I suppose it all goes back to the womb."

Adam did not like this talk of wombs. "Could I get you an aperitif?" he asked. "I think we have some Cinzano."

"We have no Cinzano," Pete said.

"Yes, we have no Cinzano," Adam sang. Then he said, "Well, what do we have?"

"There is wine, of course, and tomato juice."

"Tomato juice would be lovely," said Caroline.

"Yes," said Arden. "Please."

Pete stood up.

Arden said, "Let me help you." Together they went through the swinging door into the tiny kitchen, a sort of shed that had been built onto the millhouse at some distant point; it had no windows, just a rusted exhaust fan that no longer worked but through which leaked a little fresh air. A piece of slate, which stood on top of an old kneehole desk, served as a counter. A small, ancient, noisy refrigerator occupied the kneehole. A hot plate and toaster oven stood on the counter. A single spigot in the stone wall emptied into an old porcelain sink that stood on an iron stand beneath it. Most of the porcelain was worn away, revealing an iridescent subderma, smooth and pearly as the inside of a shell, veined with rust.

Pete rummaged in one of the desk's drawers and extracted a tin without a label. "This is either tomato juice or lard," he said, and began to poke a hole in its top with an awl.

Arden watched him. "Don't you have a can opener?" she asked.

Pete looked at her, but did not answer.

"What's wrong?" asked Arden.

"What do you mean, what's wrong?"

"I can tell when something's wrong between you and Adam. Is he still upset about last night?"

"No," said Pete. "Or perhaps yes, I don't know. What he's really upset about is the lunch."

"Because you burned it?"

Pete was a good cook, and this fiction rankled him. "I did not burn it! There was nothing to burn. He forgot to tell me you were coming until just before you arrived. And so to punish him I told him there was no food. Just one tin of soup."

"Why do you want to punish him?" asked Arden.

The answer was obvious and inexplicable, so Pete merely shrugged.

"Do you really only have one can of soup?"

"No. There's plenty of soup. But I want it to seem a miracle." Pete succeeded in penetrating the can's metal skin. He sniffed at the thick maroon juice that spunked from the hole. "It smells bad," he said. He dabbed his finger and tasted it. "It's nasty," he said. "Wouldn't you rather have a glass of wine?"

"Yes," said Arden, "I would."

"I think we all would," said Pete. He extracted a bottle of wine from the refrigerator, deftly opened it, and put it and three glasses on a little silver tray. "Why don't you take this out and leave me to my soup?"

"Are you sure I can't help you?"

"Yes. And don't give it away. There was only one tin of soup, re-member."

Arden liked Pete. Sometimes it was Arden and Pete versus Adam and Caroline. "I saw no tin at all," she said, with a laugh, and pushed through the door.

Adam and Caroline were standing by the window, whispering. Arden put the tray down on the low table in front of the sofa and poured wine into the three glasses. "The tomato juice had gone bad," she announced, "so we decided on wine. Would you like a glass, Caroline?"

"Yes, please," said Caroline.

"Adam?"

"I could have told him the tomato juice was rancid. It's been there for a hundred years, if a day."

"Then why did you not?" asked Caroline.

"Because he would have told me to shut up," said Adam.

"But you know he is right," said Caroline. "You really should shut up, sometimes."

"Of course I know," said Adam. "The problem is I have no self-control. I blame it on my parents. I was brought up well enough to know what not to say but not strictly enough to resist saying it. I was indulged and spoiled. Shamelessly. Until a certain age when a certain brother was born and I became unbearable and then I was just ignored. 'Go and play out of doors,' my mother would say, pushing me outside and locking the door behind me. They actually locked me out of the house, for hours and hours. In all sorts of weather. Can you imagine?"

"Yes," said Caroline. "I can."

"I would go to the garage and let the chauffeur interfere with me. Chauffeur interfere. That sounds very nice, doesn't it? It would be good in a poem. Or as a title: *The Interfering Chauffeur*."

Arden took a glass of wine from the tray and sat on the couch. She felt she wanted to drink it more than she wanted to serve them theirs. I suppose that makes me selfish, she thought, but so be it. She sipped the wine. It tasted very good: cold and clean. She shuddered slightly at the thought of the rancid tomato juice and drank more wine.

Pete appeared from the kitchen. He began to clear off the round table, which was stacked with books and dated newspapers and magazines.

"May I help?" asked Arden.

"No, thanks," said Pete.

"How is the soup coming?" asked Adam.

"Quite nicely," said Pete, and returned to the kitchen.

"Well," said Adam, after a moment. "Perhaps we should talk about this biography."

"Jules did not want a biography," said Caroline.

"That was my feeling too," said Arden.

"While I think it is very noble of both of you to consider Jules's feelings, I think such consideration is rather beside the point."

"Why is that?" asked Caroline.

"Jules is dead," said Adam, "as I seem to be constantly reminding you."

"I do not need you to remind me of that," said Caroline. "I know very well he is dead."

"Good. I am glad to hear it, as I had begun to wonder. And as he is dead, I think we should stop worrying about what Jules would or would not have wanted."

"But isn't that exactly our role as executors?" asked Arden. "I thought it was."

"No, my dear. Your role as executor is to manage his literary estate."

"And how can we do that without considering him?"

"Jules and his literary estate are two separate things. They are not one indivisible entity. He wrote a book. He was not his work. It was not him. It is a product."

"I think it is more than a product," said Arden.

"But you will admit it is separate from him?"

"Of course, in the most literal way."

"Why don't you tell us why you want this biography," said Caroline.

"Why do I want this biography? It is very simple! It is no great mystery. Let me try to put it simply: this biography, this authorized biography, which is guaranteed to be published by what I assume to be a reputable if somewhat . . . well, somewhat dingy university press, this biography will help immeasurably in making sure that Jules's work is not lost or overlooked. For work to survive, it must be read in context of the life. It was fine for Jules to stay private while he was alive, fine for him to want that, but if we don't allow some public investigation of his life, I am afraid his work will die with him. Disappear. And I do not wish to be responsible for that. I feel I owe my brother that much. That is what I can do for him now."

"Even if it is against his wishes?" asked Caroline.

"He made me his executor. As he did you and Arden. Somewhat perversely, of course, but nevertheless that is what he did. He has entrusted and empowered us. While he was alive it was all right for him to act in other than the best interest of his reputation. That was his decision to make, and I respected it. But he is dead. It is our decision to make now. We must do what we think is best."

"I wish I could find the letter he wrote me about this," said Caroline. "He was reading someone's biography—I can't remember whose; Maugham's, perhaps—and he said he couldn't bear for his life to be, well, I forget his words, but he compared it to a corpse being publicly exhumed."

"But you don't understand!" exclaimed Adam. "He will not have to bear it. He is dead! He bears nothing now!"

"Yes, I see your point," said Caroline. "It must seem foolish to you, but I am afraid I cannot concede. There is so little we can give the dead, beyond respecting their wishes. In fact, it is all we can give. It is all I can give, and I intend to give it."

"What about you, Arden?"

"I see both sides," said Arden. "I understand—I think I understand—both of your positions. And I think if there is a mistake to be made, the greater mistake would be in disregarding Jules's wishes. If you're right, Adam, and it's a mistake not to take advantage of what a biography would offer, that's the mistake I'd rather make. That mistake hurts no one, really. It can be changed in the future. But the other mistake is hurtful, and cannot be changed. You cannot take something out of the world once it is put in, but you can add things, later, if you want."

They were all silent a moment, and then Pete appeared with steaming and fragrant bowls of soup. They all stood up.

"It smells delicious, Pete," said Caroline.

They sat at the table and began eating the chicken rice soup, to which Pete had added lemon and cilantro and wine. It was delicious. They all agreed on that.

As it was all uphill, it was a slower walk back to the big house. And the two women were stunned by the heat and the wine they had drunk before, during, and after lunch. They would take naps when they got home, both of them, drowsing on large old beds in bedrooms at different ends of the house. They often did the same thing at the same time, unwittingly, for they were more alike than they cared to know, and there was something real between them, a rhythm, like love, that allowed them to live together as peacefully as they did.

They walked in silence, the sun on their bare arms and legs. Caroline carried her hat, trailing its ribbons. They passed the field of wildflowers, but the butterflies had disappeared. The flowers were left behind, however, like an image in a mirror that remains reflected after its subject passes.

"I'm glad that it's been decided," said Arden.

Caroline murmured something.

"I think we've made the right decision," said Arden. "I don't think a biography would make much difference anyway. I'm not convinced by that. It's better to proceed cautiously. I shall tell him we have no interest in a biography at this time."

"Yes," said Caroline. "Tell him that."

"I'll write to him as soon as we get home," said Arden. "We mustn't keep him waiting." As she said this her mind made a little leap, and a field appeared beside the field in which she had been thinking: She could write the biography. They couldn't stop her from doing that. And what else was she to do with her life? It was the project that she needed, that would give her direction and purpose, save her from this aimless fretting. She supposed she could do it. It was just a formula after all, a gathering of information, a filling-in of blanks, a compiling and arranging of facts. It seemed impossible but it must not be, as biographies were so often written. And with Adam and Caroline around it wouldn't be difficult to find out what she needed to know. Really, among the three of them, they knew everything. Or everything that would go into a biography. Adam knew about Jules's childhood and the past, and Caroline knew about the rest. And who better to write it than she? Some graduate student from Kansas who had never known Jules and never set foot in Uruguay? No wonder he wants to pick our brains, she thought. We mustn't let some stranger do it. I must write him at once and say no.

"I shall write him at once and say no," said Arden.

"Yes," said Caroline.

They turned into the drive and saw Portia, walking home from school, a ways ahead of them. She was trailing her cardigan in the dusty road and hopping along, singing. Some of her piping notes were carried back to the two women.

Arden called out her name.

Portia stopped hopping and singing and turned around. The two women caught her up. Arden leaned down and kissed her.

"Where have you been?" asked Portia.

"Having lunch with Uncle Adam and Pete," said Arden. "How was school? Pick up your sweater, darling. Don't drag it. Here, give it to me."

"What were you singing?" asked Caroline.

"Did you hear me?" asked Portia.

"Yes," said Caroline. "It sounded lovely."

"It was just a song," said Portia. "Well, not a song, really. I was making it up. Oh, before I forget. I've got to bring some yarn to school tomorrow. Sister Domina is teaching us knitting."

"Knitting?"

"Yes. It's either knitting or decoupage. But Sister Julian's doing the decoupage, so everyone chose knitting. So then we had to count off because there weren't enough needles and I was an even, and evens are knitting. Ana Luz and Paloma are knitting too. Marta is decoupage, but she's going to pretend the varnish makes her sick and get switched. Ana Luz showed her how to be sick."

"You must teach me to knit," said Caroline. "I would like to knit a nice, warm gray sweater to wear when it rains." She drew her arms around herself as if she were chilly. "I used to have the loveliest gray sweater. It was my sister's. I wore it when I painted, which was stupid of course, but I felt good in it. It must have been full of turpentine because one day I dropped my cigarette on it and it went up in flames. Luckily I got it off before it burned me. That's when I stopped smoking. Although it's really drinking I should have stopped. I only dropped the cigarette because I was drunk, you see. But there is only so much we can give up."

"We're knitting scarves, I think," said Portia. "Not sweaters."

CHAPTER FOUR

The dog was standing on top of the picnic table, which meant it was time for dinner. The dog communicated in odd ways. When she wanted to go outside she tipped over a wastebasket. The dog was looking toward the kitchen, as if she knew Omar was at the window. I should bring her inside and feed her, Omar thought, but first I must call Deirdre. I must call Deirdre. It was the thing he had been avoiding doing all afternoon. He must call Deirdre before he fed the dog. He picked up the telephone that hung on the wall and dialed her number. She answered in her usual slightly breathless way.

"It's me," said Omar. "Listen, I've got to talk to you."

"I hate that expression: talk to you. Why can't it be with? Why can't you talk with me? Am I to say nothing?"

"I want to talk with you," said Omar. "It's important. I want to see you. Can we get together?"

"When?"

"Now. Soon."

"I was going to go to Lucy Greene-Kessler's lecture about the simian aspects of *Mrs. Dalloway*."

"The what aspects?"

"Simian, I think. But I could be wrong."

"There are no simian aspects in *Mrs. Dalloway*," said Omar.

"Of course there are. You can find aspects of anything in Virginia Woolf. Or Lucy Greene-Kessler can. I could meet you at eight-thirty. But what is this about? What's happened? You sound like something is wrong."

"Something is wrong," said Omar. The dog jumped down from the picnic table and then immediately jumped back up. This meant feed me *now*.

"You haven't burned anything down, have you?"

"No," said Omar.

"Then what?"

"I'll tell you when I see you. I have to explain it. It's complicated."

"Wrong and complicated. That doesn't sound good. Are you okay? Can this wait until eight-thirty?"

"Yes," said Omar. "It will take me a while to get downtown. Assuming the car will start."

"You should get a new car."

"The car is presently the least of my problems."

"Oh, my. Is the complicated wrong thing something medical?"

"No," said Omar.

"You're not going to die or anything, are you?"

"No. Well, eventually. But no sooner than I thought. I think."

"Good. Where do you want to meet? How about Kiplings?"

"All right. Fine. Although I haven't got any money."

"I do. I'll see you there at eight-thirty. A little before, maybe. I'll try to sneak out. Once Lucy gets going she never looks up."

Omar parked behind the bank, in the lot reserved for customers. Although it was empty, as it was evening and the bank was closed, the sign that threatened that the cars of noncustomers would be towed at their expense made him nervous. In most public matters he was by nature literally and pridefully obedient. Two girls were playing hopscotch on hastily chalked squares in the far corner of the empty lot. Omar got out of the car. The girls knelt down and watched him cautiously as he crossed the parking lot, as if he might do them some harm. He smiled and waved at them but they just crouched and stared. When had children stopped trusting him? Why?

He walked up the alley to the street. He stopped outside the bookstore to cruise the free-books box but he couldn't deal with it: it always depressed him, these books out on the streets, begging to be taken home, like dogs at the pound, books that had filtered down through the economic system and arrived, irrevocably, at the bottom, in a box on the sidewalk. He walked past the shoe store that mysteriously stayed in business even though the shoes in the window never changed. An old couple ran the store and one of them was always sitting inside, smoking. Tonight it was the wife. Omar looked at the shoes behind the transparent yellow shade that was kept perpetually lowered, so the shoes were observed through a sort of jaundiced screen. They were mostly the kind of shoes old ladies wore when their feet got arthritic and gnarled, but most of the old ladies Omar saw in the grocery store now wore sneakers.

Just past the obsolete shoe store was Kiplings. Kiplings was an Indian restaurant for people who were leery of foreign food. It was Indian cooking filtered through British imperialism and modified for Americans. It was a fairly dismal, awful place but some of the curries were decent and the beer was cheap, and if you drank enough of it the place seemed less awful and dismal. Deirdre was sitting at the bar drinking a Bass Ale with lime, a combination she liked that always slightly revolted Omar. Just the thought of it made the inside of his mouth blanch. He sat down beside her. She kissed his cheek and laid her hand on his shoulder. "How are you?" she asked.

"Okay," he said. "How are you?"

"Awful. I passed by the bookstore and found out they ordered the wrong translation of Turgenev for my 201 next semester. They claimed the one I wanted wasn't available so they went ahead and ordered the Constance Garnett translation. I can't stand Constance Garnett, she's so Victorian and British, she makes everything sound like Dickens. I can't teach it. I'm furious. And they're such dopes down there. They don't understand that all translations are not alike."

"That's too bad," said Omar.

"I'm sorry. I know it's no big deal, but it makes me furious. Constance Garnett! Oh, and before I forget: it was influences of the Crimea in *Mrs. Dalloway*. I hate it when people put books in a historical context."

"Why?"

"Because it's unfair to people like me who know no history. A text should exist outside history. I mean, really, the Crimea! And why is it always *the* Crimea? Explain that to me."

"I think it's like the Balkans," said Omar.

"Well, that makes sense," said Deirdre. "That makes perfect sense: *the* Balkans. Because there are several Balkans, there are many Balkans. But there is only one Crimea. I think."

Omar said nothing.

"I'm sorry," said Deirdre. "It just infuriates me. I'm sorry." She shook her head. "So what's with you? What's wrong? Tell me."

"Should we get a table?" asked Omar.

"Are you hungry? Do you want to eat here?"

"Yes," said Omar. "Let's sit down."

They sat in a booth and ordered what they always ordered: a chicken madras, a vegetable curry, and a pitcher of beer. "So what's wrong?" Deirdre asked. "Tell me."

"It's about the fellowship," said Omar.

"What about it?"

"There's a hitch," said Omar.

"How can there be a hitch? You already got it."

"I know," said Omar. "But something's happened. Or rather, something's not happened."

"What? Tell me."

"I didn't get authorization."

Their beer arrived and Deirdre carefully filled two glasses, waiting several times for the foam to settle before she poured more. When she was angry with Omar she tried to take a "time out." It was a technique she had read about in a women's magazine she did not admit to reading. You were supposed to allow your anger to settle so that it would not stain your discourse. And so their conversations were often interrupted by these momentary silences while Deirdre became inordinately preoccupied with some meaningless task. Like carefully pouring the beer.

When the two glasses of beer were finally and equally full she said, "What?"

"I got a letter from the executors today. They're not granting me authorization."

"I thought you got authorization a long time ago. I thought you couldn't apply for the fellowship unless you had the authorization and cooperation of the estate." She sipped her beer.

"You couldn't. So on the application I said I had authorization. I didn't realize you had to have it, I thought you just had to have applied for it. And I got the dates mixed up and apparently mail to Uruguay takes longer than I thought. And I was sure they would say yes. I mean, why wouldn't they say yes? I have perfectly decent credentials and it's not like everyone in the world is working on a biography of Jules Gund. I'm sure people aren't racing to Uruguay beating down their doors. That's why I picked Gund. Nobody's ever heard of him."

"Omar, don't be stupid. Of course people have heard of him. He won the Americas Prize. He wandered into the jungle and shot himself in the head."

"I don't think it was the jungle."

"What do you mean?"

"I mean I don't think there's a jungle in Uruguay. I think it's more of a savanna. Or a veldt. Or a pampas, maybe."

"Whatever. People have heard of him. And the people who have heard of him are exactly the kind of people who write biographies. And race down to Uruguay. What did they say?"

"Who?"

"The executors! Have they given authorization to someone else?"

"No," said Omar.

"Well, that's good. So you could still get it. What did they say? Exactly."

"That they don't see the need for a biography at this time, nor at any time in the future."

"You keep saying they. Who are they?"

"There are three executors. I think that's part of the problem. Gund's wife, his brother, and this American woman he lived with at the end. She's the one who wrote me."

"And they're all down there in Uruguay?"

"Yes."

"That must be cozy."

"It's all very tortured and incestuous, I'm sure. It would make a wonderful book. And now it looks as if I'll never write it because I'll have to give back the fellowship because I lied on the application."

"But you're sure there's not another authorized biography?"

"Yes. At least that's what the letter said."

"So there is a chance that you could get authorization?"

"Yes, I suppose: theoretically there is a chance. Although this letter sounded very definite."

"Well, it's your only chance. Otherwise you'll have to give the fellowship back, and that means— Well, you know what that means."

"What?"

"It means you don't write the book, you don't get the book published, your contract isn't renewed, you lose your job, and you won't be able to get another job, at least not teaching. And what else can you do?"

"Nothing," said Omar.

"Exactly. So you've got to make this happen. Otherwise you'll end up selling shoes in a mall. And in a way, you haven't really lied on your application."

"How do you figure that?"

"Well, like you said, if you got the dates confused and if you really thought in good faith that you would get authorization, I'm sure you can get around it. And if you get them to change their minds and grant you authorization, then you won't have lied. I mean, you will have lied, but only temporarily, and they'll never need to know. The executors didn't cc the fellowship committee or anything evil like that, did they?"

"Not as far as I know."

"Well, it's really your only chance. If they see no need for a biography now you have to show them that there is a need. Make them think there is a need."

"Is there a need? I don't think the world is really crying out for a biography of Jules Gund."

"Fuck the world! The need is yours. Do you want to keep this fellowship, Omar? Do you want to write this biography?"

"Yes. Of course I do."

"Because sometimes it seems as if perhaps you don't. Sometimes it seems as though . . ."

"What?"

"I don't know. I just don't understand how you can fuck up like this. I mean, how could you get the dates wrong? And of course it takes forever for a letter to get to Uruguay! That's what Federal Express is for."

"Federal Express goes to Uruguay?"

"Federal Express will go wherever you pay them to go. If you want something to happen, Omar, you have to make it happen. Do you want this to happen?"

"Yes," said Omar. "I told you: yes."

"Then you have to make it happen," said Deirdre.

Although Deirdre lived only a couple of blocks from Kiplings, Omar drove her home.

"Do you want to stay over?" asked Deirdre.

"No," said Omar. "I've got to go home. I forgot to feed Mitzie."

"That stupid dog," said Deirdre.

"She's not stupid," said Omar.

"Yes she is. She's the stupidest dog I've ever known."

"I'm not going to argue with you about the intelligence of Mitzie," said Omar.

"I'm sorry," said Deirdre. "I know I'm being cranky. I'm sorry. It's just that . . ."

"What?" asked Omar.

Deirdre ran her finger through the mist that had collected inside the car window. She did not want to be mean. Just wait, she thought. Wait until you don't feel mean. Don't say anything while you're angry. She rolled down the window and erased her traces. "It's just that, well, this seems awfully symbolic to me in some way."

"What?"

"This business with your fellowship."

"What do you mean?"

She turned away from the window and looked at him. She put her hand on his leg. "I mean, it scares me a little. I think if you want things, you make them happen. Or at least you try to make them happen. And sometimes I think you don't want things enough. You just let things go wrong, you don't try, and I think, Well, maybe he

43

doesn't really want it, what does he want, what does he really want?"

"What are you talking about? Are you talking about the fellowship?"

"Yes, but it's not only the fellowship. It's—well, it's practically everything you do."

"That's not true," said Omar.

"What about the car?" asked Deirdre. "And your apartment? What if Yvonne hadn't let you use her house? What would have happened then?"

"I would have found another apartment."

"Yes, and probably burned that one down too!"

"It didn't burn down," said Omar. "Besides, it was an accident."

"I guess what I mean is that I don't really believe in accidents," said Deirdre. "Accidents happen because someone is not paying attention or is making mistakes. I mean the fire occurred for a reason. It wasn't spontaneous combustion. And you did throw water on it."

"It was a fire, okay? I panicked. And I didn't know you're not supposed to throw water on a grease fire."

"But Omar, you should know! There are just these things you should know. Things you need to know to cope in the adult world. Sometimes I wonder if it's because you were brought up in Canada. That the social welfare net stopped you from becoming a responsible, autonomous adult."

"So you think I'm to blame for the fire?"

"This isn't about the fire! Let go of the fire."

"But you said it was. You said it was everything I did."

"I was exaggerating, all right? I was exaggerating for effect. It's something I do. You know that."

"I know. But sometimes, when you say things like that, I wonder . . ."

"What?"

"I wonder if you really love me. I think, how can she say something like that to me, like You fuck up everything you do, how could she say that to me if she loved me? Or not how but why? How *and* why."

"Listen," said Deirdre, "I love you. You know I love you. This isn't about that. In fact, I say things like that to you because I love you."

"It doesn't sound like love. It sounds like anger."

"Of course it sounds like anger! It is anger! I'm angry, Omar, but that doesn't preclude love. They can coexist, you know. I am capable of feeling several emotions simultaneously. I'm a complex person. Life is complex. Love is complex. It isn't simple. It isn't about just one thing at a time."

"Why are you so angry?"

"I'm angry because you fucked up the fellowship! I mean, how could you fuck up a simple application? Why didn't you get authorization? Why did you lie?"

Omar was silent a moment. It looked as if he might cry. But then he spoke. "You know," he said, "you're an extremely capable person. You're hardworking and organized and you've always gotten everything you wanted. That's you. That's who you are. I'm not like that."

"But Omar, you make it sound as if being capable is some intrinsic talent. It's not. Being capable is about wanting to be capable. It's about making an effort to be capable. It's about following through. We're not talking about painting the Sistine Chapel. We're talking about using FedEx when it's necessary."

"Well, the fact is that I've fucked up," said Omar. "As apparently I always do."

"And now you feel sorry for yourself and you want me to feel sorry for you too. But I won't. I can't. If you really wanted to get this fellowship, and write this book, if you really wanted everything that is predicated on your doing those things—and I don't want to be brutal, but a lot of important shit is predicated on your doing those things—if you really wanted to do it, you would do it. You wouldn't let this stop you. You'd get authorization. You'd go down to Uruguay and not come back until you got authorization. You're so ready to give it all up."

"I'm not," said Omar. "I just don't know what to do."

"Go to Uruguay! You have the fellowship money, don't you?"

"Yes. But I should give the money back."

"No! Use the money. If you give it back, it's all over. Get authorization: go down and meet with the brother and sister and wife."

"It's the brother and wife and mistress."

"Whoever. Whomever? Whatever: charm them. Change their minds. You could go down over break. By next semester everything could be fine."

"Or I could be arrested for spending the fellowship money under false pretenses."

"They're not going to arrest you, Omar. They'll just fire you. But if you don't do it, they'll fire you too. I really don't think you've got any choice."

"I wonder how much it costs to fly to Uruguay? And where would I stay?"

"Well, there are answers to these questions. Call the airlines. Buy a guidebook."

"If I did go down there, I could start my local research."

"Let's not get ahead of ourselves," said Deirdre. "Look, I'm going in. I've got twenty-five so-called essays to read for tomorrow. Go home and think about this. Call me in the morning." She opened the door and stepped out onto the sidewalk, then leaned back into the car through the open window. "And I'm this way because I love you, Omar. If I didn't love you I wouldn't be like this. I wouldn't care about you. I care about you and I love you and I want you to write this book. I know you can. I want you to be successful. I don't want you to be one of those professors who are always wandering around the halls searching for their office with egg salad spilled down their front. Okay? Is that clear?"

"Yes," said Omar.

"Then kiss me," said Deirdre, leaning farther into the car.

Omar had been evicted from his last apartment after a fire had gutted the kitchen. Fortunately, Yvonne Mailer, a history professor, was spending her sabbatical year in Turkey and was looking for someone to house- and dog-sit and as she was a woman who did not listen to local gossip she knew nothing of Omar's incendiary past and was more than happy to leave her keys with him and fly to Istanbul. Her house was about ten miles outside of town in what once had been a lakeside community of summer homes called Hiawatha Woods, but the dam that contained the lake had been sundered by a tornado in 1982 and so now the lake was replaced by a marshland through which meandered a torpid stream. Yvonne's home was the only one that had been winterized and was inhabited year-round, and so living there, among the empty dwellings, made Omar feel like a caretaker at some out-of-season summer camp.

The house was cold when he returned to it. There was a woodburning stove in the living room, and Yvonne had assured Omar that if properly maintained and securely shut, the stove could be left running all night long or in one's absence, but after his recent experience with fire Omar was afraid to leave it burning out of his sight. And so he wasted a lot of time, and was often cold, as he was constantly extinguishing flames only to rekindle them hours later.

When he got the fire burning he went into the kitchen and fed Mitzie, giving her more than usual to make up for the delay. The dried food cascaded into the bowl, making a tintinnabulation that usually prompted Mitzie to come scurrying from wherever it was she snoozed. But when the bowl was full and the silence had returned the dog had not appeared. Omar called her name. He walked through the small rooms of the little house, looking for her in the places where she usually slept, but she was nowhere, and then he thought: Could I have not let her in when I left? Did I leave her outside? He could not remember letting her in the house but that did not mean he had not. But she was not in the house. He opened the kitchen door and turned on the spotlight that illuminated the weed-choked clearing. Mitzie was not there. The picnic table on which she liked to stand was an empty stage. He called her name and then listened, but heard nothing that sounded comfortingly canine: no bark, no jiggling of dog tags, no quadrupedal pitter-patter. He went back inside and put on his coat and grabbed the flashlight and then walked out into the dark woods. There were rumors that lapdog-eating coyotes roamed the woods. He called the dog's name again and again, walking forward in the illuminated nimbus the flashlight cast at his feet. He looked back to make sure he could still see the lights of the house behind him and realized he had left the fire burning. Should he go back and extinguish it? Had he closed and latched the little metal oven door? Of course he had. But he could not remember doing it. Why didn't he remember more of what he did? Surely the fire was safe and contained. He turned away from the house and walked farther into the woods.

Suddenly his feet descended into the soft, wet earth and he could not lift them. He must have been walking toward the drained lake bed instead of around it. Quicksand, he thought. He had sunk up to his knees. My new shoes! He tried to lift just one foot out of the muck and succeeded, but he could not find solid ground to rest it on while he extracted the other. His foot resettled itself in the unfirm earth. He could no longer see the lights of the house and had lost his sense of direction. Don't panic, he thought. He stood still for a moment. At least he was not sinking further. And then he realized that he was, slowly, sinking. He saw a little sapling growing within arm's reach and grabbed hold of its thin, adolescent trunk and tried to use it as leverage to extract his feet. He succeeded only in pulling the tree from the earth. He stood still for a moment, guiltily clutching the little tree, as if he might be apprehended, and then he tossed it into the darkness. He tried then to move his feet subterraneanly, shuffling toward more solid ground. But the ground in which his feet were ensconced clutched them possessively. And then he tried again to lift one foot out of the muck and lunge forward and lift the other before the first had a chance to resettle itself and in this way he finally regained terra firma. He sat down to catch his breath and realized he had dropped the flashlight. He could see it shining in the muck a few feet away, taunting him. When he had regained his breath he set off through the woods. As the road circled the lake, he knew he would come out on it eventually, and could find his way home from there.

He approached the house from the front. It had not burned down. It looked a little like a house in a fairy tale: the windows shone with light and smoke cutely wafted up from the chimney. Mitzie sat on the porch and watched him approach, patiently, as if they had been out for a walk together and she had raced ahead and returned first. Omar stood for a moment. It was not that he was afraid to enter the little house, it was more that he felt he had somehow forfeited the right. It's not my house, he thought. It's not my dog. He wished that something was his, unequivocally and irrevocably his, but he knew that nothing was. It had never occurred to him, or troubled him, before, but here he was, twenty-eight years old, standing in front of a house that wasn't his in a deserted community surrounding a nonexistent lake watched by a dog he neglected. Mitzie looked at him curiously and then padded down the front steps and walked toward him as if she knew it was her place to welcome him. She sniffed at his muddy pants and then sat down and gazed up at him. He reached down and palmed the warm, furred dome of her skull. She whined. And then they entered the house together. It was now warm: the fire sang from inside the stove. Mitzie found her dinner. Omar took off his pants and shoes and sat down in the living room and listened to her eat. When she was through she came out of the kitchen and laid her head on his lap. For a dog who communicated in odd ways, her message was clear: he was forgiven. Dinner had been eaten and they were both home and it was warm, and everything, as far as it concerned Mitzie, was all right.

"Maybe I should call him," Deirdre said. And then, because Marc Antony did not look up, she said it again.

Marc Antony's real name was Michael Anthony but Deirdre called him Marc Antony. He was her roommate. She really didn't need a roommate—at least not financially—but she liked having someone around she could talk to, and since she didn't want Omar to live with her until he had responsibly lived on his own—and who knew when that would be—she got a roommate. Marc Antony. Marc Antony was a very good roommate. He was quiet and clean. He liked to bake, and dust bothered him, so he actually dusted. He was going to law school. He was cute, too, but gay.

Marc Antony was sitting at the kitchen table reading one of his big, boring law books. I could never go to law school, Deirdre thought. I'd die of boredom. At least I get to read novels. Although mainly what she read was students' essays. She was drinking some coffee, trying to wake up a little before she started grading her 101 essays. Although there was really no need to be awake to grade them.

"Marc Antony, I said maybe I'll call him," she said again, loudly.

"Who?" he said. He did not look up. He did this: tried to stay disengaged. It was the only bad roommatey thing about him.

"Just talk to me for five minutes," Deirdre said. "Five minutes. Then I'll leave you alone."

"Three minutes," he said. He closed his book and looked at his watch. "Go," he said.

"Omar," she said. "I'm talking about Omar, of course. Who else would I call? He's the only man I would call at"—she looked at the clock on the kitchen wall—"oh my God it's eleven-thirty already. At eleven-thirty. I was mean to Omar," she said.

"You're always mean to Omar," said Marc Antony.

"That's not true," said Deirdre. "I'm not always mean to Omar. I love him."

"I didn't say you didn't. I just said you're always mean to him. Whenever I see you together you're always at him about something. Always hectoring him."

"I don't like that word, *hectoring*. Besides, I don't hector him. I nudge him."

"Well, you just admitted you were mean to him."

"I know. I was. And that's why I'm upset. I don't like it when I'm mean to him."

"Then don't be."

"I tried, really I tried. But you see, it's impossible to be with him and not be a little mean. Sometimes. He's so exasperating. He fucked up his fellowship and now he might lose it."

"So. You have to realize that what happens to him happens to him. That he'll learn from his mistakes or he won't and there's nothing you can do about it."

"You don't think I can hurry him along that learning curve a little?"

"No. You have to accept his pace. As a teacher you should know that."

"But he's not my student."

"Then don't treat him like your student."

"You think I treat him like a student?"

"Yes. Like a student. Or dog. Like a dog student. A dog student in obedience school."

"But when he does something, well, something stupid like this, like fucking up his fellowship, how should I respond? I mean, assuming you know everything?"

"Be understanding and encouraging. Be sympathetic. Be helpful."

"Wow. Understanding, encouraging, sympathetic, and helpful. Simultaneously? I think that's a little beyond my ken."

Marc Antony was glancing at his book.

"So do you think I should call him?" Deirdre asked.

"Yes," said Marc Antony. "And your three minutes are up."

Deirdre went into her bedroom and called Omar. His line was busy. She waited about five minutes and then called again. This time he answered.

"It's me," she said. "Who were you talking to?"

"When?" he asked.

"When? Now. Five minutes ago. I called you and it was busy."

"Oh," he said. "I was talking to the airline. I called to get information about flights to Uruguay. It's not that expensive. I mean, it's expensive, but not as bad as I thought."

"Are you going to go?"

"Yes. I think so. I reserved the ticket. I have twenty-four hours to decide. I'll go right after New Year's."

"Listen, Omar. I called you because I feel bad about the way I was tonight. I'm sorry if I was mean to you."

"No," said Omar. "I don't blame you. If I were you, I would be disgusted with me too."

"I'm not disgusted with you! Omar! I could never be disgusted with you. You can never be disgusted with someone you love. You can be annoyed. I was annoyed, I admit it, and I'm sorry that sometimes when I'm annoyed with you it triggers these other, negative emotions, but I want to stop that, really I do. I want to help you. I want to be understanding. I want to be understanding and helpful and a few other things I can't remember at the moment."

Omar said nothing.

"Listen, maybe I should come with you. I think I could help you. I've had more experience than you with stuff like this, and—"

"No," said Omar. "I think I should do this myself. In fact, I think it is very important that I do this myself."

"Why?"

"Because. It's important for me. I got myself into this situation and I should get myself out."

"But if somebody else can help you— If you need help from somebody, it's okay to take it. It's stupid not to."

"Do you think I'm stupid?"

"No," said Deirdre. "Of course not! That's not what I meant. I meant letting pride stop you from accepting help, when you need help, is stup—— isn't wise. There's nothing wrong with letting people help you."

"I appreciate your offer," said Omar. "But I don't want help with this."

"You appreciate my offer?" said Deirdre. "What does that mean? You appreciate my offer? Omar, it's me, Deirdre. You don't appreciate my offer. Don't ever say that to me again."

"All right," said Omar. "I won't."

"Omar, don't get all weird and distant. I said I was sorry. I want to help. I think you need my help. I think it would be good for us if we do this together. It could be very good for us. It could be fun, and exciting. To go to Uruguay, and solve this problem, and be together and in some place that isn't Kansas. I don't think you should risk going by yourself."

"You don't think I can do this by myself?"

"Of course I do! I have complete confidence in you. Of course you can! I just think it would be better, safer, and more fun if we go together. Better for both of us. Individually and as a couple."

"That's funny," said Omar. "I think it would be better for both of us, individually and as a couple, if I go by myself. I really do."

"You sound uncharacteristically certain about this. What's happened since I left you? Since you left me?"

"I almost drowned in quicksand," said Omar. "I saw my life

pass before my eyes and I did not like what I saw. I have resolved to change my life."

"What were you doing in quicksand?"

"Looking for Mitzie."

"Mitzie was in quicksand?"

"No. I was. Mitzie was home waiting for me. Mitzie is much smarter than me."

"Than I. But no, Omar! You're much smarter than Mitzie."

"Thank you," said Omar.

"Listen. It's been quite an evening. What with the Crimea and Constance Garnett and quicksand and all. Let's go to bed. Well, let's you go to bed, I still have to read my 101 essays, but you go to bed and we'll talk about this tomorrow. Let's not resolve all this tonight. Let's talk again in the morning. Okay?"

"All right," said Omar. "I am tired. Exhausted, in fact."

"It amazes me that you can sleep at a time like this," said Deirdre. "If I were in your position, I'd be up all night. Of course, I'll be up all night anyway."

"Well," said Omar. "Good night."

"Omar? I am sorry about before. I do want to help you. In whatever way I can. Okay?"

"Yes," said Omar. "Thank you."

"I can feel you withdrawing."

"I'm not withdrawing. I'm just tired. I want to go to bed."

"All right," said Deirdre. "Do you know I love you? I love you, you know."

"I know," said Omar. "I love you too."

"I wish you had stayed over," said Deirdre.

"Tomorrow night," said Omar.

"Okay. Sleep well. I'll talk to you in the morning."

He said good night and hung up. Deirdre looked out the window. The movie theater across the street was closing. A guy on a ladder was changing the title on the marquee from one stupid movie to another. For a moment, when the two titles were combined, it looked like gobbledygook. Gobbledygook. Once Deirdre wrote "Gobbledygook!" in the margin of a particularly illiterate student's essay. The student complained and Nicholson Garfield, the department chairman, told Deirdre to limit her comments to remarks that were within academic parameters. Deirdre showed him the definition of *gobbledygook* in the dictionary. He told her not to be clever at his or the students' expense.

Deirdre lay back on the bed. She could tell when the movie theater lights went out because they stopped reflecting on the ceiling of her bedroom. It was rather dark then. After a moment, she got up and turned on the light. She sat down at her desk and began to read her students' essays on the role of fate in *Tess of the d'Urbervilles*.

CHAPTER FIVE

Omar had always intended to learn Spanish before he went to Uruguay, but going to Uruguay was always something that was going to happen in some indefinite future, a time before which he would certainly have plenty of time to learn a foreign language. But of course it had not worked out that way: here he was in Montevideo and he spoke not one word of Spanish. Well, maybe a word or two.

He decided that it was too easy to get places. I really should not be in Montevideo so soon. It was better before planes. If I had had to take a boat to Uruguay, I could have learned Spanish on the boat. I would have taken a Spanish boat and spoken with the sailors. And learned a sort of crude but serviceable Spanish that would impress the natives for its authenticity.

It was a problem, not speaking the language. He had hoped that people would speak English or French, of which he spoke a little, but they did not. At least not the ones he had come in contact with. Perhaps if he stayed at a more expensive hotel his chances of encountering English-speakers might increase, but he could not afford to waste his money on extravagances. Hence the Hotel Egipt. It was really not such a bad hotel. Not having a window was a little weird. Actually there was a window, but when Omar drew the curtains aside he saw that it had been bricked over. If he spoke Spanish he could perhaps ask for a room with a window. *Por favor, yo*— what was want?—*desiro? uno cuarto con la* window. Or maybe saying "I want" was rude. He should say "Can I have." May I have. But in Spanish.

Omar had been in Montevideo two days. Two days of eating all his meals at the little coffee shop—well, he supposed it wasn't called a coffee shop in Spanish—beside the hotel. For breakfast he had *huevos revueltos,* and they were aptly named: they were revolting. The yolk and the white were only lackadaisically intermingled and strange things (maybe bits of mushrooms, which Omar hated) were chopped up and added to the eggs. He wanted to say "No things in the eggs: just eggs." *Sólo huevos.* Did that mean only eggs or one egg? So he picked all the things out and ate only the eggs and hoped that if he did this often enough they might catch on and leave the things out. But when you picked all the things out there wasn't really much egg. Just enough to hold the mess of things together. For lunch he had *sopa de tortilla* and *cerveza.* And for dinner he had *arroz con pollo.* And more *cerveza.* He kept going to the same place because he thought his chances of learning the language were better if he interacted with the same people repeatedly. The same waitress worked all three meals, so she had served him six times, but she did not speak. Could she be dumb? It would be his luck to frequent a restaurant with a dumb waitress.

Two days had gone by, two nights at a hotel and six meals, and Omar had accomplished nothing. It was not that he had not tried. But he could do nothing until he got to Ochos Rios and no one seemed to know where that was or how to get there. Or at least that is what Omar assumed from his confusing visits to the bus and train station. He had shown his slip of paper with the address carefully printed in block letters to ticket sellers and they had all shaken their heads and waved their hands dismissively. Could it be that it was a place impossible to get to? Could there be such a place? He had never been able to find it on a map, but he had assumed that was the fault of the maps he had consulted. He knew it existed because he had sent mail there; it had been received because it had been responded to. Perhaps he should write them a letter asking for directions. Of course, it would be much better if he just showed up; if he wrote them first they could tell him not to come, which they could not do if he was already there. They could tell him to go away but they could not tell him not to come. Of course, by refusing authorization they had already told him not to come, in a way. But he couldn't think of it that way. What he had to do was get there and then count on his charm and their mercy. And pray that their mercy was greater than his charm.

Or maybe he should spare himself the ordeal of getting there and being rejected in person. They could be crazy and dangerous, he supposed. Who knew? Perhaps they had guns and shot strangers. It might be better to admit defeat and fly back home. He could tell Deirdre he had seen them, pleaded with them, and been refused. There was no way she would ever know he had not. Of course, he would be ashamed to do that. Like all things, it was a matter of choice: the shame of going home at this point or the probable mortification of continuing.

CHAPTER SIX

Arden and Portia were filling a hole in the drive with gravel when they heard a car stop outside the gate. They turned around to see somebody clamber out of it with a suitcase. The car sped away, and the person, who was a young man, stood there in the hot sun and roiling dust, just outside the gate.

"Who is that?" asked Portia.

"I don't know," said Arden.

"Is he coming to us?"

"I don't know." She waited a moment, but the man just stood there, looking around himself. He seemed a bit dazed. He put the suitcase down on the road and dabbed at his face with a handkerchief. Then he picked up the suitcase and began walking toward them up the drive.

"He's coming," said Portia.

"Yes," said Arden. Who can it be? she wondered. Getting out here with a suitcase. As the man drew closer he revealed himself to be rather good-looking, tall and slim with dark hair and features and skin. He looked tired and dirty and his clothes were rather a mess.

"Buenas tardes," said Arden, as he approached them.

"Yes," he said. *"Buenas tardes."* He put down the suitcase, as if it were impossibly heavy. And then he said, *"¿Habla usted inglés?"*

"Yes," said Arden.

"Oh, good," he said, and smiled. His teeth were very white. "I am looking for—is this Ochos Rios?"

"Yes," said Arden. "This is Ochos Rios."

"My name is Omar Razaghi. I am looking for Arden Langdon."

For a moment Arden didn't answer. She didn't know what to do. He was a strange man on the road toting a suitcase.

Portia answered. She looked up at her mother and said, "That's you."

"Yes," Arden admitted. "That's me."

"Oh, good," said Omar. He smiled again. "I'm lucky. I'm very happy to meet you." He held out his hand.

Arden didn't particularly want to shake it, but she did. It was easier to shake it than to ignore it.

"I wrote to you a couple months ago," Omar said. "About the biography of Jules Gund. And you wrote me back. Do you remember?"

"Yes," said Arden. "Of course."

"Good." He seemed to not know what else to say.

"And . . ." Arden prompted.

"Yes," said Omar. "And . . . and I wondered if I could talk to you? About the book? You, and the other executors. Not now, but at a time that would be convenient to you."

"But didn't you get my letter?" asked Arden. "We decided not to authorize a biography."

"Yes, I know," said Omar. "But I wondered—if . . . well, I'd still like to talk to you."

"You've come all this way to talk to us?" asked Arden. "Or did you just happen to be passing by?"

"No," said Omar. And then he said, "Well, yes, in fact I have. But I really just want to talk to you. I'm sorry to appear like this. I mean suddenly, out of nowhere. I was going to call you but I couldn't find a public phone and then someone was driving this way and I thought it might be easier, better, if I just . . ."

"Arrived?"

"Yes," said Omar. "I didn't know what to do. It's been very difficult to get here. But I can come back. If you tell me when, I can come back, and we can talk then. Is there a time I can come back to talk to you?"

"And where—where are you staying?"

Omar looked around, as if a hotel might suddenly present itself. "I don't know," he said. "Somewhere near here, I hope. Is there a hotel in town?"

"No," said Arden.

"Well, there must be one somewhere," said Omar, almost petulantly. "If you'll tell me when to come back, I'll go and find a place to stay."

"But you're on foot," said Arden. "And there isn't a place for miles. Who drove you here?"

Omar looked back at the road, but the car had long since disappeared. "I don't know. A man I met in Ansina. I gave him five hundred pesos."

"Five hundred pesos! You're crazy."

"Yes," said Omar. "It seemed a lot. But there was no other way to get here."

"No," said Arden. "I suppose there wasn't, not from Ansina. But now that you're here there's nowhere else for you to go. So you might as well come up to the house with us. You can stay there until we can get you back into town."

"But I don't want to intrude. Really, I can sleep outdoors, or something."

"Don't be ridiculous," said Arden. "You cannot sleep outdoors. Look at you. Come up to the house. Here, put your suitcase in the wheelbarrow."

Omar put his suitcase and knapsack in the wheelbarrow, and

then began wheeling it up the rutted drive, behind the girl and woman. He felt exhausted, too tired to even worry about making a good impression.

"Why did you take the bus to Ansina? Why didn't you come to Tranqueras?" asked Arden.

"No one in Montevideo seemed to know how to get here. Finally a woman told me to take the bus to Ansina and get a ride from there. I didn't know what else to do."

"Ansina!" said Arden. "I don't know what she was thinking."

"Neither do I," said Omar.

"Well, you got here," said Arden.

"You seem very far away from everything," said Omar. "Is there a town nearby?"

"Yes," said Arden. "Tranqueras. Well, about ten miles from here. But you came the other way, didn't you?"

"I suppose," said Omar. "I was about to get nervous. I wasn't sure where that man was taking me. There's been nothing for miles and miles. Just forest."

They turned a corner in the drive and the house came into view. It was very large, made of brick, which at some distant point had been painted yellow, with a mossed-over slate roof. It had a classical, elegant façade, and looked very out of place in the unkempt landscape. Omar stopped for a moment and looked up at it. "Wow," he said.

"It's a monstrosity, isn't it?" asked Arden.

"No," said Omar. "I think it's beautiful."

Arden and Portia started walking again, but Omar did not move. They paused and looked back at him.

"What's wrong?" Portia said.

"Nothing," said Omar. "It's just that—I never thought I'd be here. I mean, you read a book and think all about this place, but you don't really think it exists, you don't really think you will be there—at least I never thought, never—"

62

Arden took the wheelbarrow from him. "Come," she said.

"No, no," he said. He fought her for possession of the wheelbarrow. "Let me."

She let him take it. They walked the rest of the way up the drive in silence. There was a flight of stone steps leading up to the front door.

"You can leave the barrow here," said Arden. "I'll take it around back later. Just grab your bags."

Omar took his bags and followed them through the door.

Caroline was descending the stairs from the tower as Arden climbed them. Arden heard her and waited on the landing.

"Who was that?" Caroline asked. "I saw you coming up the drive with a man."

"It's the biographer!" exclaimed Arden. "The one who wrote to us."

"What's he doing here?" asked Caroline.

"He wants to talk to us. He wants us to reconsider. He's come all the way from Kansas."

"He's come all this way for that?"

"Yes," said Arden. "Apparently."

"Is he mad?"

"Apparently," said Arden. "He took the night bus to Ansina and paid someone five hundred pesos to be driven here. And he has no place to stay."

"So he's staying here?"

"At least for tonight. What else could I do?"

"Nothing, I suppose. He's not crazy in any dangerous sort of way, is he?"

"No," said Arden. "Just misguided. He's taking a bath. I told him we'd have dinner about seven-thirty. Should I call Adam?"

"Yes," said Caroline. "No—wait. Maybe it would be better if

tonight it's just us. Adam—well, you know Adam. It might be calmer if it's just us, at least at first. With Adam things will be difficult."

"Yes," said Arden. "I was thinking the same."

"Have we got anything decent for dinner?"

"I was going to make a risotto. And baked eggplant."

"What's he like?" asked Caroline. "He looks dark. Is he African?"

"No. He's Egyptian or something, I think."

"How old would you say he is?"

"Oh," said Arden. "It's hard to tell. Twenty-five. Thirty? He must be desperate to have come all this way. Or crazy. I think he's a little stunned."

"Perhaps he's not very bright," Caroline suggested.

"I think he's just addled. It's probably coming on the night bus. He said he would sleep outdoors! Apparently he thought there would be a hotel in town. A Holiday Inn, no doubt."

"Well, it's a new face at the table, if nothing else." Caroline began to reclimb the stairs, but turned around. "Let's have some decent wine tonight. I'm tired of plonk."

"What do you want?"

"How about champagne?"

"Champagne? Won't that give him the wrong idea?"

"I don't really care what idea we give him. It's just an excuse to drink the champagne."

Arden was about to slice the eggplant when she heard the water draining out of the tub upstairs. She laid down her knife and then climbed the back stairs, and walked down the hall. The door was closed and she knocked.

"Yes," Omar said.

"It's me," said Arden. "Arden Langdon."

She waited, and after a moment Omar opened the door. His hair was still wet and uncombed. He had on a clean pair of pants and a pressed shirt but was barefoot. The shirt was unbuttoned and a slice of his dark, hairy chest was exposed. He smelled clean and fresh.

"Hello," he said. He had closed the shutters and the room behind him was dark. He had opened his suitcase on the bed. She noticed that it was neatly packed.

"Was your bath all right? Was there enough hot water?"

"Yes," said Omar. "Thank you."

"You must be tired. Could you sleep on the bus?"

"Not really," said Omar. "But I don't feel tired. I think it's the excitement of being here. Of getting here. I wasn't sure I would. In fact, for a while I was sure I wouldn't. It isn't an easy place to get to."

"Yes," said Arden. "I know." She paused for a moment. "I'd like to know why you've come," she said. "I'm sorry to be rude. It's just that it's odd to have you here and not really know. Are you really here to try to change our minds?"

"Yes," said Omar.

"Why?" asked Arden.

"Because I need to," said Omar. "I want to write a biography of Jules Gund. And I can't write the book without your authorization."

"But of course you can. People write unauthorized biographies all the time."

"Well, yes," said Omar. "Theoretically, I could. But you see, it's complicated. It involves a fellowship, and the university press, and they won't give me the money or publish the book unless it's authorized."

"Oh," said Arden. "That is a problem. No wonder you're here."

"I'm sorry to be trouble," said Omar.

"You're not trouble," said Arden. "I'm just sorry you've come all this way. Because you won't change our minds. I'm afraid our minds are well set."

It was Omar's turn to say "Oh."

"I'm sorry."

"I think I could write a very good biography. And I'd like to work closely with you, and respect your wishes. That's what I wanted to tell you all. I understand that things are complicated, and I'd be willing to be, well, tactful, you know, or silent, as you wanted."

"Oh, no," said Arden. "It isn't out of a wish to censor or silence that we're withholding authorization. You mustn't think that. That's not it at all."

"Then why?" asked Omar.

"I'm really not at liberty to say," said Arden. "I'm sorry to be so vague, but you must take my word for it. You'd be wasting your time if you thought you could change our minds. And I just don't want to see you wasting your time."

"But I've come all this way," said Omar. "Can't I at least talk to you all?"

"Oh, of course," said Arden. "I won't prevent you from doing that. Caroline will be joining us for dinner. And you can see Adam, tomorrow, perhaps. He lives quite close by."

"And do you all feel the same?"

"I suppose not, since we're all different people. Quite different people, as you'll see. But our decision is mutual, if not our reasons."

"Oh," said Omar.

"I'm sorry to bring bad news. I just didn't want you to get your hopes up, now that you're here. I thought you deserved to know what the situation is."

"Yes," said Omar. "Thank you."

"I'll let you finish dressing. I'm sorry to have barged in on you like this."

"No," said Omar. "I appreciate your talking to me. It's kind of you. You're different from what I expected. Much different."

"How?" asked Arden.

"Younger. I guess I supposed all executors were ancient and intimidating."

"Oh, I hope I'm not that," said Arden. She thought, I mustn't let him flirt with me.

"And you're beautiful," said Omar. "I didn't think executors would be beautiful."

"So your strategy is to flatter us all?" asked Arden.

"Oh, I'm too stupid to have a strategy," said Omar. "If I had a strategy, I wouldn't be here in the first place."

Omar finished dressing, but it was still too early to go to dinner. He stood by the window and looked down through a chink in the shutter. He could see a clothesline on which was hung what seemed to be an inordinate amount of women's intimate apparel. Brassieres and panties fluttered radiantly in the twilight. Omar quickly closed the shutter. In a little while he would have to go down there and have dinner with them. And be charming. If I don't get authorization after this, he thought, what will I do? I can't go back. But there is nothing else you can do. You must go back. Maybe it isn't so bad. Deirdre was exaggerating. He could return the fellowship money. What was left of it. The balance he could borrow from his parents, although they had never forgiven him for not going to medical school. They had warned him about becoming an academic and they were right. Perhaps that would make them kindly disposed: when people were right, and you admitted you were wrong, they were inclined to be charitable. But he mustn't give up so easily. Just because Arden Langdon told him it was useless didn't mean she was right. In fact, maybe she was trying to scare him off. It was odd of her to come to his room like that. She's only one out of three.

Maybe she never even told the others about his letter. And of course she would not want a biography. She was the villain, the mistress, the home breaker. Or was it wrecker: home wrecker?

At 7:30 Omar appeared in the courtyard to find Portia setting a round table. The courtyard was empty except for the table, a fountain at its center—a round basin in which a spilling urn stood atop a fluted column.

"Hello," he said.

"Hello," said Portia.

"My name is Omar," said Omar.

"Yes," said Portia, "I know."

"May I help you?"

"Do you know how?" asked Portia.

"Not really," said Omar. "But I can follow your example."

"It goes fork, fork, knife, spoon. It would go fork, fork, knife, spoon, spoon on top, but we're not having soup."

"Do you usually have soup?" asked Omar.

"No," said Portia. "Not with dinner. Do you?"

"No," said Omar.

"We have soup every day at school," said Portia.

"Where do you go to school?"

"The convent of Santa Teresa. She was the little flower of God."

"Was she?" asked Omar.

"Yes," said Portia. "She drank her own sputum."

"Why did she do that?"

"To mortify herself," said Portia.

"Oh," said Omar.

"The spoon goes on the outside," said Portia. "Fork, fork, knife, spoon."

"Ah, yes," said Omar. "Sorry."

"Who is your favorite saint?" asked Portia.

"I don't think I have one," said Omar. "I adore all saints equally. Who is yours?"

"Saint Agnes. They say that roses and lilies fell from the sky when she prayed. I would like to see that. When I pray, I ask God to drop something."

"I hope nothing too large."

Portia laughed. "No," she said. "Just a feather or something."

"And does he?"

"Once a little paint fell off the ceiling."

"Really?" said Omar.

"But the paint is always falling," said Portia. "Hey! Why are you folding the napkins like that?"

"You don't approve?" asked Omar.

Portia studied them for a moment. "I suppose they're all right," she said.

"Should I do them like yours?" asked Omar.

"No," said Portia. "Why are you here?"

"I want to talk to some people here," said Omar.

"Who?"

"Your mother and uncle and . . ." Omar did not know how to characterize Portia's relationship to the wife. "And Mrs. Gund."

"About what?"

"A book I am writing. A book I want to write."

"What kind of book?"

"A biography," said Omar. "Do you know what a biography is?"

"Yes," said Portia. "Of course. I read a biography of Helen Keller. She was blind and deaf and dumb. Dumb doesn't mean you're stupid, it means you can't talk. Only grunt." She grunted. "Are you writing a biography of my father?"

"I hope to," said Omar.

Arden appeared with a tray. On it was a bottle of champagne and several glasses.

"He helped me set the table," said Portia. "Look how he folded the napkins."

"Very nice," said Arden.

"He's writing a biography," said Portia.

"Is he?" asked Arden.

"Yes," said Portia. "Of Jules."

"Is he?" asked Arden.

"I only said I hope to," said Omar.

"Would you like a glass of champagne, Omar?" asked Arden.

"Champagne?" asked Portia. "Why champagne?"

"Caroline wanted champagne. Why don't you go up and tell her that dinner is ready? Now that the food is cooked and the table is set she may make her entrance."

Portia entered the house.

Arden looked at Omar. "Champagne," she said. "Yes? No?"

"Yes, please," said Omar.

Arden poured two glasses of champagne and handed one to Omar.

"Thank you," he said.

"Sit down," said Arden.

Omar sat. "Cheers," he said, lifting his glass.

"Yes," said Arden. "Cheers."

They both sipped from their glasses.

"It's very kind of you to let me stay here," said Omar. "I want to apologize again for intruding."

Arden shrugged. "In a way I admire you for showing up like that."

Omar seemed to blush a little. He sipped his champagne.

"Not many people would have come all this way on the basis of so little," said Arden.

"No," said Omar. "But there was nothing else I could think to do."

"So you came all this way."

"Yes," said Omar.

"Well, I think that entitles you to at least a glass of champagne."

They were silent a moment. Omar looked around the courtyard, then up at the house, which surrounded them. "I like your house very much," said Omar.

"It's falling apart," said Arden. "Of course, everything is falling apart, but things seem to be falling apart here a bit more quickly than usual. One day it will all come tumbling down, I'm sure."

"Is it very old?"

"No. The decay makes it look older than it is. It was built in 1935, when Jules's parents came over. It's supposed to be a replica of their *schloss*. They wanted the comfort of familiar architecture, so they tried to re-create a bit of Bavaria here in the new world. I think something got lost in the translation, though. Quite a bit, in fact."

"Why did they come here?" Omar asked.

"To get away from Hitler," said Arden. "Jules's mother was Jewish."

"Yes, of course," said Omar. "I knew that. I mean why here, why Uruguay, why this spot?"

"Oh," said Arden. "Jules's family was in the mining business. There was a magnesium mine near here. Or a supposed one. They came under the pretense of running that. Uruguay let them in because they brought money with them, and promised to keep the mine open, and people employed, for a certain number of years. And they built this house, and dammed the river, and made the lake, and brought the gondola and almost everything they owned across the ocean."

They were silent a moment and then Omar asked, "How far is it to the lake?"

"About three miles," said Arden. "Maybe a bit farther. The road's washed out, so you have to walk. There's a shortcut through the woods."

"And is the gondola still there?"

"Yes," said Arden. "It's rotting in the boathouse. There is a key here somewhere. Or was. Things disappear."

"I would like to see it," said Omar.

"It's rather hideous," said a voice behind them. They both turned and saw Caroline standing in the doorway, very beautiful in a blue dress with a black silk shawl. She wore a necklace of hammered silver leaves, and silvered leaves hung from her ears. "Or at least I always thought it was hideous," she continued. "Gondolas look so silly away from Venice."

Omar stood up as she approached the table. "Hello," he said.

"Hello," said Caroline. "I am Caroline Gund. I'm afraid I don't remember your name."

"Omar Razaghi," said Omar. He shook her hand. "It is a pleasure to meet you."

"You have surprised us," said Caroline.

"I'm sorry," said Omar.

"Oh, don't be sorry," said Caroline. "We have so few surprises here. Champagne! Another surprise! How good it looks."

"You're the one who wanted champagne," said Portia.

"Yes, but it is still a surprise. We do not always get what we want. Perhaps you would pour me a glass, Mr. Razaghi."

"Ah, yes," said Omar. "Certainly."

He poured a glass and handed it to her.

"We don't usually drink champagne," said Caroline. "Lest you get the wrong impression."

"It's very good," said Omar, somewhat stupidly.

"Yes. I think if you're going to drink champagne, you might as well drink the best," said Caroline. "It is the one thing about which I am a bit of a snob. I used to be that way about clothes, too, but living here prevents that. For some reason one can get quite decent champagne here for very little. I'm sure it is contraband of some sort. It is one of the advantages of living in a godforsaken, lawless place like this: strange things wash up on the beach."

"What beach?" asked Portia.

"I was speaking metaphorically," said Caroline. "Alas, we are all too far from *la playa*."

"You live in Kansas?" asked Arden.

"Yes," said Omar. "For several years I have. I am getting my Ph.D. there. Or trying to get it. I'm afraid my succeeding is somewhat contingent on writing this book."

"Have you always lived in Kansas?" asked Arden.

"No," said Omar. "I was born in Iran. My parents left when the Shah was deposed. We moved to Toronto, Canada. I lived there until I started graduate school."

"Iran, Canada, Kansas—where is your home?" asked Caroline.

"I don't really know," said Omar. "Kansas now, I suppose."

"You will stay in Kansas?" asked Caroline.

"It's difficult to get a job teaching college," said Omar. "If they offer me one, I suppose I will stay there. Or go wherever I can find a job."

"That seems a bit strange to me: to allow a job to decide where one lives. Surely you are not so cowed by reality as that?"

"I'm afraid I am very cowed by reality," said Omar.

"Oh," said Caroline. "Why is that?"

"Oh, I don't know," said Omar. "I'm just trying to get, well, you know, some things straightened out, get a foundation, I suppose, and then I hope to be less cowed."

"Oh, but once you get a foundation, you will be chained to it. It will become an anchor, a deadweight. No. Now is the time to break free from all that. Now, before it is too late."

"Caroline," said Arden, "would you help me in the kitchen for a moment?"

"Certainly," said Caroline. "Although I cannot imagine what help I might be."

In the kitchen Arden said, "What are you doing?"

"What do you mean?" asked Caroline.

"Why are you flirting with him?"

Caroline laughed. "Flirting? I haven't flirted in years. Surely I have forgotten how to flirt."

"Well, it seems to be coming back to you."

"I'm only trying to be friendly. We might as well be friendly, now that he is here. He is so pathetic, coming all the way from Kansas. I am simply trying to be nice to the poor boy. And, after all, it is you who invited him here."

"I did not invite him here! I wrote him and told him no. He just appeared out of nowhere. What was I to do?"

"Exactly as you did. It is nice to have a new face at the table. And it is rather an interesting face, don't you think?"

"I hadn't noticed," said Arden.

"Hadn't you? Well. And what help can I be to you?"

"What?"

"You said you needed my help in the kitchen," reminded Caroline.

"Oh," said Arden. "I just wanted to talk to you. Warn you. I think we've got to be careful. If we're too friendly, he'll think we've changed our minds."

"I can be friendly without changing my mind," said Caroline. "If he thinks that just because I am friendly I have changed my mind, that is his problem."

"Yes, but it would cruel to mislead him."

"Well, you be unfriendly, then. Surely we don't both have to be? Doesn't he deserve a little friendliness after such a long journey?"

"I don't mean to be unfriendly," said Arden.

"Then what do you mean?"

"I mean to be a little less charming."

"Why?"

"Oh, forget it! Be however you like! But you will have to tell him no this time. I wrote the letter. That was difficult enough. I refuse to do it again. You can be the one to tell him no in person. He said if he doesn't write the book he can't get his degree. Did you hear that?"

"Yes," said Caroline. "And I think we are doing him a great favor. The last thing he needs is that degree. It condemns him to a miserable life in Kansas."

"Well, it's his life. I think we should let him lead it where and how he likes."

"So you have changed your mind? Is that what this is all about?"

"No, I haven't. And it's because I haven't that I think we shouldn't give any indication of softening . . . I can sense him getting hopeful. I think the champagne was a mistake."

"Champagne is never a mistake," said Caroline.

Arden returned to the table with the risotto and eggplant and a loaf of bread. Caroline brought another bottle of champagne.

"Did you enjoy your stay in Montevideo?" she asked Omar, as they began eating.

"I wasn't there very long," said Omar. "Only two days. And I was mostly preoccupied with finding out how to get here. It was not easy, with my Spanish. I spent most of my time in Montevideo at the bus and train stations. In vain."

"How unlovely it sounds," said Caroline.

"It was like a dream," said Omar. "A nightmare, I suppose. This whole journey has been like a dream. I still can't believe I'm here. I don't feel like I'm here."

"Where do you feel like you are?" asked Arden.

"I don't know. I don't feel anywhere. I feel a little weird, as if I were floating. Perhaps it's the not sleeping last night. I haven't slept very much since I got here."

"You must be tired," said Arden.

"I'm not," said Omar. "I was before, when I first arrived this afternoon, I felt exhausted. But now I'm not at all tired." He looked up at the sky. "It's so beautiful here. Look at all the stars."

They all looked up at the sky.

"There's the Southern Cross," said Portia.

"Yes," said Omar. "You seem to have more stars here."

"It's just that it's so dark," said Caroline. "They're easier to see. And we are, perhaps, at this time of the year, a little closer to them then you ever are in Kansas." She took her shawl off the back of her chair and wrapped it about her shoulders.

"Sister Julian says the stars are the eyes of angels," said Portia.

"Perhaps they are," said Caroline. "The angels press their faces against the black window of night and look down at us. Is it with longing, they look? Or concern? Or perhaps with derision. I wonder."

Arden put Portia to bed and then returned to the kitchen to wash the dishes. They were stacked in the deep sink. She looked at them for a long moment, as if they were an exhibit in a museum of domesticity. She had drunk too much champagne and felt exhausted. She sat and rested her head upon the table, her forehead pressed against her forearm. Oh, she thought. Something is going wrong now.

Caroline sat a long while in her studio, looking at her version of *Madonna of the Meadow*. Sometimes you do things you do not understand. Why did I behave as I did at dinner? Why did I wear my necklace of hammered silver leaves that Jules brought me from Mexico?

It does not look like a meadow to me.

She went to the window. She saw the light dimly pushed through the shutters of Omar's window.

He is still awake. He has come so far, and cannot sleep. Why does traveling, coming far, excite us? Has it to do with what we leave behind or with what we encounter?

But she was wrong: Omar was not awake. He had simply fallen asleep with the light on.

CHAPTER SEVEN

Omar slept quite late the next morning. The loudly ticking clock on the bedside table claimed it was 10:20. The house was quiet in a way that suggested there was no one about—in fact, the quiet suggested that the planet might have been evacuated while Omar slept. In the kitchen he found evidence of life, if not life itself: a loaf of bread, a pot of jam, and a small bowl of honey were placed on the table in a way that clearly indicated they were at his disposal. The bread was rather stale but the jam and honey were delicious and awoke in Omar a ravenous appetite, for he had, out of a nervous, ridiculous politeness, declined second helpings of last night's risotto. With no one there to see him, Omar spread quite a bit of jam and honey (alternatively) on slices of the bread. The honey was dark and fragrant and curiously spicy. The jam was made from cherries, and had some pits. While washing his plate in the sink he saw a note on the counter:

Dear Omar,

I am in the garden, which is through the courtyard and down the gravel path, behind the oleander hedge. Caroline is up in her studio. It may be best if you come find me.   *Arden*

Why, he wondered, would it be best to find Arden? And did this mean he was meant to go find her, or only to find her if he were inclined toward company? I won't think too much about this, Omar thought. I'll just go find her, like a normal person would, after reading this note. I will behave like a normal person for as long as I possibly can.

He opened the kitchen door, and stepped out into the courtyard. The table they had eaten at the night before was cleared but the tablecloth was still spread across it, mottled by faint stains. One of the mushroom-shaped corks from the champagne bottles sat, conspicuously alone, on the linen. Omar picked it up and slipped it into his pants pocket. I will keep this, he thought, as a souvenir of my first night at Ochos Rios.

The oleander hedge was clearly visible when he emerged from the courtyard. He walked down the gravel path through a formal garden that had been neglected and was subsequently casual: flowers and weeds erupted in the spaces among the overgrown miniature privet bushes. This garden was bordered by a massive oleander hedge through which an arch had been incised, mirroring the one in the courtyard wall. Omar passed through this second arch and discovered the garden, which was large, and surrounded by a flimsy chicken-wire fence. Arden Langdon was crouching in the center of the garden, wearing khaki pants, a faded madras blouse, and a straw hat with a large brim. Her feet were bare. Omar stood just outside the fence and watched her. She was moving down the row in a slow, shuffling squat, gently pulling the weeds out of the earth, shaking the dirt from their roots, and tossing them into a metal bucket she nudged along in front of her. She reached the end of the row and stood up, put her hands on her hips, and arched her back. She saw Omar.

"Good morning," she said. "So you've arisen."

"Yes," said Omar. "Good morning."

"Did you find the bread and jam?"

"Yes," said Omar. "Thank you. It was delicious."

"I hope it was enough for you."

"It was plenty," said Omar.

She walked down the row she had just finished weeding and stood near him, just inside the fence. "Did you sleep well?" she asked. Her face was a little dirty and the hair around her temples was moist. She smelt of earth.

"Marvelously," said Omar.

"Good," she said. She smiled, and touched the back of her wrist to her temple. "You can come in if you want. There's a gate over there." She pointed. "Are you interested in gardens?"

"Well, I do not garden myself," said Omar. "But I have always had a fondness for gardens." He walked around and tried to open the gate, but could not. It seemed to be locked, or stuck.

"You've got to hold the clasp down and lift the latch up and push," said Arden. "It needs to be forced."

After a bit of a struggle, the gate opened, and Omar entered the garden. "It is a very big garden," he said. "Do you manage it all yourself?"

"No," said Arden. "Pete helps me."

Omar must have looked baffled, because she added, "Pete is Adam's partner. His boyfriend, I suppose. Adam is Jules's brother."

"And they live near here, you said."

"Yes," said Arden. "Just down the road a ways. You passed their house on your way here. It's the round, stone building. It was a millhouse."

"I wasn't very alert, I'm afraid. In fact, I was dozing. I must have seemed rather stupid when I arrived."

Arden shook her head.

"I hadn't thought I would meet anyone—I mean any of you—so quickly. I had hoped I would be able to collect my wits before meeting you. But there you were."

"Yes," said Arden. "There I was." She picked through the

weeds in the bucket, as if she had lost something among them, or as if some might not be weeds after all and should be reinserted in the earth.

"Perhaps I can help," said Omar. "Now, with the garden. I think I can manage to pull the weeds and spare your plants."

Arden laughed. "You're dressed much too nicely to garden," she said. "And besides, I'm ready for a break. You haven't had any coffee, have you? Or did you make some?"

"No," said Omar.

"Well, come," said Arden. She set the bucket down. "We'll have some coffee, if you like."

They sat at the kitchen table and drank their coffee.

"How did you become interested in Jules's work?" asked Arden.

"Well, I read *The Gondola* in a class I took on literature of the Diaspora."

"I see."

"I liked the book very much. Perhaps because of who I was—having left Iran, coming to Canada at the age I did . . . I don't know. It's a beautiful book. It touched me very deeply. I know that sounds sentimental, but it is true."

"Yes," said Arden.

"The other books did not move me so much. I liked the gentleness of *The Gondola*. Its grace. To come so far, to bring so much with you, and to be nevertheless traumatized, devastated . . ."

"Yes," Arden repeated, a bit vaguely, as if she were in a trance.

"So," said Omar, "I became interested in Jules Gund. I tried to read more—by him and about him. And there was none of either. Or nothing I could find. The woman who taught the course on the Diaspora was my thesis advisor. She encouraged me to work on Gund. And so here I am."

Arden sipped her coffee. It was a little bitter. "Do you take sugar?" she asked. "I'm sorry, I forget to ask you. Or cream?"

"No," said Omar. "I like it black."

"It's bitter," said Arden.

Omar said nothing.

"It's odd that you're here," she said, after a moment. "I mean, not just the surprise of your showing up like you did."

"How do you mean?" asked Omar.

"I don't know if I can explain it," said Arden. She held her hands together, fingers aligned, as if she were praying, and then rubbed them back and forth, lightly against each other. "It just seems odd . . . I suppose it is because I meet so few people. So that now, when I meet someone, I think, How did this happen? Why?"

"But you know why I am here," said Omar.

"Yes, of course," said Arden. She almost said, I know why you are here for you, but I do not know why you are here for me.

"I wonder if . . ." Omar began, but hesitated.

"What?"

"Last night, when you came to my room, you said there was no chance you would change your mind. I wonder if you still think that?"

"Yes," said Arden. "I think I do."

"But you're not sure?"

"I don't know," said Arden. "I'd like to help. I would. But the thing you want, it's the one thing—it's a complicated thing for all of us: Jules's life. It—well, even though he's been dead three years, we're all still very much engaged with him in some way. I don't think we're ready to let him go. Which is what you seem to be asking, in a way."

"I'm not asking that at all," said Omar.

"I know you're not. I mean, intellectually I know that. But emotionally, you must understand—or perhaps you can't—what it is you're asking."

Omar looked troubled, but said nothing. He sipped his coffee. It was bitter.

"I thought about writing a biography myself," said Arden.

"Of Jules?"

"Yes."

"When?"

"Just recently. Because of you. After we made our decision, I thought, Well, why don't I write a biography myself? I thought it couldn't be so hard. I went so far as to buy note cards. I wrote something I knew on each of the note cards, one fact about Jules on each, and I thought I would just arrange them chronologically and then elaborate upon these facts. And then fill in the blanks."

"I see," said Omar. "So that's why you don't want me to do a biography."

Arden laughed. "No!" she said. "That's not it at all. I've given up on doing a biography myself. I gave it up very quickly."

"Why?"

"There were too many blanks," she said. "It scared me, actually. I stopped out of fear."

"Fear of what?"

"Fear of what I didn't know about Jules."

"Why did that frighten you?"

She looked at him. She shook her head. After a moment she said, "Perhaps I shouldn't be talking to you about this."

"Oh," said Omar.

"Under the circumstances, I don't think it's right."

"Yes," he said. "Of course. I'm sorry."

"No," she said. "You shouldn't be. I brought it up. I don't know why. I'm sorry."

They sipped their coffee for a moment, and then Omar said, "I wonder if I could—well, at some point that was convenient, perhaps speak with all three of you together: you and Mrs. Gund and Mr. Gund."

"Of course," she said. "I'll invite Adam to dinner this evening. You can talk to us then. For what it's worth."

"It's awkward being so dependent upon your hospitality," said Omar. "Perhaps I could take you all out to dinner someplace. Is there a nice restaurant nearby?" He thought: It can't cost that much, restaurants in this part of Uruguay. But would he be able to use a credit card? Did he have enough cash? He had used so much of it paying the man who drove him here.

"I'm afraid there really aren't many decent restaurants in the area," said Arden. "We're in somewhat of a backwater here, culinarily speaking. And we can't have you spending your money on us."

"Please," said Omar. "I'd like to. You've been so kind, letting me stay here, and feeding me."

"Oh, yes!" Arden laughed. "Stale bread and bitter coffee! Like prison!"

"And champagne and jam and honey, and that delicious risotto last night. Please: I'd like to take you all out to dinner."

"Well, I'll phone Adam. He's sometimes very agoraphobic. Other times he quite likes to go out. We'll see what kind of mood he is in. He won't go out to a restaurant unless he wants to."

"Well, I hope he will say yes," said Omar. "And his boyfr——his partner, too, must join us, please, if we go."

"I'll call them," said Arden. "Now perhaps you should go up and see Caroline. I think she wants to talk to you. She's in her studio. Did you know she paints?"

"No," said Omar. "I'm afraid I know ridiculously little about any of you."

"Well, that's reassuring," said Arden.

"Caroline paints?"

"Yes. Apparently she is quite talented. Or was, I am told. But she suffered some loss of confidence and now only paints imitations."

"What do you mean?"

"She makes copies of paintings. It's not about her anymore, her art. She has taken herself out of it."

"Why?" asked Omar.

"I don't know," said Arden. "Perhaps you should ask her."

There was a special staircase that led up to Caroline's studio in the attic. Omar crossed the courtyard and opened the door that Arden had pointed out and climbed the stairs with considerable trepidation. He stood outside the closed door for a moment before he knocked.

"Yes," a voice called.

"It's Omar Razaghi," said Omar.

"*Entrez*," said Caroline.

Omar opened the door and stepped into the room. It was not at all how he had expected: it was large and full of light. Caroline was sitting near the windows, in a dilapidated wicker chair. A large book of paintings was open on her lap. "Hello," she said. "Come and sit down."

Omar sat in the chair she indicated.

"I'm sorry I've got nothing to offer you up here. Unless you'd like some scotch?"

"No, thank you," said Omar.

"Yes, it is a bit early for that, isn't it?"

Omar agreed it was.

Caroline closed the book: *The Drawings of Alberto Giacometti.* "Do you know anything about painting?" she asked, after a moment.

"No," said Omar. "I'm afraid I don't. I like paintings, very much, but I don't know a lot about art."

"What sorts of paintings do you like?" asked Caroline.

Omar looked around the room, as if he might see one that fit into this category. All he saw were a lot of canvases turned to the wall, and one displayed on an easel: a blue-shrouded Mary holding a baby Jesus. It's odd, he thought, you never see a painting like that and think, Oh, there's a mother with a child on her lap; you always know it's Mary and Jesus. He looked at Caroline. "Well, I like the Impressionists—Monet and Cézanne and van Gogh. Perhaps they weren't all Impressionists, however."

"What is it you like about Monet and Cézanne and van Gogh?"

"Well, I think their paintings are beautiful," said Omar. "I think they found something that painting could do, that nothing else could do."

"And what is that? What can painting do that nothing else can do?"

"I don't know," said Omar. "Capture a place and time, a moment, but capture it personally, subjectively, evocatively. They are about paint but not just about paint. I don't really understand abstract art."

"And that is what you think painting does: captures a place and time?"

"No," said Omar. "I mean, I don't really know. I think the Impressionists—if they were Impressionists—did that. But painting can do many things, I'm sure. I can't really speak intelligently about it; I'm sorry. It isn't my field."

"No," said Caroline. "You speak intelligently. Of course you can speak about it. I have noticed this: this hesitation to speak about anything outside of one's field. This caution. How boring it makes everything. It didn't used to be like that. People used to talk about whatever they liked."

"One gets a bit scared, in academia," said Omar. "You can get in trouble for saying the wrong thing, for being wrong."

"Well, I like what you had to say about Monet and Cézanne and van Gogh. I agree with you: they did get something right, each in his own way."

"Were they Impressionists?" asked Omar.

"As far as you need be concerned, they were," said Caroline.

She stood up, put the large book on the floor, walked over to, and looked out, the windows. They were high up, Omar noticed: the windows looked out onto the treetops, the green, sloping, glossy shoulders of the firs.

Looking out the window Caroline said, "What do you know about me?"

"What?"

She turned toward him. "What do you know about me? I feel I am at a disadvantage. I want to deal with you, but I want to do it equitably. What do you know about me?"

"Very little," said Omar. "I know you were married to Jules Gund. That you are French. That you paint. I have just learned that." He looked at her. She was looking back out the window. He could not see her face.

"I am more than that," she said.

"Yes," he said. "Of course you are."

"Your coming here," she said, "your wanting to write a biography of Jules, makes me think of that."

"Of what?" asked Omar.

"Of who I am." She turned away from the window. "Of who I would seem to be if a biography were written of Jules. If, let us say, you were to write a biography of Jules. Who would I be? A mad Frenchwoman. Who had been married to Jules Gund. Painting in an attic."

"You are not mad," said Omar, although at that moment she did look a bit mad to him: her body was tense in some potentially mad way, and the light around seemed to be bursting. But perhaps it was he. He could feel himself sweating. For the first time since he arrived in Uruguay, he felt actually, vitally there. Last night seemed like a dream.

"Am I not?" she asked, with a wild, potentially mad laugh. "What am I doing here, if I am not mad?"

"I'm not sure I follow you," said Omar.

87

"You don't follow me?"

"No," said Omar. "I don't think I do."

"What are your thoughts on marriage?"

"On marriage?" said Omar. "What do you mean?"

"What do you think of marriage? As an institution? Do you believe in fidelity? Monogamy? Divorce? Do you think men are naturally promiscuous?"

"I haven't given any of that much thought," said Omar. "I'm not sure what I think."

"How I hate that!" said Caroline. "No one is sure what he thinks. You are just afraid to say what you think."

"Yes," said Omar. "Perhaps."

"Don't be afraid. I need to know what you think."

"Why?" asked Omar.

"Because if you are to write a biography of my husband, I must know what you think about certain things."

"Like marriage?"

"Yes," said Caroline.

Omar said nothing.

"Are you married?" she asked.

"No," said Omar.

"Are you a homosexual?"

"No," said Omar.

"So we may conclude that you are an unmarried heterosexual?"

"Yes," said Omar. "We may conclude that."

"Are you romantically engaged?"

"Yes," said Omar. "I suppose I am."

"You suppose? You're not sure? How unromantic."

"No, I am sure. But why do you want to know that?"

"Because I would not want the person who writes the biography of Jules Gund to be a person who had never been in love. Or, worse yet, a person who would not admit to being, or having been, in love."

"But I thought I wasn't going to write the biography."

"Yes. You were not."

What would Deirdre do, Omar wondered, if faced with this type of lunatic interrogation? He had a vision of Deirdre pushing, or slapping, Caroline. Not that Deirdre was given to violence: it was just a vision he had. Perhaps because he wanted to push or slap Caroline? No. But he felt odd.

They were both silent for a moment.

Then Caroline said, "I ask you again: are you romantically engaged?"

"Yes," said Omar. "I am."

"I am glad to hear it," said Caroline.

"Well, I'm glad to have done something that pleases you."

Caroline smiled. "It is a woman, I assume, with whom you are romantically engaged?"

"Yes," said Omar. "It is a woman."

"For how long have you known her?"

"A little more than two years," said Omar.

"Am I making you feel uncomfortable?"

"Yes," said Omar.

"Why?"

"I don't know. It's personal, I suppose— "

"I see. You are to come here and ask us all innumerable personal questions—pardon me if I am wrong, but I assume that's how a biography gets written—and we are to ask you none? Is that how this works?"

"I didn't say you couldn't ask me questions. I just said it makes me uncomfortable. And if I don't have authorization I won't be asking you any questions anyway."

Caroline looked at him. "It is a little difficult for me to believe you."

"Believe what?"

"That you are, or have been, in love."

"I have a girlfriend," said Omar. "Her name is Deirdre. We've been together two years. If it wasn't for her, I wouldn't be here now."

"What do you mean: here, as in the man you now are, or here, as in Uruguay?"

"I wouldn't be here in Uruguay." Both, he thought.

"Why not?"

"I would have given up," said Omar. "I would have accepted your decision."

"So Deirdre convinced you to come here. She urged you to come here and change our minds?"

"Yes," said Omar.

"And if you fail to change our minds, if you return without authorization, what will she think?"

"I don't know," said Omar.

"Will she think you have failed?" asked Caroline.

"I don't know," said Omar.

"I know you don't know!" exclaimed Caroline. "Of course you don't know. You are clearly not a mind reader. I asked you, what do you think? What do you think she will think?"

"I think she will think I have failed," said Omar. "I will have failed."

"Sometimes it is good to fail at things," said Caroline. "To try, but to fail. There is nothing ignoble in that."

"I suppose not," said Omar, "but it is failure nonetheless. And Deirdre regards these matters less philosophically than you."

"Ah. She is a practical woman?"

"Yes," said Omar. "She is, among other things, a very practical woman."

"And you are not? Or perhaps you are?"

"A practical woman? No, I am not."

"Are you a practical man? I would think, in order to write a biography, one would need to be practical."

"I'm sure it helps," said Omar. "I've resolved to become practical."

"How dreary it sounds: to aspire to practicality."

"I am resolved to become it; I don't aspire to it."

"To what then do you aspire?"

"I aspire to write a biography of Jules Gund," he said. "I aspire to write a new kind of biography."

"How new?"

Omar took a deep breath. He had a feeling this was his moment. "I intend to abandon the notion of objectivity," he declared, as if he knew what he was talking about. "The objective biography is a myth. I want to write a biography that celebrates its subjectivity. In terms of biography, there was no Jules Gund. No one, real, intact Jules Gund. Certainly no 'authorized' Jules Gund. There is your Jules Gund. There is Miss Langdon's. There is mine."

"And your biography would present them all?"

"Yes," said Omar. "At least it is to that that I aspire. A truer account by virtue of, rather than despite, its subjectivity. Biography is a hoax."

"Yes," said Caroline. "I see your point."

"I'm sorry," said Omar.

"Sorry? Sorry for what?"

"For lecturing you. It's odd; it's not something I normally do. Not even when I'm supposed to be doing it. It's just that I thought if you knew what kind of book I intended to write, or at least hoped to write with your cooperation, you might reconsider your decision. I have no intention of usurping, exploiting, or hijacking the life of Jules Gund for my own purposes."

"It's interesting, what you propose to do. Yet it doesn't sound very academic. Will your university support such a project?"

"Oh yes," Omar hastened to assure her. "The weirder you are, the more they like it. You've got to do something no one else understands—then they can't attack you. If they don't understand it, they think there's a chance it might be brilliant and keep their mouths shut."

"And has this always been your approach to biography? I don't remember it expressed this way in your letter to us. You seemed to advocate a more traditional approach then."

"Yes," said Omar. "You're right. It is only since I've been here, and met you, and Miss Langdon—"

"Stop calling her Miss Langdon! Her name is Arden. And mine is Caroline. Miss Langdon: it sounds like an amanuensis."

"Yes," said Omar. "Well, it's only been since I've met you, and Arden, that I've understood things."

"So we are speaking of a recent realization?"

"Yes," said Omar. "Very recent. I came here thinking I would write the standard academic biography, but I see now that that is impossible, even distasteful."

There was a knock on the door. *"Entrez,"* said Caroline.

The door opened, revealing Arden standing in the vestibule. "I'm sorry to interrupt," she said, "but I've just spoken with Adam."

"What does he want?" asked Caroline.

"He invited Omar to have lunch with him and Pete. And Caroline, Omar has offered to take us out to dinner this evening, you and I and Adam and Pete. Adam has accepted this invitation. What about you?"

"Well, a dinner out sounds fine, but we cannot allow Omar to take us. While he is here, we are his hosts—"

"No, please, I insist," said Omar. "It would give me much pleasure to take you all out to dinner. Really it would. You must allow me! I insist."

"Adam suggested Federico's," said Arden. "I hope you like Italian food," she said to Omar.

Omar said he did.

"It was Jules's favorite restaurant," said Arden. "It's a bit of a drive, but as I told you, there are really no decent restaurants in the neighborhood."

"In fact, there is no neighborhood," said Caroline.

"Well, Adam is expecting you. He said to come at noon. Do you want to take the car or walk? He's only about a mile down the road."

"I'd be happy to walk," said Omar. "If you will show me the way."

"It's just straight down the road," said Arden. She turned to Caroline. "About dinner. Should I make a reservation at eight?"

"I seriously doubt we will need a reservation," said Caroline.

"Well, just to be sure. Is eight all right with you?"

"Yes, eight is fine. You'd better go, Omar, if Adam expects you at noon. You don't want to keep him waiting."

"No," said Omar.

"Come, then," said Arden. "I'll point you in the right direction."

CHAPTER EIGHT

Omar felt a bit loopy as he walked down the road toward Adam Gund's house. His interview with Caroline—indeed the entire morning—had left him slightly discombobulated, and he was trying to calm himself and recover his wits. Yes, he thought, I was a bit mad. But then I think she is a bit mad herself, so perhaps it was okay. Why did I say that, about a subjective biography? Was it nonsense? Do I want to write that kind of biography? Could I? Would the university publish it? He stopped walking and stood in the middle of the road. He knelt and laid his palm on the cracked tarmac. Oh, he thought, it's quiet and beautiful and peaceful here. And warm.

There was no traffic on the road, which pitched gradually downward. He continued walking down its center. Woods grew close to the road on either side, and then on one side gave way to a clearing, a sort of meadow. The road turned around the meadow and then descended more sharply; a crude stone bridge rose over a wide, shallow creek. Omar paused for a moment and looked down at the water flowing briskly over the rocks. He thought: Here I am in Uruguay, but I could be anywhere. I could be in Kansas. Although the air smelled different: there was some sort of warm, dusty scent that seemed vaguely exotic.

Omar crossed the bridge and saw the dirt lane that led to what must be the millhouse, a tall, cylindrical dwelling made of stone. He turned off the deserted road and walked down the tree-shrouded lane. A low stone wall separated the house from the lane, and inside the wall, in front of the house, was a yard paved with stones and crosshatched with moss. In this yard a man with a wire brush was vehemently scraping the paint from a wooden table. The noise this activity made, and his intentness upon it, prevented him from noticing Omar's arrival.

Omar stood outside the stone wall and watched for a moment. The man was Asian, and he didn't look much older than Omar. His dark hair was drawn back into a ponytail. His bare brown arms were sinewy and strong. After a moment he interrupted his activity, stepped back, and appraised his work. He noticed Omar. "Hello," he said.

"Hello," said Omar. "I am Omar Razaghi. I am here to see Adam Gund."

"Yes," said Pete. "We are expecting you. Come in."

Omar opened the wooden gate and stepped into the yard.

Pete set the brush down on the table and wiped his hands on his pants, and then held one out. "I am Pete," he said. "I live here with Adam."

Omar shook his hand. "It's nice to meet you," he said.

"How was your walk?" asked Pete.

"Very nice," said Omar. "I enjoyed it."

"You must be thirsty. Come in and I'll get you a glass of water."

Before this act of charity could be achieved the front door opened and an elderly man, dressed in a linen suit that looked much in need of washing and pressing, emerged from the house. He wore a fedora made of straw and a cravat at his open neck.

He carried a cane, or a walking stick, with which he pointed at Omar.

"Mr. Razaghi, I presume?" he said.

"Yes," said Omar. "Are you Mr. Gund?"

Adam held out his hand. "I have been," he said. "And seem to keep on going being Mr. Gund, much as I try to avoid that fate. Every day I wake up hoping I have been metamorphosed. For this reason I have never understood that book of Mr. Kafka's. I would be delighted to wake up an insect."

Omar shook his hand, but could think of no reply.

"So," said Adam, who seemed not to notice Omar's silence. "You have survived a night with the madwomen of Ochos Rios. You look no worse for the experience, although not having prior knowledge of your appearance disqualifies me from making such a judgment. You were not eaten alive?"

"No," said Omar. "I was treated very well. Especially considering I arrived unannounced."

"Yes, how exciting your arrival must have been. Nobody ever arrives at Ochos Rios, let alone arrives unannounced. I'm sure the women are still fibrillating. Well, your arrival here was expected and I must say you are admirably punctual. I thought instead of running the risk of poisoning you with a meal served out of our encephalitic kitchen, we would venture to the only marginally safer neighborhood cantina."

"That sounds fine," said Omar. "Whatever."

"I have a tendency toward preoccupation that makes driving an unwelcome adventure. Can you drive, Mr. Razaghi?"

"Yes," said Omar.

"How nice for us all. How exceedingly perfect you are. We must leave at once, I am afraid, for the cantina stops serving lunch at two o'clock."

"Enjoy your lunch," said Pete. "I'll see you later, I'm sure, Omar."

"Yes," said Omar. "I hope so."

"The car is this a way," said Adam, pointing with his stick.

The cantina was a modest building in a clearing of trees about ten miles down the road. Many trucks and jeeps were parked in the gravel lot in front of it. Only men seemed to eat lunch at the cantina, Omar noticed, and they all seemed to be eating large plates of big-boned chops and crude, bursting sausage. The dining room was a tin-roofed platform open on the three sides that did not face the kitchen, from where great whooshes of flame periodically erupted. Adam and Omar found a table on the far side of the room, a bit away from the more boisterous diners. The table was covered with brightly colored, plastic-coated fabric. A very pretty waitress offered them menus, but Adam declined the menus and said something to her in Spanish that was beyond Omar's comprehension.

"I have ordered us a plate of grilled meat and a pitcher of beer," he said, when the waitress had left them. "I hope that will suit you."

It had only been hours since Omar had gorged himself on the bread and jam and honey, but he found he was hungry once again. There was a wonderful smell in the air of rendered fat and spice and juicy meat, and when the waitress returned with the pitcher of glowing amber beer, which seemed blessedly lit from within, Omar felt curiously happy. It was pleasantly warm in the drowsy grove of trees, the carnivorous men around him all seemed happy and handsome, and he was in Uruguay.

"I will let you do the honors," said Adam, nodding toward the pitcher.

Omar filled two glasses with beer. He remembered Deirdre filling the glasses that evening at Kiplings, and was overcome with an urgent tender feeling for her. If it were not for her, he thought, I would not be here. In Uruguay, drinking beer with the brother of Jules Gund. He silently toasted her: Oh Deirdre!

Adam took a sip of his beer and cleared his throat. "So tell me," he said, "have you managed to change their minds yet?"

"You mean about the biography?" asked Omar.

"Yes, of course. Although I may wish you would change their minds about other things, I don't know you well enough to presume you might."

"I don't think so," said Omar. "They both still seem pretty much opposed to granting me authorization. But it is hard to tell."

"I trust you know that I am on your side in this matter?"

"I did not know that," said Omar. "I thought the decision was unanimous."

"Did Arden tell you that?"

"I don't know. I don't think so. I just assumed it, I think."

"Well, you misassume. No, I am all for this biography. I tried to talk sense to those women, but as you have no doubt discovered, it is like shouting down a well. Shouting down a well? Is that an idiomatic expression in English or did I just make it up?"

"I don't think I've heard it before," said Omar. "But English is my second language."

"What is your first?"

"Farsi. I was born in Iran."

"You mean Persia."

"Well, it was once called Persia."

"Yes, back when the world had a certain elegant order. Do you know, I never learned German until I was an adult? My parents never spoke it after leaving Germany. We spoke English at home and Spanish elsewhere, but never German. But that is beside the point. Of what were we speaking?"

"The biography," said Omar.

"Exactly. I am all for it. And Caroline and Arden can be made to agree with me."

"Can they?" asked Omar. "How?"

"Don't you worry about that. They disagree with me at this

point only because it is more interesting for them to disagree with me at this point. And in a way I am grateful for their recalcitrance, for it has brought you here to us."

"Yes, but their agreement would have done the same."

"Perhaps not so immediately, and so beseechingly. You are really too adorable! Of course you have no idea of how adorable you are, which only makes you more so. I am sure they were plumping your pillows and darning your socks all night long."

"They left me quite alone," said Omar, a bit indignantly.

Their platter of meat was delivered and set between them.

"Please, help yourself," said Adam. "Take whatever morsels you so desire."

"I don't usually eat meat," said Omar, and thus excused, helped himself to some sausage and what looked to be a lamb chop.

"It seems rather pointless to be alive and toothed and not eat meat, but your diet, whatever it is, seems to agree with you." Adam maneuvered several chops and sausages onto his plate and began to attack them with his knife and fork. He was a zealous and messy eater, Omar noticed: the pink juice ran down his chin, onto his cravat.

"No, no, no," said Adam, after a moment of concentrated gluttonous consumption. "There is a reason I have lured you here, there is a reason for our little *déjeuner sur l'herbe*. And I am sure you have guessed what it is."

The meat was delicious: tender and juicy; it was the kind of meat that made a very persuasive case for eating flesh. When Omar, who was in a bit of a blood-induced stupor, did not answer, Adam looked over at him. "Have you guessed?" he asked.

"Ah, no," Omar managed to say around a mouthful of sausage.

"We must work together," said Adam. "We must co-conspire."

"Yes," said Omar, "of course."

"I can help you with this," said Adam. He filled both their glasses with beer. "I can get the women to agree to authorization."

"Can you?" said Omar. "How?"

"Never you mind how," said Adam. "I haven't lived with crazy women for most of my life without learning a little about how to deal with them. Did you know my mother was crazy?"

"No," said Omar.

"Mad. Undone by grief. Prostrated by sorrow. Loco. Yes, I have walked many a mile with a madwoman. And Caroline and Arden are two of the maddest. They aid and abet each other, you see."

"They seem quite sane to me," said Omar, although he remembered that he had only recently wondered if Caroline were mad.

"Oh, of course they appear to be quite sane. It is the crowning achievement of their insanity: their elegant rational façades. But it is only a façade, my dear boy. Behind it is a madhouse, I assure you. Bedlam! Rattling around in that spooked house like two Miss Havishams. It makes me shiver." Adam did shiver, and forked another sausage onto his plate. "No," he continued, "you leave the mad-women to me. I will have them signing on the dotted line—I assume there is a dotted line somewhere—in no time at all."

"Well, good," said Omar. "That's great."

"Yes, isn't it great?" said Adam. "My father smacked me every time I said anything was great. Frederick was Great, he would say. Catherine was Great! Your *baba au rhum* is not great. Speaking of *baba au rhum,* do you want a flan? We had better ask for it now, before our waitress disappears. These waitresses have a maddening habit of disappearing. I think they are lured into postprandial dalliance by their customers. You look as if you could use a flan, or two."

"No, thank you," said Omar.

"You're quite sure?"

"Yes," said Omar. "I couldn't, after all this meat."

"No doubt it is the secret to your charming figure. But as I have long ago forsaken mine—or more aptly it has forsaken me—I will order a flan."

He summoned the waitress and appeared to do that.

"So," said Adam. "I will help you get the authorization you need."

"Thank you," said Omar.

"And I wonder if you would be so kind as to help me with something."

"Of course," said Omar. "What?"

Adam laid down his fork. He rubbed his napkin ineffectually on his stained shirtfront, and sat back in his chair. "There is something," he said, "that you could do for me."

"What?" repeated Omar. He was wondering if it would be piggish to take the last sausage, which had burst its skin and was leaking its savory stuffing onto the platter. No, he thought, I mustn't: I've had enough.

He looked over at Adam, and saw that he was thinking. After a moment Adam said, "It is such a long story. I don't know where to begin."

Omar knew enough to say nothing. He waited. He pushed the platter a little bit away from him. All around them men were rising from their tables; in the parking lot, trucks were backing up, raising clouds of dust. Lunchtime was apparently drawing to a hasty conclusion. The waitress arrived with Adam's flan, which wobbled prettily in a pool of syrup on a white saucer. She took the platter of meat away with her.

Adam took a bite of the flan. "Delicious," he pronounced.

A few men still lingered at tables, smoking cigarettes or cigars and drinking tiny cups of espresso or yerba maté. For a moment Adam concentrated on his flan, and Omar thought he must have forgotten the long story. But he had not. When the flan was consumed and the saucer scraped clean, Adam laid down his spoon. He patted his mouth with his napkin and then folded it carefully and laid it on the table. "I think I shall spare you the long story," he said.

"I would be interested to hear it," said Omar.

"That's right," said Adam. "I forget, you are a biographer. You thrive on narrative excrement. You prefer it to flan."

Omar said nothing.

Adam said, "I'm sorry. You must understand—or rather, I beg you to understand—that this contempt I have for everyone is really contempt for myself. But perhaps you are wise enough to know that."

Omar said nothing.

The waitress came and gave them both espressos. Omar did not know if they came automatically or if Adam had ordered them.

Adam said, "Contempt. It is such a pathetic thing, isn't it? I mean, my mind is just large enough to know that. But it is practically all I feel. It is the odious gas that fills me. One day I will float disdainfully away, buoyed by contempt. Icarus flew too near the sun."

"Yes," said Omar.

Adam smiled, sadly, at his espresso cup. Something had shifted: Omar noticed they were the only ones left in the cantina. A few men stood about in the parking lot, but all the tables were empty, and the light had changed all around them, grown just a bit less harsh.

"Do you know the story of Icarus?" Adam asked.

"Yes," said Omar, although suddenly he thought perhaps he did not: was there more to it than wings made of feathers and wax melting in the heat of the sun? Of course there was more.

"My parent were refugees," said Adam. "Of course, you know that. They brought certain things with them when they came to Uruguay."

For a moment Omar thought this had something to do with the story of Icarus but then he realized it did not. "What things?" he said.

"Both my parents came from wealthy families. My mother, especially. My mother brought some paintings with her, paintings which were not supposed to leave Germany. And jewels."

"Are they yours now?" asked Omar.

"What interesting, methodical questions you ask. You will make a fine biographer, methinks. To answer your question: I believe they belong to me," said Adam. "They were my mother's. In some way, they belonged to Jules, too, of course, but Jules is dead. I suppose they belong in some way to Caroline. Perhaps they belong in some way to Arden. But I think they mostly belong to me. Neither Caroline nor Arden knows these things exist. Jules did not know. My mother did not feel safe here. She did not feel safe anywhere after she left Stuttgart. She did not feel safe on this planet. Unlike Arden and Caroline, she had reason to be crazy. I would like to sell these things now. I would like you to take these paintings and this jewelry back with you to New York, and give them to a man there, who will arrange for them to be auctioned."

"Oh, I don't live in New York," said Omar, as if this disqualified him from everything.

"I assume you pass through New York. Or can arrange to go there. If you have gotten yourself here, I am confident you can get yourself to New York. You merely need to go to New York and give these things to a man. I will give you his address."

"Is it legal?" asked Omar.

"Is what legal?"

"This whole thing . . . taking these things out of the country, taking them to New York."

"It is moral," said Adam.

"But not legal?"

For a moment Adam did not reply. Then he said, "You know, of course, that my mother was a Jew. You know they came to Uruguay to escape Hitler. They waited a bit too long. I think they thought for a while that since my mother had married a gentile, things might not be so bad. But things were bad. They realized this, and finally came here. It was the only place they could come to at that point. Do you know the conditions of their coming here?"

"No," said Omar.

"Well, first of all, my father had to buy a mine. A failed mine, a spent mine, a mine he did not want. And he had to pay a lot of money for it. My mother was not allowed to bring any of her family's possessions out of Germany. They finally let her leave, but she could take nothing with her. So she smuggled these things. These few paintings, these few jewels. I want to sell them now. Do you know why I want to sell them now?"

"No," said Omar.

"I need money for Pete. I need money to give to Pete so he may leave me."

Omar said nothing. Then he said, "This sounds very personal and complicated. I don't think I want to get involved with all of this. I don't think I should."

"Oh," said Adam. "Oh," he said, again. Then he said, "Remind me: what is it you want?"

"What?"

"You want to write a biography of Jules, no? You want authorization to write a biography of my brother. Is this not something you want?"

"Yes," said Omar. "I want that."

"But you don't want to get involved with personal or complicated things?"

"It just sounds like it could get messy," said Omar. "And dangerous."

"And you don't want things to get messy or dangerous?" asked Adam.

"No," said Omar.

"It has been my experience that sooner or later things always get messy or dangerous," said Adam. He stood up and paid the waitress, who was wiping tables with a rag and a spray bottle of cleaning fluid. Omar watched him give her a bill; she gave him change from the pocket of her apron. Adam returned to the table but did not sit down.

"I'm sorry," said Omar, after a moment. "It's just that I'm no good at these things."

"You're scared," said Adam. It was a statement, not an accusation.

"Yes," said Omar.

Adam put his hand on Omar's shoulder. "You can be scared," said Adam. "The thing is not to let being scared stop you from doing the right thing, or from getting the things you want. That is what makes cowards." He removed his hand. "But enough of this now. I am sleepy," he said. "I want to go home, and take a siesta."

They were silent on the ride back to the millhouse. Pete was where they had left him. He walked over to the car and helped Adam out of it. "Did you have a nice lunch?" he asked.

"Delicious," said Adam, "but stupefying. At least I am stupefied. I want to be prone: prone and unconscious."

"Thank you for the lunch," said Omar.

"You're welcome," said Adam. "Thank you for the pleasure of your company. Perhaps you would help me up the stairs, Pete." He turned to Omar. "Pete does things like help me up the stairs now and then. He is so good to me."

"Let me help you," said Omar. "There is something I want to tell you."

"Is there?" asked Adam.

"Yes," said Omar. "There is."

"Well, you need not help me up the stairs. We can talk without my experiencing that particular mortification."

Omar looked at Pete.

"Excuse me," said Pete. "I will go."

"No." Adam touched Pete's bare forearm. "Stay. Pete may hear whatever you have to say to me, Mr. Razaghi. We have no secrets."

"It's only that— I just wanted to say that I'd do what you asked me to do. Of course I'll do it. It seems the right thing to do."

"Does it?" asked Adam.

"Yes," said Omar. "I am sure it is the right thing to do."

Adam pounded his walking stick twice upon the cobbles beneath them. "Good," he said. "I feel revivified. I believe I have sufficient strength to drag myself to my bed without the help of either of you burly youths. I leave you here." He turned and walked, quite briskly, but with apparent effort, into the house.

When he had disappeared, Pete said, "I'll walk you back up to the big house. Or would you rather walk alone?"

"No," said Omar, "of course not."

Pete laid down his tools and they set off up the narrow lane toward the road. They did not speak. There is a way that people displace their attention to one another onto the landscape that, when done simultaneously, is sometimes an effective and satisfying substitute for communication.

Omar had to urinate badly; he had intended to ask for the lavatory at the millhouse, but the scene there had not accommodated such a request, and he had figured he could pee on the wayside once he had gained the road, but here was Pete sharing the road with him. They walked silently up the lane and turned onto the main road.

Omar could wait no longer. "If you'll excuse me a moment, I will visit the bushes," he said.

Pete looked at him blankly. "What?" he asked.

"I need to visit the bushes," Omar said. "Nature calls."

"Oh, yes, of course," said Pete. He laughed, but not unkindly.

Omar ventured a way into the scrub and urinated vehemently against a tree. It was odd how good it felt.

When he returned to Pete's side something had shifted between them—the low call of human nature had freed something, and their silence was more companionable.

After a moment, Omar said, "How long have you lived here?"

Pete looked around them, as if Omar meant this particular spot. "About six years," he said.

"Where are you from, originally?" Omar asked.

"Thailand," said Pete. "Bangkok."

"I've never been there," said Omar.

Pete didn't say anything for a moment. Then he said, "My mother was a prostitute. So was I, for a while, as a boy. A German man brought me back to Stuttgart with him when I was seventeen. I met Adam there."

"What was Adam doing in Stuttgart?"

"He was living there. He was managing director of the Stuttgart Opera. I had a job there, building sets. When he came back here, I came with him. To do this, he must adopt me. Legally, I am his son."

"Do you like it here?" asked Omar.

"Yes," said Pete. "I have a little business. I find old furniture and then make it look older. A lady comes twice a year from New York City and buys whatever I have. She says I have a very good eye. And I help Arden in the garden. It rhymes. And I take care of the bees."

"What bees?" asked Omar.

"There is a hive at Ochos Rios. Behind the garden. I will show you."

"The garden is very large," said Omar.

"We make it a little bigger every year. It is a lot of work, especially at this time of year. It's winter now, where you come from?"

"Yes," said Omar.

"You live in the United States?"

"Yes," said Omar.

"Which state is yours?"

"A state called Kansas. It's in the middle of the country. The center."

"And it's very cold there?"

"Yes," said Omar. "Now, it is. It is probably snowing." He mimed snow by twinkling his fingers.

"Why do you pick that? A cold state? All the states are not so cold, are they?"

"No," said Omar. "Some are warmer than others."

"Then why not pick a warm state? I think Florida is warm. I was in Miami once. Miami is nice."

"Yes," said Omar. "Florida is warm."

"But you don't like Florida?"

"I've never been to Florida. I live in Kansas because it's where I'm teaching."

"And you want to write a book about Jules?"

"Yes," said Omar. "A biography. Did you know Jules?"

"Yes," said Pete. "When I first came here, Jules was alive. I am the one who found him, when he was dead. I knew where he would go."

"How did you know?" asked Omar.

"I don't know. I just knew."

"Where was he?"

"A place in the woods. Not far from the lake."

"Near the gondola?"

"The gondola is in the boathouse," said Pete.

"Was this place in the woods near the boathouse?"

"No," said Pete. "It was the other side of the lake."

"Did you know he would be dead?"

"Yes," said Pete.

"How?"

"He had taken the gun," said Pete. He touched the top of Omar's head, palmed it. "This had come off," he said. "Like an egg."

They walked the rest of the way in silence, and reached the gate of Ochos Rios. It was only yesterday that I arrived here, thought Omar. It seemed days ago.

"Where are the rivers?" he asked Pete.

"What rivers?"

"The eight rivers. Isn't that what Ochos Rios means: eight rivers?"

"Yes," said Pete. "But there are no rivers. It is just a name."

CHAPTER NINE

From a window in the tower, Caroline watched Pete and Omar walk up the drive. She felt in Omar's presence a threat—not merely, or perhaps not even fundamentally, because of the book. It struck more deeply and vaguely than that. In some instinctual way, before she had even intuited the threat, she had thought she could rise up and meet or deflect it—that explained her behavior with Omar last night and this morning. But now she wasn't sure. They seemed to be chattering gaily, Omar and Pete, like two old friends. Omar glanced up then and saw her in the window. He raised his hand in a combined wave and salute. The familiarity of the gesture shocked her. She stepped away from the window. She stood there, feeling and thinking nothing. Lately she felt this often: this stasis, this vacancy, this sitting or standing still and feeling emptied out, hollow. It was not unpleasant. It did not scare her: it was a sort of contentment, a hiatus, a satisfaction of nothing.

Caroline found Arden in the kitchen, where she appeared to be making bread. Caroline secretly felt that the point of much of Arden's domestic activity was to irritate her: they could easily buy their own bread.

She stood in the doorway for a moment, and then said, "I just wanted to let you know that I won't be joining you for dinner this evening."

"Why?" asked Arden. She did not look up. "Aren't you feeling well?"

"I'm feeling fine," said Caroline. She thought: She pretends it is such hard work, making bread.

"Then why won't you come to dinner?"

"I see no point in it. I will not change my mind about this. It is a waste of my time, and his."

"He just wants to talk to us," said Arden. She stopped fussing with the dough. "To all three of us. To make his case. He's offered to take us out to dinner. He's come all this way to do that. It will seem rude not to go. It is rude, I think."

"His coming here is rude, I think. We should not indulge him. I shall not," said Caroline.

"Well, it makes no sense for us to go out to dinner, then," said Arden. "The whole point was for him to be able to talk with all three of us. If you don't come, it is pointless."

"Why especially me?"

"Because it is you he must convince."

"I have just told you I will not be convinced."

"Well, if you are so sure of it, there can be no harm in coming to dinner and listening to him."

"He must convince you as well," said Caroline. "Or have you changed your mind?"

Arden kneaded the dough. "I think I have," she said.

"Ah," said Caroline. "He has charmed you. He has—"

"He hasn't charmed me!" Arden exclaimed. "I have changed my mind."

"Call it what you will," said Caroline.

Arden said nothing.

"Why have you changed your mind?" asked Caroline.

"Why do you ask me? So you can make fun of me?"

"No," said Caroline. "I'm sorry. I'm not making fun of you. Truly, Arden, I'm not. Why have you changed your mind? I sincerely want to know."

"I don't really know," said Arden. "My reasons for objecting were muddled, as you know—it was an instinctual response to say no, to agree with you. And now I feel differently. I don't know precisely why. I think Jules would like him. I think he will understand Jules. I feel it should happen, now, the book."

"You don't honestly think it is because he has charmed you?"

"Do you think he is charming?"

"No," said Caroline. "I do not. But I would not be surprised if you did. I think you are more susceptible to charm than I."

"Why?" asked Arden. "You think I have no mind of my own?"

"No," said Caroline. She paused. "I think you are lonely." She said it kindly: it was a statement, not an accusation.

Arden glanced down, deflecting her face, but then raised it. Her cheeks and throat were red. "Perhaps I am lonely," she said. "Perhaps his coming here has made me feel that I am lonely. Yes—perhaps that. But changing my mind is separate from that; it is not about that."

"Perhaps I should not tell you this—"

"What?" Arden demanded. "Tell me what?"

Caroline considered. And then she said, "Did you know that he is in love with someone?"

"No," said Arden. "I did not know that."

"He told me this morning. He has a fiancée. Well, perhaps they are not engaged. He did not say that. She is a fellow academic."

"Why do you tell me that?"

"I don't know. I thought you should know."

"Why?"

Caroline turned toward the door. "Forgive me if I have upset you."

"You have not upset me," said Arden. "Although I'm sure that was your intention."

"You are mistaken, Arden."

"It seems a shame," said Arden.

"What?"

"To do what you're doing, withholding authorization, out of spite."

"I don't follow you," said Caroline. "I do nothing, as far as I know, out of spite."

"I see it differently," said Arden.

"No doubt you do," said Caroline. She turned around and walked down the dark corridor, into the front hall, but paused at the bottom of the stairs, her hand on the banister. It cannot be left in this way, she thought. She retraced her steps to the kitchen door. Arden was rolling out the dough, flushed and intent, and did not look up.

"Arden," Caroline said.

Arden looked up then, and said, "Yes?"

"I am sorry if I have offended you. I don't really understand what we just said to one another."

Arden said nothing. She pressed her fingers into the dough.

"I don't want this to cause trouble between us." She noticed that Arden was crying and stopped talking.

"What's wrong?" she asked.

Arden shook her head and sat down in a chair. She put her elbows on the table and hid her face in her hands, awkwardly: palms out, fingers splayed, for they were covered with flour. Caroline crossed the room and stood beside her. She laid her hand, tentatively, on Arden's back. "What's wrong?" she repeated.

Arden revealed her face; her cheeks were wet. She shook her head again. "Nothing," she said. "I don't know—I'm just emotional."

Caroline removed her hand. She could not remember touching Arden before. Surely she must have, but she could not remember it.

She dampened a cloth at the sink and handed it to Arden. "Here," she said.

Arden took the cloth and pressed it against her eyes, her cheeks. "Thank you," she said.

Caroline stood there for a moment. "You're welcome," she said. She touched Arden again, quickly and lightly, on her shoulder and then she turned and left the room, not pausing this time, and not returning.

Arden sat in the kitchen while the bread baked. She drank a glass of water and then made rings with the wet glass on the stone table. The rings faded. She thought if she sat there quietly, long enough, the shaken mess of her mind would comprehensibly settle, like glittery snow in a glass dome.

Had she made a mistake? Had Omar simply charmed her? Was she betraying Jules? Jules had never said to her he did not want a biography. Perhaps he had said something to that effect in a letter to Caroline twenty or thirty years ago. It did not signify anything now. If we were held to everything we wrote in letters thirty years ago—No, if that was the only reason, it was not enough. She had been right to err on the side of caution initially, but the very fact of Omar coming this far changed everything. He was not a charlatan or a monster. It would be simply mean, perverse, to withhold authorization from him at this point. Perhaps it was not spite—she should not have said spite—but there was something twisted and perverse in Caroline's response. Yet it made sense: Caroline had so little to hold on to, so of course she was fierce with it. I must allow her that, thought Arden: it is how she reminds herself that she was loved.

Adam awoke to hear someone calling his name. He lay on the bed for a moment, slightly disoriented. Then he heard his name again, shouted up from below. It sounded like Arden. Of course it was Arden. She was the only one who would stand in the hall and bellow his name. He roused himself and stepped out onto the landing. Arden was standing inside the door, head thrown back, gazing up at him.

"I'm sorry," she called. "Did I wake you? Were you napping?"

"Yes," he said. "I'm afraid I was."

"Well, I'm sorry," she said. "But it's important. Something's happened."

"What's happened?" he asked. "Wait. I'll be right down. There is no need for us to scream at one another. Perhaps you could make some coffee, if you can find the coffee. It has lately gone missing."

"Of course," said Arden. She disappeared into the living room.

Adam returned to his bedroom. He stood in front of the mirror and yawned. There was nothing worse than being roused untimely from a nap. These awful, interfering women, he thought. Running about like headless chickens shouting something's happened! The sky is falling! He combed his hair and straightened his clothes, which had suffered from both his lunch and his nap, and went downstairs.

After a moment Arden emerged from the kitchen with two cups of coffee. "Your milk's gone horribly bad," she said, "so we'll have to drink it black."

"I prefer it black," said Adam.

She handed him his cup and sat on the sofa.

"Where did you find the coffee?" he asked.

"In the bread tin," she said.

"Ah," he said.

"There are all sorts of things in the bread tin," she said, "except bread."

"It would be rather depressing to keep one's bread in the bread tin," Adam said. "So something has happened?"

115

"Yes," said Arden. "And I thought we should talk before this dinner."

"What has happened?"

"Well," said Arden. "I have changed my mind."

"How has this happened? The effect of Mr. Razaghi is potent! He has hardly been in our midst twenty-four hours. This coffee is very good. When I make coffee, it never tastes this good."

"You must measure it correctly," said Arden. "How was your lunch with him?"

"Nice enough. I found him charming in a slightly stupid, dewy-eyed, bushy-tailed way."

"He is not stupid," said Arden.

"I've no doubt he seems quite wise to you," said Adam.

"I have never claimed to be smart," said Arden.

"It is the wisest thing about you," said Adam.

"I like him very much," said Arden.

"So do I," said Adam. "He is very pettable."

"What do you mean?"

"I mean it would be nice to put him in a cage and feed him nuts. And pet him."

"I don't know what you're talking about. He's not gay, if that's what you mean. He has a fiancée. Or girlfriend. Or something like that."

"Oh, I'm sure he has something like that. We all have something like that. So he has changed your mind?"

"I have changed my mind," said Arden. "But there is a problem. Caroline refuses to go out to dinner with us."

"Why?"

"She says there is no point in her going. She will not change her mind. She seems very certain."

"Of course she seems very certain. Caroline is always certain. It is what I most admire about her. She is just certain about different things at different times. Often diametrically opposed things. There will come a time when she will find it is more fun to cooperate. And she will change her mind, just as you have sensibly done."

"It is the right thing, isn't it?" asked Arden. "I mean the biography, and letting him do it. You don't really think he's stupid, do you?"

"Oh, you don't need to be smart to write a decent biography. Only dogged. And he is dogged, we know that. He has proved that by coming here."

"I'm quite excited about it, now," said Arden. "How long do you suppose it will take?"

"Years and years, I'm sure," said Adam. "It will take him as long as he can find grants to support the writing of it. It's the writing of it that will support him, not the publishing."

"Well, I hope he won't take too long," said Arden. "I want to read it. But now listen—what should we do about tonight? The whole point of going to Federico's was to give him an opportunity to make his case to all three of us. Should we cancel it?"

"We shall certainly not cancel it," said Adam. "We shall go and have a nice dinner with him. Caroline can mope in her tower and feel righteous. She is so very good at it. We can drink champagne with the adorable Mr. Razaghi."

"All right, then," said Arden. She stood up. "We'll pick you up at about seven-thirty. Is Pete coming?"

"I don't know," said Adam. "He's disappeared. I assume he will come."

"Do you think if you talked to Caroline, she would come?"

"No," said Adam. "Let's forget about Caroline for the nonce, and have a happy time."

CHAPTER TEN

Omar appeared in the front hall, promptly at 7:00, as he had been instructed. He was wearing a jacket and tie. He had interfered with cologne and pomaded his hair. He sat on one of the pewlike benches beside the door and tried not to sweat. It seemed very warm. After a moment, a door on the right side of the first gallery landing opened and Arden appeared. She was wearing a sleeveless striped silk shirtdress in sherberty shades of orange, red, and lilac; it was rather old-fashioned, and reminded Omar of a box of colored pencils—or a section of such a box. She looked very beautiful, and she knew it, for she blushed as she walked down the stairs.

"I'm afraid Caroline is not going to join us," she said.

"Oh. That's too bad," said Omar.

"She's—well, I won't make excuses for her. She's being difficult. But Adam and I are happy to speak with you. And dine with you."

"Good," said Omar. "Thank you. You look very beautiful."

"Thank you," said Arden. "So do you. Should we go? Just let me say good night to Portia." She disappeared down the hallway toward the kitchen. Omar opened the door and stepped out onto the portico. It was that lovely time of day when everything—the trees, the façade, even him, he knew—seemed gloriously lit. After a moment he heard the door open behind him. "There you are," said Arden. "We're going to take Adam's car. So we've got to walk down to the millhouse, I'm afraid."

"That's fine," said Omar.

"If you don't mind, I think I'll take off these damn shoes," said Arden. "They weren't really made for walking. At least around here."

She bent down and unstrapped her shoes—beige, open-toed sandals with a heel. She carried them in one hand as they set off down the drive. "You must be tired of all this walking," she said.

"No. I like walking."

"So do I, but I get so tired of this route. It doesn't change much, day to day."

"In some ways that's better: it's less distracting."

"I would welcome a little distraction," said Arden.

"Are you bored, living here?"

"No," said Arden. "It's quiet, and I like that. And I think it's a good place for Portia to grow up. I don't want her to have all that junk that surrounds kids in the States. But there's no avoiding some of it. American popular culture is so pernicious, especially when it comes to kids. Of course, the price you pay for that is no culture at all." She laughed.

"But do you like it here?"

Arden looked around. So did Omar. The setting sun filtered thickly through the alleys of pines. The two stone pillars of the gate were covered in climbing wild roses. The air was fragrant.

"Yes, I like it here," said Arden. "I had a lot of drama early on in my life, a lot of moving around and inconstancy. Perhaps that's why I like it here. No doubt Portia will grow up wanting just the oppo-

119

site. You moved around, too, didn't you, when you were young? From Iran to where?"

"Toronto. Canada. And then I lived in Berkeley, California, before I went to Kansas."

"What were you doing in Berkeley?"

"I worked in a restaurant."

"As a waiter?"

"No, as a busboy."

"And then you went to Kansas?"

"Yes."

"And what about your parents? Are they still in Toronto?"

"Yes," said Omar. "My father is a surgeon. He's very tyrannical, conservative. He has never forgiven me for not going to medical school. I come from a long line of doctors."

"But aren't you getting a Ph.D.? Won't you be a doctor then?"

"If I write this book," said Omar. "But it's not really the same. At least not in my father's eyes."

"What about your mother? Is she proud of you?"

"No," said Omar. "She would like me to be a doctor too. What about your parents? Where are they?"

"They are both dead," said Arden.

"Oh," said Omar, "I'm sorry."

"I don't really miss them," said Arden. "They weren't very good parents. Or people, for that matter. Well, my mother I hardly knew. She died when I was five. I think she killed herself, although technically it was an accident. I went to live with my grandmother then."

"Where was that?"

"Ashland, Wisconsin. Nowhere, like here. I loved my grandmother. But then she died, and I moved to England, to live with my father. Or go to boarding school and visit my father. And now he is dead too. They are all dead."

Omar said nothing. They passed through the gate and turned onto the road.

"I'm sorry," said Arden. "I must sound morbid."

"No," said Omar.

"It's just that I hate the past," said Arden. "I hate *my* past."

"Why?" asked Omar.

"It seemed so stupid. So random. There was no logic to it, or evolution. It was just bouncing around. That's what I want to give Portia: a sense of stability, of home. I mean a home in every sense: even geographically. I think it's important to be allied with a place: to think you come from someplace specifically. Do you feel that way about Iran?"

"No," said Omar. "Not really. We left there when I was ten. And Toronto never seemed like home, either, because there was always this idea that we might return to Iran one day, if things changed . . ."

"What about Kansas?"

"I've only been there a couple of years," said Omar. "Perhaps when I have been there longer . . ." He remembered how he felt that night standing outside Yvonne's house, the night he had lost Mitzie.

"I felt at home here as soon as I arrived. I don't know why. Perhaps because I was pregnant, and needed to feel that way. Also, I think I was ready for it in some strange way. But in any case, it stayed, that feeling. It's odd: sometimes I have, or think I have, memories of being here as a child." She shook her head. "It's very odd."

"It is odd, how memory works," said Omar. "And déjà vu."

"Yes," said Arden. "I don't believe in the afterlife, or in reincarnation, or anything like that, but I do think this life is more—more powerful, more complex than we think. I feel it sometimes, as if there is some incredible richness, complexity, lurking just beyond the wall. Some other level of living, of engagement."

Omar said nothing. She is talking about love, he thought.

"I'm not making any sense, I know," said Arden. "I don't know what I'm talking about."

He wondered if she really did not.

Adam was ready when they arrived. He, too, was nicely dressed. Arden drove; Adam sat beside her and Omar sat in back.

"Is Pete not joining us?" asked Arden.

"Apparently not," said Adam. "He has not returned from wherever he was."

"He was in the garden this afternoon," said Arden.

"He was in the garden this afternoon: it sounds so biblical," said Adam. "I think I finally understand this sad propensity you, and so many others, have, to till this miserable earth. It is Eden you are after, vainly trying to regain a paradise lost."

"It is not in the least about religion," said Arden.

"Oh, but it is, my dear," said Adam. "The nice thing about getting old is that you lose that sentimental attachment to the earth. I do not need to muck about in the soil, fertilizing carrots, to feel safe. Or saved."

"Must you disparage everything we do?" asked Arden.

"Oh, I don't. I admire you very much. I think you drive very well. And dress nicely. I think you are a wonderful mother. And you make excellent coffee. In fact, your talents are infinite."

For a while no one said anything. And the landscape they passed through seemed in some way reflective of their silence: the road was straight, though it rose and fell with the gentle swells of the earth, and the woods that bordered it were unremarkable.

"You seem to live very far from anything," Omar said, after a moment.

"What an astute observation," said Adam.

"Federico's is in Tacuarembó," said Arden. "It's not far from here. Not terribly far."

Adam turned around in his seat so he was facing Omar. "Federico's has been here forever," he said. "By that I mean it has been here as long as I. I came here with my parents, and Jules. Often, of a Saturday night, the Gunds would dine at Federico's, *en famille*. They were a little pathetic, a little sad, our dinners at Federico's. A desperate attempt to retain Europeanness, normalcy." He turned back around. "Just to give you some historical perspective," he said.

Federico's looked alarmingly like Ponte Vecchio, the Italian restaurant Deirdre and Omar sometimes frequented in Lawrence, when their budget allowed a splurge. Omar wasn't sure what he had expected, but he had thought that an Italian restaurant in Uruguay would be different from an Italian restaurant in Kansas. At some level he believed that everything in Uruguay had to be different from everything in Kansas, such was his notion of the two places, and the fact they were not so different, and in some ways almost identical, was vexing.

The restaurant appeared to be quite empty. In fact, it was empty.

"I'm so glad you thought to reserve a table," said Adam.

Arden laughed. "Well, you never know with Federico's," she said. "It's either no one or the world."

Omar was preoccupied by trying to find some sign that indicated the establishment welcomed credit cards, particularly Visa. He thought he had enough cash to pay for the meal, unless of course it was hideously expensive. But it did not look like the kind of restaurant that would be too expensive. He noticed two dead fish in the aquarium beside him in the entryway, which he took to be a good sign.

A man in a tuxedo appeared out of the gloom in the back of

the restaurant—it was very dimly lit, relying mostly on candles guttering in wine bottles for illumination (a technique also favored by Ponte Vecchio). The man looked rather funereal from a distance, and his glum expression did not alter as he drew near. He grabbed a few menus from atop the aquarium and said, *"Tres?"*

"Sí," said Arden. *"Tenemos una reservación. A nombre de Gund. Para cuatro personas, pero sólo somos tres."*

The man seemed, understandably under the circumstances, uninterested by this information. He led them through the sea of empty tables to a circular booth along the back wall.

"Muy bien," said Arden. *"Gracias."*

Omar, who had understood everything Arden had said, felt empowered. Perhaps he was learning Spanish. Perhaps it really did just come to one, like getting a suntan or acclimatizing oneself to a new time zone.

"Sí, gracias," he said to the maitre d'.

Arden scooted into the booth and sidled toward the middle; Omar and Adam flanked her. She picked up the menus the maitre d' had somewhat flung onto the table and handed one to each of them. "Everything is good here," she said to Omar.

"It would be more accurate to say that nothing is better than anything else," said Adam. "But first we must order a drink. Will you join me in a cocktail, Mr. Razaghi?"

At some sedimentary level Omar thought that perhaps it might be best not to drink at this very important dinner—he did not hold liquor particularly well and was still feeling a bit stupefied from all the beer he had drunk with lunch—but his immediate response was affirmative: he would like a cocktail, so he said yes.

Adam snapped his fingers in a way that suggested he had spent much of his life summoning waiters (and others) in this fashion, and a waiter immediately materialized beside their table. They ordered drinks (martinis for Adam and Omar, a glass of wine for Arden) and turned their attention back to the menus.

124

Omar was mainly concerned with the prices and was trying to convert them into dollars in his head. He was delighted to find that the place was absurdly cheap—entrees for as little as $1.50! Oh, wait: he did the math again, and realized he had neglected to shift the decimal point to the right. Entrees were $15.00. And up. Well, it was still within his means. He didn't suppose the drinks and wine could cost that horribly much.

Adam put his menu down first. After a moment, Arden, apparently decisive, discarded hers. Omar was looking for the cheapest pronounceable thing; luckily he could discern the Italian origins of the dishes through the Spanish scrim. He, too, lowered his menu.

Their drinks arrived. Omar couldn't think quickly enough to make a toast—would toasting Jules Gund be in poor taste?—but the moment passed, as they all seemed more eager to sip their drinks than to make, or acknowledge, a toast. Toasting really is a ridiculous custom, thought Omar. It's like saying "God bless you" when someone sneezes.

"I'm sorry Mrs. Gund couldn't join us," he said, carefully lowering his precariously full martini. He had ordered a martini because after Adam had ordered one it seemed the easiest thing to do.

"Are you really?" said Adam. "I'm surprised you know her well enough to miss her company."

"I don't really," said Omar, remembering his talk with Caroline that morning—in a certain way, he knew her quite well, and was glad she was not there. "It's just that I wanted an opportunity to talk to all three of you, together."

The waiter came to take their order. When he had been dispatched—Adam's summoning of waiters was not a singular phenomenon; he dispatched them with equal panache—another party had entered the restaurant, and for some reason watching them be seated was preoccupying. After a moment Adam turned to Omar and said, "What is it you want to tell us?" as if he had no idea what had brought Omar to them.

For a moment Omar's nerve failed him, so he took another sip of his drink. Why do they fill the glass so full? he wondered in panic. His main object was drinking it down to a level where it could be more easily handled, although he was glad he had followed Adam's lead and ordered a martini: it really was a lovely drink. He noticed that Adam's martini had already sunk to a very safe level.

"Well," Omar began, "I suppose I'd like to talk to you about why I want to write a biography of Jules Gund, about the importance of the project to me, and to answer any questions or address any reservations you have. I feel confident that if I explain things properly to you, you will see no reason to withhold authorization."

Omar noticed that Adam had returned his attention to the large party that had recently entered the restaurant. "Is that Suki Schmidt?" he asked Arden.

"Yes," said Arden. "And Willem and Willem's brother Brat and I don't know who else. Perhaps it's Brat's wife and her sister."

"I thought she and Willem were divorced."

"They were," said Arden. "But they reconciled."

"How terribly stupid of them. They were always at each other."

"Yes," said Arden. "But they were unhappy apart. Apparently they missed it."

"What?"

"Being at each other."

"They were awfully good at it," said Adam. "She once shot him, you know. And hit him too. In the stomach, I think."

"Yes, he has one of those plastic bags now," said Arden.

"Violence is terribly underrated," said Adam. "It's so—so expeditious. I'm always asking Pete to smack me. 'Just smack me,' I tell him."

"Pete would never smack you," said Arden.

"Yes, I know," said Adam. "Yet I think we would be so much happier if he did. Did you ever smack Jules?"

"Yes, in fact," said Arden. "Once or twice."

I should be taking notes or something, Omar thought. I should have brought a tape recorder. Suddenly it seemed exhausting, impossible: How do you write a biography? he wondered, when there is so much, when there is everything, an infinity, to know. It seemed impossible. It was like compiling a telephone book from scratch. He sipped again from his martini.

"You often had that smacked-about coital glow," said Adam.

"Oh, Jules never smacked me," said Arden. "You're mistaken if you think he did."

"Oh, I never thought he did. I assumed the smacking was all yours. What about you, Mr. Razaghi? I understand you are affianced. Does your fiancée smack you? Or you her? Although you don't appear to be the smacking type. Or perhaps you are both above all that?"

"I am not engaged," said Omar.

"Pardon me," said Adam. "I have been misinformed. My sources err."

"Who told you I was affia—— engaged?" asked Omar.

"A little bird," said Adam. "A big bird. A blue bird. A swallow. A bat."

"Well, I am not engaged," said Omar, thinking: Why I am saying it like that, as if they are accusing me of something? It must be the martini. He glared at it a moment, then sipped from it.

"There is something so repellingly Victorian about any couple," said Adam. "The smugness, the sense of sanctity and safety and superiority; it's why God invented smacking. I am sure the Victorians were constantly smacking one another. It's why they wore all those hideous clothes: to hide their bruises."

The conversation seemed to have veered into territory beyond Omar's ken, and he felt that he—and his martini—had contributed to its waywardness. So he decided to sit quietly and collect his thoughts.

"Perhaps you should tell us, then, why you want to write a biography of Jules Gund," Arden suggested.

Why did he want to write a biography of Jules Gund? It was a very reasonable question, especially under the present circumstances. Of course, it presumed he wanted to write a biography of Jules Gund, but of course he did. He would not be here if he did not. But suddenly, for the first time in the entire process, he was not sure. Did he want to write a biography of Jules Gund? Could he?

"Well, as I told you," he heard himself saying, "I am extremely interested in his work. Although he wrote only one book, I think it is an important book. It deserves to be more widely known, and read, and I think a biography would help in that regard. Really, the fact that he wrote only one book does not matter."

"He wrote another book," said Adam.

"Adam . . ." Arden warned.

"What?" asked Adam.

"He published only one book," said Arden. "*The Gondola*. That is what counts."

"Well, it depends who is counting."

"He wrote other books?" asked Omar.

"No," said Arden. "He worked on other books, but none of them—he did not finish another book. There is only *The Gondola*. Go on with what you were saying."

Omar was flustered. Other books? What did they mean?

"Why do you want to write a biography of Jules?" Arden prompted.

"Well," said Omar. "I think *The Gondola* is an important historical and artistic document. And his life was interesting—in many ways, it is a quintessential life of the century."

"How do you figure that?" asked Adam.

"His life bridges worlds and cultures and religions. All of the great conflicts of the century are apparent in it."

"I see what you mean," said Arden. "His being half Jewish, and European, but raised Catholic in South America . . ."

"Exactly," said Omar. "And then there is, of course, his personal life."

"But all that applies to me as well," said Adam. "And my being homosexual, well, that's certainly more a twentieth-century story than wives and mistresses, which sounds very nineteenth century to me. Why not write my biography?"

"I don't doubt for an instant that your life is every bit as interesting and relevant," said Omar. "And I encourage you to write an autobiography. But as someone interested in the politics of literature, it is natural I am more interested in the life of Jules Gund. And of course it is perhaps important to repeat that there is considerable academic interest in a biography of Jules Gund. As you know, the University of Kansas Press has already committed to publishing the book, on the basis of my dissertation."

"How many copies will they publish?" asked Adam.

For God's sake, thought Omar, why don't you ask me how many pages the book will have? "I don't know," he said. "Although I'm sure their print runs are commensurate with other university presses."

Perhaps Arden heard the edge of frustration in his voice, for she leaned toward the table—she had sunk back into the banquette's gloom—and said, "I have changed my mind, Omar. I have decided to authorize the biography."

"Really?" said Omar. "Thank you."

"I am sure you will write a fine biography," said Arden. She raised her glass of wine to him.

"But what about Caroline?"

"You must still convince Caroline," said Arden.

"I wish she had come tonight. How can I convince her if I can't speak with her?"

"You assume Caroline is rational. She is not. She will not be convinced in that way," said Adam.

"Then how can I convince her?" asked Omar.

"You cannot," said Adam.

"But then—don't you need to be in agreement? Can you grant authorization without her?"

"I said you cannot convince her," said Adam. "I did not say she would not be convinced. I hope you have not forgotten our little agreement?"

"No," said Omar. "Of course not."

"What agreement?" asked Arden.

"It does not concern you," said Adam.

"If it concerns the authorization, it concerns me," said Arden. "What agreement have you made?"

"It really does not concern you," said Adam. "Isn't that correct, Mr. Razaghi?"

"Please call me Omar," said Omar.

"Isn't that correct, Omar?"

"I'm not really sure what concerns who. Whom."

"Well, rest assured that what we spoke of earlier does not concern Arden. Or Caroline."

"What are you plotting?" asked Arden. "If you are plotting something, Adam, I must know. Otherwise I won't cooperate."

"I am plotting nothing," said Adam. "I do not plot. Perhaps we should drop the subject, and enjoy our dinner. If you'll excuse me a moment, I will go say hello to Suki and Willem." He left the table and crossed the dining room.

Arden said nothing. She was fingering the stem of her wineglass, staring straight ahead.

Omar did not know what to say. Arden looked very beautiful. Her hair was pulled back into a chignon and she wore pearl earrings and lipstick. It was clear she had gotten dressed specially for the dinner, and there was something a little bit sad about it, Omar thought: that she looked so beautiful, with lipstick, her hair styled, her pocketbook sitting on the banquette beside her—all for what? This dinner with him and Adam in a crummy restaurant. She looked defeated and sad.

"I'm sorry," he said.

She turned to him and smiled. Perhaps she was not sad. "Sorry? Sorry about what?"

"About—I haven't been plotting with Adam. Really, we haven't."

"Oh," she said, and laughed. She had a lovely laugh: gushing, natural. "I'm not sure I believe you. Adam is always plotting. I'm used to it."

"There's just something he wants me to do for him," Omar said. He felt better having said it. He did not want to have secrets from Arden.

"You don't have to do anything for him, you know. Be careful. It will all be fine."

"What about Caroline?"

She looked away: over at the other table, where Adam stood talking. She shook her head. "Caroline must make up her own mind," she said. "The more you try to persuade her, the more she'll resist."

"Well, I'm glad you've changed your mind," said Omar. "Thank you."

She looked at him again. "I haven't changed it to please you," she said. "You mustn't think that."

"No," said Omar.

"I just—in thinking about things, it seems to me that a biography is the best thing for Jules. It's for Jules I've changed my mind, not you."

"Of course," said Omar.

At the millhouse, Adam opened the car door. "Do you want to come in for a nightcap? We have a bottle of chartreuse lurking about, I believe."

"I've had plenty for the night," said Arden. "And Ada is staying with Portia."

"You can take the car back with you, if you want," said Adam. "Pete can fetch it tomorrow. Walk me to the door, then, Mr. Razaghi," said Adam. "These cobbles are treacherous at night."

Omar got out of the car and helped Adam from his seat. Adam took hold of Omar's arm and led him across the dark, cobbled yard.

"Well," Adam said. "One down and one to go. Perhaps you did not need me with Arden, but Caroline is a stickier wicket."

He was speaking rather loudly—they had drunk a bottle of Prosecco with dinner—and Omar was afraid that Arden would hear. "I don't think I had anything to do with Arden changing her mind," he said.

"Nonsense! Of course you did. Don't underestimate the effect of your charm."

Omar said nothing, but blushed in the darkness. He felt Adam's grip upon his arm tighten. "I once had charm like yours," Adam said. "Strange as it may seem now. But charm spoils with age. Like cheese, or beauty. Or at least for me it did. Some people manage to retain one or the other or, rarely, both. But I think you will find this prize requires a price. The price is selflessness, forfeiture, abstinence. There is something a little pathetic about ending up old and beautiful and charming, I think: it indicates, to me at least, a waste of resources, or at the very least, a serious misappropriation of them. I think I have very appropriately divested myself of these resources. For charm and beauty are more valuable commodities in the young. There's little the ancient can buy with them. For this reason, I do not mind being old and ugly: it seems apt."

"But you're not ugly," said Omar, emboldened by liquor.

"How charming of you to say that," said Adam. "Thank you. But don't squander your charm on me."

"No, thank you," said Omar. "Thank you for all your advice, and help."

"I think in retrospect you'll come to see I've done nothing for you," said Adam, "but while you are feeling obliged, I hasten to remind you of our agreement."

"Of course," said Omar, "I haven't forgotten."

"Well, we can talk about all of that later. Tomorrow, perhaps. Now, I need my bed. Perhaps you could open the door for me, for it sticks a bit, and responds well to brute force. A quality, like charm and beauty, I presently lack."

The door was recalcitrant but Omar managed to push it open. Adam stepped inside.

"Charm and brute force. What a delicious package you are."

Omar remained on the stoop. "Good night," he said.

Adam turned back toward the door. He put a hand on either of Omar's shoulders, and kissed him on his cheek. "Good night, dear boy." He turned and slowly walked up the dark stairs. Omar pulled the door shut and crossed the yard. Arden had left the car and was sitting on the stone wall. She had once again removed her shoes. He sat beside her. It was cool and she had put on a sweater he had not realized she had. Perhaps it had been in the car. "Is it all right to walk back?" she asked. "I feel like a walk, and some fresh air—but we can take the car if you want. You must be tired."

"No," said Omar. "I'd like to walk."

Arden stood and began walking up the drive. Omar followed her. They were silent all the way up the lane. They crossed the bridge over the stream, which they could hear gushing in the darkness beneath them. They paused there, as if by mutual agreement. Arden said, "What will you do now?"

Omar wasn't sure exactly what she meant, and he did not want to think about what he could, or should, do. He said nothing.

"Well, you're welcome to stay here as long as you need to," said Arden.

"Thank you," said Omar.

Arden began walking again, and Omar followed her.

"There is one thing I'd like very much to do," he said.

"What's that?"

"I'd like to see the gondola."

"Oh," said Arden. "Of course you may see it. It's a hike, though,

I warn you, now that the road's washed out. I told you the road was gone, didn't I?"

"Yes," said Omar. "When did that happen? How?"

"It was about five years ago. Jules's father had built a lake for the gondola by damming the river. That river"—she motioned behind them—"but farther up. Of course the dam, like everything, was neglected. It broke in a storm and the road up to the lake was washed out, and we've never bothered to fix either."

"But you can still get there?"

"Yes, on foot. There's a path."

"How far is it? How long does it take?"

"A couple of miles, I suppose. Uphill. About an hour or so. We can go tomorrow, if you like. It's a nice walk."

"Thank you," said Omar. "I'd like that."

"After breakfast, then. We can bring a lunch with us."

"May I bring my camera?" asked Omar.

"I don't see why not," said Arden.

Omar said, "It's odd."

"What's odd?"

"Where I live, in Kansas—where I live now—I live in a house on a defunct lake."

"What do you mean?" asked Arden.

"It's the same as here. There was a lake created by a dam, but the dam broke, so the lake is gone. Just a creek and marsh. It's odd that the same thing happened here."

"Yes," said Arden, "I suppose." And then she said: "Do you live alone?"

"Yes," said Omar.

"But you have a girlfriend, I understand?"

"Yes, I do," said Omar.

"What's her name?"

"Her name is Deirdre."

"That's a pretty name," said Arden.

Omar did not respond.

"And is she also an academic?"

"Yes," said Omar. "She is."

"Is her field literature?"

"Yes," said Omar. "It is."

"Forgive me if I'm being rude," said Arden.

"You aren't being rude," said Omar. "I'm sorry if I made you feel that. Really, you weren't."

"I don't meet new people often. I don't know how to behave anymore." They were silent a moment, walking side by side, and then Arden turned slightly toward him. "Are you happy?" she asked.

It was an odd question, thought Omar, perhaps she did not know how to behave anymore. But there was something about the moment that allowed it: or it was not the moment so much as the sum of moments, the entire day, stretching back behind them in the darkness, as if the day was a road they had walked along. "I suppose I am," said Omar. "I have no reason not to be. Although I'm concerned about the book, of course, and authorization—"

"No," said Arden. "I mean apart from all that. I mean in your life, living in Kansas, getting your degree, teaching—does all that make you happy?"

The answer was no, but for some reason Omar was unable to admit that, for admitting to unhappiness seemed tantamount to admitting to failure, for after all, wasn't it? If he was unhappy, unhappy living in Kansas, getting his degree, teaching, wasn't it all his fault? Yes. If he was unhappy there was no one to blame but himself. And that was failure. But was he really unhappy? He had never thought so before, exactly. Instead of saying no, he said: "It's odd to come so far away from your life, like this. To step out of it. Imagine if you came to Kansas—"

Arden laughed.

"I know," said Omar. "I can't imagine you in Kansas."

They arrived at the gate and turned up the drive.

"I feel like I've been here longer than one day," said Omar.

"Yes," said Arden, "it feels longer."

"I understand why you would want to stay here. Or at least I think I do. It seems very perfect here, in a way."

"How do you mean?"

"I don't know. It's hard to say. It's just that everything seems perfect. Everything seems in its place. Even the trees, the gate, the house, all the things in the house, and the quiet—I don't know. I'm a bit drunk, I think."

Arden smiled in the darkness.

"You look so beautiful tonight," said Omar.

"I've changed my mind. You can stop flattering me."

"No!" said Omar. "Really. I mean it. I wouldn't flatter you. I mean I wouldn't flatter you for mercenary reasons. I'm not like that."

"I know," said Arden, "but you shouldn't, nevertheless."

"Why not?" asked Omar.

"Well, for one thing, you have a girlfriend, don't you? I don't think she would like it."

Omar thought of Deirdre. It was hard to think of Deirdre, perhaps because he was drunk, and the distance, it was almost as if the distance affected his ability to imagine her. "I don't think she would mind if I said you were beautiful," he said.

Arden said nothing. They approached the house. A soft light glowed from the windows in the tower but most of the others were dark, and they stood outside the front door, in the darkness. The trees all around them murmured and exhaled their piney scent.

"I wish we could walk now, to see the gondola," Omar said.

"Now? In the dark?"

"Yes," he said.

"But you wouldn't see it. There are no lights up there."

"I want to keep walking," said Omar.

"I've got to go in," said Arden. "Ada is staying with Portia. You can walk about all you like."

"I think I will walk a little."

"Fine," said Arden. "Don't get lost." She turned away from him, abruptly, without saying good night or anything else, and entered the house. Omar stood outside and watched the lights turn on. Then he walked down the drive, to the point where it curved, and he turned and looked back up at the house. He could see it looming there in front of him, the yellow bricks glowing palely in the dark. He stepped a ways off the drive into the towering trees. He lay down on the ground, looking up through the embrasures of their quivering tip-tops at the stars.

Adam was sitting in the dark living room when Pete returned. Pete turned on the light and saw him: "Why are you sitting in the dark?" he asked.

"I was waiting for you," said Adam.

"Why were you waiting for me?" asked Pete. "Why were you in the dark?"

"Where have you been?" asked Adam.

"In Huerta."

"And what brought you to Huerta?"

"A table," said Pete.

"You missed the dinner," said Adam.

"I'm sorry," said Pete. "I didn't think I would be away so long."

"It does seem rather a long time to be contemplating a table. Was it a particularly fascinating table?"

Pete went into the kitchen and rinsed out a dirty glass, then filled it with water and drank it all, quickly. Then he filled it again and returned to the living room, sipping from it. "Do you want something?" he asked Adam.

"There are many things I want," said Adam.

"Do you want something I can get you?" asked Pete.

"I want you to be happy," said Adam.

"I am happy," said Pete.

"Are you?"

"Yes," said Pete.

"If I were you, I would not be happy," said Adam.

"Well, you are not me. And who would you be happy being? No one, I think."

Pete sat down on the sofa across from Adam. A low table intervened, and Pete raised his legs up, one and then the other, and rested them on the table. He sighed, and leaned back into the cushions. "How was the dinner?" he asked.

"Mildly diverting," said Adam. "Arden has changed her mind. I have always liked that expression: 'changed her mind.' Like hats: as if one takes one mind out and puts another mind in. I would like to change my mind."

"Change it about what?"

"I mean entirely. Like a hat."

"I like your mind. I would miss it," said Pete. "Why did Arden change her mind?"

"Because she thinks it would be fun to play with Omar Razaghi."

Pete said nothing.

"Of course we all want to play with him, each in our own way. The problem is that Caroline is contrary, and thinks it would be more fun to bait him than to aid him."

"And you?" asked Pete.

"I just find him amusing."

"Well, I am glad you are amused."

"Tell me about the table," said Adam.

"What table?"

"The table that has occupied you in Huerta this entire evening."

"You don't believe there is a table in Huerta, do you?"

"Of course I believe there is a table in Huerta. I believe there are many tables in Huerta."

"It was actually not a table. Or not only a table. They are building a new courthouse in Huerta. Very modern, and ugly. They are auctioning all the contents of the old courthouse. There are some beautiful things. Including tables. Beautiful benches. And on the way back I stopped at Mordachei's, and had dinner, and drank some beer."

"Alone?"

"Yes," said Pete.

"You spoke with no one?"

"Why are you asking these questions? I don't have a secret life."

"I know," said Adam. "I wish you did."

"Why?" asked Pete.

"Well, not secret. Not necessarily secret. But another life, or at least a bit of a life, I wish you had that."

"I do," said Pete. "I have more than a bit of a life."

"Sometimes I think it was wrong of me to bring you here."

"I happen to like it here," said Pete. "I'm happier here than anywhere else I have ever been. I wish you would not worry about me in that way. I'm not a pet."

"I didn't mean that," said Adam.

"I think you did. You're not responsible for my happiness."

"Of course. Yet it concerns me, nonetheless."

"I think you should worry about your own happiness."

Adam chuckled, darkly. "Oh, I have given up on that!"

"You pretend you have, but you have not."

"How do you know?"

"It is cowardly, I think," said Pete. "It is the one thing about you that I don't like."

"What?"

"That you pretend happiness does not matter. That it is somehow beyond, or behind you. That you are past it." He paused. "It is a little too easy, and selfish."

"Selfish?"

"Yes," said Pete. "Selfish, and a bit mean. What about me? Don't I make you happy? Can't I make you happy? At least sometimes?"

"Of course you can," said Adam. "Of course you do."

"Then don't say you are not happy. Don't say happiness does not matter."

"I'm sorry," said Adam.

Pete stood up. "I'm tired," he said. "Are you ready for bed?"

"Go up," said Adam. "I will be there in just a minute."

Pete replaced his glass in the kitchen. He passed back through the living room and paused in the doorway. "Are you coming?" he asked.

"In just a minute," said Adam.

"Did I upset you?" asked Pete.

"No," said Adam. "Well, yes, a little. But it is fine. I am fine. Thank you for what you said."

"Come up," said Pete. "Please, come up now."

And to his surprise, Adam did.

CHAPTER ELEVEN

Caroline was drinking tea at the kitchen table when Omar appeared the next morning. "Good morning," he said.

"Good morning," she replied. "Portia missed the bus so Arden drove her to school. She should be back shortly, I think. There is coffee in the pot."

"Thank you," said Omar. He poured himself a cup of coffee and sat at the table.

"I understand you and Arden are off on an excursion," said Caroline.

"Yes," said Omar. "We're going to see the gondola." He sipped his coffee. It was very hot. He blew on it.

"Did you enjoy your dinner at Federico's?" asked Caroline.

"Yes," said Omar. "It was a very nice dinner."

"And Arden has changed her mind," said Caroline.

"Yes," said Omar.

"You know, I have been thinking about it all. And I am confused. You confuse me. Perhaps I misjudged you yesterday, but you seemed different."

"How did I seem?"

"You seemed compassionate, and moral."

"You think I am immoral?"

"Well, I wonder what kind of person would write a biography of a man against that man's wishes. Or those of his wife, for that matter."

"I'm sorry," said Omar. "I just fail to see how a letter a man wrote thirty years ago—"

"Twenty."

"Twenty, then. Whatever. But I fail to see how feelings expressed at that time have any bearing on this matter."

"How convenient for you."

"And even if they did, other matters take precedence."

"What matters are they?"

"I mean that if Jules had never written a book it would be different. But he did. And it was published to considerable international attention. He joined in public discourse."

"And so he lays himself open to the scourge of biography? By publishing one book?"

"Yes," said Omar. "And I don't think biography is necessarily a scourge."

"I think you're simply rationalizing, making excuses. I wish you could read his letter."

"So do I," said Omar.

"I'm sure you do. I'm sure you'd like to read all his letters to me."

"I would, in fact," said Omar.

"And that doesn't seem strange to you?"

"What?"

"That you feel you have the right to read the letters my husband wrote me?"

"I don't think it's a right," said Omar. "It would be a privilege."

"Well, you shan't have that privilege," said Caroline.

"I'm sorry you feel that way," said Omar. "And actually, your aversion to the biography concerns me more than Jules's."

"Because Jules is dead, and I am an executor."

"No," said Omar. "You always think the worst of me, don't you?"

"Then why?"

"Because I care about what you think. Of course I don't want to write this biography without your blessing."

"Then don't write it."

"I won't. I can't. But I think that is a shame. I think it's an important story, and deserves to be told. And Adam and Arden agree with me."

"In matters of morality, the majority does not rule."

"Why must you make this a moral issue?"

"Because it is," said Caroline. "I don't believe that you cannot, or will not, see that."

Omar said nothing for a moment, and then he said, "Is it only this letter from Jules, or are there other reasons?"

"The letter is the primary, and I feel, a more than sufficient reason."

"But you have other reasons?"

"Yes," said Caroline. "Of course I do."

"Would you share them with me?"

"I don't want to seem unkind. Although I suppose, in your eyes, I already do. How sad. I am not an unkind person."

"I don't think you are," said Omar.

She smiled at him.

"You seem very young to me," she said.

He did not refute her perception.

"Beyond my feelings concerning Jules's letter, I feel you are not well suited to the task. I would not authorize any biography of Jules, but a biography written by you gives me especial pause."

"Why?" asked Omar.

"You are too unlike him. You won't understand his life. You won't understand me. You are not Catholic. You are young. You are callow. And I think you will get it all wrong."

"But with your cooperation I will not get it wrong. It is only if you fail to help me that I will get things wrong."

"You don't understand what I mean. I don't mean wrong about fact. I realize you are an academic, and it is a factual life you intend to write, but nevertheless, it is a life. A life. Everyone seems to keep forgetting that. And a miserable life. He suffered enough in it."

"But good biographers are often unlike their subjects," said Omar. "In fact, I think it is preferable. It allows for dispassion and clarity."

"Dispassion? Yesterday you told me something quite different! Yesterday you said you wanted to write a subjective, passionate biography. Omar, you're floundering. You don't know what you're saying, or doing. Admit it: there's no shame in it. The shame is in doing the wrong thing."

Omar said nothing.

Caroline reached out and touched her hand to his. "You don't need to write this biography," she said. "I know you think you do, but you don't. You can not write it. You have that option."

"But I don't," said Omar. "You don't understand. Everything depends upon my writing it."

"What is everything?"

"My job. My career. Perhaps my relationship with my girl-friend."

"I'm sorry, I'm truly sorry, you find yourself in this predicament. I can believe that from where you sit it does appear that everything depends upon your writing this biography. But I assure you everything does not. Whatever holds you to writing this biography is not important. Now is your chance to let that all go. This is an opportunity to change your life, Omar. You must take advantage of it."

"I don't want to change my life," said Omar. "My life may be difficult, but I like it how it is."

"Well, I cannot compromise myself simply to make life easier for you."

"I know," said Omar. "I'm not asking you to do that."

"I thought you were," said Caroline. "What is it, then, that you are asking me?"

Omar looked at her. It should not be this difficult, he thought. The fact that it was this difficult meant that there was something wrong, something inherently and fundamentally wrong. He should have sensed that earlier, and never come here. He was wrong to have come. He should have returned the fellowship money. Deirdre had been wrong. It was not the right thing to do. Nothing really depended upon it. Nothing that really mattered.

"I ask nothing of you," he said.

Caroline looked at him. He felt his face shaking, but then he felt it harden, a sudden hardness surged through him, an odd, foreign strength. And he looked back at her with this strength in his eyes. Caroline shrugged. She stood up from the table and crossed the room to the sink and rinsed her teacup beneath the tap and then overturned it in the dish drainer. Then, without looking again at Omar, she opened the door. Omar watched her walk across the courtyard and disappear into the door that led to the tower.

She is right, thought Omar. I don't agree with everything she says and I don't really understand her, but fundamentally she is right. Perhaps she is right morally. But I am not a bad person, Omar told himself. I have no ill intentions. What I want to do is perfectly acceptable and morally innocuous. He put his face in his hands. But why did God invent Caroline?

Arden found him sitting at the kitchen table that way when she returned from town. "Good," she said, "you're up. Did you sleep well?"

"Yes," said Omar. He did not look up at her.

"What's wrong?" asked Arden. "You look—is something wrong?"

"No" said Omar. He looked up and tried to smile. "Nothing's wrong. I'm sorry. I'm just a bit hungover, I think. I'm not used to drinking so much."

"Neither am I," said Arden. "Although it doesn't seem to have—"

"And perhaps it's the traveling too," said Omar. "I just feel a little strange."

"You look pale," said Arden. She came close to him and put her hand on his forehead. "You don't feel warm."

"I'm sure I'm fine," said Omar. "The coffee will wake me up."

"Do you still want to go—or perhaps, if you aren't feeling well, we shouldn't walk up to the gondola this morning."

"No, I want to," said Omar. "It will be good to get some exercise. It's what I need, I think."

"Are you hungry?" asked Arden. She sat down at the table.

"No," said Omar.

"Would you like some bread and jam? Or eggs?"

"No, thank you," said Omar. "The coffee is fine."

Arden stood up. She had brought a bag of groceries back with her and she began to empty it, stowing its contents in the cupboards and ancient refrigerator. "Portia is angry with us," she said. "She wanted us to wait till she came home from school, so she could join us."

"We can wait, if you'd like," said Omar.

"No," said Arden. "She'll only slow us down."

CHAPTER TWELVE

They passed through the courtyard arch, down the gravel path across the formal garden, through the oleander hedge, around the garden, through an orchard of fruit trees, and then climbed up a small ridge into a forest of mostly deciduous trees. It was quiet and hot; there was no breeze and the trees only obscured and filtered the warm sunlight, they did not seem to mitigate it. There was no sign of a path; in fact, there was no indication that anyone had ever set foot thereabouts before, but Arden walked purposefully, switching back and forth among the trees.

"I thought there was a path," said Omar.

"There is a kind of a path later," said Arden. "Not through here."

"Is this your land?" asked Omar.

"Yes," said Arden. "We've tried to sell it but no one will buy it."

"How many acres do you have?"

"I don't know. A lot, I think. Hundreds. And there was more before, when they still owned the mine."

"When did they sell the mine?"

"I don't know. I think in the fifties, but I'm not sure."

"Is the mine still operating?"

"No," said Arden. "It's been shut for ages."

"What did they mine?"

"Bauxite," said Arden.

"What is bauxite?"

"An ore, I think. It's used to make aluminum."

"I don't understand how all that works," said Omar.

"Neither do I," said Arden. She paused, glanced around, and then headed in a slightly different direction. She was walking more quickly than Omar had imagined they would walk. As far as he knew, there was no hurry, but Arden moved as if there was.

After a moment Omar said: "May I ask you a question?"

"Yes," said Arden. She slowed her pace a little.

"I just wondered if you knew—do you think there's some reason Caroline doesn't want the biography to be written? I mean some reason other than the letter from Jules?"

"What do you mean?" asked Arden.

"I mean, do you think there's something, something about herself or Jules that she does not want written about?"

"Oh," said Arden. "Something shameful? No, I don't think that. Although of course it's possible, but it had not occurred to me. Do you think that?"

"I don't know," said Omar. "I don't know her. I just don't understand her recalcitrance."

"Perhaps it is not to be understood," said Arden.

"But don't you think everything can be understood? If you look at it closely and carefully enough?"

"No," said Arden. "That has not been my experience. Although it seems a practical approach for a biographer to take. A necessary approach, in fact."

"I don't just mean about the biography. And I'm not a biographer. At least not yet. And at this rate, never. No, I mean about life in general, and people. I mean, people often behave mysteriously or inexplicably, but if you know them well enough, and know enough about them, you understand why they do what they do."

"I'm not sure people are as rational as all that," said Arden.

"Do you understand Caroline's opposition?"

"Yes," said Arden. "But not in a rational way. I can't explain it to you, but it makes sense to me. It's complicated, I think. It's not just one thing, or two things. It's the whole world, her whole world, being how it is."

"Oh," said Omar. Then: "She told me this morning—or she implied—that I was immoral. That it was immoral of me to write the biography."

"Did she?" asked Arden. "I'm not surprised, though. It's always her last resort: the moral high ground. Caroline in her tower looking down on us all."

"Do you think biographies are immoral? I mean essentially, intrinsically immoral?"

"No," said Arden. "But perhaps I'm too stupid to understand how they are. But you mustn't let Caroline's arrogance affect you. It's how she bears her loneliness, by convincing herself she's better than everyone. She's very proud. It's why she stopped painting, I'm sure. She couldn't bear the idea of being a mediocre painter, so she stopped. She thinks it's better to not paint than to paint something mediocre. It's very sad, and stupid. She's thwarted, and so now she likes to thwart others. She does it all the time with me, but I don't mind it. Or I try not to mind it. Neither should you. Really."

They emerged from the woods onto a derelict dirt road that rose through denser and more varied forest. Arden explained this was the road to the lake that had been washed out, and they followed it upward; it hugged the side of the hill and when the woods fell away Omar could see the house at Ochos Rios below them. They had come farther and higher than he had thought.

They stood for a moment, looking down at the house.

"Do you know why it's called Ochos Rios?" he asked Arden.

"It means 'eight rivers,' " said Arden.

"I know. But there aren't eight rivers, are there?"

"No," said Arden. "Perhaps there were, at some point. A lot of place-names here are names from Spain. Or elsewhere."

"Was it named by Jules's parents?"

"Oh, no," said Arden. "At least I don't think so. I'm sure it was named when they got here. Before they got here."

"Yet you said they built the house."

"I think there was a house there—the wing where the kitchen is now. They added the rest." She turned around and pointed into the woods on the other side of the road. "There is the path, but come up here a ways, and you can see where the road is washed out."

He followed her up and around a corner to where the road abruptly ended. It was a scene of devastation, and it was hard to imagine that the little apathetic stream wandering through the bottom of the scarred chasm that divided the road had been responsible for the alteration of the landscape. They stood at the edge of the precipice and looked down into the ruin.

"It was odd," Arden said, after a moment, "the night the dam broke. We heard it first. Although of course we didn't know what we were hearing: a strange noise in the distance. A sort of thundering, but not in the sky. It was frightening: hearing it coming closer and not knowing what it was. I never realized how little we control the earth until I moved here. Even at the house it's evident. The way things grow, so unbelievably quickly; the way the house is constantly cracking and moldering and disintegrating. At night I hear the slates sliding off the roof and crashing in the courtyard." She looked at him. "Do you believe in God?" she asked.

He told her no.

"Sometimes I think, or feel, the earth doesn't want things to last; it wants everything to crumble and for all of us to go away. It wants to get back to where it was before it all started, back to the garden with the fruit and the animals, before God got ambitious and ruined it all. He should have left well enough alone. He should have rested on the sixth day, not the seventh." She shuddered, and turned away from the abyss.

They retraced their steps, and found the path, which climbed up the rocky forested slope. The path was narrow and they had to walk in single file, Arden in front of Omar. After a moment Omar said, "I don't suppose I could see the other book—the manuscript— you mentioned last evening."

Arden paused for a moment but continued walking. She did not turn around. "No," she said. "That is not possible. Adam should not have mentioned it."

"How many are there?"

"One. Just one."

"Have you read it?"

"Yes," said Arden.

Talking to her back, not being able to see her face, emboldened Omar. "What is it about?" he asked.

Arden was not looking at him. She was looking ahead of them. "It was about a man who lives in a large house in the middle of nowhere with his wife and mistress. He was not a particularly inventive writer, Jules."

"Most writers aren't," said Omar.

Arden said nothing.

"Was he still working on it when he died? Or had he finished it?"

"It was finished," said Arden.

"And was it Jules who did not want it published? Or . . ."

"Or us? No, it was Jules. Adam should not have mentioned it. I shouldn't have said anything. You must forget it. It does not exist."

"You mean it has been destroyed? The manuscript?"

"You must forget it," said Arden. "Please don't mention it again."

"Okay," said Omar.

They walked silently for a while then, climbing up through the woods. Presently the ground leveled and the woods thinned and they walked out into a large clearing of grass and reeds and thorny bushes.

Arden paused at the edge of the clearing. "This was the lake," she said. "It was large, but not very deep. Of course, it couldn't be deep for the gondola. The pole needs to touch bottom." She mimed a gondolier's action.

They stood there for a moment, looking out over the hot, bright expanse of low brush.

"The boathouse is on the other side," she said, pointing. "In those trees. Come." She set off down the path, and Omar followed her. In the middle of the clearing was a shallow, muddy stream, which they both hopped over. In the trees on the far side of the clearing was a long, low wooden building, raised up on stilts, with two barnlike doors facing them. "The door is around back," said Arden.

"Wait," said Omar. He felt suddenly odd. He felt as if he might faint. Was it the heat? The altitude, perhaps? The exertion of climbing with nothing but coffee in his stomach? Perhaps, he thought, but he knew it was something more than all that.

"What's wrong?" asked Arden.

"Nothing," said Omar. "I just feel a bit odd. Perhaps it's the altitude."

"We aren't very high up," said Arden. "We aren't high at all." She laughed. "Come, sit in the shade over there."

She led him to what had been the bank of the lake, and they sat on the shaded ground next to the boathouse. Arden fished out the bottle of water she had packed in her bag and handed it to Omar. He drank some and then handed the bottle to her. She drank.

"Do you feel better?" she asked.

"Yes," he said. He stood up in attempt to illustrate his recovery, but Arden remained seated. Omar looked out over the emptied lake basin, trying to picture it otherwise, but he could not: he had a literal mind. "What was it like?" he asked.

For a moment he thought Arden had not heard him, because she did not reply. He turned around and looked at her. She, too, was gazing out over the defunct lake.

"It was a lake," she said. "It looked artificial. You could tell it had been made by man, not God. It was too perfectly oval, or something. We swam in it, sometimes, although it was muddy and full of weeds. And snakes."

"Did you ride in the gondola?" Omar asked.

"No," she said. Omar could tell by her voice that she was remembering something.

"Never?" he asked.

"No," she said. "It wasn't used. Not after Jules's father died. I don't know why, really, but it wasn't. I never saw Jules or Adam in it. Perhaps they didn't know how, but I think it was something else."

"It's an amazing thing," said Omar. "To have brought it here with them. To have escaped with it."

"They didn't," said Arden.

Omar turned around.

"They didn't bring it with them," said Arden. "They brought hardly anything with them. The gondola didn't come until after the war."

"But in the book—" Omar began, and stopped.

"It's a novel," said Arden.

"Yes, I know," said Omar. "I just assumed— So the lake wasn't built until after the war?"

"No," said Arden. "At least I don't think so."

"Oh," said Omar. He sat back down beside her. For a moment they did not speak, but both looked out over the sunstruck landscape, as if there were something to discern in it. Then Arden said, without turning her head, "Did you know I was an actress when I was a child?"

"No," said Omar. He looked at her. Her face was passive yet intent and her eyes were focused on something far beyond them, as if there were enemies on the far shore only she could see.

"Yes," she said. "After my grandmother died, and I moved to England. My father was a director. He was a bit of a drunk, and I was scared of him. He taught me to act by scaring me. Cry, he would say, and I would cry." She looked quickly at him, then resumed her face-off with the horizon. "I was always an orphan in the movies, or a sick girl. A girl who cried. People like to see girls cry in movies. It was all there, everything he wanted, just beneath the surface. Sometimes I think we're born with a finite store of emotion. When I was on ships as a child I'd think about how everything, all the food, all the water, all the supplies, was stored somewhere, how it could all run out, how every day the ship was getting lighter, the food passing through us and being flushed into the ocean. And the ship buoyed up by its increasing emptiness. I thought growing up was like that: a process of being hollowed out, emptied. That adults were quick and mean because their emotions had been deplenished. I thought it was a good thing, worth aspiring to. And so I would cry when my father told me to cry, take after take, as many takes as it took, and it was all real, I wasn't faking it, and in some way I thought I was freeing myself from that sorrow. That it couldn't come back."

Again, she glanced at him, and again looked away.

"You make me think of all this. It's odd. I don't understand it."

"What don't you understand?" asked Omar.

"I don't cry anymore. I mean, not at all, for years. Not when Jules died. Not when—" She shook her head. "Never. Never, in years and years. But in the last few days, since you arrived—"

She did not finish. Apparently she could not.

"Why?" Omar asked.

She looked at him, directly, and her face was tense and full of emotion. "I don't know," she said. She smiled a little. "I don't even know what it is. Fear, perhaps. Or sorrow. I don't know if it's you. Or if it is you, why."

"I'm sorry," he said. "I'm sorry if I've upset you. Perhaps I shouldn't have come here. I just seem to have upset everyone. I was just thinking, this morning, that I shouldn't have come."

"No," she said. "Don't you see? It's if you hadn't come—"

They were sitting side by side, on the ground, rather close to each other. Perhaps they were touching. They felt as if they were touching. They were touching. Arden's hand was on Omar's cheek, and then—it was like falling in a dream: inexorable and terrifying but simultaneously euphoric—they were leaning their faces toward each other, closing their eyes, and kissing.

And then they sat there, struck, wondering, silent. Omar's hand was on Arden's leg. And then after a moment, they turned again toward each other, and kissed again.

Then Arden stood up. She brushed herself off, although she was not dirty. She could not look at him. They had kissed, but they could not acknowledge it. "Let me show you the gondola," she said. She nodded toward the boathouse.

Omar stood up and followed her around back, where she stood unlocking the padlocked door. She pushed it open and motioned for him to enter. He walked past her and into the boathouse. She stood standing, just outside the door, in the daylight.

It was dark and cool in the boathouse and it smelled of silt and rot. The few windows were grimed over. Omar turned back toward the door. "Aren't you coming in?" he called.

"No," Arden said. She looked pale, or perhaps it was just the brightness of the sun on her, the difference in light.

Omar understood that she did not wish to see the gondola, and suddenly he was scared to see it himself. As if seeing it would change something, or alter him.

"I don't like it in there," Arden said. "It gives me the creeps. But go, look. I'll be out here." She disappeared from the doorway.

Omar turned around. There was a canoe and a rowboat sitting on the wooden floor, and past them, overturned on risers, the gondola. It was smaller than he had thought it would be. He walked around the other boats and touched its hull, whose color he could not discern in the gloom. He squatted and tried to look up into it. It was too dark to see anything, but he could smell the moldering leather and velvet. And suddenly he felt foolish—or not foolish, he felt wrong, like he was committing a sin. He felt that his desire to see the gondola was inappropriate, almost prurient. He felt ashamed of himself.

And it made him sad, there was something very sad about the fact of it there, overturned, locked up in darkness beside the absent lagoon.

It took him a moment to adjust to the light outside. He did not see Arden anywhere. For a moment he thought she had left him there. He looked all around, and finally saw her standing behind him, back in the shade of the trees. She walked down the slope and passed him without speaking. She went and locked the door of the boathouse, and picked up her bag, which she had left on the ground. Then she walked past him again, down toward the edge of what had been the lake. She stood there, in the hot, bright expanse, waiting for him to join her.

When they emerged out of the woods into the little orchard they found Pete on a ladder, trying to shroud a tree in netting to save the fruit from the birds.

"Hello," he called to them.

They had not talked all the way down, so Pete's interruption was welcome. They went and stood beneath the tree he was netting. "Do you need help?" Omar asked.

"Yes, thanks," said Pete. "It might be easier with two."

"I'll leave you, then," said Arden. She walked back toward the house.

Pete climbed down the ladder. "Where have you been?" he asked Omar.

"We went up to see the gondola," said Omar.

"Did you like it?" asked Pete.

It seemed an odd question: it was not something you liked or disliked. "I am glad to have seen it," said Omar.

"Come," said Pete. "I will show you the hive."

It stood in the long grass at the edge of the field of fruit trees. It was made of wood and looked like a dresser. Slender vertical drawers could be pulled from it. Pete pulled out one containing a honeycomb thronged with swarming bees. The bees crawled onto his hand, covered it, like a buzzing glove. He held it out toward Omar but Omar shrieked and shrank back. Pete laughed. He waved his hand in the air as if he were making slow figures with a torch. The bees drowsily flew from it. He replaced the drawer in the hive, and stood beside Omar. They watched the bees turn about in the air and return to the hive, flying in through the bottom.

Pete reached up and pulled a peach off a tree and handed it to Omar.

"Thank you," said Omar.

Pete selected one for himself. They were small peaches, bursting ripe, with very thin, pale blushing skins. The flesh was pale, too, and tasted a bit like banana. Perhaps they were something other than peaches. Pete ate his in a few big lunging bites, holding it out in front of him so the juice would drip on the ground. He sucked the flesh from the stone and then threw it toward the woods. He lay down in the long grass on the sun-dappled ground beneath the trees and put his arms behind his head. His T-shirt rode up and exposed a stripe of skin around his middle. He tugged the shirt back toward his pants, but it ascended as soon as he returned his arms behind his head. He closed his eyes. Apparently he meant to nap.

Omar finished his peach and tossed the pit into the tall grass. He wasn't sure what he was meant to do. Stay, or leave Pete. But it was nice to just stand there. In the quiet he could hear the hive humming. He had to urinate. He walked off a ways and peed into the long grass.

He walked back and sat near Pete. After a moment Pete opened his eyes and sat forward. He looked toward the hive, around which a few bees were still hovering. "How old are you?" asked Pete.

"I'm twenty-eight," said Omar.

"So am I," said Pete. "We are like brothers."

It occurred to Omar that brothers would not likely be the same age, but he said nothing.

Pete stood up. So did Omar. "Let me get another ladder," he said. "I'll be right back."

Omar sat down. He watched Pete walk back toward the garden. He was alone. He could hear the hive humming, it was a low, gentle rumble. He could almost feel it. I have kissed Arden, he thought. He lay back in the grass. He heard Pete return with the ladder. When he sat up Pete had leaned both ladders into a tree, one on either side.

"It will be easier if we are both up in the tree," he said. He began to climb one of the ladders. Omar got up and walked over to the tree. It was the one Pete had taken the fruit from. The tree was full of fruit. Some of it was rotten. Omar climbed the ladder, which wobbled beneath his jouncing weight. The limbs of the tree were not strong but they were supple. He could not see Pete through the dense foliage. The buzzing was coming from the tree, too: it was full of bees.

"I will throw the net over the top," said Pete. "Try to catch it and pull it down, okay?"

"Yes," said Omar. He could hear Pete struggling with the net. And then a whoosh as the net landed on the tree.

"Do you see it?" Pete called.

"No," said Omar.

"Shit," said Pete. "Let me try again."

Omar waited and heard Pete throw the net again. This time part of it hung down, not far from him.

"Do you see it?" asked Pete.

"Yes," said Omar. "Let me grab it."

"Be careful," said Pete.

Omar reached out for the net. He felt a burn on his hand, as if he had reached into a flame. And then he was falling.

PART TWO

That golden evening I really wanted to go no farther;
more than anything else I wanted to stay awhile . . .
                              —Elizabeth Bishop, *Santarém*

CHAPTER THIRTEEN

He understood that he was in a hospital and that something was very wrong with him. He could not move; it hurt, even, to think. And he would struggle out of the arms of sleep only to fall almost immediately back into them, but they did not hold him well, they kept dropping him, he would fall through sleep into something deeper and darker, and then he swiftly rose up once again to consciousness and opened his eyes. A woman stood and looked down at him. She was speaking but he was underwater and could not hear her.

He realized they had taken him out of his body and put him in something else. He told her this. He asked her for his body back.

The next time he woke there was a doctor leaning closely over him, as if they might kiss. Can you feel this? the doctor asked, tenderly touching his cheek. If you can feel this, blink your eyes.

He blinked.

The doctor took his hand away. Can you feel this? he asked again. If you can feel this, blink.

He tried to explain how they had taken his body away but the doctor would not listen. He only repeated himself: Can you feel this? If you can feel this, blink.

Dr. Peni entered his office and sat down behind his desk. The woman sat across from him as women do in these situations, her face blank with tension, waiting. For a second he enjoyed her beautiful fervency and his power over her. He touched two fingers to his desk, tapped them lightly. "Well," he said, "as you know, he has regained consciousness. That is a very good thing."

"Yes," said Arden.

"We remain concerned by his fever. And there is, I am afraid to say, a certain amount of paralysis."

"Paralysis?"

"Yes. You see, the poison affects the central nervous system, shuts it down. That is why it is so important to introduce the serum immediately. Because of the delay in this case, there is a certain extent of paralysis. If you are keeping bees, you should really have some serum available."

"Is it—will it be permanent?" she asked.

"It is impossible to know at this point. The body can respond quite miraculously. Or sometimes, not at all. He is young and in good health. I am inclined to be optimistic, but without further tests it is impossible to know the extent of the damage that was made to the nervous system."

"Have you talked to his father? I understand he is a doctor."

"Yes, he called here this morning. A most unpleasant man."

"But you got the information you needed?"

"Yes," said Dr. Peni. "The young man—may I ask: is he related to you?"

"No," said Arden. "He was a guest, visiting us. A friend."

"I see," said Dr. Peni. "A special friend, I would imagine."

Arden looked puzzled. "I'm not sure what you mean."

"I'm sorry," said Dr. Peni. "From your demeanor, I assumed he is a special friend of yours. Your concern seems deep. But perhaps I assume too much. I thought if he were a special friend, you might like to see him."

"Oh," said Arden. "May I?"

"Yes," said Dr. Peni. "He is conscious, but unresponsive. His brain—well, we know nothing yet. But it might be good if you see him. Good for him, I mean."

"Yes," said Arden. "I would like to see him."

"In that case, let me take you to see your friend."

He's got it all wrong, Arden thought, as she walked behind him down the hall. He thinks we are lovers, but perhaps it is good he thinks that—if he thinks Omar is loved, he will try harder to save him. For me, she thought. He will save him for me.

She cried out when they entered the room. It could not be—something awful had happened—he was bloated and had an old man's face, an ugly face—

"You know Señor Miquelrius?" asked Dr. Peni.

"Oh!" said Arden, realizing. "I thought—I thought that he was Omar."

Dr. Peni laughed. "No," he said. "Your friend is here." He indicated the screen around the other bed. "If you'll come this way, we'll let Señor Miquelrius enjoy his beauty sleep." He drew aside the screen so they might stand beside the bed. Omar did not look well, but he at least still looked like himself. His eyes were closed. Dr. Peni raised one of Omar's lids, and peered into the exposed eyeball. He let the lid close. "He is sleeping," he announced. He held his stethoscope to Omar's chest, and listened. "It sounds well, his heart," he said.

Arden looked down at Omar. It was as if it were the first time she had ever looked at him. She let her gaze fall on him.

"Perhaps you would like to touch him?" Dr. Peni wondered aloud.

"What?" Arden asked.

"If you would like to touch him, you may," said Dr. Peni. "Gently, of course." He indicated with a forefinger Omar's cheek. "Here, perhaps."

Arden reached down and laid the backs of her fingers against Omar's cheek. Omar responded to the contact by moving his head slightly on the pillow; a gentleness passed across his face. They both saw it. Dr. Peni smiled.

But when she returned to the clinic the next day, Omar was once again comatose. Dr. Peni was troubled by his loss of consciousness, but assured Arden that Omar's vital signs were all good. A loss of consciousness is sometimes in the body's best interest, he explained to her: it is how the body heals itself. It would be good, he thought, if Arden talked to him: the sound of speech was good stimulation for even a comatose brain. He led her to Omar's room, and left her there.

Señor Miquelrius had been sent home, and the white screen had been removed from around Omar's bed. Arden sat on a metal chair beside him. For a long while she merely watched him; his face was bloated a bit, as if he had been inflated, and there was an ugly crust around his eyelids. He breathed with effort. There was a washbasin in the corner of the room with cloths stacked upon it; Arden ran one beneath the tap, wrung it out, then gently touched it to Omar's face.

Talk, she thought, talk to him, but she could not speak. She sat there, for a very long time, thinking of what she should say, knowing it did not matter what she said. But it did matter. She felt it did matter. Even if she were only dropping rocks into a well, they would stay there, in his unconsciousness. It seemed dangerous, almost criminal. To speak to someone who could not resist. And then she thought her silence was perverse, ungenerous, cruel. Why could she not speak to him? If it could help him why could she not speak?

"I'm sorry," she said.

She sat there looking at him. She wondered if perhaps being near him was, in some way, as beneficial as speech. Who knew how the subconscious was affected? She reached out and touched his bare arm, which lay atop the blanket, but quickly withdrew her hand. I have no right to touch him, she thought. She stood up and tossed the moistened cloth into the basin. She left without saying goodbye to Dr. Peni.

Deirdre's phone number, which Arden had found listed in Omar's passport, was written on the little pad on the phone table in the front hall, and Arden dialed it immediately upon entering the house. She had spoken to Deirdre the night of the accident, told her what had happened: Omar had been stung by a bee and had an allergic reaction, fallen out of a tree and broken his right wrist, but that he would be fine.

The phone was answered by a machine that asked her to leave a message.

"This is Arden Langdon," she said. "I don't wish to alarm you, but I'm afraid Omar is once again in a coma. I suppose Dr. Peni is in touch with Omar's father, but I thought I should call you. I think you should come here. Please call me back as soon as you can."

She hung up the phone and stepped through the open French doors into the courtyard. There, she thought: That is the end. If his girlfriend comes, nothing can happen. He will not die and I will not fall in love with him.

The tablecloth was still on the table. It had only been three nights since they had drunk champagne. She gathered it into her arms. It was stained; it would need to be bleached.

CHAPTER FOURTEEN

Omar had had trouble getting to Ochos Rios because fundamentally he did not believe he could get there; Deirdre was not hobbled by doubt, and her intrepidness was coupled with a sense of emergency. She arrived there two days after receiving Arden's summons—there being Tranqueras, the nearest town. The closer to the destination, the more difficult the journey: there seemed to be no way to proceed beyond Tranqueras—or at least no commercially sanctioned way. In her haste to depart and therefore arrive, she had not adequately questioned nor listened to Arden's directions and had assumed that the house—Ochos Rios—was in the town, not ten miles distant.

She thought that perhaps she could call Arden and ask to be picked up in town, or given instructions for concluding her journey, but there seemed to be no public telephones available. Under other circumstances Tranqueras would have been a charming place to languish: there was a single street of shops, a parklike square in front of a church, a small market of flip-flops, batteries, and skinny, badly plucked chickens, and a café with a few tables set out directly upon the broad cobblestoned street. It was in front of this café that Deirdre alighted from the bus. She sat at one of the tables beneath an umbrella that advertised German beer. A young man, formally dressed, emerged from the café and approached her. Deirdre's Spanish was quite good: she had studied it in college and spent a semester in Seville. She ordered an *agua mineral,* after being told that the *bebida típica de la región* was Coca-Cola.

When the waiter returned with her water she asked him if he knew Ochos Rios; he did. Did he know how to get there?

It was a distance, he admitted, but there was always someone driving out in that direction, especially in the evening. She could not wait until then? Ah, yes: an emergency. Well, in that case—

Deirdre took the crammed school bus full of chattering girls out to Ochos Rios, and alighted from it, with Portia, at the bend in the road outside the gates.

"We have to walk from here," Portia explained.

"Is it far?" asked Deirdre.

Portia pointed up the drive and said, "It's about as far again as you can see."

"Oh," said Deirdre.

"Is that far?" Portia wondered.

"Yes," said Deirdre, "in my case it is."

"You can leave your suitcase here, if you want," said Portia. "And get it later with the wheelbarrow."

"I prefer to carry it," said Deirdre.

They began walking up the drive.

"Do you know how Omar is?" asked Deirdre.

"He was stung by a bee," said Portia. "And swelled up like a balloon. He couldn't breathe." She mimicked gasping. "He's at the hospital."

"I know," said Deirdre. "That is why I am here."

"Are you his mother?" asked Portia.

"No," said Deirdre. "I am his friend."

"His girlfriend?"

"Yes," said Deirdre. "Is he better, do you know?"

"I don't know," said Portia. "Where do you live?"

"In the United States," said Deirdre. "Do you know where that is?"

"Yes," said Portia. "My mother lived there, before she came here. And my grandmother lived there but she's dead."

Deirdre put down her suitcase. "Let's rest a minute," she suggested. She sat down on the case. "Have you seen Omar, since he was stung by the bee?" she asked.

"Yes," said Portia. "He was lying on the ground kicking his feet. His shoes came off. Then he fainted. Pete and my mother had to carry him to the car. They dropped him once. He's heavier than he looks, they said."

Deirdre stood up. "Let's go," she said. "Would you like to help me?" she asked Portia.

"Yes," said Portia.

"Then carry this," said Deirdre, handing over her backpack.

Portia left Deirdre in the front hall and went in search of her mother. She found her in the garden. "Hello," Arden called, as her daughter approached. "You're supposed to change out of your uniform before coming outside."

"Omar's girlfriend is here," said Portia. "She took the bus with me."

"What?" asked Arden.

"Omar's girlfriend came on the bus with me. She's in the house, waiting for you."

"On your school bus? Are you sure?" asked Arden. "I don't think she could have gotten here so soon."

"She says she's Omar's girlfriend. She's from the United States. She made me carry her backpack."

Deirdre waited until the child disappeared and then looked around her. The room in which she waited was large, with doors and windows on two sides. Its ceiling was three stories high. In the center of this room was a large wooden table, the apron of which was intricately carved and inlaid with mother of pearl. On this table was a large vase of rather dead flowers. The parquet floor was badly scuffed; many of the pieces had become dislodged or had disappeared. In one corner, beneath the curved staircase, was a little table with an antique rotary phone on it, and a pad of paper, on which was written Deirdre's number.

Deirdre was trying to open the French doors out into the courtyard when she heard someone close a door above her. She stepped back into the center of the room and saw a woman descending the stairs. For a moment she thought it was Anaïs Nin. And then she remembered that Anaïs Nin was dead and that she was in Uruguay and that her brain was muddled with travel and fatigue and worry. She felt for a second as if she might cry, but something about the woman's calm, silent gaze quieted her. The woman, who appeared to be between fifty and sixty, was quite beautiful. She had a serene face. Her hair was parted in the middle and loosely drawn back and knotted, so that it hung in two wings beside her face. She wore an indigo linen dress that had no waist and came to just below her knees. A necklace of amber and silver beads hung almost to her navel. The woman came down the stairs slowly, holding her spine straight, so that the heavy necklace barely moved, and she did not speak until she had gained solid ground.

"May I help you?" is what she said.

"Hello," said Deirdre.

The woman repeated her greeting. She smiled in a patient, unfriendly way.

"I'm Deirdre MacArthur. Are you Ms. Langdon?"

"No," said the woman. "I am Caroline Gund."

The wife, Deirdre thought.

"May I help you?" the woman said again.

"I'm a friend of Omar Razaghi's," said Deirdre. "I've come to see Omar."

"Oh, Omar," said the woman. "Omar is not here. He has had an accident."

"I know!" said Deirdre. "That is why I am here. Do you know how he is?"

"I am afraid I do not," said the woman. She touched the dusty surface of the large table with two fingers and then rubbed them together. There was something condemnatory about the gesture, as if Deirdre were responsible for dusting the furniture. "You have come from—where?"

"From the United States," said Deirdre. "Kansas."

"Ah, yes, Kansas. People from Kansas keep appearing here. Unexpectedly," she added.

"Miss Langdon knew I was coming," said Deirdre. "She asked me to come."

"Did she?"

"Yes," said Deirdre. "Do you really know nothing about Omar? Is he still in a coma?"

"I think he has regained consciousness. But Arden knows more. I have somewhat absented myself from the affair."

"Oh," said Deirdre.

"You have only just arrived?"

"Yes," said Deirdre. "I have only just arrived. I've been traveling for hours and hours and hours. Days."

"I would show you to your room, but I am not at all sure what room is yours. Arden is the innkeeper. But I could offer you a drink, of water or whatever else might please you."

"Thank you," said Deirdre.

"Water? Or something stronger? You look as if the latter might be—how should I say? Appreciated? Required?"

"Water would be fine," said Deirdre. "Perhaps something else later."

"Of course," said Caroline. "Excuse me." She opened the door beneath the stairs and disappeared down the dark hall toward the kitchen.

Deirdre sat on one of the benches beside the door. She saw the child and another woman crossing the courtyard. She stood up.

Arden opened the door and entered the hall. Portia dawdled by the fountain. "Hello," Arden said. "I'm sorry I wasn't here to greet you but I had no idea of when you might arrive. You've come sooner than I thought. I am Arden Langdon." She held out her hand, and then, seeing how dirty it was, withdrew it. She laughed. "I'm sorry. I've been in the garden, and—"

"Hello," said Deirdre. "Do you know how Omar is doing?"

"Yes, yes," said Arden. "He's doing better, I'm happy to tell you. He's regained consciousness; he's been conscious for twenty-four hours at least now. I haven't seen him today, but Dr. Peni—that's the doctor who's treating Omar—called at noon with quite a good report. I didn't go on the chance you'd arrive."

"When are visiting hours?" asked Deirdre. "When may I see him?"

"Oh, it's rather a relaxed establishment in that regard," said Arden. "There are no visiting hours. I think you could see him at anytime."

"Now?" asked Deirdre. "Could I see him now?"

The door beneath the stairs opened, revealing Caroline holding a glass of water.

"Oh, Caroline," said Arden. "Hello. Have you met Deirdre?"

"Yes," said Caroline. "This water is for her." She handed Deirdre the glass of water. "I'll leave you in Arden's hands now. She is, as I said, the innkeeper."

She slowly ascended the stairs.

"I could use some water too," said Arden, as she watched Deirdre gulp her own. "Let's sit in the kitchen for a moment. It's through here." She opened the door beneath the stairs and motioned down the hallway. Deirdre picked up her bag.

"Oh, why don't you leave that here?" asked Arden. "Unless you want it for something."

Deirdre lowered the bag and followed Arden down the dark hallway into the large, bright kitchen. Arden took a bottle of water out of the refrigerator and refilled Deirdre's glass and poured a second glass for herself. "Sit down," she said, nodding toward the table. "I'm just going to wash my hands."

Deirdre sat at the table. It had wooden legs and a stone top. A fresher-looking bouquet of flowers erupted from a glass jar at its center. Deirdre laid her hands flat against the tabletop.

Arden fondled her soapy hands beneath the rush of water from the tap and turned to look at Deirdre. "You got here so quickly. How was your journey? Portia told me you came on the school bus from town. How clever of you."

"The man at the café suggested it," said Deirdre. "He was very kind. And so are you, calling me, and letting me stay here. I appreciate it."

"Well, I wish it wasn't unpleasantness that brought you here," said Arden. She turned off the water and then dried her hands with a white towel. "Although I suppose nothing else would. But as you see, we've got plenty of room. Or will see, when I show you the house. I'm sorry I haven't made a bed for you but it won't take a minute."

"I can sleep in Omar's bed," said Deirdre. "I don't want to trouble you."

"It's no trouble," said Arden. She sat at the table, and drank her glass of water. It had never occurred to her that Deirdre might sleep in Omar's bed. No, she must have a bed of her own.

"Where is Omar?" Deirdre asked.

"Oh," said Arden. "The clinic is just outside Tacuarembó. It's about a thirty-minute drive from here. Why don't we—well, perhaps you'd like to freshen up? And we'll go."

"I hate to be so dependent upon you," said Deirdre. "Is there a place in Tacuarembó where I can stay?"

"Oh, please," said Arden. "You mustn't feel that way. You must stay here. It's really no problem. As you'll see, there's very little for you to interrupt. There's a bathroom upstairs you can use. And we'll put your bags in a room. Have you really only brought the bag in the hall?"

"Yes," said Deirdre.

"You travel light," said Arden.

"I didn't really pack," said Deirdre. "I was in such a rush—"

"Well, if there's anything you need, you must tell me. I think my clothes would fit you. Come, I'll show you the bath."

In the car they were silent for a long time, Arden driving, Deirdre sitting beside her, looking out the window. They passed no buildings or houses or people or other cars.

"How did it happen?" asked Deirdre.

Arden glanced at her. "What?" she asked.

"How did Omar come to be stung?" she asked.

"Pete and Omar were netting a tree in the orchard. Omar was very kind to help. He was up on a ladder, and apparently he was stung. We have a hive, we keep bees," said Arden. "Pete and I. Pete is Jules Gund's brother's companion. I don't really know what happened. I was in the house. We had gone for a— But poor Omar was stung, and— Did you know he was allergic to bee stings?"

"No," said Deirdre. And then she said it again, "No."

"I think it was immediate, his reaction. Pete came running in; he couldn't move Omar by himself. At first we didn't know he had

175

been stung. We thought he had just fallen from the tree. They realized that at the clinic, so he didn't get the serum as soon as he should have— But you see it's a distance to Tacuarembó, and then they had to summon the doctor when we arrived, and it all took time. It was awful. But you mustn't worry. He's going to be fine, Dr. Peni assures me." She looked over at Deirdre, who was clutching the little strap that hung from the car's ceiling. "There's something I should perhaps tell you," said Arden.

Deirdre looked over at her. Arden was looking straight out at the road, intently serious but her preoccupation was artificial, Deirdre could tell. "What?" Deirdre asked.

"It's about Dr. Peni," said Arden. "It's really silly, but you should know, I think. He's taken very good care of Omar. Extraordinary care."

"I'm happy about that," said Deirdre.

"Yes," said Arden.

"What is it?" asked Deirdre.

"Dr. Peni thinks Omar is my—well, I suppose he assumes he is my lover. I never told him that, he just misinterpreted my concern, and I didn't correct him."

"Why not?" asked Deirdre.

"I felt it was in Omar's best interest," said Arden. "Dr. Peni is a bit of a romantic, a chauvinist really, and well, he is like men here. He likes to see the world in a certain way. He saw Omar and me in a certain way that appealed to him, I think, and I sensed it would help Omar, so I didn't correct him. Of course, now that you're here, we shall, but I wanted to explain."

"No," said Deirdre. "Whatever works best for Omar. I don't care what the doctor thinks."

"But he'll wonder who you are, coming from the United States, appearing like this."

"I could be his sister," said Deirdre, "or a friend. It doesn't really matter. Must you explain it? Let him think whatever. If he assumed something about you, he will assume something about me, won't he?"

"I suppose he will," said Arden.

"Let's leave it alone, then," said Deirdre. "At least for now. At least until we're sure Omar is out of danger. I will be his sister. Or I suppose I can't be his sister, as I look nothing like him. Who can I be?"

"A friend," said Arden.

"All right," said Deirdre. "I will be a friend." She looked at Arden. "A close friend," she added.

Arden led Deirdre down the hall; the door to Omar's room was open. Omar was asleep. The bed Señor Miquelrius had abandoned had been assumed by a young man—a teenager, in fact—who sat up in bed, eating his dinner from a tray. He looked over at the two women standing in the doorway.

"Good evening," said Arden, in Spanish. "We're here to see Omar."

The boy had nothing to say about this. He returned his attention to his meal.

"Go and sit with him," said Arden. "I don't think you should wake him, but sit. You can maneuver that screen if you want some privacy." She pointed to the screen of white cloth panels that now leaned against the wall.

"Thank you," Deirdre said.

"I'll be in the waiting area," said Arden. She turned and walked down the hallway.

Earlier, from her tower, Caroline had watched them drive away. She sat looking out the window for a long while after the car had disappeared and the dust in the drive had settled.

Then she got up and walked down the stairs and across the courtyard. Deirdre's bag remained in the hall. She went out the front doors and walked down the drive.

She walked to the millhouse. She knocked, but opened the door before her knock was acknowledged. She stood inside the door; the living room was empty. She looked up. "Hello," she called.

After a moment Adam appeared on the uppermost landing. "Caroline," he said, "hello."

"Hello," she said again, rather stupidly, as if they could spend the rest of their lives greeting each other.

"I suppose decorum necessitates my descending."

"I could come up," said Caroline.

"Didn't the ancient Colette receive guests in her bedroom? I am not so decrepit. Yet. And besides, all the liquor is at ground level. I will descend." He began to do that. Caroline went into the living room and sat on the couch.

"Where's Pete?" she asked, when Adam finally entered the room.

"Pete has taken his truck and is scavenging," said Adam. "I hope that since I have exerted myself by coming downstairs you will mix the drinks."

"Mix them?" asked Caroline. "Meaning you want a cocktail?"

"A cocktail! What a lovely word. If only we could have a cocktail, a proper cocktail, properly, sitting on barstools somewhere. But liquor is liquor wherever you go in the world. It is one of the great comforts. Perhaps it is the great comfort. Why don't you go in the kitchen and mix us cocktails."

"What do you have? What do you want?"

"Nothing. It would take an alchemist, alas. There is a bottle of vodka. And some wine."

"Which do you want?"

"Oh, the vodka, I think, if you can find ice. If you can't find ice, the wine."

Caroline disappeared into the kitchen. Pete's absence was illustrated by the mess. Fortunately the bottle of vodka had risen above the mess and there was ice, though rather furred, in the freezer.

She returned with two glasses of vodka rocks, and handed one to Adam.

"I say 'to what do I owe this pleasure,' because really, you know, it is a pleasure." He raised his glass. "To the pleasure of you," he said.

"How sweet you are," said Caroline.

"Do you know," said Adam, "often I think, often I say to myself: You must radically change your life. Now, before it is too late. Now, now, now. Extraordinary things often happen in the last few chapters, don't they? Do you ever think of your life as a novel? I do. It was something that started with me quite early. I thought—I suppose it was when I left here, for the first time—I thought: You must live your life as if you are the hero of a novel. You must always do something interesting, always earn your space on the page. It is very hard to live one's life like that. Novels are so deceitful in that way: they leave so much out. The years of tedium, of happiness perhaps, but tedious happiness. Or tedious unhappiness."

"Actually," said Caroline, "I want to talk to you about something in particular."

"Shut up, in other words," said Adam.

"Yes," said Caroline.

"I desist," said Adam.

It was silent then, just the two of them regarding the transparency of their drinks.

And then Adam said, "About what, in particular, did you wish to talk?"

"I'm not sure," said Caroline. "About allegiances, perhaps."

"Allegiances?" asked Adam.

"Yes," said Caroline. "I think that's the word. I've just been thinking. Today, and perhaps for longer than today. Longer than today, in fact, I'm sure. Since this business of authorization and the biography, I suppose."

"Allegiances?" Adam said.

Caroline said nothing. They had a strange way of talking to each other, although perhaps it was not so strange, perhaps people who have lived almost exclusively together, and shared certain experiences, perhaps people like that all talk in this eliding way, like stones skipping over the flat surface of water. After a moment spent sipping her vodka, she said, "Perhaps it isn't allegiances I mean. I don't know what I mean."

"You usually do," said Adam.

"I know," said Caroline. "It's all this business with the biography. I don't mind that you've agreed to it—really, I don't—but I'm bothered by how things stand."

"How do you mean?" asked Adam.

"I mean I don't like feeling opposed to you, or Arden. You, especially. In some way I am forever opposed to Arden. But not you. Never you. That is what I meant about allegiances. I have always felt you were my ally, Adam, always. And if I thought you were not—"

"But of course I am. Caroline, really. This biography is nothing. It is nonsense. It is a divertissement."

"I don't see it like that. I know you do, and perhaps you are right, but I don't. I can't."

"And I respect how you feel. So does Arden. I daresay even the boy himself respects how you feel. There is no problem, my dear. Don't worry."

"I can't help it. You see, something has shifted. I don't know what, or where. I don't know if it's inside me, or outside. But I feel—I no longer feel comfortable. Right."

"Whatever do you mean?"

"Do you think I am a fool?"

"I think we are all fools."

"Adam! No. Please, don't be like that. Please. Help me. I am trying to—I need to speak seriously. For once."

"You are not a fool, Caroline. You are a wise and gracious woman."

"Do you think—honestly, tell me honestly, please—do you think I should have stayed here?"

"What do you mean?

"You know what I mean. I mean after Jules came back, with Arden. Do you think I was right to stay?"

Adam shrugged. "I did not judge you. It was your affair, yours and Jules's."

"But I want to know. Judge me now."

"I don't think you can look back like that. It's futile."

"I disagree. How do we know—how do we know anything about ourselves, if we do not look back?"

"I think why we want to know anything about ourselves is a better question. I prefer to know as little as I can about myself."

"Adam!"

"I'm sorry. No, I don't think you were wrong to stay. I did not think so then and I do not think so now. This was your home and Jules was your husband and you had every right to stay."

"Was, was . . ." said Caroline.

"Yes," said Adam, "was."

"What about is?"

"Oh, is. The less attention paid to is, the better."

"I haven't been paying very much attention to it. It is what we do here, isn't it?—go on and on, and let life happen elsewhere, to others."

"They are welcome to it."

"Don't you like life, Adam?"

"Yes, I like life. I would not want to live forever, but for a little while, life is fine."

"And are you happy living here? Or do you wish things had gone differently? Do you wish you had stayed in Stuttgart?"

"At my age I do not seek or expect happiness."

"Forget happiness, then. Do you wish you were in Stuttgart? In Europe?"

"No," said Adam.

"Why not?"

"You have to care—or pretend to care—about everything: politics, fashion, culture. It is exhausting. Why? Are you thinking of moving back to Europe?"

"No," said Caroline. "Not really. I am thinking—wondering— why I am here. What keeps me here. If this is where I belong."

"What scary things to wonder. I'd stop it at once, if I were you. And I'm not being glib. I am speaking seriously."

"I'd like to stop it. I'd like to be like you."

"You are here because this is where your life has brought you. You don't belong here. Nothing keeps you here. No one belongs anywhere, least of all here."

Caroline stood up and looked at the window, at the rocky stream that ran behind the millhouse. After a moment she said, "It's not the letter."

"What?" asked Adam. "What letter?"

"Jules's letter about not wanting a biography. That's not what's making me resist this."

"Is there really a letter?"

She turned away from the window and looked at him. She shook her head. "No," she said.

"It did sound a poor excuse to me," Adam said.

Caroline said nothing.

After a moment, Adam said, "Then what is it?"

"I think it is guilt. Or shame, perhaps."

"About what?"

Caroline straightened a quilt that was folded over the back of a couch. "About so many things," she said. "About everything."

"Well, that narrows it down."

Caroline did not smile. She laid her hands on the smoothed quilt.

"I don't understand," said Adam.

"I know you don't," said Caroline.

"It is Jules's guilt, Jules's shame—"

"No," said Caroline. "Not entirely."

"Well," said Adam. "Of course. We are all guilty. You do not get to be our age without amassing a burden of guilt. But I do not think a biography written by Mr. Razaghi will delve too deeply into the moral caverns of our lives, or expose us in any way we would rather it did not. That is the beauty of the authorized biography. You have nothing to be scared about, my dear."

"I'm not scared!" said Caroline, somewhat fiercely. "Of course I am not scared. You don't understand. Even if the book tells nothing, I don't want it, because I will know it tells nothing."

"I don't think I follow you," said Adam.

Caroline returned to her chair. She picked up her glass and shook it, looking for any vodka that might remain. Then she put it back down on the low table between them. "Do you know how I met Jules?" she asked Adam.

"You met him on the boat, didn't you? Coming back from France?"

"No," said Caroline.

"Then how did you meet him?"

"I never took the boat. I flew home. I flew back to New York but Margot wouldn't. We had almost crashed going over, and she hated planes. She took the boat, and met Jules." She paused. "When I went to meet her at the dock they were together and I could tell she had fallen in love. They were so beautiful together. Margot was very beautiful, she was the beautiful sister, and he was—he was very beautiful too. You know what he was like then. He stayed in New York that summer. Of course I fell in love with him, and he knew it, we all knew it, I suppose, but it was clear that he was Margot's and I was just adoring him. It was understood. And then something happened, something shifted between us. It didn't feel safe anymore, what I felt, or what I felt he felt." She stopped.

"And that is your great, awful secret: that you stole your sister's boyfriend?"

"I know it sounds inconsequential, but it was not. It was an awful thing to do. It was a crime, a sin."

"Falling in love with someone is not an awful thing," said Adam. "There is no morality about it. As they say: all is fair in love and war. The world would be a very boring place were it not. I think you are being a little absurd, Caroline."

Caroline shook her head. "I have never talked to Margot since then," she said. "And my mother never forgave me, either. My sister and my mother, both. And then all I had was Jules and here, and then I stopped loving Jules, because how could I love Jules? But I was too proud, too ashamed to let him go. It is what killed him, I think."

"Jules killed himself," said Adam.

"Yes," said Caroline, "that is what we all let ourselves think, of course. But it is not the truth."

"And you are afraid that if this biography is written—what? You will be exposed? We will be exposed? I think you overestimate the powers of Mr. Razaghi."

"It has nothing to do with Mr. Razaghi's abilities."

"Then I don't follow you."

"Adam, do you think it's odd that we've never talked about Jules's death? Or perhaps you and Arden have. Have you?"

"No," said Adam.

"And you don't think that's odd? My husband, your brother, the father of her child—and we don't talk about it?"

"No, I don't think it is odd. What is there to say?"

"I don't know. We must find what there is to say by saying it. But talking to Mr. Razaghi, selling him a life that was not Jules's, which is what you will do, both you and Arden, I know it, I can hear it all already, the fake version we all have, that ceases to seem fake because we have embraced it for so long—that is not what should happen now. That is not what should ever happen. I will not allow it." She stood up.

"I don't know what you're talking about. Really, I don't. What fake version? I have never lied about Jules. I am not implicated in his death. And I resent your implying otherwise. Jules was always melancholy. Always, he was born with it. He tried to kill himself once when he was seventeen, did you know that?"

"No," said Caroline.

"He did. In the garage with the automobile. And don't forget my mother was mad. Of course, her life didn't help much, but she was a bit mad to start, and Jules got some of that. And he wrote a book that was acclaimed and then spent twenty miserable years trying to do it again, and failing over and over again. It is no wonder to me that he destroyed the manuscript and walked out into the woods. I don't think there is any great mystery about his death. No: I don't think there is so very much to talk about."

"Well, what about that—what you just said: that he tried to kill himself earlier? Why did you never tell me that?"

Adam thought for a moment. "I don't know," he said. "I suppose I assumed it was private, it was his, to tell you or not. And in a way you are right: we did not talk about it. It was a bad thing that had happened and we did not talk about bad things. It was how my parents dealt with their past."

"By not talking about it?"

"Yes," said Adam. "And I am their child. And it is a little late in the game for me to start talking."

Caroline laughed.

"Why are you laughing?" asked Adam.

"It just sounds odd, what you said, because you talk all the time."

"You know what I mean," said Adam.

"Yes," said Caroline, "and it is a little sad."

"Well, a lot of things are a little sad," said Adam.

Caroline remained standing. After a moment she said, "I don't want this book to be written because it won't be an honest book. It will not tell the truth. Perhaps no biography does. I doubt it. But I do not want a false book about Jules. A pretend book."

"It need not be so complicated. Again, I think you misunderstand the kind of book Razaghi will write. He is a hack. He is concerned with dates and places. None of this concerns him, Caroline."

"Yes," said Caroline, "I know. Exactly. None of it concerns him: you express it so well. Better than I. It will be a hollow book. It will be all that is left of Jules and it will be hollow, false." She stood there for a moment, but Adam said nothing. He did not know what to say.

"I'm sorry," he said, after a moment. "I don't know what to say."

Caroline shrugged. She turned and walked out of the room. Adam heard the front door open and close. He sat there for a long time. Then he heard Pete's truck pull up. Good, he thought: Pete is home. He tried to stand up but he felt very tired, and a bit dizzy. How much vodka had he drunk? He leaned back into the cushions, closed his eyes.

Deirdre entered the room. An aluminum chair stood at the foot of each bed; Deirdre pulled the one at Omar's bed around to the far side and sat facing the door. The boy in the other bed studiously ate his meal. He looked very healthy, princely: he was wearing maroon silk pajamas with an indecipherable monogram on the jacket pocket.

Omar lay in the bed, his head off the pillow and oddly askew, as if he had been thrashing about in his sleep; his body was twisted beneath the thin white blanket, but he slept peacefully. Both of his hands were wrapped in mittens of gauze. He was wearing green nylon pajamas patterned with a hideous purple paisley. For a long while Deirdre just sat there, neither talking to nor touching Omar. A nurse came into the room and took the tray from the boy in the other bed. She looked at Deirdre and nodded, but said nothing. When she had left the room, the boy in the other bed took a book off his bedstand and turned on the lamp over his bed, and then lay down on his side facing away from Deirdre, giving her privacy.

She reached out and touched Omar's arm but he did not stir. She leaned closer and whispered his name into his ear, then studied his face, which remained stilled, passive. She grasped his hand. She felt two things, strongly, simultaneously: she felt a deep, almost debilitating affection for him, the sweetness of him, the goodness of him, the loveliness of him; and she felt also the foreignness of him, his strangeness, his otherness, all the uncharted regions of him she did not know. After a while he withdrew his hand from hers but did not awaken.

She sat there, feeling very tired herself. The boy in the next bed reached up and turned out his lamp, put his book back on the table, and assumed a position that suggested he would soon be asleep. Deirdre stood. She replaced the chair at the foot of Omar's bed. From there she regarded Omar. She wished he would wake up so she would be certain he was not still comatose. Of course, they would not lie to her about that.

After a moment she left the room and walked down the hallway. When she came to the end, she realized she had been walking in the wrong direction. She turned around. She passed the room. Of course he was still lying there, as she had left him. She had irrationally thought her absence might awaken him.

Arden Langdon was sitting by herself in the waiting area, just sitting, not reading a book or a magazine. Deirdre saw her from down the hall. There was something odd about the absolute still-ness, the infinite patience, with which she sat.

On the way home, they said nothing. In the lobby, Arden had asked Deirdre if Omar was awake, and Deirdre had said no, he was not. We can come back tomorrow morning, Arden had said. He will be awake then.

Deirdre fell asleep in the car, her head leaning against the door. Arden thought the cessation of motion might arouse her, but it did not, so she was compelled to reach over and touch Deirdre's shoulder, softly shake it.

"Deirdre," she whispered, "we're home. Well, I'm home. You're here."

Deirdre opened her eyes. They were parked at the top of the drive, on a grassy verge beside the house. There was a little light left in the sky, soft, late-evening light, and it poured itself across the miles onto the baked yellow wall of the house. For some reason that seemed absolutely correct and necessary, Arden kept her hand, for a moment, on Deirdre's shoulder. Arden knew, instinctually, how and when to touch people. It was a gift, a talent she had.

"Come in," Arden said. "And we'll make a bed, and you can sleep."

CHAPTER FIFTEEN

Deirdre awoke the next morning in a strange bed in a strange room. It was very quiet. For a moment she thought she was in some sort of sanatorium—the linoleum floor and white metal bed frame seemed quaintly therapeutic; I have TB, she thought, and have been sent to a sanatorium.

Then she saw her suitcase opened on the floor and remembered that she was at Ochos Rios, in Uruguay, and that it was Omar who was incapacitated. She looked at her watch, which was, besides a ceramic lamp and a glass of water, the only thing on the bedside table. There was something oddly lovely about the glass of water: the tumbler itself was delicately etched with a garland of braided flowers, and the water was curiously bright and clear. Schools of tiny bubbles clung to the sheer inside wall. It was 10:40. She had slept for hours and hours. She got out of bed and stood in the center of the room, looking around. There were three doors, one per wall, and on the fourth wall was a window with a rather ugly and ancient venetian blind drawn, and drapes made from heavy brocaded fabric that did not at all suit the utilitarian, therapeutic mood of the room. They looked like drapes that had been cut down, made over, from other more majestic drapes. They were not drawn. Light leaked prismatically through chinks in the lowered blinds, forcing itself, as if by desire, into the room. It must be very bright outside, Deirdre thought. She parted two lengths of dusty blind and peered out: an unkempt lawn sloped sharply down toward a piney forest. A dog was sitting on the lawn, carefully eating a very large bone. She tapped softly on the glass but the dog did not respond, and she had the odd feeling he was in another world, that it was all other worlds, through the window and behind each of the three doors.

Deirdre hoped that one of the doors might reveal a bathroom. Alas, none did: one opened into a large closet empty save for a pomandered, wizened, unidentifiable fruit that hung on a satin ribbon from the long rod. There was something totemic and disquieting about it hanging there, all by itself, in the dark closet. Another door opened into an identically sized room where in place of a bed there was a long worktable piled high with bolts of fabric and an ancient sewing machine. The third door opened out onto a long corridor, with perhaps a dozen closed doors set along its length. Many chairs of different breeds were set along either side of the hall, between the doors, and it was clear that they served no purpose, that no one sat on them waiting, but they themselves were waiting.

Deirdre now vaguely remembered visiting a bathroom along this hall the night before. How tired and exhausted she had been! She hoped she had behaved all right. She set out in search of the bathroom. She knocked on the door across the hall and when no one answered she opened it. This room, which seemed to be roughly the same size and shape as her bedroom, was empty except for a large wooden table set before the window; on the table was a small, velvet-curtained proscenium stage of the kind used for puppet shows. Marionettes hung, like torture victims, along the walls. There was something creepy about this room—something creepy, at least, to Deirdre—and she quickly closed the door. Even as a child—especially as a child—she had always hated the dumb, staring faces of dolls. She could never pretend that they were alive, and had disdained girls who did.

The room beside the sewing room was another bedroom, similar to hers. She recognized Omar's suitcase closed, but not latched, upon a chair. The bed was neatly made. She stepped inside and closed the door. She looked into the suitcase. On top of the clothes were a few books: Hermione Lee's biography of Virginia Woolf (which Deirdre had given him, along with a watch, for Christmas), and Spanish and English editions of *The Gondola*. There was also a small, cheap notebook with a pen jammed into its spiral. Deirdre opened this notebook and recognized Omar's careful, somewhat old-world writing. Apparently it was a journal. She looked around the room, and convinced she was alone, began reading:

Well, I got here. Here being Montevideo, which I suppose is really neither here nor there, but I'm still amazed I got this far. Although I think the trip here was the easy part. I feel a little scared and lost. But excited too. Montevideo is half-great and half-ruined, like most places in the world. I've just been walking around. I'm staying in a pretty terrible hotel but it's cheap. My room has no window. It feels very safe, like a cocoon, but it's a little scary. Like you could disappear in it. Like in addition to the window the door could be subtracted and you would be stuck inside. It's a very basic room: floor, walls, ceiling, bed, wardrobe, chair. A lightbulb on a chain hangs from the ceiling. I'm sitting up in bed now, writing this. I could be anywhere in the world. The sheets are stiff and scratchy but clean. They smell of bleach. The bed creaks when I move.

Now that I'm here (although it's only Montevideo) and nothing has really been accomplished yet or changed, but now that I'm here, this far, I feel like things will be okay. I mean whatever happens. I thought about writing them from here, saying I was coming. Send a telegram or some-

thing like that. But I think it would be better if I just show up. I'm sure
that there is some way I can present this so that they will be willing to
give me authorization. Unless they're totally insane and irrational.

On the plane they gave us all free champagne. Little miniature bot-
tles. The woman next to me didn't want hers so I got two. I'm keeping
the extra one to drink with Deirdre when I get back, when all this has
been straightened out, when I've got authorization, and everything is
okay again. And we can celebrate. It's only a little bottle but we can
drink it together.

I'm tired and it's hard to write sitting up in this bed. Needless to say
there is no desk.

That is all there was written in the book.

"There you are," said Arden, when Deirdre entered the kitchen. "I
was just thinking about waking you, but felt odd doing so. Did you
sleep well?"

"Yes, thank you," said Deirdre.

"You were exhausted," said Arden. "I mean really exhausted.
Physically exhausted. Emotionally, too, no doubt."

Although Deirdre knew that exhaustion was a neutral state, she
felt in Arden's pronouncement a judgment, as if some weakness on
her part had allowed, even fostered, the exhaustion.

"I'm feeling much better now," she said.

"And did you find the bathroom? I hope there was enough hot
water for you to shower properly."

The shower had been tepid, slurring toward cool as it evolved,
but it had nevertheless been much enjoyed by Deirdre, as showers
after extended periods of travel inevitably are. "It was fine," she
said. "I'm in love with your house. All the old fixtures, and furniture—"

"Their charm wears thin after a while," said Arden. "I loved it
all when I first came too." She said this in a way that made it clear

that she still loved it all, but had the time-deeded prerogative to make complaints. "What would you like for breakfast? Everyone eats such different breakfasts, but we have most anything you'd like."

"Coffee would be wonderful," said Deirdre.

"Yes, of course," said Arden. "But what else? You must be starving. You ate nothing last night."

Deirdre realized she was famished. "I suppose I am a bit hungry," she allowed.

"Of course you are," said Arden. "How do you like your eggs?"

"Scrambled," Deirdre said, "but let me do it. Really, let me. Just show me—"

"Nonsense," said Arden. "Unless you don't trust me. But eggs I can manage." She laughed. She poured coffee from a percolator into a mug and set it before Deirdre, and nodded at the milk and sugar waiting on the table. Then she busied herself with the making of the eggs.

The coffee was very good: dark and fragrant and intensely flavorful.

Arden returned to the table with a plate of eggs and bread and fried potatoes. She set the plate down in front of Deirdre, then filled a mug with coffee for herself, and sat at the far end of the table.

"Thank you," said Deirdre. "It looks delicious."

Arden sipped her coffee with a vague smile on her face.

"How long have you lived here?" asked Deirdre.

"About ten years," said Arden. "Eleven, now, I suppose."

"And are you from Uruguay? Were you born here?"

"No," laughed Arden. "I was born in England. My father was British, and my mother was American. She was an actress."

"So you grew up in England?"

"Yes, except for a bit in Los Angeles and Wisconsin. Mostly in boarding schools. My parents were both rather self-preoccupied. They divorced soon after I was born."

"Does your mother still act?" asked Deirdre.

193

"I think not," said Arden. "She's dead."

"Oh, I'm sorry," said Deirdre.

"It happened quite a long time ago," said Arden.

"I wanted to be an actor," said Deirdre, "but I could never relax on stage. I always looked tense, they said."

"I see," said Arden.

"Do you mind me asking you questions?" asked Deirdre.

"No," said Arden, "of course I don't."

"It's just that it seems so interesting to me—your being here. How did you get to Uruguay?"

"God brought me," said Arden.

"Oh," said Deirdre.

Arden laughed. "I joined one of those awful Christian missionary groups when I was in college. I was a bit of a mess. I think I mostly did it to hurt my father, who was passionately irreligious. The group I joined was called Joyful Noise. We traveled around the world giving concerts and smiling brightly and converting heathens. I shook the tambourine."

"And you came to Uruguay?"

"Yes," said Arden. "We were touring South America by bus. My God. Can you imagine? I made it as far as Montevideo, where I came to my senses. I've always loved Montevideo for that reason. I couldn't go home, so I arranged to go to the university and that's where I met Jules. He was teaching there. And then I came here."

"You've had an interesting life," said Deirdre.

"Well, it's quieted down. It took me a while to find my home. I had never had a home before I came here. Neither of my parents had time for homes."

"And it's just you, and Portia, and Caroline living here?"

"Yes. An odd home, I know. Adam and Pete live just down the road. Adam was Jules's brother. Pete's his companion. It was Pete who was with Omar when he had his accident. He feels very bad about all of this, of course. He feels responsible."

"Do the bees sting often?"

"I suppose," said Arden. "I'm often stung." She looked down at her hands and bare forearms, as if for evidence. "No one has ever responded to a sting like Omar. I've never seen anything like it. I really thought he was going to die."

"Did Omar get a chance to speak with you?" Deirdre asked.

"What do you mean?" asked Arden.

"I mean, about the book. The biography. And authorization." She heard the curtness in her voice. "I just wondered," she amended.

"Yes, he did," said Arden. "And he changed our minds. Well, he changed my mind, and Adam's. Well, Adam was already in favor of it. He changed my mind. Caroline's mind is not changed. She still refuses to grant authorization."

"How did he change your mind?" Deirdre asked.

"I don't really know if he did," said Arden. "I mean, my mind has changed, and I suppose it is because of him, but I'm not sure. You see, Caroline claims Jules wrote her—soon after *The Gondola* was published—that he never wanted to have a biography of himself written. I think he was reading a biography at the time—I don't know whose—and was disturbed by it. Biographies can be disturbing. Well, when Omar's letter first arrived, I was persuaded to withhold authorization on the basis of that, but now . . ." She picked up Deirdre's cleaned plate and carried it to the sink. She rinsed it under the tap and then turned and faced Deirdre, who remained sitting at the table. "Now that seems like a less compelling reason. It was such a long time ago he wrote that letter. Jules is dead. This biography can't hurt him. And Omar is alive, and the biography can help him. It seemed rather simple to me."

"So it's to help Omar that you changed your mind?" asked Deirdre.

Arden looked over at Deirdre, and smiled. "Yes," she said. "I suppose that is why. I'm sure you're anxious to see him again.

Should we go? I don't mean to rush you, but I'd like to get back here before Portia returns from school."

"I feel so terrible you have to drive me there," said Deirdre. "I wish I could drive myself."

"Everyone wants to be so self-sufficient these days," said Arden. "It's a bit sad."

"It's just that I hate imposing—"

"But it isn't an imposition," said Arden.

Deirdre thought she was in the wrong room, but the number on the door confirmed she was not. This time the screen was set around the boy's bed and voices murmured from within the cocoon. She walked around the shrouded bed and saw Omar lying awake. "Deirdre!" he said.

She sat on the bed and kissed him. "Hello," he said.

"My God. Why are you here?"

"Arden called me. You were in a coma. And you were paralyzed. Can you move everything?"

"Yes," said Omar. "I think so."

"Have you walked?"

"No," said Omar.

"How do you feel?"

"A bit odd. Groggy. I think it's the medication."

"What about your poor hand? Does it hurt?"

Omar looked down at his gauze mitt. "No," he said. "It just itches. I can't believe you've come. There's really no reason. And my God—how much did it cost?"

"Don't worry about that," said Deirdre. "What's important is that I'm here, and that you're okay."

"The nurse told me someone had visited me last night. I couldn't imagine who it was. I mean other than Arden. Why didn't you wake me?"

"They told me not to. Has Arden been visiting you?"

"Yes," he said. "Have you met her?"

"Of course," said Deirdre. "I'm staying there."

"Isn't it amazing? I mean the house and everything."

"I think it's spooky," said Deirdre.

"Have you met Caroline?"

"Yes. Briefly."

"And Adam?"

"No," said Deirdre. "I just got here last night."

"I don't know why Arden called you. I'm really fine."

"I don't think you were, though. She was very worried. Do you remember what happened?"

"No," said Omar. "I don't remember anything from that day clearly. I was a bit sick, hungover, I remember that. We had gone out to dinner the night before."

"Do you remember that?"

"Yes," said Omar. "We went to this restaurant. An Italian restaurant. Adam, Arden, and me. Caroline wouldn't come. She's been difficult."

"Yes, I've heard," said Deirdre. "But I hear Arden has changed her mind. And the brother too. Congratulations!"

"Yes," said Omar. "Although the brother—Adam—was for it from the beginning, I think. But Arden has changed her mind. But I don't think Caroline will. Although Adam says . . ."

"He says what?"

"He says—he told me he could change her mind for me. That he would change her mind for me. If I . . ."

"What?"

"Nothing," said Omar. "I don't really remember."

"What?" said Deirdre. "Omar, I've come all this way. What's going on? I can't help you unless I know what's going on."

"Nothing's going on," said Omar. "There's another book, though."

197

"What do you mean?"

"Jules wrote another book."

"Was it published?"

"No."

"Have you read it?"

"No. But supposedly it's based on their ménage."

"That's great. If you hurry, you can have the biography published simultaneously. That would be fantastic."

"They don't want to publish the book."

"Why not?"

"I'm not sure. It's supposed to be a secret, I think. Adam blurted it out and then Arden told me to forget about it. So don't mention it."

"Okay," said Deirdre, "but that's very exciting news."

"I know," said Omar.

They heard the screen around the other bed being moved and were silent. A doctor and nurse emerged from behind it. The nurse left but the doctor washed his hands in a basin in the corner of the room and then came and stood beside Omar's bed.

"I am Dr. Peni," he proclaimed, extending his hand. "And you are a friend of our poor stung Omar?"

"Yes," said Deirdre. She shook his hand, which was still damp.

"You are from the United States?"

"Yes," said Deirdre.

"You are a good friend, to come so far."

"I'm very concerned about Omar."

"Of course you are. We are all concerned. But I think all the news is good news. He has been conscious for two days. I think for good now. You won't be leaving us again, will you, Omar?"

Omar said he would not.

"You see," he said, turning to Deirdre. "You must not be worried. You are too beautiful to worry. All the women who visit Omar are beautiful. No wonder he makes such a recovery. I can claim no credit: it is the beauty of women that has healed him."

Deirdre did not approve of the direction the doctor was taking. "Is his paralysis all gone?" she asked.

"Yes, Omar's sensation has returned, to every part of his body. He will soon be fit as a fiddler. And ready to fiddle again. You must not worry about Omar," he said. "I will reassure you."

"I don't want you to reassure me," said Deirdre. "I want you to tell me the truth."

"Oh, but the truth is reassuring. The truth is always reassuring," he said.

Although Deirdre did not agree with this statement, she knew that it would be pointless to refute it. "How is his health?" she asked. "He seems to have some memory loss."

"His health, under the circumstances, is fine. All his organs are functioning normally. His loss of memory is a temporary and normal result of brain trauma. It will all fall back into place, rather quickly, I imagine. But we must all be patient. Omar is fortunate to be so loved and befriended. It plays a great part in his recovery, I assure you. I play my part, which is, of course, instrumental, but we cannot underestimate the human part. Are you a religious person, Miss—"

"MacArthur," said Deirdre. "Deirdre MacArthur. No, I am not."

"If you were, I would urge you to pray for your friend. You do your work and I do mine. But in this case we shall leave the prayers to others." He patted Omar's head, shook Deirdre's hand again, and then left the room.

Driving back in the car, Deirdre said to Arden: "Does Mr. Gund live near you?"

"Do you mean Adam?" asked Arden.

"Yes," said Deirdre. "I suppose. Jules Gund's brother. The other executor."

"Yes, he does," said Arden. "Not far at all."

"Do you think I could see him?" asked Deirdre.

"Of course," said Arden. She glanced over at Deirdre. "About what?"

"Oh," said Deirdre. "I would just like to meet him. And there is something—something private—I would like to discuss with him."

"Of course," said Arden. "I can drop you there on our way back."

"I hate to cause trouble for you," said Deirdre.

"You aren't," said Arden. "It's on the way."

Arden parked in front of the millhouse. "Perhaps I should come in with you, just to make sure he is here," she said. "And introduce you."

"Thank you," said Deirdre.

The two women got out of the car and approached the house. Arden knocked on the wooden door. After a moment she opened it and called Adam's name.

He was coming down the stairs. "Come in, come in," he said. "Who's this?" he asked, upon seeing Deirdre through the open door.

"This is Deirdre MacArthur," said Arden, "Omar's friend from Kansas. We've just been to see Omar. And Deirdre wanted to have a word with you."

"Did she?" said Adam.

"Yes," said Deirdre, "although I could come back at a more convenient time if you would like."

"No, I am hopelessly free for the rest of my life," said Adam. "Now is fine. In fact, I was going to walk up to the big house this afternoon for a chat with you."

"Then I'll leave you," said Arden. "Do you mind walking back to the house, Deirdre? It isn't very far."

"Of course not," said Deirdre. "Thank you."

Arden went out and closed the door.

"Come sit down," said Adam. "It is so merry having all these guests. First Omar and now you. We are unused to so much company."

Deirdre followed him into the living room. "Would you like something to drink? Something cold? Something hot? Something tepid?"

"Something cold would be nice," said Deirdre. "Just some mineral water, if you have it."

"Yes, yes," said Adam. "Sit down." He indicated the sofa and disappeared into the kitchen, returning a moment later with two glasses of water. He handed one glass to Deirdre, who had not sat down. "So you are Omar's paramour?" he asked. "It is almost palindromic: Omar's paramour. Or is it merely anagrammatic?"

"I think it is neither," said Deirdre. "Nor is it the word I would use to describe our relationship."

"I think words are very bad at describing relationships," said Adam. "At least my relationships. They are all too complicated for mere words."

Deirdre said nothing.

"Please, sit down, my dear," said Adam. "You look as if you might bolt. It is upsetting me."

Deirdre sat, but rigidly, as if in compromise. Adam sat opposite her. "I did not mean to offend you. I can see you are offended. I suppose you are Omar's partner or significant other or something *moderne* like that. But it sounds very dreary to me! How much nicer to be a paramour. You should consider it."

"I will," said Deirdre.

"Perhaps you are not the paramour type," said Adam.

"Are you?" asked Deirdre.

"Yes, I was: in my youth. And I was a youth for a very long time. Perhaps it was the effect of being a paramour. It retards the aging process, but it does not, alas, stop it: I woke up one morning and I was an old man. You are aging more gradually, which is, I think, a blessing: there is nothing worse than waking up one morning and discovering that you are decrepit."

"It is better to become decrepit gradually?"

"Yes," said Adam. "You don't notice, then. Unless you are foolish enough to look at an old photograph. For this reason I have destroyed all old photographs of myself."

"I should think some people would want to be reminded of their beauty," said Deirdre.

"It is better to remember it in one's mind's eye," said Adam. "Beauty remembered is more potent than beauty recorded."

"Have you really burned all your old photos?" asked Deirdre.

"No," said Adam, "but I will do so as soon as you leave. I shall build a fire—a pyre—in the yard and immolate my past. I think people should leave the world very cleanly, with nary a trace. It is rude to leave things behind—it is like littering, I think. I shall leave nothing behind."

"Did Jules Gund leave lots behind?"

"Don't tell me you're writing a biography of Jules Gund too!"

"No," said Deirdre, "I just wondered. Are there lots of letters, and photos, and manuscripts, and stuff?"

"Perhaps you should write the biography. You show more interest than our poor Omar. How is he? Have you come from visiting him?"

"Yes," said Deirdre.

"And how is he?"

"He seems well, considering."

"Considering what?"

"Considering his accident," said Deirdre.

"Aren't we all."

"Aren't we all what?" asked Deirdre.

"Aren't we all well, considering our accidents," said Adam.

Deirdre did not reply.

"You seem to me to be a sensible woman," said Adam. "Do you consider yourself to be a sensible woman?"

"Yes," said Deirdre. "I suppose I do."

"It is a novel experience for me: talking to a sensible woman. I am so practiced in the art of dealing with hysterics."

"We don't much like that term," said Deirdre.

"Oh," said Adam. "Don't we? Who is we?"

"Women," said Deirdre. "It implicates our wombs. It is a term that reeks of male oppression."

"Wombs! I am surrounded by women who are preoccupied with wombs."

"I was merely speaking of the Latin roots of the word," said Deirdre. "I am not preoccupied with my womb. Or the wombs of others."

"And I am so glad to hear it. I meant to say that I am unpracticed in the art of speaking directly, as everything we say to one another here at Ochos Rios is convoluted at best. And I want to speak to you plainly, and directly."

"Please do," said Deirdre.

"I will try. The day before poor Omar encountered his poisonous bee, I had a talk with him. Actually, several talks, but it is one of our conversations that concerns me."

"About the biography?" asked Deirdre.

"Yes," said Adam. "among other things. In fact, we made a little bargain. And I am worried that in his present infirm state he may forget his obligation."

"It is about that little bargain that I have come to see you," said Deirdre.

"Ah! So he has not forgotten. He has told you about it?"

"Yes," said Deirdre. "He mentioned it."

"Good. Then he has not forgotten."

"I think perhaps he has. I mean, he remembers you made a bargain, but he doesn't remember the details."

"It is really quite simple: My mother brought paintings with her when she came here—fled here—from Germany. I would like to sell these paintings now. Omar agreed to take them to New York City for me, to a dealer who would arrange their sale."

"Do you mean smuggle them?"

"No."

"And Omar agreed to do this?"

"Yes, he did."

"You said it was a bargain. What was your part?"

"I guaranteed him authorization. I convinced Arden to change her mind."

"In other words, you blackmailed him."

"Smuggle . . . blackmail. You have a romantic imagination. No doubt you read too many nineteenth-century novels."

"No: I am a modernist. And Arden told me she changed her own mind."

"Of course Arden thinks she changed her own mind. That is the only way to change someone's mind—to allow them to think they have changed it themselves. Caroline will think the same."

"Perhaps you should forget this bargain, which seems both coercive and ridiculous to me. Perhaps you might concern yourself instead with Omar's recovery."

"Of course that concerns me! I am not heartless. But by all accounts he is out of danger and progressing splendidly. I am sure he will be gathering honey in no time."

Deirdre stood up. "I am glad to hear that," she said. "If you'll excuse me, I think I will return to Ochos Rios. I am feeling tired."

"Wait," said Adam. "Please."

Deirdre had headed toward the door, but she turned around. "What?" she asked. "You know, I think it was really wrong of you, manipulating Omar like that! I'm sure what you've asked him to do is illegal. I will not allow him to do it. And besides, he is the wrong person to do something like that. It would be better if you found someone else."

"I agree with you," said Adam.

"Oh," said Deirdre.

"It is precisely about that that I wish to talk to you."

"About what?"

"About Omar being all wrong for the job. About finding someone else."

Deirdre said "Oh" again, and loitered near the door.

"Will you come sit down? For just a moment. You don't look tired at all."

"I am tired," said Deirdre, somewhat petulantly. But she sat back down.

"I asked Omar to transport the paintings to New York for sale—which is, I assure you, my moral right to do—because he was the only person available to transport them to New York. But I agree with you, he is hardly the ideal man for the job."

"What do you mean: moral right? Is it legal or not?"

"You are obsessed with semantics. It is the curse of the academic mind. Try for a moment to rise above it."

"Yes, tell that to the border guards! Tell them to rise above it!"

"Calm down. May we forget, for a moment, the legality of the issue? Or can your mind see no other perspective?"

"I don't know why you're telling me all this. If you think Omar is going to transport the paintings, you're mistaken. And neither am I. So it is pointless to talk about this any further."

"You seem so sure of yourself. You will not even listen to me? What better thing have you to do?"

"I'm tired," said Deirdre. "And I'm worried about Omar. You've no idea how worried I am. He is not well. I cannot concern myself with smuggling paintings at a time like this."

"I have never understood that expression: a time like this. Surely you mean at this time, not a different time similar to this time?"

"Now who is obsessed with semantics?" Deirdre stood up.

"You are a less interesting person than I thought you were," said

Adam. "Although I like you. You are invigorating. It is a shame you have no sense of adventure. You submerge your life: you read too many books—or perhaps you don't even read books anymore. You probably just read criticism of books: you live vicariously. You come all the way to Uruguay, but do not concern yourself with what you encounter here. You will regret it all your life. Or no: it will take you a while to regret it—one day, when you are old and decrepit like me, you will think, Why did I not smuggle those paintings?"

"So it is smuggling. I was right."

"I prefer to think of it as private relocation."

"Why must it be done privately?"

"In order to maintain provenance, the paintings must seem to have remained in Germany. The man in New York has someone who will take them there—smuggle them, as you are so fond of saying—and then they will be sold there. The jewelry is another matter. That can easily be sold in New York."

Deirdre stood up. "Well, I'm sorry," she said, "but neither Omar nor I will be able to help you with these transactions. You must consider your little bargain with Omar dissolved. I am sure we can get Caroline to agree to authorization without your help."

"Are you sure?"

"Well," said Deirdre. "We can only try. Honestly try, without resorting to bargains and blackmail and manipulations."

"You shall take the high road, so to speak," said Adam. "Yet it seems odd to me—odd and a bit stupid even, if I may be so blunt—that you would alienate me in this way. After all, what is stopping me from changing my mind?"

"Oh," said Deirdre. "I understood that you wanted the biography. I did not think your support was variable or to be bought. I did not think there was any issue there."

"There are issues everywhere, my dear." Adam stood up. "While I admire your gumption, I think it would be best if this situation is resolved between Omar and me. The agreement was made with Omar; it is up to him to dissolve it. Well. I have so enjoyed our chat, but I usually take a siesta about this time. Will you excuse me?" He left the room, and Deirdre heard him climbing the stairs.

She waited a moment, but it was quiet. She went out into the hall, but he had disappeared. She felt foolish standing there, so she went out the front door. She was not sure how to walk back to Ochos Rios. She supposed she should walk up the lane to the road and then head in either direction. One of them was bound to be right.

CHAPTER SIXTEEN

How tiresome these people were, Deirdre thought as she walked toward Ochos Rios. Poor Omar, having to deal with them. It was really a good thing she had arrived, and could straighten things out. Perhaps his accident had been a blessing in disguise.

The school bus was letting Portia off at the gate as she approached. Portia waited for her, clutching her satchel.

"Hello," called Deirdre.

"Hello," said Portia. "Where have you been?"

"I was visiting your uncle," said Deirdre. They began walking up the drive. She tried to think of something nice to say to Portia. She was about to say what a pretty dress she was wearing when she noticed Portia was wearing a uniform. She could think of nothing else, so she said, "How was school today?"

"Good," said Portia.

"Omar and I are both teachers," said Deirdre.

"Are you nuns?" asked Portia.

"No," said Deirdre. "We don't teach at a Catholic school. We teach at a university. A public university."

"Oh," Portia said. Apparently she was not interested in the subject.

"What do you want to be, when you grow up?" Deirdre asked her.

"I want to be a nurse," said Portia.

"Why not a doctor?"

"I would rather be a nurse."

"Why?"

"Because then if the people die it's not your fault. If you're a doctor it is. But if they do get better the nurse helps them."

"Oh," said Deirdre. Then she said. "I saw a nurse today. In the clinic where Omar is."

Portia looked at her. "Of course," she said. "That's where nurses work."

"Yes," said Deirdre. They did not speak the rest of the way; the nice thing about children was that you could ignore them if you wanted: they didn't take it personally.

Arden was waiting in the front hall. She hugged Portia and said to Deirdre: "Dr. Peni called. He said he might release Omar tomorrow. If he has a quiet night."

"Oh, good," said Deirdre.

"But he said he couldn't travel for at least a week. That he'd have to spend most of his time in bed, resting."

"I suppose I should stay here, then, and go back with him. Is that all right?"

"Of course," said Arden. "How was your talk with Adam?"

"It was fine," said Deirdre.

"I don't suppose he offered you lunch. You must be hungry."

"Can I have my snack?" asked Portia.

"Yes," said Arden. "Can I get you something?" she asked Deirdre.

"No, thank you," said Deirdre. "I'm tired. I think I will take a nap now."

"Of course," said Arden. "We'll eat around seven. Do you eat meat?"

Deirdre said she did, and asked if Caroline would be present at dinner. Arden said she was not sure.

Caroline did not join them for dinner. "I would like to talk to her," said Deirdre, as the meal concluded. "Do you think I might?"

Arden paused. She knew that Caroline considered social interaction she had not herself initiated an intrusion, but she saw no reason to protect Deirdre from Caroline. She was trying very hard to like Deirdre, as she thought not liking Deirdre would be petty and mean-spirited, but she was finding it difficult to like Deirdre. She was perfectly nice, considerate, polite, appreciative, even helpful— she helped with dinner and offered to help with the cleaning up— but there was something just a bit unperceptively aggressive about Deirdre that put her off. Like this asking to see Caroline. And asking to see Adam. She was, after all, the guest here, and it seemed odd to Arden that she was initiating all the meetings. She had been very unforthcoming about her meeting with Adam: Arden had asked her about it again at dinner and her reply had been equally terse and vague. Arden supposed that meant it had gone badly, as so many meetings with Adam were apt to go, and she felt that Deirdre would not fare much better—or worse, perhaps—with Caroline. In a way, she did want to protect Deirdre by dissuading her from accosting Caroline (for that is how it would seem to Caroline), but then she thought: Is it Deirdre I want to protect or Omar? And she thought: This is absurd, I should just stay out of it all.

She told Deirdre that she would probably find Caroline in her studio in the tower at the top of the stairs.

Something about climbing up to the tower intimidated even Deirdre. She paused outside the closed door and tried to listen, to intuit if Caroline was in fact there. But before she could discern any sound the door opened.

"Hello," said Caroline. "I thought I heard someone coming up the stairs." She was wearing a man's white dress shirt, untucked, over a pair of beige slacks. She had her hair pulled back and twisted and stuck up with a paintbrush.

"Yes," said Deirdre. "I hope I'm not disturbing you."

Caroline corroborated this supposition by not refuting it. She just stood there, holding the door open, smiling a bit oddly at Deirdre.

"I wanted to talk to you," Deirdre continued. "But I can come back, or meet you elsewhere later . . ."

"No, no," said Caroline brightly, having seen the effectiveness of her pause. "Come in. Now is fine. Come in and sit down."

Deirdre entered the studio. She looked around for a painting to compliment, but all the canvases were turned toward the wall. There was only one painting visible, resting on an easel, a rather insipid-looking still life, one of those paintings Deirdre hated, in which a bunch of hard-to-paint things that didn't belong together (in this case grapes and dead rabbits and a crystal decanter filled with wine) were thrown together on a table so the artist could show off. "It's very nice," said Deirdre, nodding at the painting.

"It's a Meléndez," said Caroline.

Deirdre was not sure if this referred to an artist or a technique—she had mostly snoozed through Art History—so she said nothing.

"Sit," said Caroline, as if Deirdre were a dog.

There was a low, modern—well, fifties—couch mostly covered with art books, and an easy chair facing it. Deirdre shifted a pile of books and sat on the couch. Caroline sat opposite her.

"It's lovely," Deirdre concluded. "Those grapes look delicious!" She realized this sounded absurd, but Caroline's wary, silent regard of her was unnerving. "Do you only paint still lifes?" she asked.

"No," said Caroline, without amplification.

Deirdre looked around for another painting to comment on, but her initial impression was accurate: all the other canvases were turned against the wall. It seemed to Deirdre that although Caroline sat facing her, smiling faintly, she, too, was also, somehow, turned against the wall: there was something absent, almost hostile, about her presence. "What a lovely room," said Deirdre. "It must be wonderful to paint up here."

Caroline acknowledged this remark by slightly amplifying her tight-lipped smile. Then, after a moment, she said, "Would you like a drink? I have some scotch."

"Please, yes," said Deirdre.

Caroline got up and went over to a table, where she poured some scotch, neat, into two glasses. "Water?" she asked. "I'm afraid I haven't got any ice or soda."

"A little water, please," said Deirdre. She watched Caroline pour water from a plastic bottle into one of the glasses, and return with the drinks. She handed one to Deirdre and sat back down.

"How is Omar? I assume you've seen him."

"Yes," said Deirdre. "He's doing well, considering. I believe he will come home tomorrow—well, come here, I mean."

"Ah, good," said Caroline. "And then you will leave?"

"Not for a week," said Deirdre. "The doctor says he can't travel for at least a week."

Caroline said "Ah" again.

Deirdre sipped her drink. "Mmmmm," she said. "Thank you. It's lovely." Then she remembered she had said the painting and the room were lovely. Lovely, lovely, she thought: everything can't be lovely or she'll think I'm simple. She sipped again. "Smoky," she said. "Is it single malt?"

"Yes," said Caroline. "Laphroaig."

Deirdre could feel the warmth of the scotch spreading in her. Her father had called alcohol "Dutch courage." Take courage, she thought: be brave. She took another sip and then said, "You must wonder why I want to speak with you."

"In fact, I don't," said Caroline, pleasantly.

"Oh," said Deirdre. This was a rather dampening response. But, courage. "Well," she said, "may I tell you?"

"Of course you may." Caroline laughed.

She's really horrible, thought Deirdre, she's enjoying this. These people are awful. They're all thwarted and poisonous. They need lots of therapy.

"Well," she said, "I'm aware that you are the only executor who is withholding authorization. I don't know what Omar has told you, but I'd like to assure you that he intends to work very closely with you all on the biography, and respect your wishes. You have nothing to fear."

"I do not withhold authorization out of fear," said Caroline.

"Of course," said Deirdre. "I didn't mean fear, per se."

"What did you mean?" asked Caroline.

"I meant—I meant . . . well, why are you withholding authorization? Perhaps if you told me, I could address your concerns."

"I have already discussed this with Omar. Several times. Forgive me if I do not see the need to discuss it with you."

"I'm sorry," said Deirdre. "I don't mean to be rude. Really, I don't. It's just that if you knew what this meant to Omar, how very much is dependent upon his getting authorization and writing this book, I think . . ."

"You think what?"

"I think you might reconsider. At least, I hope you would consider reconsidering."

"But my decision has nothing to do with Omar. I don't doubt for a moment what this means to him. After all, his coming here—well, what better illustration is there of his need? But I am not concerned with his need. I have other—different allegiances in this matter."

"To Jules Gund, you mean?"

"I don't think it is really any of your business, what I mean. But, yes—to Jules Gund. And to myself, for that matter."

Deirdre thought for a moment. It was all going wrong. These people were impossible. She had wanted to fix it all for Omar. It was a gift she wanted to give him, the authorization. She had pictured herself handing him the form, complete with its triumvirate of signatures, when he returned from the hospital. Perhaps they would have a little celebration, to welcome him home and toast the biography. And he would be so pleased and grateful. If only these people listened to reason!

She looked over at Caroline and said, "I'm sorry. I think I'm wasting your time."

"Time is not such a precious commodity here," said Caroline.

"Yes," said Deirdre. "But nevertheless. I feel you've made up your mind. There's really no point in me, or Omar, talking to you."

"We made up our mind months ago. Before Omar came here. We made up our minds then."

"But Arden changed her mind," said Deirdre.

"Yes," said Caroline, "she did. But I will not change mine."

"Then I am wasting your time," said Deirdre.

"If that is the only reason you are talking to me then yes, I suppose you are," said Caroline. She seemed a little hurt.

Deirdre stood up. "I'll leave you, then. I'm sorry to have bothered you."

"You have not bothered me," said Caroline.

I wish I had, thought Deirdre: I wish I could. "Thank you for the scotch," she said.

"You're welcome," said Caroline. She stood up and opened the door. "Good night," she said.

Instead of going back into the house Deirdre crossed the courtyard and walked out through the arch in the back wall. She didn't really want to deal with anyone at the moment, not even Arden. There was something a little weird about Arden, too: something she couldn't put her finger on. She seemed to think too much about everything she said and did, so it all came out perfect.

The sun had not yet set but the tall, dark pines planted all around the house created an early dusk. If I lived here the first thing I'd do is cut down some of these trees, Deirdre thought. She walked out the gravel path and through the arch in the hedge. She paused at the garden fence. A sprinkler set up on a sort of platform in the middle of the garden cast long, shaking spurts of water. The plants were all dripping in the fading light. The air smelled of herbs. Some large black birds—crows perhaps—were pecking at the moist earth.

She stood there until it was dark, or almost dark. The sprinkler went off by itself. It must be on a timer, she thought. It was very quiet then. She had not realized what a racket it had made. She looked up at stars that were just beginning to appear, pricking themselves into the sky. She shivered, although it was not cold: just a little cool, a breeze. If Omar does not get authorization, what will happen? she wondered. What will happen to him? To me? To us?

She closed her eyes. The scent of herbs again, and pine, and wet earth. She felt like she wanted to pray but it went no further than that. But for Deirdre that was quite far.

CHAPTER SEVENTEEN

Omar was delivered to them the next morning in a station wagon masquerading as an ambulance. He had been heavily if not excessively drugged for his journey and arrived in a stupor from which he did not recover until early evening. Deirdre made him some soup—well, she reheated soup that Arden had made—and brought it up to him.

He was lying in bed, a bit glassy-eyed, but alert. His gauze mitt had been removed, revealing an elastic brace that covered his right wrist and palm but left his fingers and thumb free.

"Oh, it's you," he said.

She was irked by this response—who else would it be?—but tried to remain bright and cheerful. "Yes," she said. "I've brought you some soup. Are you hungry?"

"Yes," he said, "a bit. What kind of soup is it?"

"Avocado and cress," said Deirdre. "I think it's supposed to be cold but I heated it up. I thought something hot would taste good to you." She put the tray with the bowl of soup and bread and glass of water down on the little table beside his bed. "Why don't you sit up?" she asked. "Wait, I'll get another pillow from my room. I'll be right back."

When she returned with the pillow Omar was sitting up, eating the soup. "It's very good," he said.

"Good," said Deirdre. She sat beside the bed and watched him eat. He appeared to be very hungry, although his braced hand prevented him from eating neatly or expeditiously.

"Do you want me to help you?" she asked. "Perhaps I should feed you? You're making a mess."

"No," he said, "I'm fine."

She took the napkin off the tray and tucked it into his collar, spread it over his front. He was wearing the purple paisley pajamas again. "Where did you get these pajamas?" she asked.

"I don't know," he said. "They just appeared at the hospital."

"Perhaps they're Jules Gund's," said Deirdre. "Arden might have brought them. Perhaps you're wearing Jules Gund's pajamas."

"I think they're just hospital surplus," said Omar. "Probably some dead guy's."

"I should have brought some pajamas from home for you," she said. "And a bathrobe. I wasn't thinking."

"I don't have any pajamas," said Omar.

"I know," said Deirdre. "I meant, I should have bought some, and brought them with me."

"These are fine," said Omar. "I like these."

"Omar, they're hideous."

He looked down at them. "No," he said. "I like them. I want to take them home with me."

She decided not to argue with Omar about the hideous pajamas. "Well," she said. "How do you feel? You were terribly drugged. I don't know what they gave you. I think that doctor is a bit of a quack. As soon as we get home, you must see a doctor and have a thorough physical exam."

"I'm fine," said Omar. "Is there any more soup?"

"No," said Deirdre. "Eat the bread. Listen, Omar. We need to talk. Are you okay? Is your head clear and everything?"

"Of course," said Omar.

Deirdre moved her chair closer to the bed. "Well, we need to talk strategy. We need to strategize. I've been trying to push things along since I got here but it hasn't been easy. They're all a bit mad, I think. Adam and Caroline mostly, but Arden, too, although at least she's agreed. It's the other two we have to concentrate on."

"Adam's agreed too. He was for it from the beginning. And I told you, he said he would help with Caroline—"

"That's what we need to talk about. Omar! I talked to Adam yesterday. He told me about your bargain. I can't believe you would agree to that. You didn't, did you?"

Omar said nothing.

"You told him no, didn't you?"

Omar shook his head. "No. I told him I'd do it. The way he talked about it made it seem okay. And he said he would convince Caroline and Arden. I don't know. Maybe I was stupid. But it seemed like the only thing to do."

"Omar! You're crazy. It's smuggling. You'll go to jail. Remember *Midnight Express?*"

"He said it wasn't. I really don't think he'd ask me to do something that was dangerous, or illegal. I know that sounds naive, but I trust him."

"Well, I don't. And you're not smuggling things out of the country for him. I told him that. He got a bit testy and threatened to change his mind—"

"Deirdre! Adam can't change his mind. If he changes his mind, there's no way I'll get authorization."

"Don't worry. I think he was just being contrary. I don't think he likes women. Strong women. He's one of those homosexuals who find women intimidating, I think."

"Well, then you shouldn't talk to him. Everything was fine. He liked me."

"Of course he liked you. You're cute and you were going to smuggle for him. What's not to like? But that's not the way to get authorization, Omar."

"Well, what do you propose?"

"I don't know. That's why we have to talk. Caroline is even more difficult, because she's genuinely loony, I think. She can't be reasoned with. I tried."

"I wish you had just stayed out of it," said Omar. "I was doing fine. Everything was fine."

"Everything was not fine, Omar! You were in the hospital and on the way to jail. That is not fine!"

"Well, I was doing it. I was doing it my way. And it was working."

"But it wasn't working, Omar. If it was working I wouldn't be here."

"I didn't ask you to come here," said Omar.

"Oh," said Deirdre. "I'm sorry! I'm sorry I flew twelve thousand miles or whatever because I heard you were in a coma—a coma! I'm sorry I've hung out with a bunch of lunatics for three days trying to convince them to authorize a book you need to write. I'm sorry—"

"Stop," said Omar. "I'm sorry. I didn't mean it. I just meant I wish you wouldn't treat me like a baby."

"Then don't act like a baby! Don't agree to smuggle contraband! Don't fall out of a tree!"

"Falling out of the tree was an accident."

"You know what I think about accidents."

Omar attempted to throw the crust of bread he was eating across the room, but his injured wrist prevented it from traveling beyond the foot of the bed. "Yeah, and I'm fucking tired of you making me feel guilty! I'm not a moron. I'm not inept. Accidents happen to people, Deirdre. We're not all perfect like you."

Deirdre retrieved the bread. She put it on the tray, and wiped her hands. "I'm not perfect," she said. "I know I'm not perfect. I don't think I'm perfect. And I'm sorry if I've acted that way. I'm just trying to help you, Omar. Because I love you."

"I know," said Omar. "I'm sorry."

"Do you really wish I hadn't come?"

"No," said Omar.

"Because I can leave. I can leave whenever you want."

"No," said Omar. "I want for you to stay."

She took the empty bowl of soup from him and put it back on the tray. She took the napkin and began to wipe his face but he pushed her hand away.

"Omar!" she said. "You've broken your wrist. Please let me wipe the soup off your face."

"Okay," said Omar. He submitted to this indignity and then turned away from her.

"Why are you so angry? Are you sure you feel all right?"

Omar said nothing.

"Omar?"

He turned to look at her. "I'm sorry," he said.

"No," said Deirdre. "Don't be sorry. Just—" She reached down and touched his face. "Just rest," she said.

Arden and Pete were working in the garden. Pete was hoeing and Arden was weeding. It was amazing, how quickly the weeds grew, Arden thought. It seemed almost impossible. It was almost as if you could watch them.

Suddenly she was aware of being in shadow. She looked up to see that Pete was standing above her, hands resting on the hoe.

"What?" she asked.

"Will you miss them?" asked Pete. "When they are gone?"

"Who?" she said, although of course she knew who, but she did not want to speak to Pete about them, she did not want to speak to anyone about them, she just wanted them to go away.

"Omar," said Pete. "Omar and Deirdre."

Arden sat back on her haunches. For a moment she felt blinded, but then she realized Pete had shifted and the sun was shining full in her face. She closed her eyes. Pete shifted again and the shadow returned. She opened her eyes.

"No," she said. "Why would I miss them?"

"I think I will miss them," said Pete. "I mean Omar. I will miss Omar."

"It must be lonely for you here," said Arden. She pulled a weed from the ground and dropped it into the bucket. She crumbled a little clotted earth between her fingers.

"Do you love him?" asked Pete.

Arden looked up at him. "No," she said. She shook her head. "No," she said again. "I don't love Omar." She stood up. "I've got a headache," she said. "I think I'm going to lie down."

She took off her gloves and tossed them in the bucket, on top of the mound of weeds. She left the bucket there, in the middle of the row.

In the kitchen she saw the saucepan in the sink. This irritated her. Why had Deirdre heated the soup? It was supposed to be cold, it was best cold, the freshness of it, the flavors would all be compromised by heat—but you are being absurd, she thought: it doesn't matter at all. It doesn't matter.

She went upstairs and lay on her bed. It was awkward having Deirdre here. It was a strain for her. But it was good. If Deirdre were not here, she would have to be nursing Omar, and that would not be good. With Deirdre here she could avoid Omar. She would avoid him and then he would be gone, in less than a week, he would be gone. Perhaps he would not leave. Perhaps Caroline would change her mind, and he would stay to work on the book. Deirdre would leave, but he might stay. For quite a long time, perhaps, working on the book. But Caroline would not change her mind.

She was sure Omar did not remember their kiss; she almost did not remember it herself, so completely had the immediately ensuing emergency obliterated, superseded it. Yet she knew it had happened, they had kissed, sitting up there, outside the boathouse, in the hot sun. They had kissed. Perhaps he did remember. Or perhaps he would remember, and it would mean nothing to him. It is hard to know what a kiss means. She did not think Omar was in the habit of indiscriminately kissing women, but that did not mean that their kiss had meant anything in particular to him. Meant anything! How stupid she was. How pathetic. It was these years of living alone, living away from things, people, men. These years of not being kissed. She had had one affair since Jules's death. It was with the brother of the van Deleer sisters, friends of Caroline. He had come to visit them for a month; she had been invited to dinner, and somehow they had ended up in bed together. Although it had not seemed very curious at all at the time: from the moment she encountered him on the van Deleers' loggia, where they had drinks before the meal, she had known, and she had known that he had known, that they would sleep together. His name was Henrik. It had been very nice, but he had gone away, of course, at the end of the month. He had a wife in Cape Town, and a daughter, who was oddly enough named Portia. Of course she had fallen in love with him, it was impossible for her not to have under the circumstances, but it was a heady, superficial love that did not leave much of a stain. She had kissed him that first night, the first night she met him at the dinner party. She had got up to use the bathroom after dinner and he had followed her; as she emerged he was waiting in the shadows of the dark hall; he stood there waiting, watching her. To return to the party she had to walk past him. The hall was narrow. She thought for a moment he was waiting for the toilet but he was not, he was waiting for her. She thought: It is stupid to pretend I don't want this; I won't do that. I won't be like that. I want this. She walked toward him, in the dark narrow hall, and kissed him.

The sisters van Deleer found out, of course, and never much

liked her after that. Arden was sure they had probably told Caroline, but Caroline never mentioned it to her.

The attraction had been very clear—very apparent, overt—with Henrik, but with Omar it had not been clear. It was all murk, weird fumbling and murk, and then that one odd, sunstruck kiss. Perhaps, she thought, we do love each other in a way, for the kiss had been—what? Real? Yes, the kiss had been real, so perhaps we do love each other, but it is not a practical love. It was all right. The fact of it happening doesn't mean anything: it doesn't mean it's meant to be acknowledged, or fostered, or consummated. Consummated! She thought of what it would be like to make love with Omar. He was very beautiful. His skin, and hair and eyes . . . she was touching herself, gently, in the strange half-light of her bedroom. Why had Pete asked her if she loved Omar? What did Pete know? Had Omar spoken with Pete? While they were netting the trees? What had he said? Had he told Pete he loved her? That they had kissed? She got up off the bed. She went into the bathroom and washed her face with cold water. She looked at her face in the mirror. Sometimes she could look at herself and see that she was beautiful, but she was never sure. Something always looked wrong. It went back to when she had been in movies: it was awful, seeing her huge face on the screen. She had not been pretty then.

She went back out to the garden. Pete was still intent upon his hoeing. She stood outside the fence and called to him.

He turned around. "What?" he said.

She motioned him over. "Come here," she said.

He thrust the hoe upright into the earth and walked over to the fence. There was sweat on his face. He wiped it with his bare arm. He stood there, waiting for her to speak.

She looked away. She looked past the garden, at the orchard, at the netted trees. They looked ugly: the netting was plastic, orange, synthetic. It was a shame they had to be netted. Perhaps they could find some netting that was not an eyesore. That was invisible.

"What?" said Pete.

Still looking at the trees, Arden said, "Did Omar say anything to you, the other day, when you were netting the trees?

"What do you mean?" asked Pete.

She turned to him. "Why did you ask me that, before?"

"What?"

"Before," she said, "what you asked me about Omar?"

"I just wondered," said Pete.

"He didn't say anything to you? About me? The other day?"

"No," said Pete.

"Oh," she said. And after a silence: "I just wondered. It seemed odd, that you would ask me that."

"I'm sorry," said Pete. "I just thought, if I were you . . ."

"If you were me, what?"

"I might love him."

"Well, we hardly know him, do we, Pete? He's only been here a short time. He has a girlfriend. And he's leaving soon—"

"Yes," said Pete. "All of that is very true." He went back to his hoe. He pulled it from the soil and resumed his work. After a few moments he stopped and turned around. Arden was still standing by the fence. Pete smiled at her.

Caroline stood in the middle of the kitchen, gazing around her vacantly, as if she had never seen a kitchen before. "Oh, there you are," she said, when Arden came in from the garden. "I just wanted to let you know I am going away for a few days."

"Where?" asked Arden.

"To Gianfranco and Donatella's. I don't feel comfortable here, with all these invalids and hangers-on lurking about."

Gianfranco and Donatella Norelli were an Italian couple who owned a vineyard about a hour from them.

"Fine," said Arden. "When are you leaving?"

Caroline looked at the clock. "It's rather late now. I suppose I shall wait till the morning."

"How long will you be gone?"

"Until they leave," said Caroline. "You must call me when the coast is clear."

"I'll do no such thing," said Arden. She was looking at the saucepan, which was still in the sink. She could not help thinking about her delicious cold soup, heated . . .

"What?" said Caroline.

"I'm just . . . Go if you want, go, but don't give me orders. Don't tell me what to do."

"Goodness," said Caroline, "it sounds as if you're the one who needs to get away from here. You're welcome to join me if you want."

"Are you going to leave without talking to him?"

"Who?"

"Omar!" Arden almost shouted. She banged the saucepan in the sink and then filled it with water.

"Why should I talk to Omar? I have talked rather a lot to Omar."

Arden wanted to say, If you go you can't change your mind. But of course that's why Caroline was going, she thought; she's afraid if she stays here she'll change her mind.

"You're afraid if you stay here, you'll change your mind," she said.

"No," said Caroline. "I'm afraid if I stay I'll lose my mind. I'll have people accosting me at all times of the night and day, trying to do that, yes: change my mind, but I do not want my mind changed. I want these people to go away, but as they only incapacitate themselves and multiply, I will go away myself."

"Fine," said Arden. "Go."

The next morning, Deirdre brought Omar's breakfast to him on a tray.

"Where is everyone?" he asked.

"Who?" asked Deirdre. "Who is everyone?"

"Caroline and Adam and Pete and Arden and Portia. I've seen no one but you since I've been back here."

"They're all busy doing whatever it is they do around here. Forging paintings and raising killer bees. Do you know there's a weird voodoo-ey puppet theater down the hall?"

"No," said Omar. "Have you been opening doors?"

"I was looking for the bathroom. And next to my room is a sewing room, with one of those old pedal machines."

"So?"

"I'm just reporting." She put the tray down on the bedside table. "Why don't you take off those pajamas? And I'll see about getting them washed." Or destroyed, she thought. "Do you want to take a bath?"

"That might be nice," said Omar.

"There's a nice tub down the hall," said Deirdre. "I'll go fill it."

Omar heard the taps squeal as they were opened and the water thunder into the tub. But it was several minutes before Deirdre returned. She closed the door and leaned against it. "Oh, no," she said.

"What?"

"Caroline's bolted."

"What do you mean?"

"I was filling the bath when I saw her walk by with a suitcase. I followed her downstairs. She's going to stay with some friends for a while."

"For how long?"

"She was vague. Her suitcase was rather large."

"Is she still here?"

"No, she drove away."

"Why didn't you stop her?"

"What was I supposed to do? Tackle her?"

"But I need to talk to her. I've got to talk to her. If I can't talk to her, it's all over."

"I know," said Deirdre. "I panicked. But what could I have done?"

"Where has she gone?"

"I told you to—to visit friends."

"I know, but where? How far? She's not leaving the country, is she?"

"I have no idea."

"We've got to find out. Ask Arden. Is she around?"

"Presumably," said Deirdre. "Somewhere."

"Will you tell Arden I'd like to talk to her?"

"All right, but you should take your bath first. Shit! Your bath. It's still running."

CHAPTER EIGHTEEN

Two days later Pete drove Omar to Las Golondrinas, which was the name of the vineyard where Caroline was visiting her friends. It had not been easy to arrange: at first Caroline refused to take his calls, but he persisted and finally she got on the phone to tell him to stop harassing her and her friends. Omar promised to desist if she would speak with him for fifteen minutes. Somewhat miraculously, she agreed.

Of course, Deirdre had wanted to accompany him, but Omar had refused to let her. And somewhat miraculously, she had agreed. So here he was speeding across the range in Pete's battered pickup. The fields spread out as far as Omar could see in every direction. They were dotted by shallow pools around which willow trees gathered, and often in the shade of these trees cattle lolled.

"It's very beautiful," Omar shouted over the noise of the truck and the wind rushing through the open windows.

"Yes," Pete agreed.

"It is like Kansas," said Omar. "Very flat."

Pete slowed down and stopped: a herd of cattle was being moved across the road by two men on horses.

"Are those gauchos?" asked Omar.

"Yes," said Pete. He leaned over and fished a pack of cigarettes out of the glove box. He offered them to Omar.

"No, thanks," said Omar.

"Don't you smoke?" said Pete.

"No," said Omar.

Pete put a cigarette in his mouth and pushed in the dash-board lighter. "I only smoke in the truck. I like to smoke and drive."

"You drive around a lot, looking for furniture?" asked Omar.

"Yes," said Pete.

"To the ranches?"

"Sometimes the ranches. But mostly to the little towns, where people have old furniture. They think it is not nice, they want new things, so they sell me the old things for very little."

The lighter popped, and Pete held it to the tip of his cigarette. There was the sudden, pleasant warm smell of tobacco. The cattle completed their migration. The gauchos waved at them. Pete waved back and continued driving. "So," he said, "you need to see Caroline about your book?"

"Yes," said Omar. "Arden and Adam have agreed, but Caroline has not."

"Caroline is stubborn," said Pete.

Omar agreed. "What was Jules like?" he asked.

"I did not like Jules," said Pete.

"Why not?" asked Omar.

Pete shrugged. He flicked his cigarette out the window. "I don't think he was a very nice person," said Pete. "He did not seem very happy. He always had a face like this—" Pete scowled.

"What did he do?" asked Omar.

"What do you mean?"

"What did he do with his time?"

"He traveled a lot. To Europe and the United States. And when he was here he was always writing. Always in his study, but I think he was mostly drinking. But I did not know him for long. Only a few years. I think he was happier before I came here."

"You came with Adam?"

"Yes, from Germany."

"Do you like it here?"

"Yes," said Pete. "It reminds me of Thailand a little bit. More than Germany. I did not like Germany. Not the place and not the people. Here is nicer."

"This is like Thailand?" asked Omar.

Pete looked out at the fields. "No," he said. "But the weather is nice. It was too cold in Germany. I hate the cold."

"Then you would not like Kansas."

"Do you like the cold, and skiing?"

"No," said Omar.

"In Germany everyone is skiing."

"I like the sun and the beach," said Omar.

"Yes, that's very nice," said Pete. "There are nice beaches here, in the south. You should go there before you leave. Does Deirdre like the beaches too?"

"She likes to swim, but she doesn't like to take the sun," said Omar.

"I love to feel the sun," said Pete. He stuck his bare arm out the window, and rotated it in the hot breeze. "Perhaps we should go to the beach, now. We could keep driving. There is a good road."

"But Caroline is expecting us at Las Golondrinas," said Omar. "I have to talk to her."

Pete withdrew his hand. "I would like to show you the beach," he said. "Maybe some other time."

"Yes," said Omar. "That would be nice."

"So you will be back?"

"I hope so," said Omar. "It depends what happens with Caroline."

"I hope she will say yes, then."

"Yes," said Omar. "So do I."

They were quiet a moment, both gazing out at the road bisecting the landscape in front of them, and then Pete said, "Omar, Adam told me there is no letter."

"What?" asked Omar. He put his hand on the dashboard.

"Adam told me there is no letter from Jules, about the biography. It is Caroline pretending."

"When did he tell you that?"

"The other day. I came home and he was upset. He was angry at Caroline. And he told me she made up the letter."

"Why doesn't she want the biography, then?" asked Omar.

"I don't think Caroline is very happy. Like Jules." He made that face again. "There could be any reason. With unhappy people it is always complicated."

"Yes," said Omar.

Pete looked over at him. "Maybe you should ask her to see this letter."

"That's a good idea," said Omar.

After a while they drove off the main road and onto a dirt road. They stopped in front of a low metal gate that was swung shut across the road. "You must open the gate," said Pete, "and then close it after I have driven through."

"Okay," said Omar. He got down from the truck and pushed the gate open. Pete drove through and stopped. Omar closed the gate and climbed back into the truck.

"This is Las Golondrinas," said Pete.

"What does it mean, Las Golondrinas?"

"It is a bird. I'm not sure what you say in English. A little bird that sings and flies." They crossed over a wide but shallow stream. The wooden bridge clacked ferociously beneath the truck. Then they climbed up through vineyards. The house was on top of a hill that rose up out of the flatness. It was surrounded by large trees, and several outbuildings. The house was two stories, made of stucco, and painted almost pink. Pete parked the truck in the shade of one of the acacia trees. They heard a dog barking, and then he appeared, charging the car: a large copper-colored dog, with a cowlick all the way down his spine.

A woman came out of the house and clapped her hands. "*Cállate*, Faustus," she yelled at the dog. "It is all right," she called to the men in the truck. "He is all bark and not bite." She was about fifty, casually dressed in jeans and a tank top. Bare feet. Her hair was dyed blond.

Omar got down from the truck but Pete waited until the woman had grabbed the dog by the collar. He was still barking. "*¡Cállate!*" she shouted again, and hit him hard on his snout. He shut up then.

"Come out, come out," she said, rather impatiently, to Pete. "He won't hurt you."

Omar appeared from around the truck. "Hello," he said to the woman. "I am Omar Razaghi."

The woman went to shake his hand and discovered his infirmity. "I've had an accident," said Omar.

"Apparently," she said, laughing. "I am Donatella. Gianfranco and Caroline are around back. We were just sitting down to lunch."

"Oh, I'm sorry," said Omar. "We didn't mean to interrupt your meal. We can wait here until you are through."

"Nonsense," said Donatella. "There is plenty for you both. But your trip has made you a bit a dusty, I think. Come inside first, why not?"

They ate lunch—a very delicious lunch—on a patio covered with wisteria at the back of the house, overlooking the vineyards. When Caroline had finished her espresso, she stood up and tossed her linen napkin onto the table. "Well," she said, "perhaps Omar and I should take a stroll." After the lovely leisure of the meal her abruptness seemed a little weird, as if it were Omar who had been setting the pace, languishing, and needed to be hurried. She wore white tailored slacks and a pink cotton shirt with a wide squared neck. She had perched her black-framed sunglasses atop her head during the meal, but she lowered them now, and smiled at him with her mouth.

He stood up. "Of course," he said, "that would be great. Excuse me. Thank you again, for the delicious lunch," he said to his hosts.

Caroline had already stepped down from the patio and was walking away from the house, down a gravel path beneath a pergola that was also overhung with wisteria. Omar caught her up.

They walked for a moment or two in silence. Flicks of sunlight fell through the leafy canopy above them and dappled the ground, dappled Caroline's nearly bare shoulders. She had picked a blossom from the vine and was methodically dismembering it: first the petals, then the stamens.

"Thank you for letting me see you again," he said.

She shrugged. "I'm sorry you had to drive all this way. Or Pete—poor Pete."

"It was just that I had an idea I wanted to share with you."

"What idea is that?" she asked.

"Well, you know what the situation is. Arden and Adam have both agreed to authorize the biography. And you have not."

"Yes," said Caroline.

"I don't know what your reasons are—"

"But I have told you!" She turned to him, exasperated. "I have a letter from Jules, stating very clearly, in no uncertain terms, that he did not wish a biography—"

"I know there is no letter," said Omar.

"What?"

"Please don't pretend there is a letter from Jules. I know there is not."

"How do you know that? Who told you that?"

"Pete told me. Adam told him."

Caroline tossed the little wrecked flower to the ground. "They had no right to tell you," she said.

"It doesn't matter," said Omar. "Until just now, I believed in the letter. What I wanted to say was that I don't know your reasons, and I don't need to know your reasons. Your reasons are private. If you don't want a biography of Jules I understand. You have that right. But Arden and Adam have a right too. I have a right."

"I think you have no rights in this matter—"

"No," said Omar. "I do. I have the right to write a biography of Jules Gund. You have the right not to cooperate with me. That is my right and that is your right."

"And I have the right to withhold authorization," said Caroline.

"Yes," said Omar, "you do. But that will not stop me from writing the biography."

"I thought you cannot write it without authorization."

"That is incorrect. Only my grant is dependent upon authorization. And the publication by the University of Kansas Press. But I can still write a biography of Jules Gund. And I can have it published elsewhere."

"But can you? Will you?"

"Yes," said Omar.

"I think not. I think you are bluffing."

She turned and continued walking down the path. Then she paused again, and turned to him. "You said you had an idea. What is your idea?"

"My idea is that you grant me authorization. And then share with me what you like. Or nothing, if that is what you want. Don't talk to me. Don't show me Jules's letters to you. Don't cooperate at all. I will work with Arden and Adam and other sources. I can even put some sort of disclaimer in the book, that you have not sanctioned the biography."

"Yes, and then I will look like a monster."

They had reached the end of the shaded alley. Another gravel path bisected the one they stood upon, and beyond that the land fell away steeply in a series of terraces, down to where the vineyards spread out in the effulgence of midday. A carved stone balustrade ran alongside this path, and behind that, cypress trees were planted at regular intervals, separating the vista into panels. They loitered for a moment, beneath the leafy carapace, looking out at the view.

Then Caroline went and sat in the sun on the balustrade with her back to the view. "How tiresome this all is," she said. "Let's just sit for a moment."

Omar stepped out into the brightness and leaned against the stone wall, a few feet away from Caroline. She had twisted herself around, away from him, so she could look out over the regiments of vines.

In other circumstances, it would have been a lovely moment: the nice meal on the patio, the delicious rosé wine, the little gold-rimmed cups of espresso, the walk down the trellised alley, the warmth of the rocks beneath them, the faint but powerful scent of earth and wisteria and verbena. And small birds—perhaps golon-drinas, Omar thought, for they sang and flew—twittered in the leafy canopy. A green lizard raced away from them down the wall, and then froze, radiant. It moved its head in small ticking motions, like the hands of a clock. Suddenly, it plunged off the wall, into the jumble of weeds below them.

Caroline spoke, but as she was still turned away from Omar, he could not understand what she had said.

"Excuse me," he said. "I couldn't hear you."

She stood up and then sat back down, facing him. "What else did they tell you?"

He remembered how she had seemed mad to him that morning he had visited her in her studio, and he felt that possibility again; there was a wild tension within her that her calm hauteur could not completely mask.

"Nothing," he said.

"Well," she said, "whatever happens, I will seem a monster."

"What do you mean?"

"I mean if you write the book, I will seem a monster, and if you don't write the book, I will seem a monster."

"You will not seem a monster," said Omar. "You are not a monster."

"You don't know me," she said. And then she said it again: "You don't know me."

"I know you a little," said Omar.

She was looking down, fingering some fuzzy lichen that grew on the rock, but then she looked up at him. He could see his face reflected in the dark orbs of her sunglasses. "Do you know why Jules killed himself?" she asked.

"No," he said.

"Do you know he wrote another book? After *The Gondola*?"

"Yes," said Omar.

"So they told you that? They've told you everything?"

"No," said Omar. "I just know there is another book, based on—on your situation, but that Jules did not want it published."

"Who told you that?"

"Arden did. Adam mentioned the book, and Arden told me what it was about."

"And she said Jules did not want it published?"

"Yes," said Omar.

"Poor Omar," Caroline said. "Everyone lies to you."

So tell me the truth, Omar wanted to shout, but he said nothing.

"Is there not another book?" he asked.

"No," said Caroline. "There is not another book. Jules wrote another book, a book about our situation, as you say. He worked on it for years. It might have been a very beautiful book, who knows? But it does not exist anymore."

"What happened to it?" asked Omar.

"It was destroyed," said Caroline. "I burned it."

"Oh," said Omar. Then he asked, "Why?"

Caroline appeared to wince. She lowered her face. She put her hand flat on the stone beside her and looked at it. "I don't know," she said. "Perhaps I felt I had given him too much, and needed to take something away. Or perhaps I had not given him enough, and wanted to take something away. And it is awful when you cannot make something yourself, not a child, not a painting, and someone else makes something out of your stuff—" She drew her hand into a fist and then slowly released it, patted the stone. "Or maybe not that at all. Perhaps simply because I hated him. Or hated myself. Or Arden. Or hated all of us, everyone. Or maybe because I loved him, and couldn't bear that. I really can't say. But I am sure you will figure it all out, and explain it to me. For there must be an explanation, of course: everything makes sense, or can be made sense of, with people like you around to do that for us. To pick up the pieces and put them back together, even if they have been shattered. Or burned."

Omar said nothing. It was hot there, in the sun. He wished he had not drunk the wine at lunch. Dr. Peni had told him not to drink any alcohol for at least ten days. But he had been so nervous and it had looked so good. Caroline stood. She moved across the walk and paused beneath the trellised canopy of flowering vines. "I will grant you authorization," she said. "It is worse to try to stop you. It does me more harm, I think. More harm to me. So go, and write your book. Explain it all to us. Explain ourselves to us. How grateful to you we will be." She turned and walked up the shaded alley, toward the patio, where Donatella and Gianfranco and Pete still loitered, laughing, at the table.

They were silent driving away from the house. Pete stopped at the gate; Omar got down and opened it and let the truck pass though, then closed it behind them and returned to the truck. He felt tired and sick. They passed over the clattering bridge and when the noise of that subsided, Pete asked, "How did it go, your talk with Caroline?"

"She said yes," said Omar.

"So you have got what you wanted?" asked Pete. "What you came for?"

"Yes," said Omar.

They turned onto the hard road and drove for a ways in silence, and then Pete said, "You don't seem happy, that you got what you wanted."

"I don't feel very well," said Omar. "And I'm tired."

"But you're happy?" asked Pete.

"No," said Omar, "I am not happy."

Pete said nothing, but after a moment he reached out and patted Omar's leg. Then he put both hands on the steering wheel and concentrated hard on driving, although the road was perfectly straight for as far as they both could see.

Pete dropped him off in front of the big house and then drove away. Omar went upstairs to the bathroom and was sick. He rinsed his mouth and washed his face and went into his room. He took off his pants and lay on the bed.

He wished he could talk to Arden; he would like to ask Arden what he should do. But he knew that Arden was avoiding him. She was sorry she had kissed him; she hoped he had forgotten it. But he had not forgotten it. It had seemed like a dream but it had not been a dream. They had walked up to see the gondola and kissed outside the boathouse. She had put her hands on his face . . .

The door opened, and Deirdre came in. She turned and closed the door behind her and then stood, looking at Omar on the bed. "What's wrong?" she said.

Omar wiped his cheeks but said nothing.

"What's wrong?" she repeated.

"Nothing," he said.

"Of course something is," she said. "You were crying. You are crying."

He covered his face with his hands. She came near the bed and touched his bare leg with her hand. He was wearing boxer shorts and lying on top of the bedspread; it was warm in the room. "Please tell me what's wrong," she said.

"I don't know," he said, after a moment.

"Are you sad about something?" she asked.

"Yes," he said.

"Did Caroline say no?"

"No," he said, "she said yes."

"Then I don't understand. Why are you sad? Or are you relieved?"

"I'm sad," said Omar.

"Why?" asked Deirdre. "Tell me. What are you sad about?"

"I don't know," he said. "Everything, I think."

"But everything is okay, Omar," she said. He felt her sit beside him on the bed. "You have nothing to be sad about. You've got authorization now, you can keep the grant, you can write the book. Everything is fine. In three days we'll be back in Kansas and everything will be normal again. You can start teaching and researching. You have nothing to be worried about, or sad about. Why are you sad?"

Omar shook his head—his hands still covering his eyes.

Deirdre gently removed his hands from his face, and smoothed his hair back from his forehead. "It must have been difficult," she said, "talking with Caroline. And traveling. And you're not well yet. You shouldn't have gone. But I'm so proud of you, Omar! What a wonderful thing you've done. How did you convince her? What did you tell her?"

Omar shook his head. "I don't want to talk about it," he said.

"Okay," said Deirdre. After a moment she said, "Omar, are you okay?"

"Yes," he said.

"I'm just so worried about you," said Deirdre.

"Why?"

"I don't know. I don't understand it. You seem different. Maybe it's just what's happened, and being here, I don't know, maybe when we get home everything will be back to normal again. I mean, not normal, not exactly the same, of course, different, of course, but—"

"But what?"

"I don't know." Deirdre was quiet for a moment, and then she said, "I've been thinking. I've been thinking maybe you shouldn't go back to Yvonne's. I don't think you should be alone out there. Especially in the winter, with your car, and the snow, and your wrist— Maybe you should move in with me. I think it would be good for us to live together. I think it's time. What do you think?"

"About what?"

"About living together."

"I don't know," said Omar. "Before you said I was too irresponsible to live with."

"That was before," said Deirdre. "Things change. Things have changed."

"How have they changed?" asked Omar.

"They have— Oh, Omar: I've changed. We've both changed. I've realized how much I love you. How much I admire you. And need you." She paused. She touched his moist cheek, gently, with the back of her hand. "And want you," she said. "I'm sorry if I sometimes behave in a way that doesn't make all that clear. I'm sorry because it's all true, it's all there, beneath everything else I say or do, there are always those feelings for you, always. Do you understand?"

"Yes," said Omar.

"Good," said Deirdre. "I think when we get back we should try to do things differently. I think living together would be a good change. Don't you?"

"I don't know," said Omar.

"Well, we can think about it," said Deirdre. "We don't have to decide now."

"No," said Omar.

"Do you want to sleep?"

"Yes," said Omar. "Maybe, for a little while."

"Okay." Deirdre stood up. "Do you want something to drink? Some water?"

"No, thank you," said Omar.

Deirdre stood beside the bed. "I'm glad we had this talk," she said. "Please don't be sad. And congratulations, Omar. You've done a wonderful thing. I'm very proud of you."

She left the room, quietly closing the door behind her.

Omar felt better that evening, and he and Deirdre went for a walk, down the drive, through the gates, and along the road toward the millhouse, where it was just road and woods and sky. It was a warm, still evening: the falling sun struck the trees along one side of the road almost brutally, turning their green into gold. They loitered there, in the middle of the road, their shadows cast wildly behind them. They had not talked much on this walk, and they did not speak at all as they stood in the middle of the deserted road. Omar knelt down and touched the macadam, which was still warm from a long day's worth of sun. "I remember the first time I walked down this road," he said.

"When was that?" asked Deirdre.

"My first day here. No: the second. I was going to see Adam. I remember I was very happy, for some reason, walking down here. Hopeful." He stood up. After a moment, he said, "I think I've decided something."

"What?" asked Deirdre. "What have you decided?"

Omar looked down at the road. For a moment Deirdre thought he might crouch and pet it again. But he did not.

"I've decided—I think I've decided I don't want to write a biography of Jules Gund. I think I want to forget about all of this."

"Omar? What do you mean? Why do you think that?"

He shook his head. "I don't know," he said. "It just seems pointless. I don't want to do it. I think I'd be bad at it. I'd do a bad job. It seems wrong."

"Wrong? How wrong?"

"I can't explain it. I don't understand it. Just wrong. But really wrong. It's like a pond where everything has settled, so it's still and clear, and if I were to— I'd just stir everything up, I'd make a mess."

"Omar! That's ridiculous. In the first place, it isn't all still and clear, and in the second place—I think you're just confused. And tired. The shock you've had; all these days, this experience—it's been too much for you, Omar. Don't think about any of this now. When we get home, and you feel better, you'll feel differently, I think. Everything's a bit askew for you here, I think. You're too close to it all, somehow."

"I don't think it's a matter of perspective," said Omar.

It seemed to Deirdre an odd thing for Omar to say.

"Well," said Deirdre. "Can't you wait and see? Please, Omar— there's no need to decide anything now. Just let's get out of here, get home, and when you're feeling better, when you're feeling yourself again, then you can think about all this. But not now. Not here. Promise me. Please, promise me."

Omar said nothing.

"Please, Omar. Promise me. Promise me you won't say anything to anyone here about not writing the book."

"Okay," said Omar. "I promise." They stood there for a moment, and then Omar said, "I think I will go visit Adam."

"Adam? Why?"

"I need to talk to him before I leave. To tell him I won't bring the paintings to New York."

"Oh," said Deirdre. "Are you sure you do? It was a silly bargain, Omar. I'm sure he doesn't really expect you to do it. Perhaps it's best just left alone."

"No," said Omar. "I need to tell him. I owe him at least that."

"What will you tell him?"

"I don't know. Something. That I've decided I can't do it, for, for—practical reasons."

"Well, don't say anything about the book. Remember, you promised me."

"Yes," said Omar.

"Do you want me to come with you? Perhaps it would be easier if I were with you."

"No," said Omar. "I think it's better if I go alone."

"You don't need to do this," Deirdre said. "It was wrong of Adam: he coerced you. You aren't morally obligated to explain anything to him."

"I'd just like to go talk to him," said Omar. "I'll see you back at the house. I won't be long." He turned and set off down the road toward the millhouse. Deirdre watched him, until he turned into the drive, and disappeared.

Adam was sitting on a wooden chair in the cobbled yard in front of the millhouse, drinking a glass of what looked like rosé wine. If his suit was a little less rumpled and his hair a bit more kempt, he would have looked as if he were in an advertisement. "Good evening," he said, as Omar unlatched the gate and entered the yard.

"Hello," said Omar.

"How good to see you," said Adam. "So you are up and about. No longer an invalid?"

"I'm feeling much better," said Omar.

"Would you like a glass of wine? I have the bottle here; you must fetch another glass."

"No, thank you," said Omar. "I'm not supposed to drink any alcohol."

"I'm sure a little glass of wine would be very good for you," said Adam. "It has such a tonic effect."

"I had some, the other day, at Las Golondrinas, and felt very ill afterward," said Omar.

"And you blame the wine? I'm sure it was the company. But I understand you returned victorious. The conquering hero." Adam raised his glass of wine, which glowed rosily in the dwindling light. "Congratulations."

"Thank you," said Omar. "I have actually come to tell you something."

"No doubt you have," said Adam. "People are always coming to tell me something. Never the thing I want to hear, of course. Only once did that happen, or once that I can recall. When I was as young as you—or younger perhaps; I was a student at Heidelberg—a boy I loved came to me and said, 'I have come to tell you something.' It was that he loved me, but he could not say it. He thought that by saying that, by saying 'I have come to tell you something' I would know of what he spoke. Or wished to speak. And of course I did. But I was no braver than he. I should have said, 'Say nothing: I know,' but I could not. Would not. This was back in the dark ages. They were silent as well as dark. And so we sat there, saying nothing, and our chance was lost. I don't suppose you have come to tell me you love me?"

"No," said Omar.

Adam said nothing, but when Omar did not speak, he said, "Then what is it you have come to tell me?"

"I have come to tell you that I cannot transport those paintings to New York for you."

"Cannot?" said Adam. "Or will not?"

"Will not," said Omar.

"Oh," said Adam. He regarded the pinkness of his drink. "I'm sure you have a very good reason for saying what you do."

"It's just that—well, the bargain was that you would convince Caroline to agree, but you did not. I did."

"Yes," said Adam. "The conquering hero." He lifted his glass toward Omar, and then drained it.

"Please don't say that," said Omar. "Don't call me that. You don't understand. I've decided—"

"You've decided what?"

"Nothing. That I can't—won't—transport the paintings for you. But you don't understand."

"Oh, I think I do. A bit. I understand a bit. And really, who can understand more than a bit? Who would want to understand more than a bit? Not I." Adam stood up. "It was all a bit foolish of me. The intractability of things! The older you get, how apparent it is, how it weighs upon one. You would think it would not be so difficult as it is." He addressed this tirade to the stones at his feet.

Omar was not sure what he was talking about, so he said nothing. And then he said, "I'm sorry."

"No," said Adam, looking up at Omar. "Don't be sorry. I couldn't bear your being sorry. Besides, I'm sure you have better things to be sorry for. Forget our little bargain."

"I sincerely wanted to help you," said Omar. "I do. Perhaps there is something else I could do for you."

"I cannot think of anything at the present moment," said Adam, "but if and when I do, I will not hesitate to contact you."

"I'm sorry," said Omar. "I am being sincere."

"And I am not?"

"No. I don't think you are."

Adam stepped forward, and did an odd thing: he touched Omar's cheek. "Don't be so sure," he said. "It is a hard thing to tell with me."

CHAPTER NINETEEN

Pete was driving them to Tacuarembó, from where they could catch a bus directly to Montevideo. They would spend one night there and leave the following morning.

Deirdre finished packing and closed her bag. She brought it downstairs and put it on the bench next to the front door. Then she went back up to Omar's room. He was sitting on his bed beside his open suitcase.

"Are you finished packing?" she asked.

He nodded. There was something wrong with him; he had hardly spoken to her since their conversation on the road, but she did not know what to do except to get him out of here, get him home. "Let's go down, then," she said. "Pete should be here."

"Do you know where Arden is?" he asked.

"She's in her room. She said she would come down to say good-bye."

Omar stood up. "I need to talk to Arden. I'll meet you downstairs."

"Omar—"

"What?"

"Why do you need to talk to Arden? Maybe we should just go."

"I just want to say goodbye to her, and thank her."

"You can do that downstairs."

"I want to do it privately."

"Remember what you promised me," Deirdre said.

"Yes," said Omar, "I remember." He left the room. He had never been to Arden's room but he knew where it was: it was one of the two large rooms at the front of the house, on the second floor. He walked down the hall and across the gallery to the other side of the house. Her bedroom door was shut. He knocked on it.

After a moment she opened it. "Omar," she said.

"May I come in?" he asked.

She looked confused, almost as if she thought he had already left, but she stepped back from the door and opened it wider so he could enter. She did not shut it behind him.

The room was very large. It was darker than he thought it would be; the shades were all drawn. A huge unmade canopied bed stood against the back wall, and a door beside it was opened into a bathroom. Between the front windows stood a long empire sofa, and facing it were several matching chairs. A very large, worn patterned carpet covered most of the floor, and the walls were all painted a pale green.

Neither of them said anything for a moment, but then Arden asked, "Is Pete here? Are you ready to leave?"

"No," said Omar.

"I was going to come down, and say goodbye. Portia is angry. She wanted to stay home from school, so she could say goodbye. But I told her I would do it for her. So: goodbye from Portia."

"Why have you been avoiding me?" said Omar.

She looked at him. "Oh, Omar," she said.

"Why?"

"I thought it best, with Deirdre here, not to be in the way—"

"I think I love you," said Omar.

"Oh," she said. She ducked her face a moment, then she looked up at him. "Thank you," she said. "I'm flattered you think that. But of course you don't. You hardly know me."

"But I—"

"No," she said, "listen to me. I shouldn't have kissed you. I'm sorry I did. It was wrong of me, Omar, it was wrong of us both. I like you very much, but you must not think you love me." She shook her head. "You mustn't think that."

"Why not?" asked Omar.

"Because," she said. "I can't explain it without hurting you and I don't want to hurt you. Just trust me, Omar."

"You won't hurt me," said Omar.

She stood up. "Yes," she said, "I will. And I don't want to hurt you. And I don't want you to hurt me. Please—" she touched him, lightly, on his arm. "Please, it will hurt me, it does hurt me, but it is better if you go. There is nothing to talk about, really, Omar. There is nothing to say. Let us be friends."

They heard the gravel crunching out front and a car door slam.

"Here's Pete," she said. She touched him again. "You should go. You don't want to miss your bus."

But Omar did not move. He just stood there looking at her. For a long moment they looked at each other. Then Arden went and closed the door. She came back and stood close to him. She touched him again—his arm, and then his face. He closed his eyes, moved his face against her hand, reached out, blindly, touched her, opened his mouth, found hers.

They were all three quiet in the car, almost as if they were strangers. Deirdre sat in front beside Pete. She closed her eyes and feigned sleep but Pete could tell she was awake, and he hated her a little for this deception. She is not brave or honest enough to sit beside me and not talk, he thought. In the rearview mirror he could see Omar gazing out the window. Pete looked up many times into the mirror, but Omar's gaze never shifted; he was always looking out the window, but his stare was dull, uninterested.

They arrived in Tacuarembó early for the bus and Pete offered to stay with them, but Deirdre dispatched him, almost rudely. It was not at all how Pete had imagined it would be. He had thought in some way that because he was young he was one of them; he had thought they would laugh and talk as they drove and embrace before they got onto the bus; he had thought they would stick their heads out the window and wave as the bus drove away. And he had thought—wildly, impossibly—that they might ask him to come with them. But no: they collected their bags from the trunk and then told him to go, or rather Deirdre told him to go. She was polite: she thanked him for the ride, for all he had done for them, but she told him to go. You have so far to drive, she said, there's no point in staying here with us. Who knows how late the bus will be . . .

Pete stood there for a moment, as if he were deciding, trying to think of a reason why he must stay with them, but he was not clever enough, and so of course he had to leave. He could not stay if they did not want him. Apparently they did not want him. Of course they did not want him. How stupid he had been. Thinking they might ask him to go with them, when they could hardly wait to be rid of him.

Deirdre went inside to buy the tickets, and Pete was left alone with Omar. He reached out his hand and touched Omar's arm. "I'm glad to have met you. I'm sorry you must go."

"Me too," said Omar. "Thank you, Pete." He embraced Pete. It happened very quickly, a quick hug. Over Omar's shoulder Pete could see Deirdre at the ticket window. Omar smelled clean and good, he was warm. Omar patted Pete on the back, and then broke away.

"You will come back," said Pete.

"Yes," said Omar, "I suppose."

"Good," said Pete. "I will take you with me when I look for

furniture. We will have a nice time together. And we will go to the beach."

"Yes," said Omar.

Deirdre had returned with the tickets. She displayed them as if they were prizes, as if she had fought for them. Perhaps she had. She stood in a way that indicated it was time for Pete to leave. He held out his hand toward her. "Goodbye, Deirdre," he said.

She shook it, and touched it with her other hand. "Goodbye, Pete," Deirdre said. "Thank you again for the ride here, and everything else—" She was sincere, he could tell. Perhaps he was wrong about her, perhaps she had been asleep in the car.

"You're welcome," said Pete. "Have a safe journey."

"Yes," said Deirdre. "You too."

But I am going nowhere, thought Pete. He said goodbye to Omar again and then he walked to the car. After he started it he looked for them but they had gone to sit inside the bus station. He drove away. He did not know what he had lost. Or it was not even something lost. It was the hope of something, the absurd possibility of something, lost. He drove a little way, out of Tacuarembó, and then pulled the car off the road. He just sat there, waiting. He did not want to get back so fast.

Pete was very late getting back. He had stopped in a town on the way back and drunk three beers in a bar and then napped in the car and then had stopped again for dinner in a roadside restaurant. Adam had left lights on for him. Or perhaps Adam had just left lights on: that was more likely. Pete turned out the lamps in the living room. There was a mess in the kitchen from Adam's dinner, but Pete let it alone. He was very tired. Driving at night exhausted him. It had been very dark all around him, and the car seemed to have weak beams. Perhaps one of the headlights was out. He sat for a while in the dark living room. He still felt the sensation of traveling, of the road moving beneath him. It would take a moment for it to quieten, to cease.

After a while he climbed the stairs. He was surprised to find a light on in the bedroom, and Adam sitting up in bed. He was reading Proust. He laid the fat book, splayed, on his lap and looked up at Pete.

"I heard you come in," he said.

"I'm sorry if I woke you," said Pete.

"No," said Adam. "I was waiting for you. I was worried. I thought perhaps you went off with them."

"No," said Pete. "They're gone."

"Good riddance, I say," said Adam.

Pete loitered by the door.

"Come to bed," said Adam. And then he leaned forward, because it appeared as though Pete were crying. "What is it, Pete? What's wrong?"

Pete had turned away, he crossed his arms against the doorjamb and buried his face in them. He was sobbing.

Adam got out of bed. He stood beside Pete, put his hand, lightly, on Pete's shaking back. "What's wrong, Pete?" he asked. "Why are you crying?"

"I don't know," said Pete. "I thought I was happy."

"Come to bed," said Adam. "Get undressed and come to bed."

Pete did. He undressed, turned out the light, and got into the bed. Adam held him. Adam held him and stroked his hair. He said his name, over and over again, until Pete stopped crying. Then he said, in the darkness: "It's all right, Pete. Don't worry. I understand that you must leave here."

"I don't want to leave you," said Pete.

"Yes, you do," said Adam. "You must. There is nothing here for you."

For a while Pete said nothing, and then he said, "But what about you? Who will take care of you?"

"I don't need so very much taking care of," said Adam. "Don't worry."

CHAPTER TWENTY

Their trip back was long and miserable. It seemed especially designed to psychologically flay them, to cause them to arrive home at their lowest ebbs of dignity and patience. Their humiliation began immediately and was nearly constant: the plane was crowded and they were forced to sit in the middle of the hateful five-person row in the center. "This is absurd," Deirdre hissed to Omar while they buckled their seat belts. "I don't understand why it's such a huge plane. Coming down, I was on a normal plane, with just one aisle. This is madness. Can you imagine eight hours of this?"

"There's nothing we can do about it," said Omar. "So just relax."

"That's easy for you to say," said Deirdre. "You're happily narcotized."

Omar was under the influence of sedatives prescribed by Dr. Peni. "I am sleepy," said Omar. "I just want to sleep. Wake me up in Miami."

"I can't sleep sitting up among strangers like this," said Deirdre. "Perhaps no one will sit in these two seats, and we can spread out."

"I doubt it," said Omar. "Didn't they say the flight was full when you asked to change seats?"

"Yes," said Deirdre. "It's fully booked. But someone may not turn up. Oh, no—look: a woman with a baby. Please God, don't let her sit beside me."

God was not listening to Deirdre. The woman, who was young, well dressed, and pretty, assumed the aisle seat and buckled her toddler into the seat next to Deirdre. She smiled at Deirdre as she did this, clearly waiting for Deirdre to comment on the child's darlingness, but Deirdre only managed a weak smile. There should be a separate airline for people with children, she thought, or at least a separate section of the plane for them.

The baby was given a bottle of some thick, yellowish milky substance. It looked like eggnog. It sucked at it happily and gazed at Deirdre. Deirdre turned to Omar and tried to complain to him, but he was giving his attention to the flight attendants, who were explaining the disaster procedures. Omar always gave his full attention to these speeches; he even removed and studied the safety brochure in the seat pocket, mostly because he felt sorry for the flight attendants performing to no one (for this reason he never really enjoyed the theater, for he was always aware of how keenly an audience's indifference could be felt) and partly because he wanted to know what to do in case of disaster. He wished they actually let you practice with the oxygen masks and life vests and (supposed) floating seat cushions: merely talking about it did not seem like adequate preparation.

They had taken off and he was about to fall asleep when Deirdre poked him. "Look at that," she said. "Look over there. Look what that baby's eating."

Omar looked past Deirdre. The mother was feeding the baby something pinkish from a small can.

"What is it?" Omar whispered.

"It's cat food," Deirdre hissed. "She's feeding her baby cat food."

"Why do you think it's cat food?" asked Omar.

"Because it is. I can smell it. Look at it. And that's a cat food can."

"Of course it's not cat food," said Omar. "And even if it is, it's none of your business. People have different customs here, different diets. You shouldn't be judgmental. It's her baby."

The woman smiled at them. She thought they were admiring how well her child ate. "He is a hungry boy," she said.

Omar fell asleep and awoke to hear both the baby and Deirdre screaming. Deirdre was standing up—well, trying to stand up, since her seat belt was still fastened—and flailing her arms. Apparently—very apparently—the child had regurgitated his supper all over her.

Deirdre spent an hour trying to wash and dry her soiled and stinking garments in the rest room, yet she remained damp and putrid the entire trip. In Miami they missed their connection and were forced to spend six hours seated in a lounge where one flight after another was tediously announced with identically complicated and hierarchical instructions for boarding; as soon as one flight was dispatched the entire ordeal began with another, and they decided this was Hell: the fluorescent-lit airport waiting lounge with its incessant and brutalizing public address system which did not allow them to read or talk or think. And they could not escape it because they were on standby for almost every flight, as there were so many lovely ways to get home, via Houston or Atlanta or Pittsburgh or Chicago or St. Louis, and they had been ordered to remain at all times near the podium.

Finally, after a long interval in which they had both seemed to sink into a catatonic stupor, Deirdre said, "We will not be here forever. That's what I'm hanging on to. It seems otherwise, but I know, logically, that I will not be spending the rest of my life in this place. I know that eventually, in a matter of hours or days, we will be home. There will come that moment when we climb the stairs and put the key in the lock. I am going to put myself on hold until then."

"I just want to sleep in my own bed," said Omar.

"But I thought—"

"What?" Omar asked.

Deirdre looked away from him, she looked at the board that displayed all the arrivals and departures that were not theirs. "I thought you were coming to stay with me. At least in the beginning. At least until you're well."

"But I really long for my own bed," said Omar. "You know how that is. I think I will be more comfortable there."

"Yes, but it's not really your bed," said Deirdre.

"What do you mean? Oh—you mean it's Yvonne's. You mean I don't have my own bed."

"Omar, no. I didn't mean that. I just meant that I think until you're feeling yourself again, I don't think you should be living alone. Especially so far away from everything, out there at Yvonne's. And in a way, you're right: it is Yvonne's bed. Or Yvonne's guest-room bed. You can't be sentimentally attached to a bed you've only slept in for four or five months. In fact, I bet you've slept in my bed almost as often."

Perhaps, thought Omar: he had spent many nights in Deirdre's bed. The two-month interval between the fire and moving to Yvonne's, and many nights before and after that, nights in Deirdre's bed, which always seemed to be neatly made, with clean sheets and lots of pillows. Yet it was Deirdre's bed, in Deirdre's apartment, and he wanted his own bed. It was not a matter of the number of nights he had slept in it, or who owned it, it was not about history or real estate, it was the way he felt when he lay down upon it in darkness.

He decided to use another tactic. "I think it will be quieter out at the lake. I don't want to be in your noisy apartment with Marc Antony and his new boyfriend fucking all the time."

"Omar! My apartment isn't noisy. And I didn't say they fucked all the time. I just said I heard them twice."

"In the same night. Of course they fuck all the time. Everyone does in the beginning. Anyway, it's a moot question, because unlike you I don't think we're ever going to leave here. I think we should resign ourselves to living the rest of our lives here and make the best of it."

But about that, at least, Deirdre was right: eventually they did get home. Marc Antony was to have met them at the airport, but because of the delay, they took a taxi.

Omar paid for it out of his fellowship money: it was, after all, a legitimate traveling expense.

They did not speak in the taxi. They sat on opposite sides of the backseat with their luggage piled between them (Omar was always afraid to put his luggage in the trunk of a taxi, because he believed they could charge you extra for this). As they approached Hiawatha Woods, which was several miles out of town, Omar looked over at Deirdre, who leaned exhaustedly against the far window. The pale winter light fell upon her face and illuminated her sadness. Omar was overcome with a tender feeling for her: she had done so much for him, she had traveled all the way to Uruguay and brought him safely home. "Deirdre?" he said.

She looked over at him, attempting to compose and animate her face but the exhaustion was too complete, it filled her to the brim and did not allow for adjustment. Omar had never seen her look like this: her face was drawn and blank, defeated somehow: Deirdre who was indefatigable. "What?" she said.

"Perhaps you're right," he said. "Perhaps I shouldn't be alone yet. May I stay with you a night or two?"

"Of course you may," she said. She reached across the divide of luggage. "You can stay with me for as long as you want."

He stayed at Deirdre's for three nights, and on the morning of the third night they made love. Perhaps it was something about their dreams, for they turned to each other upon waking simultaneously predisposed. It was so nice when it happened like that, so tender and spontaneous, slowly, slowly, warm in bed, in the pale light of the winter morning. And when they were finished, when they had successfully passed between them what needed to be passed, they did not speak, they just held each other and closed their eyes while the light gradually filled the room. It was the last time they made love.

That afternoon Gwendolyn Pierce, who had been house- and dog-sitting while Omar was away, drove Omar's car into the town. She left it in the bank parking lot with the keys beneath the seat. When he went to claim it, there was a note waiting for him, taped to the steering wheel:

Omar,

Welcome back and hope you're feeling better. Thanks for letting me stay here. It was great and peaceful and I got a lot of work done. It's a great place to work. Does the TV work? It seemed not to but maybe I couldn't figure out the cable or something. Everything was fine. I'm not sure about the snow on the roof, should it be shoveled off or something? It's getting pretty deep—don't know if that's a problem or not. Mitzie is fine. I let her out after lunch and couldn't find her before I left, but I'm sure she'll be waiting for you, or be back by dinnertime. I looked for her and called but had to run because I have a class at 2:00. Thanks again, Gwen.

P.S. I made a few long-distance calls to Tempe and New York City. Let me know what I owe when the bill comes. There is leftover lasagna in the refrigerator (veggie). Thought you could eat it for dinner tonight!

P.P.S. Did you hear? Garfield retired (finally) and Lucy GK is new chair (eek!).

That night, finally in his bed which was not his, in the house that was not his, deep in the silent woods, Omar lay awake, listening for any sound that might be Mitzie. He had been out much of the night, trekking through the snowy woods, looking for her, but she was gone. He thought of Mitzie, alone in the woods. He remembered from *The Call of the Wild* that sled dogs dug cocoons for themselves in the snow and slept warmly. Would Mitzie know to do that? Was it instinctual or genetic or learned behavior? Or perhaps Mitzie was dead on some road somewhere. He would take the car tomorrow and drive around the surrounding roads. Oh, how awful: first the fire and then this. There was always some tragedy about to happen, there was always something lurking, an unseen violence; he could not escape it. He was doomed. He had forgotten that he was doomed. He should know it by now, he should know it well by now, but he always forgot. He remembered drinking the champagne on the flight down, toasting himself, Deirdre, his future. What a fool he had been.

The next day he was putting up LOST DOG posters around the campus when Lucy Greene-Kessler approached him.

"Omar!" she said. "How are you?"

He turned away from the kiosk and saw her. She was wearing a loden-green cape and a mannish hat with a little gold feather in it. Her eyes were keen and gold and her cheeks were red.

"I'm fine," he said. "Well, actually I'm not. I've lost my dog." He indicated the poster. "Yvonne's dog. Congratulations, I hear you're the new department chair."

"Well, acting chair," said Lucy. "But how are you? How are you feeling? We've been worried about you. We understand you were very ill."

"Yes," said Omar. "I was. But I'm feeling better."

"You were in a coma?"

"Yes," said Omar.

"Did you manage to get any research done? It would be awful to go that far for nothing."

"I did a little," said Omar. "But I'd like to talk to you about the fellowship."

"Of course," said Lucy. "Could you come by my office later this afternoon? About four?"

"Yes," said Omar.

"Great," said Lucy. "I'll see you then. Oh, I've moved into Garfield's office. So don't go looking for me down in the basement."

"Okay," said Omar. "I won't."

Lucy had obviously spent much time redecorating Nicholson Garfield's office, which was a large room on the top floor of Dawe Hall with a windowed bay and a fireplace. She had installed a couch and some easy chairs in the bay and had replaced the paper blinds with curtains. It was all very homey.

Lucy saw Omar looking around at the changes and said, "Since I'll have to spend so much time in here, I decided to fix it up a bit, make it more like home. My home away from home! I don't know how Garfield could stand it, although all I think he did in here was sexually harass women and smoke that awful pipe. I had the windows wide open for days getting the stink out." Lucy shuddered. "I nearly froze myself to death, but at least I can breathe now. Let's sit over there." She indicated the alcove. "It's cozier, I think. I feel too much like Garfield behind this desk. He wanted to take the desk with him, which was fine with me, but we couldn't get it out of the door. And there was no way it could go down the stairs. Apparently it was hoisted through the window centuries ago, so I'm stuck with it. *C'est* hideous, *non?*"

"*Oui,*" said Omar. It was a huge desk, intricately carved, with an abundance of claw feet.

Lucy assumed a rocking chair and nodded at the couch. Omar sat down. Lucy took a shawl off the back of the chair and wrapped it around her shoulders. "It's chilly over here by the windows. I'm having maintenance come look at the fireplace. Garfield had it filled with junk. No one seems to know if it works. Wouldn't it be lovely if it does? I was thinking I could host fireside teas in here, a few members of the faculty each week, and select a topic to discuss. You might speak one week about your work with Gunk. I really think the intellectual life and the social life of the university should be more entwined." She laced her fingers together by way of illustration. "Or perhaps not just the English faculty, perhaps inviting people from other departments, bring them together, a chemist, a historian, someone from gender studies: bringing a group like that together for fireside teas, I think it could make a world of difference."

Omar allowed as how it would.

"Speaking of tea, would you like some? I can ask Kathy to brew us a pot, if you'd like. I've got some lovely loose Darjeeling."

"No, thank you," said Omar.

"Well," said Lucy, leaning back in her chair and rocking a little. "I'm so glad to hear that despite your trouble your trip was a success. I think it's wonderful you got the Siebert Petrie Award, Omar. Really, I do. Have I ever told you? You know I was on the committee, don't you? Some people—Garfield for one—were a little skeptical about your project; they didn't think Gunk was a known-enough commodity."

"It's Gund," said Omar.

"What?"

"It's Gund, who I'm working on: Jules Gund. Not Gunk."

"Gund, of course, Gund. I thought I said Gund. Whatever. My point is, I went to bat for you. Garfield was all excited by Teresha Lake's work on Hawthorne. Personally, I think we know all we need to know about Hawthorne, but someone like Gund, well, we're breaking ground here. We're on the cutting edge, and that's where I want this department to be."

Omar stood up. He looked past Lucy, out the bay windows. It had gotten dark while they sat there and the lamps along the pathways were lit. It was snowing, the flakes falling quickly and thickly, with a depressing insistency, as if they were in a hurry to bury the earth.

"I've decided not to write the biography," he said. "I've decided to return the award."

"Omar! What are you talking about? I thought you said you had done some research down there—"

"No," said Omar. "I'm sorry. I was lying. I've decided not to write a biography of Jules Gund."

"Why?" asked Lucy. "Why not?"

Omar shook his head. "And I won't be coming back next semester. I've decided to leave academia."

"Why? Is this something to do with Garfield? I'm committed to change, Omar, really I am. I want things to be different in the department."

"It's nothing to do with the department," said Omar.

"Then I don't understand. Do you have a better offer someplace?"

"No," said Omar.

"Then what?" asked Lucy.

"It's just not what I want," said Omar.

"Oh," said Lucy. "What do you mean: writing the biography or teaching?"

"Both," said Omar.

"Oh," Lucy said again. "Well, I'm sure you know what's best for you. At least I assume you do. And perhaps you're right. I mean, I was looking over all the student evaluations—one thing I mean to do is to improve the level of teaching throughout the department— and I did notice some comments about you that frankly gave me pause. Perhaps you aren't meant to be a teacher, Omar."

"Yes," said Omar. "Perhaps not."

"Well, it can be a curse, you know," said Lucy, with a faux-bright laugh. "I wouldn't wish it on anyone. Best to cast the mantle off now, before it weighs too heavily upon you, and all is lost."

"That's exactly what I think," said Omar.

"But it's such a shame: your work with Gund, and the fellowship. But perhaps he is too negligible."

"I think he is," said Omar. "I found there really isn't much there."

"Yes," said Lucy. "That's often the case with writers: the dreariness of their lives! And we critics vainly rooting through things, trying to find something—anything—in the prosaic murk. That's why it's so wonderful working on Woolf—there's so much there. Simply no end to it. But with someone like Gund, you're well out of it, I suppose. But I'll miss you. It was nice having someone from your cultural background in the program. We will all miss that."

"Well," said Omar, "I just wanted to let you know as soon as possible, so you could plan accordingly for next year."

"Thanks," said Lucy. "You will finish out the semester, won't you?"

"Of course," said Omar.

"Good," said Lucy. She shook his hand. "Well," she said, "it's back to work for me. I'm learning a department chair's work is never done. I don't know how Garfield did it. I suppose he simply didn't do it."

"Yes," said Omar. "I suppose that was his trick."

Deirdre was on her way to Tai Chi when she saw the LOST DOG poster taped to the streetlight. She recognized Omar's writing:

LOST DOG
small hairy white dog named Mitzie
lost near Hiawatha Woods on Wednesday, Jan. 16
please call 448-2123 with information

Oh God, she thought: Omar's lost Mitzie. That stupid dog! As she passed Kiplings, she glanced in the window and was surprised to see Omar sitting alone at the bar, drinking a beer. She turned around and entered the restaurant. She sat on the stool beside him.

He was preoccupied and did not look up from his beer until she touched him. "Deirdre!" he said. "What are you doing here?"

"I saw you. I was on my way to Tai Chi." She looked at her watch. She would be late now. "I saw you sitting here. What are you doing?" She helped herself to some of his beer.

"Do you want a beer?" he asked.

"No," she said. "I have Tai Chi. But what are you doing here? I saw the Mitzie poster. How long has she been gone?"

"Since yesterday. Gwendolyn Pierce left her outside. And she never came back. I don't know what to do. I called the police. They haven't found any dogs, dead or alive. So I put up the signs."

"You should have put a picture on the sign. So people would know her if they see her."

"I couldn't find a picture. Yvonne hid all her personal stuff. Or maybe she doesn't have any personal stuff. That's why I described her."

"Yes, but small, hairy, white: that could describe a lot of dogs."

"Well, it was the best I could do."

"Well, don't worry about it," said Deirdre. "It isn't your fault."

"Of course it's my fault!" said Omar. "I'm responsible for Mitzie."

"Yes, and when you went away Gwen Pierce was responsible for Mitzie. If she hadn't left her outside this wouldn't have happened. It was stupid of her. Irresponsible."

Omar said nothing. He rested his face in his hands. "You should go to Tai Chi," he said. "Or you'll be late."

Deirdre put her hand on his back. She had the feeling that he was crying but his face was covered by his hands. "What's wrong, Omar?" she asked.

"Everything," said Omar. And then he made a noise that was like crying.

"Oh, Omar," Deirdre said. She patted his back. "Tell me.

What's wrong? Mitzie is just a dog. She'll come back. And if she doesn't, well—it's not the end of the world. You mustn't be so upset about it. Yvonne will understand. It wasn't your fault. If Mitzie ran away, it's about Mitzie, it's not about you."

"It isn't Mitzie," said Omar. "I could care less about Mitzie. I mean, I couldn't care less."

"Then what is it?" asked Deirdre. "What's wrong?"

Omar gulped. Her hand bounced on his back, but she kept it there, pressed lightly against him. She could feel the warmth of his skin through his shirt. He was wearing a shirt she had given him for his birthday two years ago: a pale green shirt made of chamois. It looked very nice with his dark hair.

After a moment she said, "What's wrong?" again.

He lifted his face away from his hands and looked at her. "I just met with Lucy Greene-Kessler," he said. "I told her I was returning the grant. Or returning what's left of it. I'm not writing a biography of Gund."

For a moment Deirdre said nothing. She drank again from Omar's beer. Then she asked the bartender for a beer of her own. When the frosty pint was placed in front of her she said, carefully, quietly, "Omar, what happened to you in Uruguay? I mean, I know about the bee, but what happened to you that made you not want to write the biography? Tell me, please."

"I just realized that I don't want to write a biography of Jules Gund. I don't want to write a biography of anyone."

"But why? Why not? Did something happen? Did you find something out?"

"No," said Omar. "I can't say. I can't explain it."

"Omar, you can't let your sympathies get in your way."

"Why not?"

"Because you got authorization to write the book. That is what matters. Whatever squabbles there were between them, or whatever hesitations they may have expressed—well, you can't let that bother you. You can't let it affect you. You've got to be a bit ruthless, I think, to write a biography."

"I don't want to be ruthless. I'm giving the fellowship money back. I won't get my degree."

"How can you give the money back? You've already spent some of it."

"I'll find a way. I'll borrow it from someone. Or maybe they won't make me pay it all back. I don't know. That's not what matters. What matters is that I stop this."

"Stop what?"

Omar sat up straight and looked around the bar for a moment. They were the only ones there. He made a vague gesture around him. He said, "I've got to stop this," he said. "I've got to stop this life I am leading that is wrong for me. That is not mine."

"What do you mean, not yours? Of course it is yours. What are you talking about? Did you call the doctor? Did you make an appointment?"

Omar looked at her. "It isn't mine," he said. "I don't know what I've been doing. I'm sorry, Deirdre."

"What about us?" said Deirdre. "Do you feel that way about us? What about me?"

"I think there is something wrong there too. I'm sorry. I think I am not myself with you."

"Of course you're yourself! Omar! I love you!"

"I don't think you can love me," said Omar. "I don't think you know me very well."

Deirdre regarded her beer. It had a very thick head of foam. She watched it settle, the tiny bubbles collapsing with faint, bursting cries. Then she turned back to Omar. "It hurts me so much that you would say that, Omar. I do love you! And of course I know you. After all we've been through. I mean of course I don't know everything about you, I don't know you entirely, but no one knows anyone like that. I know you better than anyone else, I think."

Omar thought of Arden, who had kissed him. Who he had kissed. Did she know him? It had seemed, in some weird way, that she had. From the first moment he had met her he had felt relaxed in some fundamental way: it was not knowing, of course, for Arden did not know him. But what was it? If not knowing, what?

"Perhaps you do know me," said Omar. "But maybe it isn't that. I don't think you get me."

"Get you? What do you mean? Get you?"

"You always seem to want to change me," said Omar.

"I don't want to change you! If you think that, you don't understand. Oh, Omar: I love you. I don't want to change you. But I do want you to do the things you're capable of doing, the things that are in your best interest to do. Yes: I want you to do those things. And if I encourage you to do them, that isn't changing you! That's encouraging you! It's helping you."

"Perhaps we disagree on what is in my best interest," said Omar.

"Oh," said Deirdre. "Well, what do you think is in your best interest? Do you think not writing the biography and giving the fellowship money back and dropping out of the program is in your best interest?"

"Yes," said Omar. "I think it is."

"And how—I'm just curious; I just wonder—how do you think that?"

"I'm sorry, Deirdre. You know my father wanted me to go to medical school. And I couldn't do that. And I loved books, I love reading, so I thought I would get a Ph.D. in literature, but it's not right for me. I love books and I love reading but that's it. I don't love teaching or writing or anything else about this. I'm not good at it and I don't like it. I'm not like you. I am sorry, but I am not like you."

Deirdre said nothing. She drank from her beer. After a moment she looked at Omar. There were tears on her cheeks. "So what will you do?" she asked. "What is it you want to do?"

"I don't know," said Omar. "I'm twenty-eight years old and I don't know what I want to do. I don't know what I can do. I don't know anything."

"I don't want to cry here," said Deirdre. "I don't want to cry here, at stupid fucking Kiplings."

"I'm sorry, Deirdre."

"You're sorry! Oh, how I hate you! No, I don't hate you, it's just that, oh, Omar, I wanted so badly, so very very badly, for all of this to happen for you. I suppose selfishly, I suppose it was all about me, me and you, but nevertheless, I wanted it to happen for you. I was so proud of you: going to Uruguay—Uruguay!—all by yourself, and getting authorization, I could see this whole future for you unfolding, this good future, and it seemed right to me, but perhaps you're right, perhaps I don't know you or get you, perhaps it is all wrong for you, but I only wanted you to be happy, to succeed and be happy."

"I wouldn't have gone there if it wasn't for you," said Omar.

"Yes. And what did it get you? A bee sting. A coma. A miserable journey home."

They were silent a moment, and then Omar said, "I think I'll go home now. I'm tired. I still get tired. We can talk about this more, later. Can you still make it to Tai Chi?"

Deirdre looked at her watch. "No," she said.

"I'm sorry," said Omar.

"Don't be sorry."

"But I am." Omar stood up. He leaned forward and kissed Deirdre's wet cheek. "I am very grateful to you," he said.

"For what? For not getting you?"

"No," said Omar. "For loving me."

It was like a dream: his headlights tunneled the darkness, revealing Mitzie on the front porch. She looked quizzically at the car, and when he emerged from it, she ran toward him, barking, and threw herself up at him: she remembered him, she had returned, and she was happy, simply happy, to see him again.

Sometime after Omar went to bed the phone rang. He wasn't sure how late it was. He got up and answered it.

"Hello," he said.

"I'm calling about your lost dog," a woman said. "Your little hairy white dog. I have it here with me."

For a second, in his grogginess, Omar forgot that Mitzie had come back. Or maybe that was a dream. "Really?" he said.

"Yes," said the woman. "Is there a reward?"

Omar was confused. "Wait a minute," he said. He put down the phone and went to the kitchen. Mitzie was sleeping in her bed. She looked up at him curiously. He went back to the phone. "I'm afraid you're mistaken," he said. "I've found my dog."

"You're too cheap to pay a reward?" the woman said.

"No," said Omar. "That's not it. My dog is here. She came back."

"Fuck you," the woman said. She hung up.

Omar went back into the kitchen. He petted Mitzie and drank a glass of water. He ate a horrible sugar-free cookie Gwendolyn Pierce had left behind. Then he got dressed and drove into town. He parked at the bank and walked around, taking down all the LOST DOG signs. It took him a long time because he had to remember all the places he'd posted them. He wanted to make sure he got them all. He had put up twenty but could find only seventeen. Maybe someone had taken the missing three, or maybe they were still posted somewhere.

CHAPTER TWENTY-ONE

February 7, 1996

Dear Mr. Gund, Mrs. Gund, and Ms. Langdon:

I am writing to thank you all for the incredibly generous hospitality you showed me while I was in Uruguay. I apologize for descending upon you in what I now see was a very rude and inconsiderate way. My rudeness makes your hospitality all the more remarkable.

I am feeling much better now. I'm still a little tired, but every day I feel I have more energy and strength. I am very grateful for your, and Dr. Peni's, good care. Thank you.

In addition to thanking you I wanted to inform you that I will not be writing a biography of Jules Gund. I wish I could easily explain to you why I have decided against writing the biography, but I'm afraid I cannot. Suffice it to say I have decided to leave academia and pursue other avenues. I'm sorry to have bothered you with my request and appreciate the careful consideration you gave it.

I will always remember my time at Ochos Rios (despite my illness) as a wonderful period in my life. I learned a lot from all of you for which I am grateful.

Again, I apologize for the inconvenience I have caused you.

My best wishes to you, and to Pete and Portia as well.

Sincerely,
Omar Razaghi

CHAPTER TWENTY-TWO

Lucy Greene-Kessler had an end-of-semester barbecue in her back-yard. Omar was sitting at a picnic table when he felt two hands on his shoulders, gently shaking, and then massaging, him. Deirdre sat beside him. She had rather a lot on her plate: barbecued chicken and potato salad and fruit salad and macaroni salad. "Long time, no see," she said.

"Hello," said Omar.

"How are you?"

"I'm okay," said Omar. "How are you?"

"I'm fine," said Deirdre. "I can't believe you're here. You've sort of disappeared."

"I was lying low."

"Very low," said Deirdre. "Thank God for Lucy Greene-Kessler's ascension. Although I'm surprised to see you here."

"I wasn't going to come," said Omar. "But then I realized I did want to say goodbye to people."

"Where are you going?"

"I'm moving back to Toronto. I'm going to live with my parents for a while."

"And do what?"

"My father got me a job at the hospital. I'm going to be a physical-therapy aid."

"What will you do?"

"Hold people down while they're tortured, I think," said Omar.

"When do you go to Toronto?"

"As soon as Yvonne returns. The first week in June."

"Are you really going to live with your parents and work in a hospital?"

"Yes," said Omar. "For a while, at least."

"Will you wear a uniform?"

"I suppose," said Omar.

"Will you be okay?"

"I think so. People don't die of wearing uniforms, and living with their parents in Toronto."

Deirdre wanted to say: Yes, they do, in ways they do, in ways they don't know, can't see, they do. But then we're all dying, she thought, in ways we can't see and don't know. She pushed her overladen plate away.

"Do you want to go for a little walk?"

"Where?"

"I don't know. Nowhere. Around the block."

"Now?" asked Omar.

"No," said Deirdre, "years from now."

Lucy lived in a nice old neighborhood: houses with manicured shrubs and porches and seasonal wreaths or flags on their front doors. They walked up the driveway and began ambling along the sidewalk, the slabs of which were cracked and upset by the spreading roots of the large old trees that lined the street. They said nothing until they turned the corner.

"I got the job at Bucknell," said Deirdre.

"Did you? Congratulations! That's great."

"Yeah, well, it's just a one-year appointment. Totally exploitative. But I figure what the hell."

"It's a good place to teach," said Omar. "It's in Ohio, right?"

"Pennsylvania. In cow fields. No big lights, bright city for *moi*."

"When will you go?"

"Not till August. I'm teaching summer session here. Oh, Omar. Are you really going to Toronto?"

"Yes," said Omar. "At least for a while. Till I figure out what I want to do. Or what I can do."

"What do you want to do?"

"I don't know," said Omar. "That's what I'm going to Toronto to figure out. There's no point in my staying here."

"You could get a job here," said Deirdre.

"Yes," said Omar, "selling shoes at the mall."

"I just can't picture you working in a hospital."

"It's just for a while. I need to make some money. And—figure things out."

Deirdre pulled a new leaf, a fat green baby leaf, off a tree and shredded it.

"Have you heard from them?"

"Who?"

"You know who. The folk from down below." She nodded at the buckled sidewalk.

"No," said Omar.

"Do you wish— Do you still think you made the right decision?"

"Yes," said Omar.

"You don't want to talk about this, do you?"

"No," said Omar.

"Do you not want to talk about this or do you not want to talk about this with me?"

Omar shrugged. They stepped aside, giving right-of-way to a

young girl manically pedaling a tricycle. When she was past them, Deirdre said, "It's so weird. I know we're not a couple anymore, we're not intimate, we don't talk every day the way we used to, but it seems so strange, so weird, that my concern for you should just cease. Desist. Because it doesn't."

"Concern?" said Omar.

"I don't know the word," said Deirdre. "Maybe love. I don't know. It's been so hard, not being in touch with you. It's made me feel sick." She flung the pulpy bits of leaf down onto the sidewalk.

"I just want to forget about it all," said Omar.

"Us?"

"No—not that. Of course not that. I meant the end, the trip, the book, all of that. I want to forget that."

"Why?" asked Deirdre.

"No," said Omar. "Not forget it. But just let it be. Let it alone. Not think about it, or talk about it."

"I think about it," said Deirdre. "I wonder about it."

Omar said nothing.

"Omar?" Deirdre asked.

Omar said nothing.

"Omar," Deirdre said again, "can I ask you a question?"

She was looking at him, but he was looking ahead of them, down the sidewalk, which rose and fell like geological plates. He nodded his head.

"Did you— I've been thinking, trying to figure it out. You were so strange. It was all so strange. Did you fall in love with Arden? Is that what happened? I mean, besides the bee—"

They were passing a house that was built on a slight incline above the street; the lawn was banked and the walkway leading to the front door commenced in a series of steps. Omar sat down on the bottom step and covered his face with his hands; he sat down on the step very naturally, as if this were his house, as if he lived here, and was home, and had the absolute right to live his life, or a moment of it, sitting on the step. Deirdre glanced around, but the street was empty, the girl on the tricycle had disappeared. She sat down beside Omar.

Omar uncovered his face. His eyes looked a bit blurry and bruised, as if he had ground his fists into their sockets. He had lost weight, she realized; she had never noticed he had eye sockets before. He said, "I just have to get over it."

Deirdre said nothing for a moment. She was aware of the moment: she and Omar sitting side by side on the steps of some house. This is where it ends, she thought. And we won't ever know whose house it is, or what their story is, what drama is being played out behind us, up the walk and inside the green front door, past the rhododendron bushes. No: we won't ever know that.

"Or not," she said.

"What?" said Omar.

"You can just get over it," she said, "or not."

"I have to get over it," said Omar. "I have to figure out what I'm doing, or no: what I can do, and do it."

"Yes," said Deirdre. "Holding people down while they're tortured in a hospital in Toronto sounds like an excellent way to figure that out."

"What else can I do?" asked Omar.

"You can do anything you want," said Deirdre.

"Yes," said Omar, "and tomorrow is the first day of the rest of my life."

Deirdre said nothing for a moment, and then she said: "You could go and love Arden. Or try to, at least. I think it would come easier to you, than holding people down, whilst they are tortured."

"She doesn't love me," said Omar.

"How do you know?"

"She told me."

"Perhaps she was wrong. People are often wrong about these things, you know." She paused. "Present company excepted, of course. I was not wrong: I did love you, you know."

"I know," said Omar.

"Good," said Deirdre. "I worry about that." She paused, and then said, "I miss you."

"I miss you too," said Omar.

"Good," said Deirdre. She touched him. "Good."

She stood up. "For what's it worth, I don't vote for Toronto. I think you should go to Uruguay."

Omar laughed.

"What?" asked Deirdre.

"You're always pushing me to go to Uruguay," said Omar.

"Not always," said Deirdre. "Just twice." She held out her hand. "Come," she said. "We should go back."

CHAPTER TWENTY-THREE

She was late; she had missed her connecting flight in Miami, so instead of arriving in New York early in the evening she arrived there after midnight. By the time she was reunited with her baggage and had cleared customs it was 1:30 A.M. She fell asleep in the taxi and woke as it passed Yankee Stadium; she knew, or thought she knew from her distant knowledge of New York City geography, that this was wrong, that she should not be passing Yankee Stadium, which glowed hugely and palely in the night like an edifice in a dream. Perhaps she was dreaming. She sat forward and rapped on the glass—well, Plexiglass—divider. For a moment she had to think what language to speak in.

"Where are we?" she asked. "Why are we passing Yankee Stadium? I want to go to Manhattan. Jane Street, in Greenwich Village."

"This is a shortcut," the driver said. He had a beautiful face: sad, dark eyes that met hers tiredly in the rearview mirror. "There is much traffic the other way."

"It's the middle of the night!" she said. "There is no traffic!"

"It is quick, this way," he said. "I get you fast to Greenwich Village. Relax, ma'am, and you will be happy."

She leaned back against the seat, and looked out at the dark deserted city. She would not tip him.

He pulled up to the curb. "Here, ma'am. We are here."

She leaned forward and looked out at the building. It did not look the same to her, it did not look as she remembered it, but she had not seen it in over thirty years. But she had lived here once, for a year or two, late in the fifties. Had it been here? It looked so different. The number was right. "Is this Jane Street?" she asked him.

"Yes, ma'am," he said.

She paid him, and tipped him. He had gotten her there, after all, and what did she know? Perhaps Yankee Stadium was on the way. Perhaps it had moved. He lifted her suitcase out of the trunk and set it on the sidewalk. It was a lovely night, cool, the trees in succulent green leaf.

"This is your building, yes?" he asked.

"Yes," she said. "Thank you. Good night."

He got back in the cab. For a moment he sat there, watching her. Then he drove away. There was a smell of New York that she remembered. She stood there, beside her bag, on the sidewalk, breathing in the smell.

After a moment she climbed the steps into the lighted foyer. She was supposed to get the keys from the superintendent, but she was supposed to have arrived at 6 P.M. But there was nothing else to do. She did not know where there was a hotel. She supposed she could sit on the stoop until dawn, but her exhaustion emboldened her. She pushed the buzzer that was labeled SUPER. There was no response, so she pushed it again, and again, longer. She held it down. Finally a squawking voice burst forth from the intercom. "Hello!" she called into it. "It's Caroline Gund."

278

The door buzzed and she pushed it open with her foot. She slid her suitcase into the lobby and followed it. She stood there for a moment, panting, as if she had climbed a mountain. She could not remember where the superintendent's apartment was. She did not remember there being a superintendent. She could picture their apartment, in the back of the building, on the top floor. She stood besides the mailboxes. She saw the mailbox that was labeled m. des-courtieux. She touched it.

The elevator opened and a man stepped out of it, tucking his shirt into his pants. For a moment she mistook him for the taxi driver: he had the same eyes, the same sad, tired eyes.

"Mrs. Gund?" he said.

"Yes," she said.

He held up a set of keys on a ring. "Here are the keys."

"I'm sorry I'm so late," she said. "I'm sorry to wake you."

"It's okay," he said. He gave her the keys. "Do you need help?" he nodded at her suitcase.

"No," she said. "Thank you."

"I'm sorry about your sister," he said. "She was a very nice woman. A real lady."

"Yes," she said.

"She lived here a long time," he said.

"Yes," she said. "Forty years."

"Wow," he said. "Mr. Perth, in 6B, he has Hugo."

She did not understand what he meant so she merely nodded. "I'm very tired," she said.

He looked at her for a moment. "You come from where?" he asked. "Russia?"

"No," she said. "Uruguay. Thank you for the key. Good night."

He said good night and disappeared into the elevator. She waited a moment and then pushed the button, and after a moment the elevator returned, emptied, and she stepped into it with her suitcase.

She had trouble with the locks and keys, but finally the door swung open. The apartment was dark. She remembered the long hall. She remembered where the light switch was and felt for it, touched it, turned it on. She closed the door behind her and bolted it. There was a low bookcase along one wall, ceramic bowls of coins and matchbooks and Christmas ornaments and old keys placed along the top of it. Above it was a framed Paul Klee print. She put her suitcase on the worn wood floor and walked down the hall. She passed the kitchen and walked into the living room. Of course it was differently furnished, but the room itself was different from how she had remembered it. In her memory it had windows on two walls. She turned on a table lamp and looked around the room. It was very crowded with things: books and paintings and furniture and plants, but in its own way it was very neat and ordered. Everything had its spot. She opened the casement window and leaned out. All the windows were dark. Everyone was sleeping. It was quiet. Even for New York City, it was very quiet. She walked slowly around the room, touching the sofa, the chairs, the wooden tables. Dust.

She went back down the hall and got her suitcase and took it into the bedroom. She paused in the doorway. This is where she had slept with her sister, on mattresses on the floor. Margot had a job working at Bergdorf Goodman's. She had a job checking coats at a restaurant called Périgord. During the day she took painting and drawing classes at the Art Students League. In some ways it was all still there, those happy years in New York, those years that had ceased to exist, to be spoken of. Such complete neglect had fixed them in amber; they had not been muddied or distorted by recollection. She turned on the overhead light, but no light came on. She looked up and saw that there was no fixture, just wires dangling from the socket. Was the light being repaired someplace? Was it being replaced? She turned on the lamp on the bedside table. Of course, the mattresses were gone; they had been replaced by an antique wooden sleigh bed; its coverlet hastily pulled up over itself.

Margot had not had time to make the bed properly before they took her to the hospital. Caroline wondered if she went in an ambulance. How do you leave your home for the last time? Did she know she would never come back? For three weeks, while she lay dying in the hospital, her bed had waited here for her. Caroline sat down on the bed. After a moment she lowered her face to the pillow and breathed deeply, to see if she could smell her sister, to see if that, at least, remained.

She slept late and woke up, disoriented, in the sleigh bed. She lay in bed, looked around the strange room, and let the circumstances slowly rise to the surface: Margot was dead. She had come to New York to deal with her things: her apartment, her business.

She got up and showered, thinking the lilac-scented soap had touched her sister's skin. She looked at all the toiletries in the medicine cabinet: the bottles of lotion and perfume, the pots of makeup, the assorted prescription drugs. *Descourtieux, Margot. Take one capsule three times a day as needed to relieve pain.*

She decided to start with the kitchen. She found a plastic shopping bag and began to fill it with the contents of the refrigerator. She had quickly filled one bag and was starting on a second when there was a knock on the door. She paused for a moment. Who could it be? No one knew she was there.

The knock was repeated.

She went down the hall and opened the door. A young man, maybe in his early thirties, stood outside the door. He was casually dressed in jeans and had bare feet. "Hi," he said. "I'm Tom Perth. I live in 6B, next door. Are you Margot's sister?"

"Yes," said Caroline. "I'm Caroline Gund."

He held out his hand, and she shook it.

"Antonio, the super, told me you had arrived. I just wanted to let you know I have Hugo."

"Who is Hugo?" Caroline asked.

"Oh," said Tom Perth. "Hugo is Margot's dog. You didn't know she had a dog?"

"No," said Caroline.

"He's a French bulldog. I've been taking care of him ever since Margot went into the hospital."

"Thank you," said Caroline.

"I'm going to L.A. tomorrow. No, not tomorrow: Thursday. So I'll have to return him to you."

"Oh," said Caroline. A dog! What would she do with a dog? "Perhaps you would like to keep him?"

"I love Hugo, but I can't. I travel too much."

"Oh," said Caroline.

"You can't take him?" he asked.

"No. I'm just here visiting. I live in Uruguay."

"I thought Margot was French."

"She was. I just happen to live in Uruguay."

"Well, listen, I'll bring Hugo over later. Will you be around this afternoon?"

"Yes," said Caroline. "Or wait—no. I have an appointment with Margot's lawyer at two o'clock."

"Okay. I'll come over later, then. Around six?"

"Yes, of course," said Caroline. "I will be here then. Is there anything I need to get, to take care of the dog?"

"I have all his stuff. I'll bring it over. I'll see you later, then." He turned to go.

"Wait," said Caroline.

He turned back.

"Excuse me—I'm just curious—did you know my sister well?"

"Fairly well, as far as New York City neighbors go. We'd have dinner once in a while, and I took care of Hugo when she traveled."

"Did she travel a lot?"

"Yes, for her business, a couple times a year."

"I didn't know her well," said Caroline. "We were not in touch."

"She never mentioned you," he said.

"No," said Caroline. "I'm not surprised."

"You look like her," said Tom Perth.

"Do I?" said Caroline.

"Yes," he said. "Listen, I gotta go. I have an appointment for a massage at eleven. I'll see you this evening."

"Of course," said Caroline. "Thank you." She stepped back into the apartment and closed the door. A dog, she thought. Hugo. What can I do with her dog?

Tamara Shelley, Margot's lawyer, told Caroline that Margot's will had clearly broken her estate into three parts: her business, her savings, and her apartment. Her business, Descourtieux Textiles & Fabrics, Inc., which designed and imported fabric, had been left to her associate, a woman named Anna Powell. Her savings and retirement funds, which Tamara estimated totaled $400,000, was to be divided evenly among the American Cancer Society, Planned Parenthood, and the Fresh Air Fund. Her apartment, which had turned into a co-op at some point in the seventies and which Margot now owned, was left to Caroline, as was everything it contained: art, furnishings, clothes, books, jewelry.

It was a very sensible and straightforward will, Tamara concluded, and she anticipated no problems in executing it.

Caroline asked her how quickly she could sell the apartment. Tamara told her she could not sell it until the will had been probated, and she had assumed ownership, which could take from six to eight months, but in any case, she advised Caroline not to sell as the real estate market was on its way up and the value of the apartment would undoubtedly increase over the next few years. She recommended subletting, which Caroline could legally do for three out of any consecutive five-year periods. Remove everything valuable and personal from the premises, she advised, and sublet it furnished. She gave Caroline the name of several agencies that specialized in such situations, asked Caroline to sign several forms, and then bid her good day.

Caroline remembered the dog. What was she to do with him? Did the will mention him? To whom did he now belong?

The will did not mention a dog. Presumably he fell in with the contents of the apartment. Caroline was free to keep him, sell him, or dispose of him in any way she saw fit. Tamara believed both the ASPCA and the North Shore Animal League took unwanted pets.

Caroline walked out onto the busy midtown streets in a sort of daze. Why had Margot left her the apartment? And all her things? Why did she want Caroline to have them?

She found herself on Fifth Avenue; she stood for a moment and let the swarm of pedestrians flow around her. It was a beautiful day, late in the spring, with the feeling of summer. She walked up toward the park, and into Bergdorf's. Margot had worked behind a counter on the main floor that sold silk scarves and handkerchiefs. Grace Kelly had come in one day and bought a white linen kerchief beaded with Austrian crystals from Margot. Grace Kelly was dead. Margot was dead.

A girl at the Lancôme counter asked Caroline if she would like to be made up. No, Caroline said, and pushed herself out the doors and back onto the street. She sat on a bench in the park, beside a child and her mother. The child dispiritedly ate some sort of pink ice cream thing on a stick. Caroline closed her eyes and let the sun fall on her. She could feel the city around her, hear it thrumming. She had supposed she would never come back here. She had gotten Jules and Margot had gotten New York. It had seemed fair enough. Now, suddenly, she owned an apartment here. She could go back downtown and bolt the door and stand in the room and no one would know she was there or what she was doing. She could paint the walls. She could buy flowers from the market on the corner: she had seem them there, buckets of peonies, cosmos, phlox.

She was hot when she got back to the apartment so she showered again with the lilac-scented soap and pinned her damp hair up high on her head. She had bought the peonies, an expensive armful of them, their beautiful creamy fists nodding and unfurling in a Waterford vase in the living room. She had also bought a bottle of Gavi and cherries and pistachio nuts.

He knocked a little after six o'clock. She opened the door. He was wearing a white dress shirt and pale blue linen pants and had the dog on a leash. His blond hair was combed back from his face.

"Hello," she said. "Won't you come in?"

She stepped aside and he and the dog walked into the apartment.

"So this is Hugo," she said, closing the door. It was a medium-size dog, fawn-colored, with an ugly smashed face and bat ears. It gazed up at her with its imploring dog eyes. She bent down and touched its brow. It slobbered.

"Yes," said Tom. "This is Hugo. Poor Hugo. He doesn't much like the heat."

"I shall get him a bowl of water," she said. "Come!" she said, to both man and dog, and walked toward the kitchen. She filled a glass bowl with cold water and placed it on the floor. Tom unsnapped the leash. Hugo sat down and panted.

"Well, I would like a drink," said Caroline. "Will you join me?"

"Sure," said Tom.

"I'm afraid all I have is white wine," she said. "Will that be okay?"

"That will be fine," he said.

She took the wine out of the now empty refrigerator and

opened it. Margot had very nice wineglasses; she filled two of them and handed one to Tom. "Let's go sit in the living room," she said. "I think it's cooler."

Hugo had lain down on the kitchen floor. They left him there and went into the other room. Tom sat in a chair that was covered in old chintz; she sat on the sofa. She pushed the bowl of nuts toward him. "How long have you lived here?" she asked.

"Almost ten years," he said. "The whole time I've been in New York."

"And where were you before that?"

"I grew up in Maine," he said.

He stood up, and looked around the room. He went over to the window and looked out. Then he sat back down. "It feels so odd," he said. "To be in here, without Margot."

Caroline said nothing. She sipped her wine.

"What brought you to Uruguay?" he asked, after a moment.

"I married a Uruguayan," she said.

"Oh," he said. "Do you like it there?"

"Yes," she said. "Very much. It's beautiful and peaceful. I lived here, you know, with Margot. In this apartment. Years and years ago. In 1959."

"Wow," he said.

"You said you knew her fairly well?"

"I liked Margot. We got along. But we weren't exactly close."

"Was she happy, do you think?"

He thought for a moment, studying his wine. Then he looked up at her. "Sometimes I would see her at night, if she didn't close her drapes—my apartment is directly across the way." He pointed out the window. "I'd come home late at night sometimes, and see her in here, sitting where you are, on the couch, reading. She wore glasses to read. I never saw her wear them in public. Sometimes, I'd come over. We'd just talk for a little while. She'd make some tea, and we'd sit here and talk. She had very good tea; she brought it back from Paris with her. She gave me some. I still have it."

"Do you think she was happy?" Caroline asked.

"Yes," he said. "In a way. She always seemed composed and gracious, content. I think she liked her life. You got that feeling."

"Good," said Caroline. "Did she—do you know if she had friends? Romances?"

"Of course she had friends," said Tom. "She had many friends. She had dinner parties often—she was a terrific cook—and a big party every year at Christmastime. She'd use my refrigerator for her big party."

Caroline was touching her finger to the thin rim of her wineglass.

"Every time she went away, when I would take care of Hugo, she would bring me back something. Not something stupid, like most people would. Something nice. A beautiful tie, or a bowl, or antique cufflinks. She once had a shirt made for me, in Italy, from fabric she had found in a flea market. She was very generous. Some of the nicest things I have are from Margot."

Caroline put her glass of wine down on the table. She wiped at the tears on her cheeks.

"I'm sorry," he said. "I didn't mean to upset you."

"No," she said. "Please— I want to hear, I know so little about her."

"Why?" he asked. "You seem so like her. I would have thought you would be friends."

"We were," she said. "We lived here together, as I said—"

"And what happened?"

She picked up her glass and sipped the wine. He reached forward and took a pistachio from the bowl. "I fell in love with her boyfriend," Caroline said. "I married him."

"The Uruguayan?"

"Yes," she said, and smiled a little: Jules, the Uruguayan.

"Oh," he said.

"It was an awful thing to do," she said. "The worst thing, I suppose, a sister can do."

"But you did it—I'm sure you did not do it maliciously," he said.

"No," she said. "I was very young, and it happened so quickly. We got married," said Caroline. "Secretly, at City Hall, and left that same night for Uruguay. We wrote Margot letters, begging her to forgive us. Of course, she did not. She could not. I never heard from her again."

"Wow," said Tom. "And you've been in Uruguay ever since then?"

"Yes," said Caroline. "I've been back to Paris, a few times, to see my mother. But never back here. Not until now."

Hugo appeared in the open doorway. He whined quietly, and looked from one of them to the other.

"Are you ready for your walk, Hugo?" Tom asked. "He usually gets walked now," he said to Caroline.

"How many times a day does he get walked?"

"Three, usually. In the morning, about now, and then before bed. Why don't we go out, and I can show you where he likes to go."

At the corner, Tom handed Caroline the leash. "Here," he said. "You take him, he should get used to you. He gets a long walk now, over to the river. In the morning and at night you can just go around the block. He doesn't need much exercise."

Caroline took the leash and they crossed the street.

"Do you like dogs?" Tom asked.

"I don't know," said Caroline. "I've never had a dog."

"Hugo is a very sweet dog. He's very good, well-trained."

"Are you sure you can't take him? It would be so nice if you could."

Tom shook his head. "I can't," he said. "I go out to L.A. almost every month."

"What do you do?" asked Caroline.

"I write screenplays. Actually, I rewrite screenplays."

"For movies, you mean?"

"Yes," said Tom.

"I haven't seen a movie in ages," said Caroline.

"You're not missing much," said Tom.

"I don't remember that we were so close to the river," said Caroline. They had paused to cross the West Side Highway.

"You probably didn't come over here before," said Tom. "It wasn't so nice."

They crossed and began walking south along the river. "This is very nice," said Caroline. "How far can you walk?"

"All the way down." Tom pointed ahead of them. "To Battery Park."

Caroline looked out across the river. "May I ask you another question about Margot?"

"Of course," said Tom.

"Did she have—was she romantically engaged?"

"Not recently," said Tom. "When I first met her she was seeing a man. He was an attorney. He lived in San Francisco. He was married, I think. But he was in New York often, staying with her. And I think they traveled together."

"What happened?"

"I don't really know. It just ended. She didn't talk about it. I saw her going out with other men, after that, sometimes. She went out a lot—to the opera and ballet. She had subscriptions to both. She took me sometimes. She did not seem lonely. She was very independent. I think she liked being alone. She had another dog before Hugo—a dachshund. Named Fritz. He was a nasty dog."

"I'd like you to have something of hers," said Caroline. "Something—or things—from the apartment, that you like. Is there something you'd want?"

Suddenly Hugo stopped walking. He squatted like an anchor at the end of the leash.

"Hugo lets you know when he's had enough," said Tom.

"So we must turn around?"

"Sometimes he can be coaxed. But I should be getting back."

"Of course," said Caroline. They turned around, and retraced their steps. "Is there? Something you'd like from the apartment?" asked Caroline. "Anything."

"Really?" said Tom.

"Yes," said Caroline.

"There are a few things I'd love."

"What?"

"I'm afraid they're valuable."

"Good," said Caroline.

"There's the clock in the living room. I have always loved it. And the Rudy Burkhardt photographs in the hallway. I love those too."

"Good," said Caroline, "I want you to have them, then."

"What are you going to do with everything?" said Tom.

"I don't know. Sell it, I suppose."

"Be very careful," said Tom. "It's not junk. None of it. Margot had wonderful things."

"Don't worry," said Caroline. "I will be very careful."

On their way home they passed a little restaurant called Chez Stadium. Two tables were on the street, set with silverware and linen, but unoccupied. The sun was low over the river and shone directly up the street. "Is this a good restaurant?" Caroline asked.

"It's not bad," said Tom.

They parted in the hallway outside the elevator. In the apartment, Hugo seemed to be at home, to know what to do. Caroline did not. She looked at the photographs Tom wanted, and at the clock. He had a very good eye: they were lovely. But then the apartment was filled with lovely things.

She ate dinner by herself at the restaurant they had passed, sitting at one of the tables outside on the street. She was exhausted, both emotionally and physically, but it felt good, sitting at the little table on the street. People walked by and smiled at her. She drank two glasses of wine with the meal, and had a coffee afterward, just to prolong the pleasure of sitting there, on the quiet urban street, beneath the trees, in the lamplight. She felt very far away from Ochos Rios. She had thought that was her life but perhaps it was not. It was hard to know, and she was too tired to figure it all out now. She paid the check and went back to the apartment.

She was sitting in the living room, looking through the magazines that Margot had left behind, when Hugo appeared in the doorway. He stood there, looking at her.

"Is it time for your walk?" she asked.

He cocked his head a little.

She looked at her watch: it was 11:00. "Let's go," she said. They walked around the block. She wondered if he missed Margot. He seemed very self-possessed. She was beginning to like him. Two youngish women, a couple, Caroline felt, entered the building and rode up in the elevator with them.

The women both clutched some sort of program. One of them bent down and patted Hugo. "Hello, Hugo," she said. She stood up. "Are you a friend of Margot's?" she asked Caroline.

"I'm her sister," said Caroline.

"We heard she died," said the woman. "I'm sorry."

"Thank you," said Caroline, not knowing what else to say. "Where have you been?" She nodded at their programs.

"Oh," said the woman. "The ballet."

"How was it?" asked Caroline.

"It was lovely," said the woman.

The elevator stopped. The other woman pushed open the door. "Good night," she said.

"Good night," said Caroline.

In the apartment she let Hugo off the leash. He trotted into the living room and lay down on the rug. Caroline got ready for bed.

She went into the living room and turned out the lights. "Good night, Hugo," she said. He looked up at her.

She closed the bedroom door and got into bed. After a moment she heard him whining at the door. Then he scratched at it. She got out of bed and opened it. "What?" she said. "What do you want?"

He looked up at her.

She got back into bed but left the door open. She was almost asleep when she felt him jump up onto the bed. He turned around a few times and then settled himself at her feet.

CHAPTER TWENTY-FOUR

It was June, the penultimate day of school before the winter recess. Portia got on the bus and sat near the front, beside Ana Luz, but she heard her name being called from the back of the bus. She turned around and knelt on the seat.

He was sitting alone on the last seat; none of the girls had sat beside him. He was smiling, but he looked very silly sitting there, on the school bus, and for a moment she wondered if she could pretend not to know him.

Ana Luz had also turned about. "Who is that?" she asked.

"The man who came to write the book," said Portia. "The one who fell out of the tree."

"What does he want?" asked Ana Luz.

"I don't know," said Portia. "I'll go see. Save my seat."

She walked down the aisle. Giselle and Claudia and Seraphina and Teresa, sixth-formers who usually sat in the last seat and smoked cigarettes, were sitting in the second to last row, having been displaced by Omar. They glared at her as she approached. Only girls in the upper school sat—or even approached—the back of the bus. But Portia walked proudly past them; something about being allied with the mysterious stranger empowered her. She sat down beside Omar.

"What are you doing here?" she asked.

"Taking the bus to Ochos Rios," said Omar.

"I know," said Portia. "But why?"

Omar did not answer. The bus started. Teresa turned around and looked at them.

"You can go back with your friend," said Omar. "I just wanted to say hello."

"Are you staying with us again?" asked Portia.

"I'm not sure," said Omar.

"Does my mother know you're coming?"

"No," said Omar.

Portia looked at him. He looked different from how she remembered him, but she could not see how.

"How is everyone?" he asked.

"Caroline's gone away," said Portia. "And Pete too."

"Where have they gone?"

"Caroline moved to New York City. Pete is in Montevideo. He's opening a store there. Instead of selling his furniture to the American lady, he is selling it himself. He comes back, sometimes, when he is looking for new things."

"And Adam?"

"He's still there."

"And your mother?"

"Of course she is still there. I found your shoe, you know. The one you lost when the bee stung you. I found it when we cut the grass in the meadow. It had ants in it. I kept it, although my mother told me to throw it away. She said it was ruined."

Omar said hello to Teresa, who was still watching them. She turned around.

"I forgot I lost my shoes," said Omar.

"Just one," said Portia. "We took them off because your feet were swelling up, and you kicked one, far away. We couldn't find it. You look better now. You're not swollen at all."

"Yes," said Omar. "I'm all better."

"We have a medicine now. In case someone else gets stung like you. A needle. We keep it in the refrigerator. You stick it in your bum." She paused for a moment and then said, "Why have you come back?"

"Because I wanted to," said Omar.

The bus left them off at the gates. They walked up the long drive and into the front hall. "Wait here," said Portia. "I'll go find my mother." She disappeared through the door to the kitchen.

Omar stood in the hall. The large round table, which he always remembered as having flowers on it, had none: just some stacks of mail and magazines and papers. And dust: it needed to be dusted. He walked around the table and looked out through the French doors at the courtyard. The table they had eaten at was covered by an ugly black tarpaulin. It is winter here, he thought, and less lovely: the black shroud, the dead leaves skating over the cobbles. The sky had clouded over, thick, dark clouds he did not associate with the place. It looked as if it would rain.

He heard the door open above him on the gallery at the top of the curved stairs, and then he heard Arden say, "Portia?"

He knew he should step forward so she could see him, but he could not. He felt suddenly panicked, for he had done it all very quickly, without thinking: using his credit card to buy the ticket, packing the little bag, leaving the same afternoon Yvonne returned. He had told no one what he was doing, where he was going, he had just thought—for of course he had been thinking, but it was a different kind of thinking, a thinking that came from somewhere else inside him—*go there go there go there*, and as long as he was in motion it had seemed right, it had seemed inevitable, and he thought: Do not think until you get there, it will all become clear when you are there, but now he was there, he could go no farther unless he opened the French doors and fled, but he could not open the doors, he could not think, he could not move, he had gone as far as he could go and all he could do was stand there and listen to Arden descend the stairs.

He heard her stop. It seemed very long, the moment, or perhaps it did not seem long, it was a weird moment drained somehow of time and it was the quiet that finally made him turn around. Arden was on the first landing of the stairs, in the far corner of the hall, looking down at him, both hands on the banister. He was shocked by how beautiful she was. For a second he thought: She knew I was coming and has made herself beautiful, but then he realized that was absurd. Perhaps it was how she was standing on the stairs, like a woman in a painting, but her beauty shocked him. Or perhaps it was simply her presence. He had thought he would never see her again, even coming here did not guarantee it: she could have left, like Caroline, like Pete. She could have died.

"Omar?" she said.

He nodded, but stayed standing where he was.

So did she. "I thought it was Portia . . ." she said, vaguely.

"It was," he said. "It is. She's gone to look for you. In the kitchen."

"I was upstairs—" She gestured. Then she shook her head. "I don't understand," she said. "How did you get here? What are you doing here? I thought—we got your letter, I thought it was all over . . ."

"It is," he said. "The book, I mean."

"So why?—so what—what brings you here?"

"I needed to ask you something," said Omar.

"Ask me something? You came all this way to ask me something?"

296

"Yes," he said. He moved toward her but the door to the kitchen opened and Portia said, "She's not back there. She must be upstairs."

"I'm here," said Arden. She came the rest of the way down the stairs.

"Omar came on the school bus with me," said Portia.

"I see," said Arden.

"May I have my snack?"

"Yes," said Arden. "Why don't you—get it yourself, darling. Have a pear and a biscuit if you like."

"There are no pears," said Portia.

"Have a banana, then. Or an apple."

Portia stood there.

"Go," said Arden. "Get your snack."

Portia returned to the kitchen.

"I don't understand why you're here," said Arden. "Is something wrong?"

"No," said Omar.

"Then why have you come?"

"I told you," said Omar. "I need to ask you something."

"What?" said Arden.

Omar could not speak.

Arden moved toward him; they were standing on opposite sides of the round table. "What?" she asked again, impatiently, almost fiercely.

It was all happening too quickly, he had not expected it to happen so fast. He did not know what he had expected they would do but he had thought it would be days before they got to this point. He had thought she would know why he had come, and so there would be no need to talk about it until it became clear somehow, acknowledged, and then they would talk about it, almost in retrospect. She was looking at him fiercely and he realized the extent of his foolishness.

But he had come this far and he could not go back. That is why he had come, why he had done it this way, it was all about being there—being here. Here. He touched the table in front of him. He ducked his head but he looked over at her again and her fierce look had faded, her face had softened somewhat; it was slack with curiosity and patience. It had begun to rain: behind her, he could see it through the windows, falling.

He said nothing for a moment. He glanced down at the table, and then he looked over at her, but she was staring at the table. He said to her lowered face: "I think I kissed you because I love you."

She looked at him. "Do you?" she asked, and then she amended: "Did you? Think that?"

"Yes," he said.

"Ah," she said.

"Why," he asked, "why did you kiss me?"

She shook her head. Her face was flushed and she lowered it again, diverted her gaze. "I don't know," she said. "It was all very confusing, the book and you and everything."

"But you didn't love me?"

She looked at him with eyes that were half mean, half sorrowful. "I thought perhaps I did," she said.

"But then why, afterward, did you tell me you didn't?"

"Because— Oh, Omar, you don't understand. It isn't that simple, that easy. It isn't even about that, really. There's the past. And—you can't do this." Her fierceness rebloomed, suddenly, across her face. "Will you go on like this? Appearing here, intermittently, in these fantastic ways? I think you should not have come like this. I think you should leave, Omar."

"You don't understand," said Omar.

"What don't I understand?"

"Perhaps I have done it all wrong," said Omar. "I am sure I have done it all wrong. I'm sorry to have done it wrong. I wish I could have done it right. If there was anything I could give you it would be to do it right, but I don't know how to do things the right way, the way people are supposed to do things, but—does that mean I should do nothing?"

"I don't know what you're talking about," said Arden. "You appear here, out of the blue—"

"I'm talking about I love you!" said Omar. "I'm talking about I fell in love with you. And I thought, I thought I felt, I thought I remembered—although it's vague, perhaps I'm wrong—I thought I felt that you loved me. Not only when we kissed. Of course then, but not only then. The whole time. Every moment. Every moment."

After a moment he said it again: "Every moment."

Arden sat on the bench beside the door. She leaned forward and closed her eyes. She sat like that for a long time. It was very quiet and they could both hear the rain falling. Then she abruptly stood up. "I'm sorry," she said. She was speaking loudly, as if speaking loudly could keep her from crying. "But I don't love you. And you're right: it was wrong of you to come like this. To just appear, without phoning or even writing. I'm sorry, but it is wrong. You should never have come like this. You must go."

Omar said nothing. He stood there. He could not think what to say. He knew he must be very careful and say the right thing. He must not say the wrong thing. Not now, of all times. After a moment he said, "I love you."

Arden shook her head. "Go," she moaned. "Please, just go."

Omar picked up his bag, which he had left on the floor. He paused a moment inside the door, but Arden did not move: she stood there ashen, immobile. She was looking past him, out through the French doors, at the rain falling on the shrouded table.

Omar opened the door and stepped out into the rain.

Arden did not know how long she stood there in the hall. Presently the door to the kitchen opened and Portia reappeared. "What's happening?" she asked. "Why are you crying?"

Arden wiped her face with her hands. She shook her head. "Did you finish your snack?" she asked.

"Yes," said Portia.

They stood there a moment, stupidly, silently.

Portia said: "Where is Omar?"

"He's gone," said Arden.

"But I wanted to give him his shoe."

"What shoe?"

"His shoe! The one I found in the meadow. I saved it for him! I told him!"

"It's just one shoe," said Arden. "He doesn't need one shoe."

Portia said nothing. Then she said, "You were crying."

"Yes," said Arden.

"Why?"

Arden said: "Sometimes people cry when they feel—when they feel too much."

"Is that what you feel?" asked Portia.

"Yes," said Arden.

Omar was thoroughly soaked by the time he reached the millhouse. He knocked on the door, but there was no answer. He tried to open it, but it appeared to be locked. Then he remembered that it stuck, so he pushed hard and it opened. It was dark inside. If no one is here I can sleep on the couch, he thought, and tomorrow morning I'll walk into Tranqueras. I think I know the way.

He stood in the hall, dripping on the stone floor. He heard a door open far above him and a light appeared on the top landing. Adam stood there in his bathrobe, looking down at him.

"Who is it?" he called.

"It's me," Omar called up. "Omar Razaghi."

"Omar! What are you doing here?"

"I don't know," said Omar. "I came to see Arden, and—it's a

long story. I wonder if I could stay here tonight. Or if you could drive me to Tranqueras."

"I don't drive anymore," said Adam. "Besides, Pete has the car. He's in Montevideo. Come up, come up and tell me your long story. I'd descend but I'm in bed with a touch of *la grippe*. There's a bottle of scotch in the kitchen, bring it up with you. I've been longing for it all day."

"Where's the kitchen?" asked Omar.

"Straight ahead of you, through the living room," said Adam. "You might have to wash some of the glasses in the sink if you can't find clean ones. I'm afraid I am not the housekeeper Pete was. I'm returning to my bed. Hurry."

He disappeared back through the doorway. Omar found the kitchen, and the scotch, and washed two glasses, and brought them upstairs. Adam was sitting in a very large bed. He did not look well. There was one lamp lit on a table beside the bed, casting a small golden pool of light. The rest of the room was quite dark.

"Drag that chair over here and sit down. Good Lord! You're soaked. Are you wet through?"

"Yes," said Omar.

"Well, you'd better undress, and dry off. There's a nice warm robe of Pete's hanging behind the door. Put that on. But first pour me a scotch."

Omar poured some scotch into a glass and handed it to Adam. Then he went over and undressed in the gloom by the door, and put on the woolen robe that was Pete's.

"You need something for your feet. In the top drawer of the dresser there are socks."

Omar found a pair of socks and put them on.

"Now, come sit down," said Adam. "Move that chair. No, the other one. Over here, near the bed. And pour yourself a scotch, and tell me your long story."

Omar followed all of Adam's instructions save the last. He did not know where to begin, or how to tell, his story. He sipped his scotch, and then regarded it.

After a moment Adam said, "I take it you need prompting."

"Yes," said Omar. "I suppose. I don't know where to begin."

"I am, as you might have discerned by now, a traditionalist. Begin at the beginning."

"I suppose that would be when I came here last time," said Omar. "In January."

"It can't be a very long story," said Adam, "if it only began then."

"Well, of course there are parts before that, but that is when things changed."

"What things changed?"

"I think I changed," said Omar.

"How?" asked Adam. "Why?"

"I changed—in many ways. For one, I think, I fell in love with Arden."

"Did you?" said Adam. "What a silly thing to do. And what about your lovely girlfriend? Doris?"

"Deirdre. We've broken up. It wasn't right, between us."

"And so you have come back to declare your love for Arden?"

"Yes," said Omar. "You see, we kissed. The day I got stung by the bee, and fell out of the tree. We had walked up to see the gondola. And we kissed, outside the boathouse."

"How romantic. And then you were stung by a bee, and puffed up, and became comatose."

"Yes, and when I came to Deirdre was here. And I didn't know what had happened with Arden, I felt something had happened, but Arden was so weird and distant and then I went back."

"And wrote us that lovely letter telling us you had changed your mind about the book."

"Yes," said Omar. "I'm sorry about that. I mean, I'm sorry I caused you all so much trouble. Anyway, I came back to see Arden, to ask her if she loved me, to tell her I loved her, but she—she told me it was wrong of me to come. She was awful. I think I hurt her in some way. She told me to go. So I left. And it was raining and I couldn't think of anywhere else to come except here."

"And here you are," said Adam.

"Yes," said Omar. "I'm afraid I've made a mess of things. Of just about everything."

"Drink your scotch," said Adam, "and pour me a little bit more."

Omar poured more scotch into Adam's glass and sipped at his own. "What do you think I should do?" he asked. "What can I do?"

"You must go back to see Arden tomorrow. Of course she threw you out today, it was right of her. You cannot descend upon people from out of the blue and proclaim your love and expect them to reciprocate. A traditionalist like me knows that."

"What must you do, then?" asked Omar. "What must I do?"

"You must go back tomorrow and apologize. You have taken her for granted—"

"But I didn't! Really, I did not!"

"Well, it appears as though you did and that's what's important. You must go back and apologize. She may send you away again. If she does you must go away, but you must not give up. Arden loves you."

"Does she?" asked Omar. "How do you know?"

"It was apparent to me from the moment you arrived. Perhaps even before: perhaps she loved you when you sent the letter. It is ridiculous how, and how easily, people fall in love. Especially Arden: she was very ripe for the picking; if a baboon had knocked on her door she may well have fallen in love with it."

"So you don't really think she loves me? It's just, just the circum——"

"Of course she loves you. She loves you now probably as much as she ever will, because she knows you so little."

"It feels as if we know each other, though," said Omar. "There was something, some connection, right from the beginning, from the very first night."

"I'm glad I was spared witnessing that. No wonder Caroline fled. Have you heard? She has moved to New York City. She has abandoned us."

"Portia told me. What is she doing there?"

"Her sister died, and left Caroline her apartment. I cannot tell you what she does there. What did she do here? Nothing. What does anyone do anywhere? Nothing."

"Perhaps she is painting," said Omar.

"My point exactly," said Adam: "Nothing."

"And Pete is gone too?"

"Yes. I didn't need you to smuggle the paintings after all. Pete found his own way out. The woman he sold to in New York has set him up very nicely in Montevideo. He comes back from time to time, when he is in the area, looking for junk."

"Do you miss him?" asked Omar.

"How brutal you are! You are a biographer, after all. Asking brutal questions."

"I'm sorry," said Omar.

"Of course I miss him," said Adam. "But it is better this way. Isn't that what people say: it is better this way? Meaning I cannot bear it but I will. I will close my eyes and stumble forward into the darkness."

"I'm sorry," Omar said again.

Adam said nothing. He held out his empty glass, and Omar poured some more scotch into it.

"How odd," said Adam, after a moment. "I believe in God: I was lying up here, in bed, thinking about the scotch bottle all the way downstairs in the kitchen, knowing I was too weak to walk down and get it—more precisely too weak to walk back up after having gotten it—but wanting it, oh, yes, wanting it, wanting just a little bit of scotch, a wee dram to warm me, to dull me, to make me feel round and warm and content and sleepy, and then you appeared. Is that not proof of God? I know no better reason to believe."

"Is there anything else you want? From downstairs? Have you eaten?"

"I don't know what you could find down there that's edible. Why don't you go look? There may be tins of soup somewhere."

"All right," said Omar.

"And could I prevail upon you—it is really too mortifying, but I feel somehow you will not mind—there is a chamber pot beneath the bed full of my water. Could you empty it into the toilet downstairs?"

"Of course," said Omar.

He stood up and found the pot: a large ceramic bowl, beneath the bed. "I'll be right back," he said.

He carefully carried the bowl of urine down the three flights of stairs and emptied it into the toilet. Then he went into the kitchen. He could find no tins of soup. There were some apples, and a loaf of bread and jar of honey. Omar put these on a silver tray and carried them back up the stairs.

Adam was asleep. Omar stood beside the bed and watched Adam sleep. He had a dignity, a beauty, that was apparent—that was more apparent—when he was sleeping. Omar did not wake him. He took one of the apples and some of the bread and left the rest on the tray and turned out the light and went back down the stairs.

He ate the apple and bread standing up in the living room. There was an afghan folded across the back of the sofa. He turned out the lights and lay down and covered himself with it. He felt very far away from everything. But, he thought, Arden was wrong: it was not wrong to come here. Not if you understood it. She did not understand it, she did not understand him. No one understood him. That made him sad. He felt sad and alone and unconnected and lost. And cold, too: despite Pete's woolen robe and the afghan, he felt cold.

The next morning Arden waited with Portia at the gates for the school bus, and after it drove away she stood there for a moment. She did not want to return to the house. I will go see how Adam is, she thought, and began walking toward the millhouse. It had rained all night and the road was damp. A residual version of rain continued in the woods: a persistent, loud dripping.

When she turned the corner and saw Omar walking toward her, she panicked. She thought about running into the woods, hiding in the woods, but she could not. He had seen her. For a moment they both stopped walking, and stood about fifty yards apart, on the wet, deserted road, looking at each other. Then she began walking toward him, and he began walking toward her.

They stopped a few feet apart. "Good morning," she said.

"Good morning," he said. He looked down at the road, quickly, and then looked up at her. "I was coming to see you," he said. "I hope you don't mind. I was coming to apologize. I'm sorry. I'm so sorry."

"No," she said. She held out her hand, baring her palm, as if she were stopping traffic. She said no again.

He said nothing.

"I'm sorry," she said. "I was just scared." Her hand was still extended and she reached it a little farther and touched him. She clutched the lapel of his jacket and then smoothed it, then touched it again, laying her palm against his chest. Then she took her hand away. "I can't really explain it—after Jules, after what happened with Jules—I felt as if I had forfeited my right to be in love, to be loved. And I didn't think I could bear it. I'm scared. I don't know how I can bear it."

"Bear what?" asked Omar.

"The—the impossibility of it. You coming here. And then coming back, again. How could it happen? It all seems so random, so fragile. Like glass waiting to break."

She was weeping. Omar reached out and took her hand. He pulled her close to him and held her. "It seems just the opposite to me," he said.

CHAPTER TWENTY-FIVE

Deirdre wrote to Omar in Toronto care of his parents, but never heard back from him. Her one-year position at Bucknell was extended for two more years, and then once again for a fourth and final year. So she began to look for other jobs, and since a chapter from her dissertation ("Rose Macaulay, Penelope Mortimer, Nina Bawden: The Fiction of Gender, the Gender of Fiction") had been published in *PMLA*, the offers for interviews were numerous. In January she went to New York City to interview at Barnard. After the interview she had lunch with two professors; they bid her goodbye on the street corner. She had an hour or two to kill before her train departed and asked them if there was a decent bookstore around.

They directed her to a store called Labyrinth, which sold mainly university press books, and she spent a happy hour browsing through its shelves. She was about to leave when the title of a book on one of the remainder tables caught her eye: *To Go No Farther: Elizabeth Bishop's Years in Brazil* by Omar Razaghi. It was a little, ugly paperback book: black letters on a solid mustard-colored cover, published by the University of New Mexico Press. She picked up a copy and read the blurb on the back:

This book, number 13 in our series on 20th-Century South American Writers, examines the years Elizabeth Bishop lived in Brazil and the work she produced there. Through keen literary analysis of her poetry and translations, and a deft re-creation of her life in Brazil, Razaghi makes a compelling case for Bishop to be considered a writer of the Southern Hemisphere. Here is a new look at Bishop, as an author who found a home and voice far from her native shores.

20th-Century South American Writers is edited by Diogenes González-Barahona and Susan Shreve Shepard as part of the University of New Mexico's South American Literature Studies Program.

OMAR RAZAGHI was born in Tehran, Iran, in 1969 and emigrated to Canada in 1979. He has a B.A. in History from York University and an M.A. in Literature from the University of Kansas, where he was awarded the Dolores Faye and Bertram Siebert Petrie Award for Biographical Studies, based upon his work on Jules Gund. Razaghi lives in Uruguay with his wife and two daughters, Portia and Adela.

Deirdre looked at the dedication: *To Arden*. She bought five copies—they were only $1.98 each.

Deirdre got the job at Barnard and moved to New York. The following winter a man she met at a Tai Chi class invited her to the opera (*Les contes d'Hoffmann*). The second intermission found them leaning against the Dress Circle balustrade, looking down upon the crowded Grand Tier promenade, discussing the sexual politics of trouser roles. There was an area below them separated off with a row of potted trees, beyond which people sat on conspicuous display at little tables idiotically eating desserts. Deirdre was about to make a comment about the absurd ostentation of this, when she thought she recognized a woman seated at one of the tables.

"I think I know that woman down there," she said. "I want to go and say hello. Will you excuse me?"

"Sure," said her companion. "I'm going to the men's room. I'll meet you back at our seats."

"Okay," said Deirdre. She hastened down the crimson curving tunnel of stairs to the level below, and made her way through the throng toward the makeshift restaurant. By the time she pushed herself through the crowd, the woman was getting up from the table, leaving a man behind, walking toward her. For a moment Deirdre thought the woman had recognized her, but then she realized she had not. Deirdre stepped closer as the woman passed her and said, "Excuse me, are you Caroline Gund?"

The woman stopped and looked at Deirdre. She was wearing a long black skirt and lilac-colored watered silk blouse that tied in a huge bow on one of her hips. Her hair was gray now, but still long and elegantly styled. She wore a necklace of hammered silver leaves and matching earrings. "Yes," she said, "I am."

"I'm Deirdre MacArthur," said Deirdre. "Do you remember me? I met you several years ago, at Ochos Rios. I was there with Omar Razaghi."

Caroline smiled and held out her hand. "Deirdre, yes, of course. How are you?"

"I'm fine," said Deirdre. "I saw you from up there"—she turned and pointed to the gallery above them—"and I just wanted to say hello."

"Are you enjoying the opera?" asked Caroline.

"Yes," said Deirdre, "very much. How are things in Ochos Rios?" It sounded like that song: "How Are Things in Glocca Morra?"

"I wouldn't know," said Caroline. "I live here now. I moved here several years ago. Shortly after you visited us, in fact." Caroline carried a little bag, beaded with black jets. She turned it over in her hands.

"Have you read Omar's book?"

"Omar wrote a book?"

"Yes," said Deirdre. "About Elizabeth Bishop in Brazil."

"I haven't seen it," said Caroline.

"It's quite good," said Deirdre.

Caroline said nothing. She was looking at her bag.

"And apparently he's living down there. He's married Arden."

"Yes, I had heard something like that," said Caroline.

"You aren't in touch with them?"

Caroline looked up and smiled. "No," she said, "I am not in touch with them. And how are you? Are you still teaching in—where is it? Nebraska?"

"Kansas," said Deirdre. "No, I'm here in New York. At Barnard. So you don't go back to Ochos Rios?"

"No," said Caroline. "I've remarried. My life is here now."

"Are you still painting?" asked Deirdre.

"No," said Caroline. "No, I don't paint." She made a gesture with her hand, as if she were brushing away smoke. "I'm afraid you will have to excuse me. I was on my way to the ladies' room and you know how awful the lines are, and I don't want to miss the barcarolle—"

"Of course," said Deirdre. "I just wanted to say hello. It's nice to see you."

"Lovely to see you," said Caroline, "enjoy the rest of the opera." She pressed Deirdre's hand, and then disappeared into the crowd.

Deirdre went out on the balcony, where people stood about, shivering and smoking. Even though it was freezing, the fountain at the center of the plaza was perfunctorily founting, and a bright, steamy halo surrounded it. She watched the steam tumble up into the darkness, disappear.

Caroline's husband stood up as she passed by him. After she sat down he leaned over and arranged her shawl around her shoulders. She had put on perfume; he could smell it. He leaned closer and inhaled, kissed her cheek. She smiled, but she was looking straight ahead, implacably, at the gold curtain.

"Who was that? The girl you were talking to?"

"Oh," said Caroline. "No one. She mistook me for someone she knew."

Deirdre returned to her seat. She found a tissue in her coat pocket and blew her nose. Her companion took her hand. "You're freezing," he said.

"I went outside," said Deirdre. "It's cold."

"Here," he said. He took both her hands in his. He had large, warm hands. He squeezed her hands between his. "Who was that woman?"

"It was a woman I met when I was in Uruguay," said Deirdre.

"Uruguay? When where you in Uruguay?"

"A few years ago," said Deirdre. "Well, five years ago. Almost exactly."

"What were you doing in Uruguay?"

Deirdre shook her head.

"Tell me," he said.

"Oh," said Deirdre, "it's a long story."

"Tell me," he said again.

She opened her mouth to speak, but the dimming lights silenced her. The conductor appeared and was applauded. He raised his arms, and the music began.